SKY STITCHER

A.C. GUESS

Imprint: Draconis Ink

Cover by Etheric Designs

Editing by Kate Seger and Holly Barnett

Realm of Taara Map © Oakleaf Arrow Studios

Interior art by Nox Benedicta, efa_finearts, Alina Trocenko, and Breezy Jones

1st edition 2024

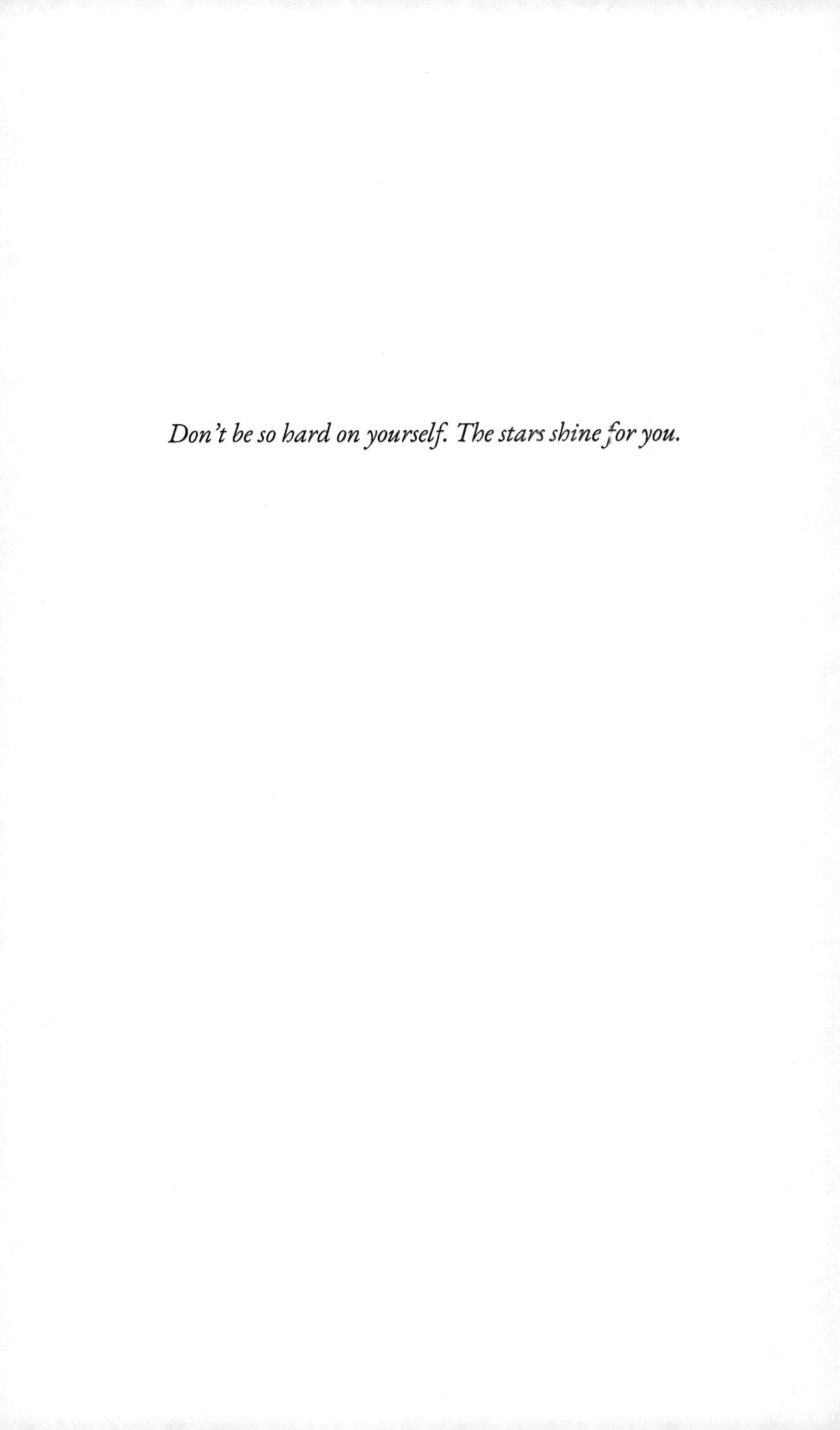

Don't be so hard on yourself. The stars shine for you.

CONTENTS

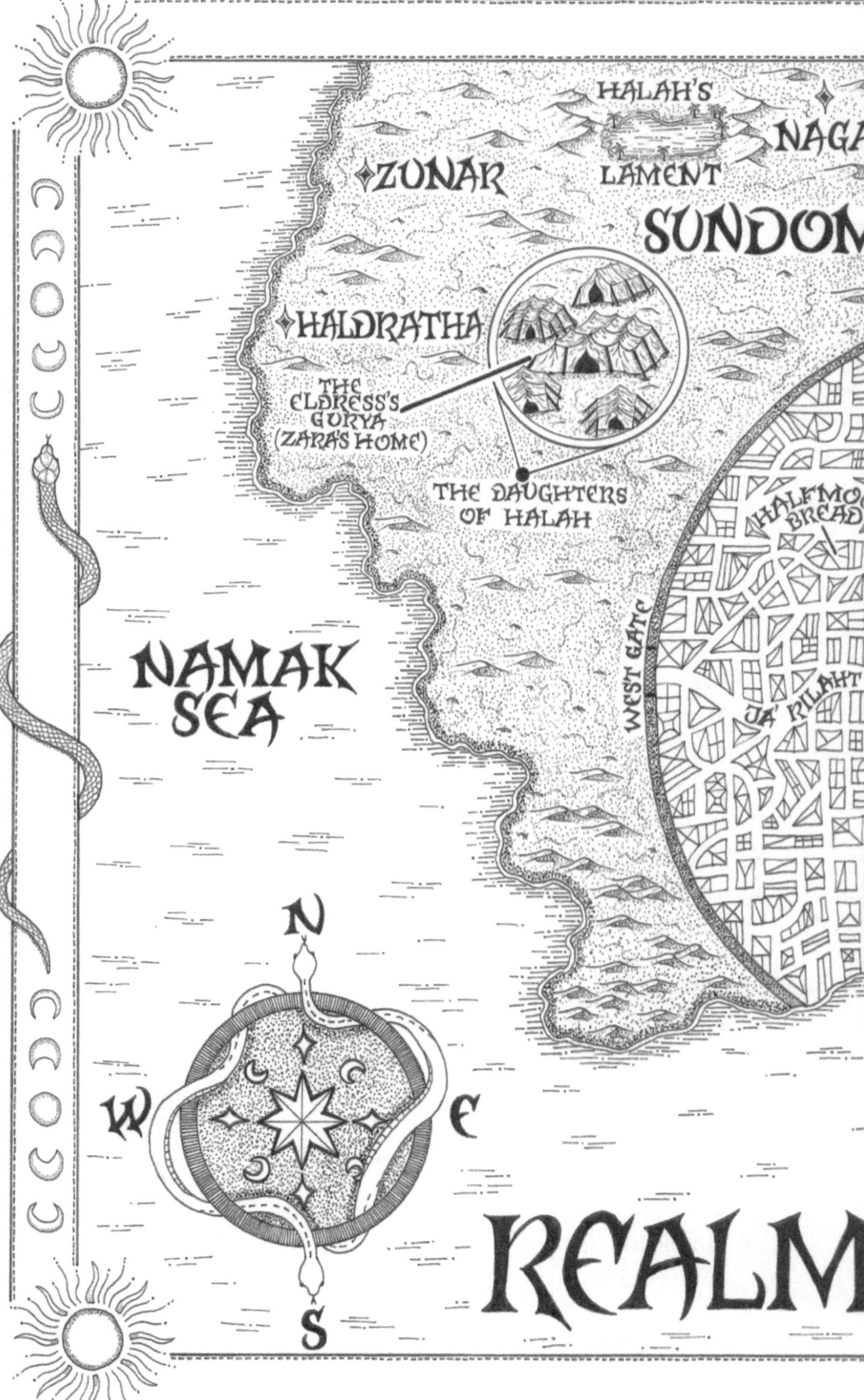

HALAH'S LAMENT
ZUNAR
NAGA
SUNDOM
HALDRATHA
THE ELDRESS'S GURYA (ZARA'S HOME)
THE DAUGHTERS OF HALAH
HALFMOON BREAD
WEST GATE
JA' RILAHT
NAMAK SEA
N
W
E
S
REALM

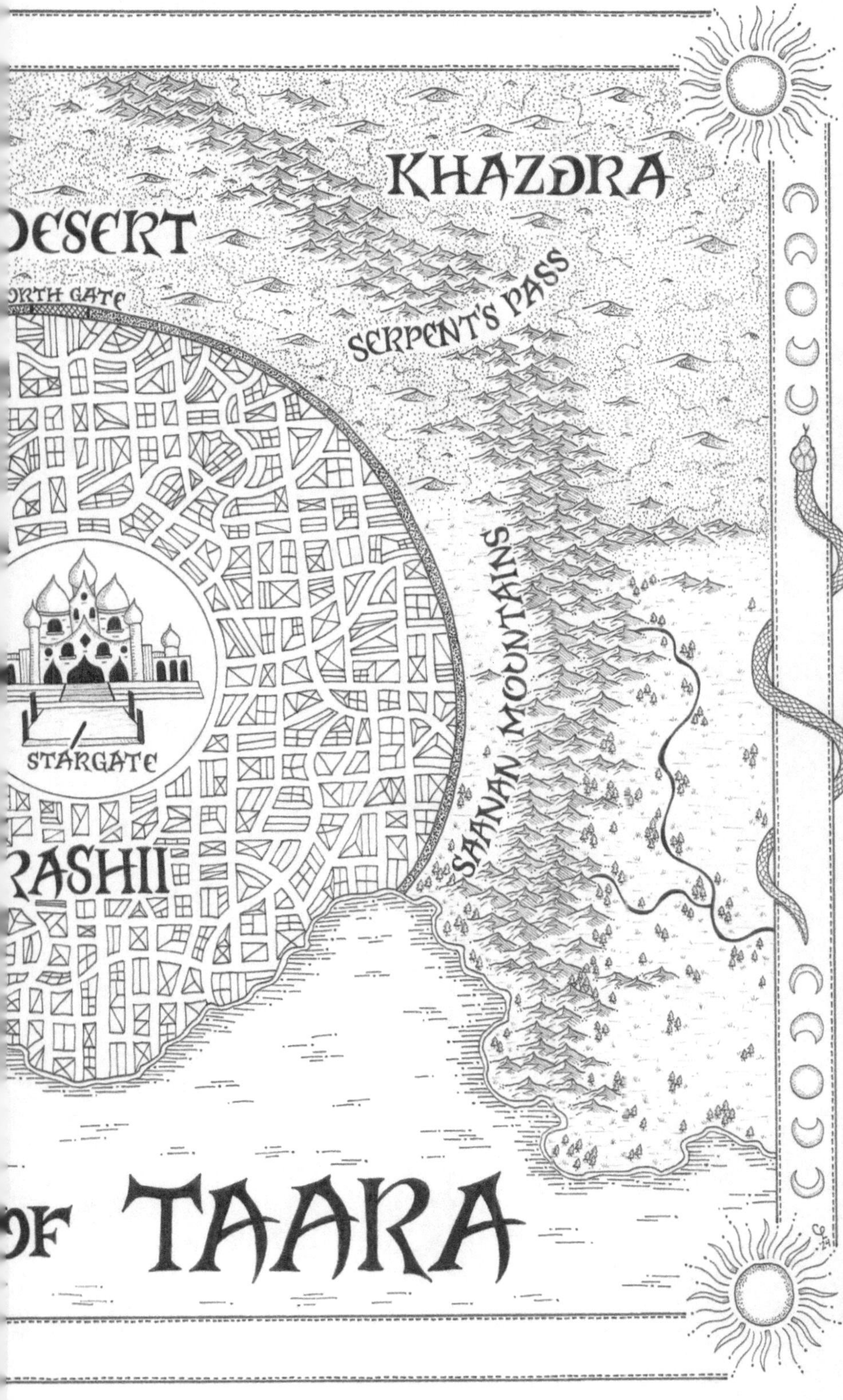

DESERT
KHAZDRA
NORTH GATE
SERPENT'S PASS
SAANAN MOUNTAINS
STARGATE
RASHII
OF TAARA

CHAPTER 1
DESECENDANT OF HALAH

I stood on the swell of the dune, shoulders squared like the descendant of Halah I was, and narrowed my eyes at the nightmarish heavens.

The sky bled.

Not with blood—not red and dripping streaks of crimson. The sky bled *black*. It oozed shadows, weeping darkness from the golden gashes between realms. I craned my neck back to calculate the extent of the damage, glaring up at the spidering veins above.

Prisha was unhappy—worse than unhappy. She was mad.

And when the goddess was mad, the monsters came.

The sand shifted beneath my feet as I stepped forward, hastening my pace across the dunes. I did not want to be caught alone in Prisha's tempest.

My tunic clung to my skin, the fabric adhering to the sticky sweat that swathed my legs. The sun's descent granted some reprieve from the sweltering heat, but the stars had not yet had time to work their magic, bathing the dunes beneath the moon in the crisp, cool glow of stardust. Still, the shiver that traced its way down my spine sent a chill through my blood.

Rustling at my feet drew my gaze.

A serpent darted away from me. I tilted my head, considering its effortless glide across the dunes, weaving through the brush like a shadow. One of Prisha's creatures, but certainly not the worst of them. I had killed far worse today.

My hand moved to the sheath at my ribs, fingers wrapping around the studded hilt. I watched the shadow wind its way between the dried roots, waiting for the window of opportunity. *There.*

The dagger sailed through the space between us, soaring toward its target with one calculated flick of my wrist. It met its mark, and the serpent writhed, its body pinned beneath the blade, life blood spilling into the sand.

The head would be dangerous for a few more hours, but the venom could not be wasted—the Daughters needed it. Perhaps Mother would spare me her usual lectures when I brought home the ingredients for the Daughters' beloved venom tea. Not that I'd be drinking any.

The venom's taste was the least offensive side effect of the brew. The worst of it—the mind-altering state that accompanied the affronting flavor. I had no aspirations to drink the tea to heighten my connection with Halah like the rest of the Daughters, but if there had been a brew to keep Halah away...to avoid her notice...

That I would drink. With gusto.

I shrugged the satchel from my shoulders and withdrew a length of heavy fabric from within, the earthy musk of leather filling the air. The material snapped as I unfurled it, and it drifted toward the sand to cover the deceased snake. Kneeling, I wound the beast into the wrapping, folding it carefully and tucking it away in my sack.

Sticky blood coated my dagger, but it cleaned up easily against the sole of my boot. I had to be careful to keep my trousers neat—Lurah hated it when I borrowed her clothes, and she hated it even more when I ruined them.

I slid the dagger back into the sheath at my ribs, then adjusted the scarf over my face. Lurah was the best weaver of all my Sisters and she knew it. Her fabrics felt like cool breezes, while mine scratched like dune nettles. Nobody ever stole my fabrics—unless you count the time Mother used them to scrub the pans.

A crackle split through the air with the snapping finality of breaking bone. I flinched, a wave of foreboding washing over me, pooling in my stomach like simmering acid, corroding my insides as my heart thumped loudly against my chest. The fabric between realms had been worsening for weeks, frayed like a worn piece of gauze stitched together too many times. There were so many gashes between realms that it had become difficult to discern the old scars from the new.

But this—this felt worse. Worse than worse.

I gasped as viscous tendrils of darkness reached through the gashes like fingers. The shadows groped, moving toward the dunes like serpentine plumes of smoke—grasping, searching, stretching the tears in the sky wider. My heart dropped into my stomach.

I covered my head with my hands, holding Lurah's silk scarf in place over my brow, and ran.

A shriek filled the emptiness of the night. *Crawlers.* The abrasive sound grated against my nerves—like knives screeching across a whetstone. I slammed my hands over my ears, wincing as the noise intensified. *How many are there?* I could not turn back to count, but I knew the answer. *Too many.* Prisha's smallest creatures were easily subdued, but I could not manage the entirety of her wrath—not on my own. Not against an army of crawlers.

I had to get away—to the safety of the Daughters and the guryas to gather reinforcements. *I have to warn them.*

A piercing wail wrenched my heart. There wasn't time.

Halah help me. Please. The Mother of Daughters didn't answer me. Of course she didn't...she never did.

Fire coursed through my veins. I raced over the dunes, my pulse hammering in my eardrums as the screeching drew closer.

Shit, shit, shit. I will be good, Halah, I promised, leaping over the slope of a dune. My lungs burned with each gulp of arid air, but I pushed myself to move past the discomfort. To move faster.

You should have drank more of that damned tea. Then maybe she'd listen to you.

Shadows stretched alongside me as the creatures closed in. I could not outrun them, but I urged my muscles forward. *I will try harder, Halah. I will be a proper Daughter—please.*

Venom and hell.

The dunes opened like an abyss before me, offering no place to hide or shelter from Prisha's curse, but the magic of the Daughters' weaving called to me, steering the internal compass within me, guiding me home.

Let me warn them, Halah. Help me get to them. For them, if not for me. Let me help them.

I sprinted as fast as my legs would carry me, forcing my sluggish muscles to ignite, urging them to propel my body forward when they only wanted to collapse and sink into the pulling sand.

Dark shapes appeared at the edges of my vision, and my heart ricocheted against my ribcage. I wasn't fast enough—if I didn't find the strength to run faster, they would end me. Prisha's crawlers would shred me and stitch the last of my soul's light into the stars to glimmer among the ancestors.

The stars above twinkled with laughter at my fate, perhaps elated I would shortly join them. Their lights—the lights of all Stitchers and Daughters from the past—shone brighter, fighting against Prisha's darkness even in their death. *Help me,* I begged. *Help me if Halah will not.*

Fleshy fingers wrapped around my ankle, and a sharp pain followed. The crawler sank its serrated teeth into my thigh, latching onto me like a leech, wholly undeterred by my attempt to fling it from my leg as I ran. My dagger sliced through its rubbery skin and it hissed. The creature dissolved, creating an oozing dribble of shadow that trailed along my leg.

More were coming—I could hear the slither of their movements even though their wails had grown silent.

Faster. In the distance, sunken between the dunes, the guryas stood like sentries in the sand, guarding the city beyond that glistened with lights more abundant than the stars. But nothing guarded the space between the crawlers and the tents sheltering my clan. Nothing except me. *Not much farther. Run, Zara.*

The sky shivered, then split, followed by the booming sound of thunder. The stitches were failing.

A fresh swarm of inky blackness descended from the tear in the heavens, tumbling like ink through water, landing on the sand and spreading into pools of shadow. I skidded to a halt.

The black pools quivered, and then, from their depths, the figures emerged. First the rigid, curved spines, then the elongated spider-like limbs, and finally, the gaunt faces with milky white eyes gleaming like moonstone. Spindly shadows consolidated into lanky, monstrous forms. A cadre of crawlers.

I whipped around, looking for an escape, but the monsters surrounded me, creeping closer on their knobbled limbs, chests dragging along the sand as they moved.

Use your weaving, Zara. The stars shimmered, as if Halah herself had whispered the words through the sky and her breath made them dance with brilliance.

My body tensed, stunned by the ethereal voice. *I can't. I don't know how.* Halah's other Daughters weaved with gentle, quiet magic under the influence of venom tea. My brand of magic was reckless. Uncontrolled. While they created, I...wreaked havoc. Surely, Halah must know that.

Try, the voice commanded. *Do not let Prisha take you, Daughter.*

Sand and wind stirred, circling me in a storm of dust. Prisha's inky curse tumbled through the gash, warping and twisting until it formed a shadowy hand. Its fingers sprawled and scrabbled across the land, searching blindly for their target. I collapsed to my knees.

The shadowy fingers seized me. I screamed and pushed against them, trying to free myself, but the snakelike tendrils writhed and elongated. Prisha's darkness wound over my limbs like overgrown vines and tethered me to the ground, restraining me as a swarm of her crawlers climbed over me.

I tucked my chin to my chest to shield my face from the whirlwind of debris and screamed as teeth sank into my back, ripping into the flesh of my arms, preparing to shred me to the last light of my core.

Another little Daughter for the sky. Another little Daughter must die. The crooning voice emanated from the shadows themselves, and my bones screamed in protest at every syllable it uttered. *Another star for Prisha's sky,* she continued, her voice as singsong as a crow's lament. *I hate you, I hate you. Now, you must die.*

The shadows wound tighter around my neck, squeezing until the pressure threatened to pop every blood vessel in my body. I couldn't breathe. My bones bent unnaturally, crushed in the goddess's grasp. *Prisha's* grasp.

Mother had warned me it wasn't safe in the dunes anymore. She'd told me it was better to stay within the guryas, under the Stitcher's protection. She'd warned me to dedicate myself to prayer like my Sisters, to beg Halah to choose a new Stitcher to replace the Eldress so we could continue our fight against Prisha.

But I ignored her—because I never wanted to be chosen. But now—

I'm dying, I registered with a surge of panic. *By the hand of Prisha.* And if it were truly the hand of Prisha, our last defenses against her had failed, deteriorating as quickly as our Eldress's aging body.

For the love of Halah, Zara, do something. Try. Try before she kills us all.

I turned my face toward the stars—beseeching the ancestors that glittered above, witnesses to my last breath. *Please.*

But I could hardly focus—my vision blurred, slipping into oblivion.

A torrent of panic surged life back through me. *No!* My body responded, pulsing with a sudden burst of raw power. I gasped, and my eyes snapped open. Tendrils of light shimmered into my vision—the invisible threads that the Daughters called on to entwine with the goddess in prayer. Normally hidden, the roots of magic now drifted in plain sight—rushing toward me like old friends, embracing me and winding themselves into my aura, banishing the black bindings of Prisha's curse.

I did not ask questions—I didn't worry or second guess or wonder why they availed themselves to me. I simply reacted, snatching as many strands as I could and winding them together, projecting their power back out through my limbs. The tendrils of magic did not function in the way I expected, in the way of the Daughters—it did not allow me to root and entwine myself in prayer to beg Halah for help. Instead, the streams of energy erupted outward, streaking toward the sky in great slivers of blinding starlight, sending Prisha's creatures skittering away. The threads pulsed and collided with the stars, knotting themselves into the fabric of the night.

Take it, a voice whispered, close to my heart. Or perhaps from my heart.

Take what? I watched in utter confusion as the stars hummed with magic, bound to me by the strange connection I'd unleashed into the sky. The stars multiplied, merging together, compacting and melding until they formed a single blinding starburst—a diamond in the heavens. A bright light erupted between Prisha's rifts, shedding an ethereal glow upon the dunes. The light trickled over me like a bath of warm milk and honey.

Take it. It's yours. The dazzling, dense flash raced toward me, and I flinched, falling backward into the sand as the luminous orb burrowed itself beneath my skin and spread into my heart. I clutched a hand over my chest, surprised by the sensation of warmth that spilled beneath my breastbone.

A light unfolds in the darkness, beginning what will have no end, the stars whispered.

No, not the stars. *Halah.* The goddess—the Mother of Daughters. The first enemy of Prisha.

You have plucked the heart of the stars from the sky, child, so it is yours. So it will be, beginning what will have no end. Use it well.

Prisha's disembodied voice hissed wildly in response. *Thief. Thief of stars! Put it back!*

The glow around my heart flickered and dulled, dampened by the toxic shadows she hurled my way. Her fingerlike tendrils billowed across the dunes, reaching out to grab me again. All around me, her creatures leered from the shadows, creeping closer, emboldened by the thick darkness choking out the last of my sputtering light.

No, I wanted to scream, but my voice failed.

I arched my back, letting a soundless shout shred through the sky as magic pulsed from my veins. Magic born of the stars. It was not the quiet, gentle weaving powers of my people—the magic I summoned burst from me like a shockwave, exploding outward in every direction from the light in my heart, decimating the shadowy creatures around me who shrieked and dissolved into nothing. Prisha's shadows hissed and recoiled when my light exploded up to the heavens. I watched, horrorstruck as the blinding flash rippled through the stitches in the sky. The sky frayed, seams splitting in the navy velvet to reveal new gashes. New fissures. As if the outburst of my magic had destroyed centuries of protection in one fell swoop. *What have I done?*

Prisha's laughter cackled, breaking something within me. *Perhaps I will let you keep your stars, after all, Sky Render. I've never met one of you before.* Her voice dropped to a bone-chilling tone that painted darkness in every crevice of my being. *Kill the Stitcher. Shred the skies. Set me free.*

No! I said, shaking my head frantically, suffocating beneath the weight of my mistake.

You must, she crooned with a serpentine hiss. *You will...It's unavoidable. You know the prophecy, don't you?*

The Prophecy of Dusk and Dawn. The last hope of our people. Of course I knew it.

A light unfolds in the darkness, beginning what will have no end, Prisha's lilting voice sang before I could respond. *You are the light. I...am the end.*

*No. That's not how it's meant to go...*My fingers groped over my chest, clawing at the light burrowed within my ribs. *No, no, no. Get it out. Get. It. Out!*

The prophecy was meant to save us...it promised a hero who'd free us from Prisha's wrath and deliver a peace with no end to the realm. But if Prisha spoke the truth, I'd condemned us to a very different fate.

What have I done? I had to fix this. I—

The light around my heart erupted, chasing her shadows away until my mind disconnected from my body, and I fell onto the sand, detached from reality as the last traces of my vision slipped and the dunes faded. *No, not now. Please don't.* But a heavy weight pushed me into the ground, exhaustion spreading like lead through my limbs.

The last stitches are failing, little Star Thief. Pity the Eldress is dying. Go and warn your Sisters...tell them what you have done. The end has begun.

I groaned, facedown in the dunes, heart racing from the last traces of a terrible nightmare. Sand had worked its way into my nostrils, settling in my throat with the viciousness of a thousand glass shards. I stirred and attempted to swallow away the sensation of hot ash, but the walls of my throat stuck together. I coughed through the discomfort and pushed myself up on my elbows.

How long have I been here?

…What am I doing here?

Lurah's scarf brushed my cheeks, and the slight graze of fabric ignited my flesh with searing pain. The stealthy rays of the morning sun had wasted no time in scorching my unprotected skin. Hastily, I adjusted the covering, drawing it over my face to shield myself from further harm. *The cursed vulnerabilities of the Daughters' moonsilk skin. Why can't we have beautiful bronzed complexions like the rest of those from the Realm of Taara?*

I got to my feet and cast my gaze upward, wincing beneath the intensity of the sun's rays. It burned high above, basking the dunes in its golden hue and sweltering heat, but at least the angry welts crisscrossing the sky had calmed to dullish gray scars. Still, something felt...off. Something I could not quite remember...a thought or a memory that skittered away like beetles fleeing the sun whenever I tried to grasp it.

I rubbed the fatigue from my eyes, staring vacantly across the dunes, letting my groggy mind attempt to make sense of my surroundings. *Is it already past noon?* A jolt of panic scattered the last dregs of my weariness, and I stood up. I'd missed morning prayer. And morning meal. And—I craned my neck to recalculate the position of the sun as I marched toward the guryas—midday meal. Shit. It must be nearly the hour for evening meal.

I grimaced, already anticipating Mother's scolding. *Where have you been? Did you say your prayers? Halah will never select a new Stitcher if we do not please her. Think of your Sisters—your family.* I waved away the onslaught of imagined reprimands, but doubled my pace. Best not to keep Mother waiting any longer. At least I had the venom to help pacify her inevitable fury with me.

I marched toward the guryas, my hair sticking to the back of my neck and sand invading every thread of my tunic. Attempting to shake the dust from the garment, my hands wavered on the frayed fabric. My gaze settled on the slashes through the embroidery—the loose strands flailing in the wind like little soldiers that had fallen out of rank, waving their flags in defeat. *Venom and hell. Lurah will murder me for ruining her tunic. What did I do?*

Trailing a finger over the torn threads, I landed upon a slash in the fabric and found the long claw marks that had ripped through my skin. My fingers brushed over the crusted blood coating the wounds, and I winced, jolting with the memory of the crawler's haunting faces, their sharp claws raking over my skin and the earsplitting screeches in the night. *Did that—did that truly happen?*

Have I gone mad? The unsettling possibility presented itself in my mind. But the memory of the crawlers' fine, razor-like teeth flashed back to me, glinting in the moonlight while their eyes glowed with unrelenting malice.

Perhaps it had been real. There had been...so many of them. My heart pulsed with a violent throb of realization. *I should have died.* All the warmth drained from my face.

Am I dead?

No, a definitive voice within me answered, one buried by confusion, heat exhaustion, and general disbelief of the wild story my memories attempted to weave for me. *You stole the heart of stars and ripped stitches from the skies.*

My heart skipped a beat and a leaden weight sank into my stomach. *Thief of stars.*

No, no, no. Panic wedged its way into my throat, choking me until my eyes widened and my ears hummed with the rushing of my own pulse. I pawed at the fabric of the scarf hanging loosely over my sternum, searching for any trace of the ethereal glow, but the only thing sparkling between my breasts was my own sweat. The sun beat down on my brow, and I shook my head at the ridiculous notion. *Thank Halah.*

Clearly, the hours in the hot sun had compromised my lucidity. My memories were as hazy as a dune storm, at best—how could I think that any of that had been real? Surely it was just a nightmare. That was all.

Still, something like an iron fist gripped my heart, squeezing and constricting until the pain made my breath hitch. The fear... the fear had been so real last night. And the sky—I'd—I'd made everything worse. Prisha had spoken to me—

Venom and hell, I cursed. *I need to get back to the guryas. To the Stitcher. I have to warn them about what I've done.*

If I even did it.

But my heart galloped at an uncomfortable pace and a warmth spread through my chest. I looked down again, startled by the dazzling light nestled just below my sternum, pulsing with unfamiliar power. *The heart of stars. It's real.* I snapped Lurah's scarf around myself as if the simple gesture could somehow erase the truth I'd seen with my own eyes.

What did it mean? Had Halah...chosen me? *Surely not.* That was not how the choosing went according to the Eldress's rambling tales. But Halah...had spoken to me. Or the stars had? *Something* had changed.

Tentatively, I loosened my deathlike grip on Lurah's scarf and examined the unfamiliar pulse of power beneath my breastbone. Its warmth flowed through me, seeking out the tendrils of energy that seeped into our world from the rifts, feeling for the delicate warmth of their presence. I marveled as it streamed from me, reaching for the ribbons of light. I'd spent so much of my life avoiding them, but now, by some strange twist of fate, I had asked them to find me. Or rather...the heart of stars *called* them to me.

Wrapping the threads around my fingers, ignoring the way my heart raced with the brush of raw power I despised, I seized them. The Daughters considered these currents to be a sacred gift from Halah, a boon to help us win the war, but I suspected Halah had deserted us long ago and left us behind to finish her fight. Just like Prisha had left everything behind to finish us.

I rolled the strands uncertainly between my fingertips, and they hummed with warmth, then burst outward. The threads streaked toward the sky, igniting like fiery bolts of lightning as my fingers reached toward the stars, following a will of their own.

My hand wavered with shock. As soon as I paused, fingers still outstretched, the light glowing beneath my breastbone sputtered, a wick drowning in its own wax. I shook my head, snapping my focus back into place until the ribbons reemerged, blazing with life. Uncertainly, I willed them to move...wondering if I could coax them to weave stitches. The strands vibrated, winding together in a wobbling duet toward the closest rift. Then, the line pulled taut. It snapped into place like a beacon, refusing to bend to my will, before the mouth of Prisha's rift slurped it into its dark depths.

Little Star Thief, caught in Prisha's web. Shred the skies, or you'll be—

Horrified, I ripped away, and as the connection between us severed, Prisha's screech howled like a gale of wind. I froze, my muscles seizing with terror, and I shoved the uncontrollable power of the heart of stars away, drowning it beneath the dark ocean of my mistrust.

Never again, I promised myself. *Never try that again.*

The rift darkened, oozing with the oily curse spewed by the goddess's hatred, then it split, pulled wider by a set of obsidian claws.

A grotesque face leered down at me, its orb-like eyes overshadowing the rest of its hellish features. The ribbons of magic surrounding me dissipated, but the damage was done. Instead of stitching the sky together, I'd summoned Prisha's attention. And in turn...one of her monsters. Leave it to me to make things worse.

The bulgroich, one of Prisha's most detestable creatures of the In Between, hurtled to the ground in a burst of starlight. The blazing comet tail trailing behind it seared my retinas, blinding part of my vision. The air rushed from my lungs as the creature blasted into me, wrapping its spider-like arms around my chest, aiming its teeth at the skin below my neck. The bulgroich did not shred its victims like the crawlers—they merely devoured hearts, keeping their prey alive just long enough to witness the blood dripping down their faces as their victim's last breaths escaped.

I tumbled, rolling to the side to free myself from its clutches. Its teeth sank into my shoulder, and my back arched as I screamed, but it didn't release me. For a creature with such a brittle frame, its grip never wavered. Its bony limbs tightened and constricted wherever it could grasp, but I wedged my elbow between its arm and gripped the smooth handle of the dagger sheathed by my ribs. Sand sprayed into the air as we wrestled for dominance, and the creature sputtered with a wailing hiss when the grains flew into its eyes. The sound was nothing compared to the anguished gurgle of its death when my dagger sank into its throat.

I pushed the creature off me and laid back in the sand, throwing an arm over my eyes to shield my vision from further damage, heaving for gulps of air that never fully satisfied my lungs.

Why would you expect to be anything other than chaos? I laughed. Not with amusement but with a bitter taste of resentment in my mouth.

Had I really just tried to master the duties of the *one* role I knew I was never suited for? And for what purpose? Morbid curiosity? Presumptuous dread? I frowned at my mind's hesitant suggestion of another possibility. A tinge of...unbidden hope? No. Not that. The confusing jumble of thoughts twisted inside my gut, but I forced them away—now was not the time to unravel such nuances.

You are not meant to be a Stitcher, I assured myself, focusing on the positives. *And thank Halah for that.*

But if the heart of stars was truly unrelated to stitching...it was something completely unknown. Unpredictable. Perhaps even dangerous. And it had inconveniently commanded the full attention of both goddesses...something I'd *never* wanted. And something I needed to fix.

Whatever I'd done—whatever I'd stolen from the sky—I could not use it again. Ever. I'd only make things worse.

The gash on my shoulder burned like fire, and I winced when I rolled over to my hands and knees, blinking the smudges of blindness from my eyes. I could not linger here. I needed food and water, and I knew I would not last against another of Prisha's creatures. *Pull yourself together, Zara. Mother's waiting.* Truth be told, her wrath was a monster far more frightening than the ones from the In Between.

And I did not look forward to enduring her anger. If she ever found out about what I'd stolen...what I feared I'd done...

I struggled to swallow the dry lump forming in my throat.

CHAPTER 3

TAPESTRIES AND TEA

Stepping into the gurya was like wading into the night sky. Darkness engulfed me, for the fabric walls of the tent absorbed every trace of light, leaving behind an endless void of blackness while the Daughters prayed. Above, the mouth of the gurya opened wide to the heavens, but no trace of the fading sunlight slipped through the gap to bask the room in its glow. The Daughters required unrestricted access to earth and sky to use their magic, but they shut out the sunlight during prayers, preferring to maintain darkness to heighten their reverence. It was a magic I didn't fully understand, but one that felt like home.

The room thrummed with the gentle weaving of the Daughters' magic as they communed with the goddess. Once my eyes readjusted to the darkness, the lumpy shadows in the curved room took on more defined shapes. My Sisters sat in total silence, eyes closed, harnessing the threads of light to transform them in prayer. As they worked, they blindly weaved a communal tapestry that rippled with new rows of stitches. *My* tapestry...the one to be presented at A'i Halajan when the elders gifted me in marriage.

My stomach soured at the reminder of the upcoming festival, and my duty to create new Daughters for the clan.

Around their ankles, the ribbons mutated to sickly moss-colored bindings, tethering them to the ground, both a part of them and distinctly foreign. Otherworldly and grotesque. The corner of my mouth twisted as I pulled Lurah's scarf tighter around my shoulders, bunching it in front of my sternum. Some gift Halah's magic was. Looked more like a curse to me.

The eerie roots pulsed with a heartbeat of their own and snaked tighter and tighter, but the Daughters did not flinch, nor did they complain. Not ever. Not even when the roots threatened to strangle them alive, or their fingers became entangled in the threads of the tapestries they weaved in their dreams. The worst was their eyes, milky white and vacant. Like the crawlers'. Mother assured me the goddess would never harm us, but still—there was a reason I favored guarding.

Mother said if we showed our daily devotions by weaving in prayer, Halah would finally choose a new Stitcher to replace the Eldress. She'd been saying that for years, but the current Stitcher had only grown more useless with every prayer-filled day. Without a proper Stitcher, nobody was left to hold back Prisha's war, and the realm would perish.

But if I did nothing to undo whatever mess I'd created last night...if I didn't warn the Eldress and ask her to wake—to restitch the tears I'd accidentally opened—the realm would perish anyway.

I needed to talk to her.

I trembled like a bucket of ice water had been tossed over my head. If I wanted to speak with the Eldress, I had to go through the proper chain of command—but the last person I wanted to speak to was Mother. The Daughters elected Loehla to the respected position of Mother long before my birth, but there were few times when *I* saw eye to eye with her. She was not an easy woman to deal with, and I didn't have time for her interference or anxieties. Perhaps another serving of tea would hold her in the trancelike state required for weaving long enough for me to talk to the Eldress without her meddling tactics.

I wiped the sweat from my palms on the pleats of my skirt and tiptoed my way through the threading Daughters, grateful they were far too immersed in their prayers to notice my revulsion.

Shivering again, I jumped over one of Juna's roots, conceding to the irrational fear that her bindings would ensnare me, too, if they noticed my presence. Best not to interfere with a Daughter in the goddess's presence, bound by roots in earth and sky.

The fire pit was still warm, though the cookfire had been extinguished to maintain the darkness for prayers. Mother thought the goddess would only contact us in the dark, as the Eldress had preached when she was still powerful enough to lead us. Something about a prophecy—but I'd stopped listening to Mother's teachings so long ago. They were almost as unbearable as the Stitcher's.

A light unfolds from the darkness, beginning what will have no end. The words pulsed in my mind, reemerging from the dark recesses of memory. *You are the light and I am the end.*

My body stiffened as I recalled the words Prisha had crooned, and a numb, tingling sensation spread through my limbs. I'd always thought that the prophecy foretold a new Stitcher, a new leader, to protect our people and deliver us from Prisha's wrath. Something *good* to hope for. But Prisha insisted the words had been meant for me.

The only end I'd begun was the beginning of *our* end. Time to fix that.

I slipped the backpack from my shoulders, careful to place it gently upon the sandy floor. But not careful enough. My shaking limbs knocked into the metal handle of a saucepan sitting on the edge of a grate set over the fire. It spun, swirling the remnants of midday meal—lorbean paste by the sweet, nutty aroma of it.

I lunged to stop its teetering progress over the edge, but knocked into the tea kettle instead, dislodging it from where it hung over the dregs of the cookfire. The kettle flew into the wooden support beam of the gurya, and the lid rattled against the ground as it rolled to my feet.

Venom and hell. What is wrong with you, Zara? Light flared at my sternum as my heart rate quickened. I hastily adjusted Lurah's scarf to hide it.

The air crackled behind me, and my shoulders slumped. Of course she'd heard me. Had she seen? I spun around, clutching the layers of scarf over my heart, not needing the light to know whose shadowy form I faced. This was her gurya to protect—her charge. And as Mother, her dwelling was most important because it housed the ancient Eldress. Any disturbance would call her attention.

Mother's roots receded, winding and twisting away to unbind her until she sat upright with a jolt, gasping sharply for breath as though she had been held below water all this time. Her eyes shot open, landing directly upon me. "Zaraya Avasya."

Full name. Perfect.

Her voice was calm and even, almost a whisper, but she had not yet mastered how to extend that same composure to her eyes. I searched for something to say, something to explain my interference during the clan's prayers, and braced myself for the inevitable implosion of her temper. Her irises flickered with—anger? Worry? I could not tell, but I knew her reaction would be unpleasant.

"You came back." She rose and crossed the distance between us, clasping my shoulders in her angular grip. The intensity of her gaze made me recoil, but her firm hold did not slacken. "You're injured."

She regarded me as though she could not entirely believe my presence, patting my arms with her hands, then retreated to collect a tin from a shelf at the outskirts of the room. When she returned, she dipped her fingers into the sticky salve, then brushed my tunic aside to reveal the jagged gash at my shoulder.

I gasped and flinched away, frightened she might shift Lurah's scarf and reveal the light I hid from her, but she merely shushed me and set herself to healing, as mothers do. Not that Loehla was truly my blood mother, but she was *Mother* to my whole generation of Sisters, and that bond was most important.

The balm soothed the burning pain into a dull but lingering ache that tingled with icy relief. Her cheeks sagged into a frown. "You missed the morning and midday prayers. It is already time for evening prayer."

Regardless of my absence, I would have evaded them. But best not to incur her wrath with such a reminder.

"I—the heat got to me." I didn't want to share what I remembered of my evening...only Halah knew the lengths to which Mother would unravel if I told her. She was not the one I needed to help with this mess. "Mother, let me see the Stitcher."

Her eyes narrowed into an austere expression of disapproval. "She is resting. Praying to Halah, as *you* should be."

"Mother, it's important. The sky—"

She waved her hand to stop me. "You spend too much time chasing the monsters, Zara. We need you here, too. The Eldress is *dying*."

My breath caught in my throat and the ground spun around me. "Dying?" If the Eldress could not help us, Prisha would win. I'd handed her a victory in a star-gilded goblet. The Eldress couldn't die. Not yet...I needed to talk to her. "Yes, but—something's wrong. The sky is worsening—more tears are opening. More of Prisha's monsters. The travelers going to A'i Halajan need protection. We should send out more Daughters to patrol the desert. The festival is starting soon, and I—"

"*The festival does not matter,* Zara. There are more important concerns."

"It matters to *me*—" My short tone gave away too much of the anger simmering in my stomach.

Mother scoffed. "Since when do you care about A'i Halajan? You have dug your feet into the sand against your union ever since it was proposed by the elders."

My gut wrenched. "I *don't* care about my union." I groaned, weaving my fingers through the hair at my temples and clutching the sides of my face. I'd agreed to marry Rali begrudgingly because it was a tolerable match and because he was kind, but the prospect of marrying him did not excite me. It was merely a duty to fulfill. Sure, the sentiments of all his letters had earned him a tentative place in my heart—kindling the small flame of hope that maybe our union *would* truly be blessed by Halah. But I did not love him. Not yet, anyway. But there could be worse—my Sisters had certainly been pursued by worse. At the very least, Rali promised I could return to the dunes to fight as soon as possible.

Still, none of that meant I had to look forward to the union.

"I care about the *people*," I amended with a sigh. "The whole thing is ridiculous...that they are crossing the desert from Haldratha or Zunar, heading to Rashii just to see *me*. They risk their necks to—"

"Then you'd best make yourself something worth risking their necks for," Mother snapped, her stern tone seeped with exasperation.

I took a deep breath, holding it in my lungs as I steadied myself, reminding myself to focus on what was important and not on what stirred my emotions. I should have been more careful earlier. At least then, the tea would be brewing instead of Mother's vitriol. "We need to protect them. If the Eldress cannot protect them, we need to patrol the dunes. We need to fight back. More monsters are coming."

And I sort of destroyed centuries of stitches and weakened the fabric of the skies and now the threat of Prisha is imminent and we're all going to die and it's entirely my fault, but please don't hate me, because the Stitcher will know what to do if you just let me talk to her. The thoughts flailed wildly through my mind, but I buried them deep down beneath the layers of panic, guilt, and self-doubt.

"We must focus on our prayers." Mother sighed. "If Halah does not bless us soon with a new Stitcher to mend the skies and banish Prisha's monsters, how much longer will the realm last?" She shook her head softly, her eyes brimming with emotion. "We do not need more *warriors* to die at the claws of her monsters. We need a new *Stitcher.* The realm needs us to protect them...and we will. But we *must* find a replacement for her. We must pray. We *all* must pray. We're nearly out of time."

Here we go again. Mother was ashamed of my lack of devotion and infuriatingly vocal about my shortcomings as a Daughter of Halah. Luckily, there were plenty of other Daughters to make her proud. If Halah cared for us as Mother insisted, surely she would choose one of *them,* and *I* could continue what I did best: fighting and orchestrating chaos.

I glanced around at my Sisters' prayerful postures, silently weaving the shared tapestry with vacant eyes as the roots twisted and writhed around their legs. All unified by their connections— like none could exist without the others. All hoping the goddess would finally reach out and bless them as her choice to replace our Eldress.

Better them than me.

I did not want to pray to the goddess, and I certainly did not want to commune with Halah. I'd had enough of Halah for a life-time, considering my last unpleasant interaction with the goddesses. It was best for all involved if I steered clear of them.

"I'll brew more tea," I hedged, sidestepping both Mother and her lecture in hopes that the offer would appease her into getting off my back. I rubbed my temples, trying to sort through the noise of concerns racing through my mind.

I reached for my satchel and withdrew the leather-wrapped package containing the crucial ingredient for our sacred tea blend. Not all of us could find the tendrils of energy without the venom tea, though some of us could. The heart of stars seemed to heighten my awareness of them, but they'd always come to me naturally, even without the brew, though I'd never wanted to use them. Probably because I spent so much time brushing them away. They were like the stray cat Mata had brought along when she returned to the clan from the city years ago. While Mata showered the cat with affection and treats, the little thing had latched itself to me, ignoring my efforts to avoid it. As if its life's sole ambition had become to endear itself to me. *I wonder what happened to that little thing...*

Mother grabbed my wrist to interrupt my musings. "You were gone nearly two days, Zara. We saw the skies...we feared—"

I paused. *Two days?* My eyes darted to the canopy above, reassessing the position of the sun. I supposed it had been nearly two—the open canopy showed the fading sun rimmed with the color of blood, casting a warm glow across the sky, though the Daughter's magic maintained the darkness within the gurya. "You *should* be afraid, Mother. It's getting worse." My gaze softened, so hopeful she would listen, yet devastated by the presumption she would not. "We should send out more Daughters to fight," I braved. "And perhaps you should pray some more."

She huffed with ill-concealed indignation. "Are you just trying to avoid me? We sent Lurah to search for you. We needed you home. The Eldress won't last much longer. You really must pray with us...no more of these excursions. Not now."

Mother hid her face then, moving toward the cook table

where she promptly busied herself in her work. I noticed the anxiety in the way she carried her shoulders—she always cooked when she was worried. The flat white circle she tossed on the table slapped against the surface, and she worked quickly to spread leftover lorbean paste across it. She drizzled it with honey, then shoved it into my hands. "Eat. You must be starving."

I bit into the bubbled crust of halfmoon bread and could not resist closing my eyes as I savored the sweet confection—the honey was a delicacy given as a gift to the Daughters at last year's festival. Mother had scoffed at it, calling it a pity present to make up for the lack of new Daughters sent to our clan last year—the most recent unions hadn't been as blessed as Halah had led us to believe. But me? I called the thick amber liquid a *little taste of heaven.*

In three eager bites, the halfmoon bread vanished, and Mother bustled about, already preparing another. I sipped deeply from the clay jug on the table, reveling in the way the water chilled my parched throat as it made its way down to my stomach. After greedily chugging half of the jug's contents, I placed it down and locked eyes with Mother. She did not even scold me. Something was wrong. Well, something *aside* from the wrongs I already knew to be wrong.

"What's the matter?" I asked.

"Everything. The Eldress. Halah. You. Lurah." She sighed heavily. "She hasn't returned." Silence fell between us, with only the humming sound of my Sisters' weaving magic to fill the air.

"She will come back." As soon as I said the words, I knew they were not true.

"Something is wrong. I can feel it," Mother said. I suddenly realized how old she had become—her eyes frosted with white film, her cheeks sagged between cascading wrinkles. The beads she wore on her ears tugged her earlobes downward, and no amount of beaded collars could disguise the years of life the loose skin of her neck implied.

"I'll go find her," I offered impulsively, needing to do something other than marinate in Mother's anxious presence. If Lurah were out there alone...she might not survive. Between Riders who patrolled the dunes hunting us, Prisha's deadly monsters, and the fact that I'd accidentally opened more tears in the sky and summoned the vengeful goddess's attention...she didn't stand a chance. I had to return her to safety before anything bad happened to her.

Then I could speak to the Stitcher.

I leaned across the table and stashed a halfmoon bread in my pocket for the way. Lurah couldn't have gotten far. She was an excellent weaver, but prayed too often to match my level of physical stamina. It wouldn't take long. And perhaps if I returned her, Mother would relax and fall back into prayer.

But Loehla shook her head, her expression hardening to reveal how deep her wrinkles had become. "No, Zara. We cannot afford to sacrifice another Daughter. We've lost too many in the dunes and to unions in Rashii. No more. Not now. I fear the war is almost...beyond hope." A teacup rattled in her hand as she held it out to me, no longer hot but still smelling strongly of nettles and spice. "Perhaps if you—"

I eyed the tea nervously and pushed past her, moving toward the entrance of the gurya before she could finish her thought. Only Halah knew what would happen if I drank that tea. I didn't need anything to enhance my connection with the goddess's magic...I'd already caused enough disasters this moon. Plus, I needed my full wits about me to rescue Lurah and return to speak to the Eldress as quickly as possible. Tucking my braids beneath one of Lurah's scarves, I fastened it around my hair and across my mouth, then turned to face Mother.

"I'll find her. Don't worry." The daylight assaulted my vision when I slipped through the opening, but Mother's hand wrapped around my wrist, her grip a bit too forceful.

"Do not be ridiculous, Zara. You must stay. *Weave.* We must pray to get an answer from Halah before the Eldress dies."

I pulled my hand away. "You know I'm not the answer we need. Let me find my Sister."

"Zara, enough! I will not lose any more Daughters today. I will not let the realm suffer because of your selfishness. It is time you stop walking around with your head in the clouds."

"*I'm* the one with my head in the clouds?" Resentment spilled from me with a short laugh. How could she say such a thing? At least I prioritized chasing the monsters to keep us safe— to keep everyone safe. What did she do? *Nothing.*

Mother opened her mouth to speak, her eyes fierce with righteousness, but I'd had enough. I leaned toward her, not bothering to dull my piercing glare for the benefit of her comfort. "You spend day and night praying to a goddess who ignores you, hoping for a solution that isn't coming. It's *not working*, Mother. But by all means, you stay here and...*pray*. Or whatever you think is best."

My lips pulled into a scowl as my eyes scanned her over with unfiltered disgust. "I'm going to find Lurah and bring her back. I'll do *my* part to save the realm by killing any monsters I come across. And *you'd* better reconsider what the realm needs because we don't have time to wait for a new Stitcher. We need to wake up the one we already have and convince her to help." I filled my lungs, realizing how much tension I held in my shoulders before I exhaled a slowly measured breath, demonstrating a return of my self-restraint. I lowered my voice. "But I can tell you with certainty, if we do nothing, thousands of people will *die*. I'm getting Lurah. Then I want to see the Eldress. And you will not stop me."

Mother sucked in a sharp breath and opened her mouth, but

whatever she wished to say in response fizzled out of existence. An arrow whizzed through the air, sailing over my shoulder so the whisper of its feathers grazed the skin by my ear. The shaft sank into the hide of the gurya with a *thunk*, pinning a blue and silver scrap of fabric to a tent pole. The material glimmered, woven with metallic threads that caught the essence of the waning sun as it tumbled downward, revealing the intricate patterns woven into the fine silk.

Lurah's work.

CHAPTER 4

THIS OLD SNAKE

Mother reached for the fabric, her eyes shifting from anger to despair. Her lips pursed in an effort to hide her shifting emotions as her fingers grazed over the embroidery.

A slip of parchment revealed itself, rustling against the smooth silk. Mother's brow furrowed when she unfolded it, and her expression changed to confusion as she read the single word scrawled across it. *Run.*

Her eyes snapped toward mine. "Outsiders. We've lingered too long."

The dry heat of the desert made my vision swim for a moment, and beads of sweat gathered at my hairline. The Daughters were a nomadic people—we moved throughout the Sundom Desert to avoid the notice of our enemies, who seemed to grow in number with every passing year. The Dune Riders had long pursued us, vigilantes driven by a misguided notion that our magic had caused the rifted skies. They blamed us for the monsters plaguing our realm and vowed to purge us from the land, but they had never succeeded in picking off more than a stray Daughter wandering the dunes.

Then there were the whispers of war brought home by Sisters returning from the city...murmurs of the northern Khazdruki who claimed the land of their ancestors had been stolen to build Rashii, and that Prisha's curse was a punishment for our wrongs. The land had been lost in a war, of course, but they didn't care for those semantics, if the whisperers were to be believed. And then there was Prisha—the most troublesome, long-standing threat of all.

The Eldress sacrificed most of her remaining energy to conceal our location from outsiders, and we never stayed anywhere longer than a few moons for our safety. But as she weakened, we risked longer waits between moves. Lurah's note—if it had even come from Lurah—meant that our location had been compromised. And it couldn't have happened at a worse time.

Venom and hell.

My stomach twisted into knots. Had Lurah been captured? Was she still alive? Should I go after her? Numbness crept from my fingertips to my limbs, turning them useless as my nerves sputtered with uncertainty. I knew we had to depart for our safety, but if we left now, I wouldn't have the chance to speak to the Eldress for weeks. The moves always sent her to a state of comatose hibernation. I didn't have the time to wait for such a long recovery. *Stall, Zara. Make a plan.* "Mother...we should call on the other elders. We should show them—"

"*I* am the Matriarch of the Daughters. We need to go. Now." She glanced nervously across the dunes, clutching the opening of the gurya in her hand. "Come." She beckoned me inside with an urgent wave of her hand.

"But is it Lurah's writing? Did she send it? Are you certain it's from her?"

"I do not know! It is Lurah's weaving, but—"

A shadow of a shiver crept up my spine, and the sky crackled with energy. Mother felt it too—her expression faltered, and her mouth opened up, her next half-formed word forgotten. I looked up. A wave of darkness swept above us, spreading to dull the marred expanse of blue sky, changing it from azure to weary gray and finally to a foreboding charcoal—much too sudden to attribute the change to sundown. Something was wrong.

"What is happening?" I whispered as the skies darkened to total blackness, so inky it completely obscured the sun from our view.

A shriek from inside the gurya startled me out of my wonder. Mother pulled me beneath the tent, and my stomach turned as my eyes swept across the room. My Sisters sat taller, their chests lifted to the sky and their heads thrown backward to revere the blackened heavens. Blue lights flared to life between them, winding together to form an interconnected web of threads, pulsing and illuminating their vacant expressions. Their rigid arms stretched out at their sides, and they jolted in unison, like a strike of lightning met each of their hearts. A haunted humming rose and dipped, filling the air and seeping into every space of the room like a heavy mist.

The lights illuminated the gauzy curtains draped in front of the Eldress's private quarters, turning them transparent. Through the hangings, the form of her crippled, weakened body moved like the shadow of a monster. Frail and gnarled, all skin and bone. A doleful, wailing groan emerged from behind the curtains—Ahma stirred. Or perhaps she was dying. *Hard to tell.*

A blinding light cracked in the center of the room, shooting straight up toward the heavens, as though the ground surged with the same electricity that descended from the sky on the hottest nights. My mind raced in competition with my heartbeat, wondering what I should do—if there was anything I *could* do—

but I was frozen to the spot. No roots gripped me as they did my Sisters, but I was every bit as restrained by my fear.

I could not blink. *A light unfolds from the darkness, beginning what will have no end.* The words flashed in my mind. Was this... was this it, then?

The rod of lightning between the Daughters surged with power, reaching up through the opening of the gurya and scattering into a shower of sparks above. They lingered like stars in the sky, then rearranged, crawling into a new formation before my very eyes. The symbol of the goddesses appeared against the heavens—a double-headed snake with vicious fangs and slits for eyes. One head for Halah—the Mother of Daughters who passed down her magic, teaching us to protect the realm from her sister. The other head for Prisha, the jealous one—the sister banished to the In Between for her crimes, fighting to find her way back to destroy our realm and exact her revenge.

The stars forming the snake's likeness shimmered as it writhed, freeing itself from its old skin and rising slowly, preparing to strike. The shedding of skin signaled the imminent passage of powers from one Stitcher to the next.

Halah was choosing.

And if she was choosing, I needed to be anywhere but here. I didn't dare call the goddess's attention for the second time this moon. But my muscles calcified into stone, and I stood staring in horror at the sky as the heaviness of dread anchored me to the spot. *Not me. Please not me.* And yet, deep down, beneath my ocean of buried thoughts and emotions, I *knew.*

Mother clasped her hands around my wrists, her eyes widening with a frenetic zeal I'd never witnessed in them before. "Zara! It is happening. It is finally happening! Halah is choosing. A light in the darkness!" My mouth gaped as I took in the scene— my Sisters humming, their faces contorted, bodies twisted into awkward positions, the lights winding through the web of pulsing energy, like little shooting stars streaking across the heavens. The stars announcing the arrival of a new Stitcher.

The lights raced toward me, too, reaching to connect me to the web of Daughters, but I slammed walls around my heart and mind, shutting them out. *Pick one of my Sisters. Any one of them. Not me.*

But then—something changed. Or stopped. Or perhaps went entirely wrong. A great collective hiss filled the air. My Sisters' bodies slumped from their rigid positions, relaxing into a more natural posture, though they did not wake. The interlaced ribbons of light dulled, then faded. A buildup of energy and a release before its culmination.

"No!" Mother screeched, sounding much like one of the desert's scavenger birds squawking to stake a claim over a stack of decaying bones. "No! Do not forsake us, Halah! Please! Do not leave yet...one of us must be worthy!" She spun on me then, the ardent flare of her gaze suggesting a woman spiraling out of control, desperate to hang on to some modicum of hope. "Weave, Zara! Pray! We must try. Do not let Halah leave us! Do not be so selfish as to condemn us without trying."

I tried to resist, suspecting what Halah had planned for me, but Mother's grip dug into my arms. She caught me off guard as she steered me toward the cook table and shoved me to the ground. I should have been able to overpower her, but shock turned my limbs to warm honey, rendering me unable to move, incapable of forcing my body to comply. Mother's fingers wound their way through my braids, and she pulled my head backward, bringing a teacup to my mouth. My body stiffened, but I could not push her off me —her grasp was unyielding. She gripped my cheeks hard and forced my mouth open, tipping the contents of the cup past my lips to compel me to commune with the goddess against my will.

No. Not me. If I weave, she will find me. I'm not meant for Stitching.

The venomous brew sloshed over my tongue, somehow more bitter and revolting in this cooled state. I lurched forward to spit out the mouthful, but Mother forced me back again, holding my jaw closed until I had no choice but to swallow. The last I saw of her was her eyes, unnaturally widened, her emotions flickering like fire in the depths of her irises.

My head dipped backward, and my chin rose to the sky, my mouth growing slack and my eyes losing focus. The tea weakened my resistance and tendrils of energy found me—rushing from the bindings that tethered my Sisters to wrap around my knees and ankles, restraining my wrists and crawling up my torso to my neck. The roots pulsed in time with my heartbeat, quickly at first, as the wave of panic rushed through me, then slowly as the venom tea took hold, dimming my senses and decelerating my breaths until I succumbed to the weight of its presence. The venom held me underwater, making the air thick and unbreathable, distorted and yet somehow peaceful as I drowned in it.

Halah's voice found me as soon as the connection took root. "Zaraya," she whispered—though not out loud. Somehow *through*. Just...*there*. "We meet again, Star Thief." Her voice contained no trace of anger, just a serene calm that floated like drifting sunfire blossom petals on the wind. Despite that, I stiffened, trying to free myself from the spell, to pull myself away from the weaving that Mother had forced upon me. "Why do you try to hide from me? Are you afraid? The goddesses cannot ignore the one who carries the heart of stars."

Bile rose in my stomach. Of course I was afraid. I would give *anything* to return the heart of stars and avoid attention for the rest of my life. *I am not meant for this.*

"You will need the power to stitch, Zaraya...do not push me away. Let me grant you that gift."

Not me. I gasped for air, though no words surfaced. But how did one tell a goddess that they were mistaken? That they were choosing wrong? That I didn't want the so-called gift she offered.

Instead, I let words I wished to scream flow through my eyes and down my cheeks as silent tears. "Do not fear your power, Zaraya Avasya, Star Thief and Last of the Stitchers. Do not be afraid. We need you."

But I was afraid. My insides *burned* with fear. Last of the Stitchers? Star Thief? I mentally clawed at the heart of stars, shredding it and forcing it deeper and deeper inside of myself where it could never be reached. Where it could never be noticed again.

A rush of air circled the gurya, stirring life into all of the weaving Daughters, lifting the haze from my eyes and returning me to my corporeal presence. My Sisters woke more slowly, blinking the trance from their eyes. I shifted uncomfortably, growing distinctly aware of everyone's gaze upon me. The web of lights shimmered and retreated, vanishing in a glimmer of dust that settled on my shoulders, marking me with the favor of the goddess. Telling the others I'd been chosen.

"Zaraya Avasya," the Eldress's voice croaked from behind the curtains, and the shadow of Ahma's hunched form stretched across the drapery of her quarters. Her voice vibrated, shaky and weak, yet somehow hinting at a well of ancient power and wisdom. "Come."

Mother reached for my elbow, swooping under my arm to help me stand, but I snatched it away from her. I whirled to face her, my lips curling into disgust. "Do you plan to take every choice away from me? Is there *nothing* I can decide for myself? *I said I did not want to weave.* I don't want *this.*"

A weird sort of whimper escaped her mouth, and she backed away, watching me with an expression of uninhibited awe.

Slowly, I unfolded myself—stacking my knees over my ankles

with the awkwardness of a newborn foal, then straightening my torso and neck. *Venom and hell. What now?* I stood, so uncertain on my feet that a single breath in my direction could topple me. The Stitcher's shadow beckoned, and I swallowed the dry lump in my throat—now sore from the harshness of venom tea. While I walked toward the Stitcher, my Sisters' heads followed me, tracking every step I made as though I were the most important thing they had ever witnessed. As though they hadn't spent the years making fun of my pitiful weaving. As if they hadn't ruthlessly teased me about the stack of love letters from Rali they'd found hidden beneath my bed mat, assuming I'd returned his gushing sentiments. As if I suddenly *mattered* and deserved their respect.

The Stitcher patted the nest of blankets that made up her bed, asking me to sit with her. I stepped closer, forcing my face to remain neutral. But inside, my stomach roiled with something wriggly as I drew close enough to see her. The Eldress's eyes met mine, clouded with milky bands as if streams of stars dwelled within them. A galaxy of wisdom contained within her soul, bestowed upon her by the goddess. Did my eyes glimmer like hers now? The thought did not comfort me.

Her skin sagged and puckered, lined with an incomprehensible number of wrinkles that merely alluded to the years she had lived. The lifetime of stitching had taken a toll on her body. It drooped and jutted in strange angles, and her skin dripped from her bones like melted wax, now stripped to a decrepit shadow of the power she once held. I wondered if I would become old and saggy, too...if the responsibilities that Halah had cursed me with would slowly consume me until nothing was left but a bag of bones and starry eyes of infinite wisdom. I choked on a sob, my lips pulling into a grimace despite my efforts to hide my disgust. I did not want this. I could not do this.

But now I didn't have a choice. Mother had made sure of that.

"Zara, come. I'm not long for this world." I did not know what she expected of me, so I shifted uncomfortably, pushing the sands beneath the woven mat with my boots. She gestured to a shimmering gown draped over her dressing screen. "I wove a dress for the new Stitcher. Put it on."

I nodded, swallowing the dry lump in my throat, and did as she asked. The dress rushed like water over my skin when I pulled it over my head. It was the softest, most cooling fabric that had ever graced my body, but the deep cut between my breasts and white hue was not the most conducive garment for my lifestyle—a lifestyle that had been completely uprooted when Halah chose me. Ahma's wrinkled mouth puckered with something probably meant to be a smile. "We have much to do. Carry me."

I recoiled slightly, uncertain if she was serious. She watched me expectantly, never blinking those milky eyes. *Venom and hell, she means it.* The Stitcher groaned and slowly propped herself up on her elbows, struggling to achieve a seated position. I swore I could hear her bones creaking as she moved. When she sighed deeply and looked as though she may topple back over, I rushed toward her and looped her fragile arms around my neck to avoid witnessing her repeat the same struggle again.

"Thank you," she whispered in a voice as grainy as the desert sands. "Now take me to stitch the skies. It is time for this old snake to shed its skin...and time for you to learn your duty."

"Ahma, I don't think—"

"Go. There isn't much time. You must learn."

I sifted through the racing thoughts in my head, contemplating dropping the Stitcher into her nest of blankets and running until the dunes swallowed me, but I waded through the gauzy drapes of her quarters and faced the room of my Sisters. They stood, eyes glued to me, then swept their hands up to the sky before gracefully lowering their fingertips to their collarbones. A sign of great respect. "Stitcher," they mumbled, an eerie reverence to their susurrous voices. "Sky Stitcher."

"You all are being weird," I murmured under my breath. Unsteady on my feet, and not just because I carried the Stitcher on my back, I moved through my Sisters. They placed their hands gently on my shoulders as I passed, treating me like some sort of divine spirit or...holy being. It was unsettling.

"Don't mind them. They are merely in awe," the Stitcher crooned into my ear, and I shuddered at the touch of her words on my neck.

In awe? I snorted air through my nose. Just yesterday, Sessu had ripped my letter to Rali from my hands to read it mockingly to my Sisters, teasing me about his superfluous affections. *Halah's blessing will shine light upon our union, though truthfully, you are my greatest blessing, Zara. My greatest treasure. Yours, Rali.*

She had laughed until tears formed in her eyes when I tried to snatch the letter back from her and continued to read. Now, she revered me. The urge to run rose to the forefront of my mind once again. Would they still revere me when they saw I'd stolen the heart of stars? When they realized I could never master the quiet, peaceful weaving of the Daughters? When they understood that my brand of magic was uncontrollable and chaotic?

There had been some sort of grave mistake.

Mother shuffled behind me, pressing halfmoon bread into my hands. I wanted to smack her away, but I numbly shoved the food into my satchel and scooped it up as I turned away, readjusting my hold around the Eldress's knees.

"You shouldn't go out there alone. I fear, with Lurah missing...that note...it's too dangerous. Let us come with you." She spoke as though nothing had passed between us, as though unaware that I might be upset with her or annoyed by her sudden change of heart, her newfound willingness to brave the dunes to fight in my honor. Apparently, now that she'd gotten her wish, she did not need to spend her days in prayer anymore. I stiffened when she spoke, my alertness heightened, but I did not turn to face her. I didn't want to see her.

"You should get the Daughters ready to move," I replied numbly, with hesitant authority. If our location had been compromised, it was Mother's duty to arrange for the Daughters' relocation, and assigning a task to keep her busy would keep her from meddling any further.

"But—"

"Listen to your Stitcher, Loehla. Mind your place," the Eldress croaked, waving a feeble hand. The simple dismissal left me feeling just a bit more endeared to her. Anyone who could tell Mother to mind her place earned my respect.

CHAPTER 5

MENDER OF SKIES

We emerged from the tent to azure skies painted with scars, bleeding the inky black of the In Between through the rifts. The last rays of daylight had reemerged from the cloak of darkness swathing Halah's choosing, but the sun drooped its weary head, searching for a place to rest among the dunes. The city of Rashii gleamed, resplendent with shimmering golden hues in the distance, and I thought of Rali. Would the union still progress if he found out I was the new Stitcher? Or would I now have to face a different lifetime of responsibility, growing old and shriveled and lonelier as the years passed? I could not decide which outcome I dreaded more.

Don't be an idiot, I scolded myself. *There are plenty of other disasters to worry about. What about Lurah? That arrow and the message...it had told us to run. Run from what? Had it even been from Lurah, or had some enemy sent it, hoping to lure us out from our shelter? Will Mother listen and prepare the Daughters to move? Will my Sisters be safe?*

I looked over my shoulder at the painted hides of the gurya.

The blue length of embroidered silk still dangled from the arrow lodged in the support beam. Were they in danger? Were we?

My heart pounded in answer.

"Ahma," I began uncertainly, not wishing to directly challenge the Eldress but unable to dismiss the concerns that lingered in my mind. "Ahma, we may not be safe. Perhaps we should allow a few of the Daughters to escort us? Or... should we wait for training until we can all move together? And we should send some of my Sisters to the city—to warn them about the new rifts."

"Do you not know who I am, child? I am the Eldress Stitcher. The mender of skies. The protector of our world. The enemy of Prisha."

I sensed she would continue with her accolades for as long as she was permitted, so I interjected, caving to the building pressure of my concern. "But, Ahma—" *You are half dead.*

"But what, Zara? Do you not trust me? I stitch the *skies*. They listen to my will. I can weave the heavens and wear the clouds as a cloak to hide us from those who wish us harm. Can you say the same, young Stitcher?"

My brows furrowed, wondering if what she said was true. I knew her magic concealed our guryas to ward off unwanted travelers and enemies, but was *that* how it was done? Ahma bent the skies to her will and hid us beneath a cloak of her magic? Was that a power typical of the Stitchers? My head reeled at the immensity of the energy likely required for such an act. Perhaps that was why she always looked so...depleted.

My eyes drifted to my hands, wondering if I'd someday learn to do that too. I laughed and wiped my palms down my sides, as if I could clean away the ridiculous notion and the nervous clamminess in one swipe. To expect to make a garment from the sky seemed...laughable. So far, all I'd managed to accomplish was to steal the stars and anger a murderous goddess. And nearly die... several times.

"Ahma, I think there's been a mistake. Halah should not have chosen...me." She should be angry with me for ripping apart the stitches, for destroying the work of our ancestors when I took the heart of stars...even if it was unintentional. It didn't make sense for her to choose me.

"Yet she did," the Eldress responded in an absolute tone, dismissing my objections. "Head further west. See those rifts? We'll use those. Hurry."

I hastened my pace, but the nagging concerns in my mind refused to be silenced. What was her plan? Did she have the strength to deal with the monsters from those rifts? I feared I did not—exhaustion pervaded every inch of my body. And what about Lurah? That warning? We should be relocating or perhaps even fleeing to the city with the other Daughters to take shelter in Rashii, warning and protecting the attendants of the festival, not wasting time training a hopeless case like me. I never thought I'd come to say it, but perhaps our time would be better served praying to Halah. Then we could ask her what in her right mind she thought she was doing when she chose me.

The sand danced around my feet, sliding beneath my soles with each step while I mulled over my worries. "I just—this doesn't make any sense. I've never been a devoted Daughter of Halah's. And I'm meant to marry that guard this year, Rali. It is written in the stars...or so you said." I left out my personal objections to the marriage and my plans to continue fighting Prisha's monsters in the dunes after our union, doubting that Ahma would approve of our untraditional arrangement or care two dune beetle wings about my reservations.

The Eldress's chest bubbled with laughter, her amusement escaping in the most unusual sound. Deep and lyrical, like the dune crickets that chirruped at night, but also deeply haunting, like the lonely moon in the sky. "No, Zaraya. A light as ardent as yours has the power to move the stars. Whatever they said does not matter any longer. You are destined for more."

Now she was speaking in riddles. I had half a mind to tell her as much, but she continued in her deep, croaking voice. "Yes, the Daughters heed the stars, but even *they* serve the goddess. And now they serve you, if I'm not mistaken. Watch how they glimmer for you when night falls. Halah chose *you*. It is time you accept that."

"But I don't want this. She chose wrong," I snapped, frustrated by her certainty, by her inability to understand my confliction. The Eldress was old and full of ancient wisdom and power. I was...Zara. Just Zara.

"Zara, you have a great responsibility. The realm needs you. When I am gone, you will be the only protector. The only one to stitch the skies and protect the realm from Prisha and her monsters. Without you, she will destroy us all. Do you wish to subject your world to such a fate?"

"There must be a way to undo it. I am better at fighting...I'm not gentle and quiet like you. Please. Let her pick someone else."

"You think me quiet and gentle? Perhaps you are not as clever as I thought."

Heat rose in my core at the insult, and with that sudden burst of energy, the ribbons of magic gravitated toward my palms, caressing my skin and humming with power. Asking to be used. I did not know how I knew, but I could feel it—I could feel my connection to it stronger than I ever had before. Light flowed from my arms, bathing my skin in a soft, warm glow.

The Eldress patted my shoulder appraisingly. "Good, yes. You see? Your power is strong...like it is a part of you already. Now use it. Send it up to the heavens and stitch that rift. The angry-looking one, over there." She waved a knobbly hand toward the sky, pointing out the seeping gash above us that crackled with gold and the oily spillage from the cursed In Between. "Put me down if you must. Focus on weaving the threads through the seam—the skies will listen."

I knew it would not work, but with my temper rising, I lowered the Eldress from my back. The least I could do was humor her...maybe *then* she would understand this was all a mistake. Maybe then she would help me find a way to undo this.

But at the slightest nudge from the heart of stars, cords of light radiated from my fingertips, beaming upward to the opening between realms. Surprise registered somewhere within me, but I fought to calm my racing pulse.

Stitch, I asked the tendrils of magic. My command was tentative...uncertain. Would the skies really listen to me, as Ahma had said? I waved my hand, ignoring the beads of sweat gathering on my brow and the vibrating sense of power that stole the breath from my lungs. The threads refused to sway to my commands. Finally, I ripped my hand from the sky, releasing myself from the strain of my effort.

"It's not working," I heaved in frustration.

The rift crackled with lightning and gaped wider as my magic receded. Molten gold lined the black space like the mouth of a monster flashing its wicked teeth, waiting to devour us whole.

Two Daughters caught in a web. Prisha will have her revenge when both are dead. A chill ran up my spine as I watched the gap stretch, Prisha's curse reaching toward the land in inky black shadows. Crawlers. My nerves ignited, banishing the sluggish fatigue from my limbs as my body buzzed with power. The dark, fingerlike shadow pummeled toward the ground, trailing against the jewel-toned sky like a stain.

Venom and hell. How can I learn to mend the skies if Prisha is summoned by every failure?

The creature spread into a flat puddle on the ground, creating a pool of darkness so complete it siphoned the vibrance of its surroundings, draining the world of its beauty.

I stepped between the creature and Ahma, drawing my dagger from its sheath at my ribs and widening my stance. The ridged back of the crawler rose up from the puddle first, hunched and so bony that its vertebrae flared into spikes like the horned beetles of the desert. The spindly limbs emerged next, followed by its head, hanging low toward the ground with milky white eyes locked on its prey.

It crawled, creeping across the dunes—slowly at first to gain its footing, then bounding forward without warning. It crossed the distance too quickly, leaping into the air with gnashing teeth and claws outstretched. The force of its collision knocked the wind from my lungs, and we tumbled through the sand. I braced my forearm against its neck, holding the creature's rabid jaws only inches away from my face, struggling against its unrelenting strength. I groaned with effort and shoved the dagger into its temple. Its skull did not resist my blade like normal bone, but succumbed easily with a shower of curdled black blood, letting the blade sink straight to the hilt. The crawler's shriek left behind a dull ringing in my ears and a silence that carried a palpable weight.

A soft shuffling of sand broke the quiet tension. Breathing shallowly, I turned and saw the Stitcher hobbling toward me, so ancient and diminished she looked like a creature of the In Between herself. She hinged forward at the hips and laid a fragile hand of bone and wrinkles on my shoulder, a gesture that felt like condescension wrapped in pity. *There, there,* I imagined her saying, though no words left her puckered mouth. She merely searched my eyes in overbearing silence, and the urge to squirm away from her piercing gaze overwhelmed me. But somehow, I remained rigid, still as a statue. Too afraid, or perhaps incapable of recoiling.

"Hmm," she murmured finally, breaking her deep contemplation. Only the tension in her jaw showed the slightest hint of her inner thoughts. I sat up straighter, still struggling to master my breath. Had she heard Prisha too? Did she know the goddess had taken notice?

"That will not do. We must teach you to do better before I expire. Why are you afraid?" She knelt at my side, her emerald and gold skirt collecting into a pool of ripples around her knees. She reached past my bent legs and extended her hand to brush the limp form of the crawler. With a burdened sigh, she closed her eyes and drew the traces of Halah's power toward her, pulling the threads of magic from the air until they glimmered about her, encapsulating her in a golden aura.

A bolt of lightning cracked at her fingertips, and the crawler's body jerked with the sudden influx of power. It withered away, crumbling to dust, scattering on winds that did not belong to the desert. The slithering form of a snake emerged from its ashes, its lithe body twisting in the sand to flee. The Eldress stood with unhurried grace and brushed the golden dust of the desert from her skirt, considering the creature as it disappeared into the shadowy dunes. But it was not fast enough.

Inspiration glimmered in the whites of her eyes, and a great inhalation expanded her lungs. Ahma's whole body swelled, growing taller and more menacing. At her full height, her shadow elongated behind her, stretching out like an ominous portent to reveal a glimmer of the power she wielded. The Eldress was not a weak, dying creature; she was a force of nature...a Daughter of the goddess. At least when she mustered the last reserves of her power. How had I ever misconstrued that?

The threads of Halah's magic shot from her fingers and struck her target, her precision enviable by even the most skilled archer. Molten gold flowed through the snake's body, electrifying it from within until only a charred and petrified form remained.

Breathing heavily, Ahma crossed the dunes with an agility I never thought her capable of, as though the brief brush with her purpose had re-empowered her.

She snapped her hand over the deceased snake, and the skies swirled, seemingly aware of the threat below. Prisha's anger crackled overhead, but the Eldress looked skyward, cast a glare that would bring any self-preserving god to their knees, and hurled the petrified snake toward the heavens. With her head tilted backward, a glint of taunting in her eyes, she stretched her arms out wide. The skies listened to her call.

The glimmering threads rippled at her command, gossamer floss weaving through the rift in a mesmerizing dance, a duet of stars and wonder. The darkness shrank away, yielding to the glowing edges of the rift until the line of gold sparked in the sky and dissipated. A smooth blue plain remained where the gash had been, completely healed of damage. Ahma turned back to me, the crooked smile on her face an echo of who she'd once been.

"Two dune beetles beneath one boot, you see?" She lifted her wiry brows to appraise her own efforts. "Stitched Prisha's creature right into the sky...may the stars swallow it whole so it will be banished from this realm forever." Her wide, toothy grin did little to ease my eyebrows back into place. They'd wandered straight to my hairline and gotten irrevocably stuck there. Ahma rolled her eyes, then made a strange gurgling sound, halfway between a sigh and a grumble. "Do not be so afraid of your power, young Stitcher. The skies will listen, but you must *mean* it. You must own your responsibilities...face them with courage."

"Ahma, you're...alarming," I whispered, half under my breath. *Venom and hell, Zara. Why did you say that out loud? To the Eldress?*

But the Eldress chuckled in her chirruping melody. "And what did you expect? I told you—Halah does not choose wrong. She does not choose the weak. She chose me, and now she's chosen you. *You* must save us when I am gone. *You* are our future." She lifted my chin in her hand, staring into my eyes with the milky streams of stars in hers. "Does it make sense to you now? Why she chose you?"

Her words were meant to assure me, but they had the opposite effect. "I don't want it. I never intended to become ancient and saggy like you, Ahma." *Again, with the truth. Shut your mouth, Zara. She doesn't need to know you assumed you'd die fighting in this war while one of your Sisters carried on to stitch the skies.*

She frowned, her jowls framing the deep creases along her lip lines, but her eyes still twinkled in contrast. "I'll remember that when I'm gone."

I couldn't tell if she was angry or amused, so I pulled my gaze quickly from her and focused on the sky. The stars emerged across the navy veil, golden orbs shimmering through the dark rifts while blackness oozed from the In Between, somewhat tarnishing the glow of their spirits. But when I swept my eyes across the heavens, the stars blinked in greeting. They flared to life despite the curse that slipped between them, the darkness that fought so hard to choke away the resplendence that made them shine. How was I to command something so inconceivably...eternal? I was no Stitcher. This was madness.

The Eldress heaved a weary sigh. "Take us home. We will try again at dayburst."

With a sense of resolute failure overturning the acrid resentment in my gut, brewing some sort of clumpy, sickening stew, I scooped the Eldress into my arms and helped her onto my back. I dared not voice it, but I'd made up my mind. Tomorrow, I'd flee to the city. Perhaps I could encourage the clan to come, too.

If I were the only hope in standing up against Prisha's curse, the only recourse against the deadly monsters and growing rifts, none of us were—how did Ahma put it? *Long for this world.* We needed time...more time than Ahma's stitches had bought us. And we needed help. We needed Halah to come to her senses and pick someone better suited for these responsibilities.

"Hurry, Zara. I am slipping."

The Eldress's bony hands clasped one another in front of my neck, and her knees pressed sharply into my hips. I knew she did not mean she was losing her grip on my back...stitching the gash in the sky had weakened her. "Get us back to the Daughters. I need their strength."

"Their strength?" I asked, hurrying back along the path we had come.

"The weaving—the Daughters all play a part in a Stitcher's magic—you and I are...simply conduits of...their...collective...effort."

Her words slowed and slurred as sleep greedily reached for her, and her hold loosened.

A lattice of golden mesh sparked above us, dissolving like a fraying ribbon consumed by a lick of flames. "Ahma," I prompted tentatively. She did not answer.

The ground began to tremble and I froze, analyzing the pattern of thumps and swishes filling the empty air, recognizing its source with a shiver of nerves along my neck. A cluster of hooded figures emerged from the dunes, pausing at the precipice of a golden hill to glare down at us.

Heart pounding somewhere in my throat and ears rather than its rightful place between my ribs, I turned and fled. Shouts erupted behind me, and the galloping sound of hooves thumping against sand pursued us. I gripped Ahma's legs closer, pushing through the slipping sands but struggling to gain the traction to run.

What was I doing? I could not outrun horses. "Ahma! Wake up! Please!"

Ahma screeched, and I nearly fell to my knees. Something

sharp brushed against my shoulder blade as she slumped forward, and a warm, sticky substance spread across my back. Her withering groan set my pulse into a frenzy. "Ahma?" I tried, struggling beneath the extra weight of her fading consciousness.

"Put me down, child," she managed, her voice a raspy wisp of steam spilling from a boiling kettle.

I gripped her tighter and spun around, casting my gaze in a wide circle. Dark figures surrounded us from every angle, closing in with weapons as sharp and menacing as the features on their faces. The Dune Riders. Hunters of the Daughters.

Run, Zara. But I turned wildly, my heart threatening to breach the confines of my ribs as I realized there were no weaknesses in their formation. They'd trapped us.

CHAPTER 6

THE DUNE RIDERS

The Stitcher's arms grew slack and unresponsive, and her body slid down my back. I crouched to the ground to set her upon the sands, allowing my hands the freedom to move to the set of daggers sheathed at my ribs. If I could not run, I would fight. I had to protect Ahma—if only because I was not ready to take her place.

A tough lump lodged itself in my throat. An arrow jutted out from her shoulder, making her look even more feeble and broken. I turned my gaze toward the Riders, my jaw locked with fury, my teeth grinding together until they ached.

Another arrow landed at my foot. Not an accident or poor aim. A warning. The cocky grin on the Rider's face made *that* abundantly clear. "What do you think you're doing, little Daughter? Running away with the Stitcher? Thought you could save her?" he asked, his words floating with the lightness of laughter at my expense.

As if he had all the time in the world, all the confidence on his side, he stretched his arms out wide and rotated cavalierly, scanning the dunes. "That was an impressive bit of magic. We knew the Stitcher concealed herself with the stars, but we have never witnessed it in action." He glanced toward the Eldress's limp form. "Or...inaction."

He gestured toward the fraying threads of gold arcing in a dome above us—the last remnants of her concealment vanishing with a *pop*.

"But where are the rest of the Daughters? Have you abandoned them?" His chin lowered as his eyes found me again, and his tone darkened. "Or are you hiding them?"

I didn't realize how shallow my breathing had become, but my lungs suddenly begged for air, roaring with the pain of my neglect. Had they been the ones who'd taken Lurah? A quick scan of their ranks sent a weight of lead plopping into my stomach, bruising my insides—I didn't see her among them. But they could have her tucked away somewhere. If they did, I'd need to find her. I couldn't let them keep her. They could force Lurah to lead them to the guryas or—I did not want to think about the other possibilities.

I needed to get back to my Sisters to warn them—or handle the Riders myself. I couldn't let them find our camp.

A realization struck me, and panic rushed through my veins. My eyes flickered down to the sands for half a heartbeat, just long enough to confirm my fear. *No.* I righted my gaze hastily and glared at the haughty Rider, but he hadn't missed the cue...the subtle body language and my haste to correct it.

A sneer spread across his face, too stretched and thin to match the rest of his features. "You've left a trail for us. How thoughtful." His eyes darted to his neighbor, then he jerked his head in the direction of my footprints in the dunes, the trail of displaced sand that would lead them straight to my Sisters.

The Rider responded with a curt nod, then raised his chin with a triumphant whistle. A dozen broke rank and moved to his side. Dangerous smirks darkened their expressions with the promise of destruction, and they set off into the dunes. Panic clutched my breast as they stirred up the path behind them, erasing the trail of footsteps that connected me with home. A home they'd ensure I'd never be able to return to.

This game had to end now.

I whirled on the man towering before me, ignoring the other Riders who remained behind, their horses chuffing as they tightened their formation around us. Ahma groaned like a slaughtered goat on the ground, her blood black against her shoulder. How much longer would she last without a healer? How much blood had she lost?

"I never thought I'd see the day," the Rider began, taking a step closer to the Eldress. I shifted, crouching closer to Ahma, and prepared to unsheathe the dagger at my side. *You will not touch her,* I vowed, still clenching my teeth to the verge of cracking them.

He stopped and stared down his arched nose, his dark brows casting deep shadows across his features to emphasize his surly facade. His lips turned downward in a sneer. "So this is the 'great' Stitcher? I see no greatness...just a curse. A plague upon our land. Stand aside, Daughter. The monster needs to die."

A knife flashed in his hand, and he swooped down, about to plunge the blade into her heart. I lurched forward and stopped the blow with my forearm, sweeping my dagger up to the unprotected space beneath his arm. He easily deflected and shoved me to the ground, pinning me with a force that made my head snap backward into a spray of sand. My ribs groaned beneath the entirety of his weight, and I could feel the air slipping from my lungs.

Do something, Zara. Now.

The cool point of his blade touched the base of my jaw. "You're a pretty thing, but not pretty enough to keep alive. Another monster that deserves to die, just like the rest of your clan."

"The only monster here is you," I seethed, fighting against him, though my heart skittered at an uncomfortable pace beneath his elbow. He clicked his tongue.

I roared to gather my strength, and a subtle light surged within me. Tendrils of energy tickled my hands, weaving through the gaps of my fingers as if to remind me of their presence. I seized them. When my palms closed around the threads, their energy hummed with life, erupting into a vibrant spray of light that knocked the man onto his ass. Sucking in the dry air to refill the desert of my lungs, I moved toward him slowly, enjoying the trace of fear that flickered in his eyes now that he no longer restrained me.

I only vaguely registered the onslaught of arrows soaring through the air, but my eyes homed in on the man before me—the one who thought himself capable of bringing down an entire clan of Daughters. An entire history of protectors. Descendants of the goddess Halah. His mouth hung open, and the whites of his eyes grew, darting nervously from side to side as he watched the threads of light swarm about me, shielding me. The ribbons wrapped around the shafts of the flying arrows, squeezing them and snapping them in midair. They drifted to the ground in a harmless circle. The splintered wood cracked beneath my footsteps, and the Rider's breath hitched in his throat.

I didn't have the strength to best the Rider in hand-to-hand combat, and I didn't have the experience and wisdom of the Eldress. I didn't have the power of the Daughters to aid me...but I did have *me*. Zara the disaster. Master of chaos and broken magic.

I lowered my voice and leaned toward him. "If you want monsters, I'll show you a monster."

Power and fury merged within me, and light exploded from my chest in a vibrant aura. I didn't know how to stitch, but I knew how to make chaos. I'd ripped the heart of stars from the sky, and I'd unwoven centuries of stitches. I could be their monster. *Help me show them a real monster,* I willed. *Help me end them.*

The heart of stars glowed between my ribs, so luminous the Riders shielded their eyes from its light. But the power expanded within me, amplifying until it spiraled out of my grasp. My eyes widened as streams of energy lanced outward from my chest, great javelins of power streaking toward the heavens instead of at my targets. The murky rift above crackled with the sound of dying stars as it ripped wider, admitting the threads of light into the oily darkness of its depths. *What is happening?* Sparks of panic pulsed through my blood.

The line pulled taut, tugging at my heart. The other side of it snaked through the In Between, wrapping and winding until it met its target, completely beyond my control. *Stop,* I begged, realizing too late that the magic had escaped my control. *Help me.*

But the heart of stars did not relent. It blazed like fire, ensnaring a dark shadow in gilded threads before wrenching it down from Prisha's rift. The black mass tumbled from the sky, hurtling toward the sand. *What creature have I unleashed now? What have I done?*

Giant wings flashed open, spreading wide to catch its descent from the heavens. The light wove through its chest, wrapping around the flickering darkness between its ribs to form a lattice of veins around its heart, binding us together.

A cloud of dust rose around the shadow when it landed with a convincingly solid thump against the sand. Huge wings spread from the dark mass, the leathery sails grazing the surface of the dunes with a whisper. He lifted his head from its bowed position, and amethyst eyes met mine.

Help me. I didn't know what lunacy possessed me to ask Prisha's creature for help or what kept me from running as fast as my legs could carry me in the opposite direction—whether it was fear, desperation, or sheer stupidity. But a silent beat of unspoken truth passed between us, as if he could understand me. As if he were capable of feeling something more than Prisha's rage.

Please.

He did not hesitate. There was no stopping to question my motives, no pause to consider my worthiness or plight. His countenance darkened, and he snapped his wings to the side, sucking away any trace of light that lingered in the night. The churning shadows of his body rippled and flowed, swirling like ribbons of ink on a starless sky. He wasn't darkness...he was the total obstruction of light—the very absence of it. Raw and powerful and undiluted.

A shiver ran up my spine.

A ribbon of energy connected us, and though it crackled and faded in the dark, its presence remained. The subtle pull and vibration of his movements crawled along the invisible bond to reach me, keeping my body hyper-aware of his presence and his actions. I tugged tentatively against the cord, and the creature responded to my call.

Absolute darkness smothered the dunes and screams shattered the quiet of night as the monster set to work. One by one, the Riders fell, victims of the force I'd unintentionally unleashed. I could not see the method of his destruction, but I could feel it— the way he killed without mercy. Without question. He worked in darkness—or perhaps with it. Or perhaps he *was* it.

What have you summoned, Zara? I'd asked the stars to give the Riders a monster, but I hadn't meant *this.*

Panic hammered through my veins as I struggled to maintain

my control over him, but the more I fought, the more he sapped away my energy. I was fading, my grip on him slipping. My knees wobbled, and the blood rushing through my veins stuttered and then slowed. The world...softened. Sand brushed against my face while my body sank, cradled by the dunes until the only sensation left to me was absence.

CHAPTER 7

HALFMOON BREAD

A winged creature loomed over me, his left arm folded across his torso, clutching my dagger in his hand. In his right, he lifted a corner of halfmoon bread to his mouth. *My* halfmoon bread.

I frowned. Had he gone rifling through my pockets? My satchel? How long had I been unconscious? And *why* had I been unconscious? Fainting seemed to have become a regular occurrence after using my power, which was mildly irksome at best, majorly problematic at worst. *Stop using that power, Zara,* I scolded. *It's too dangerous.*

He took a contemplative bite and watched me, lazily chewing with an expression of mild intrigue on his face. His amethyst eyes traced over my body with an almost...lackadaisical approach. Finally, he met my gaze. I shifted backward, stunned by the nebula of his eyes, the galaxy of stars in their depths. *Venom and hell.*

"You're awake. Finally." His throat bobbed with a swallow, and he brushed the crumbs against his black trousers. "Pity it should mean I have to kill you now."

He talks. Prisha's creature talks. Sense flooded back to my mind, and I skittered away, remembering the shadowy beast I'd pulled from the sky and the ease with which he'd decimated a full squadron of Dune Riders. I raised myself to a crouching stance, shoving aside the pounding pressure building in my ears. *What is he?* He was not a simple bulgroich or a crawler, but rather stood in front of me with the characteristics of a full-grown man. An attractive one with weathered wings. One that had emerged from a ravenous shadow of destruction. Whatever he was, he intended to destroy me and seemed fully capable of the job.

"You waited until I woke up to kill me?" I gasped. Why hadn't he just murdered me in my sleep? Did he want me to be awake and fully present for my last moments of suffering? *What kind of a monster are you?*

My heart raced as my eyes darted across the dunes, noticing the lumps that now dotted the otherwise picturesque land. Not lumps. Bodies.

Shit. I did not intend to join them.

He pondered my expression for half a second, then moved his shoulders in a casual shrug. "It didn't seem fair to kill you when you couldn't fight back."

"Stay away," I ordered, and my voice cracked with dryness as I eyed the dagger in his hand.

He lifted his brow with interest. "Pleased to meet you too, Stitcher." He flipped the blade effortlessly between his fingers and took another bite of Mother's halfmoon bread, never taking his eyes off me.

I tensed at his use of my new title. *He knows.* My pulse thrummed at a startling pace. *And if he knows, he will kill me. Or worse...he will deliver me to Prisha and doom this realm to a Stitcherless fate.* Without a second thought, before he had a chance to harm me, I lunged. Throwing my whole weight into the force of my strike, I gripped his wrist and wrenched the blade free from his grasp. Surprise registered on his face, and he fell backward, his gaze flickering to the dagger in my hand. It now hovered inches over his heart.

Hovered...but did not descend.

Venom and hell. What is going on? Resisted by some invisible force, the blade refused to move any closer to his chest. I gasped at the unexpected opposition and strained against it, letting my eyes find his while my nerves sparked with sharp, electrical surges of panic. He cocked his brow and tilted his head to the side, seemingly unperturbed by my effort to skewer his heart. In fact, his eyes, now creased with the hint of a smile at their edges, glinted. The essence of stardust and laughter glimmered within.

My muscles quivered with strain, and my face flushed, but the dagger would not budge. It would not cross the small yet infinite barrier between us, rejecting my efforts to plunge the blade through his heart. Finally, I rolled away and rose to my feet, exhausted but not spent enough to let him kill me. The ember of resistance still flickered deep in my soul.

"Who are you? What are you?" I managed between ragged breaths, holding the blade in front of myself in warning. My knees bent slightly in a crouch, shaking from nerves or fatigue, or perhaps a combination of the two.

The creature from the In Between sat up and neatly folded his black wings behind his back. His deep-set eyes held mine, their intensity never wavering. Astral power rolled within them, giving the impression that I was staring into a stream of stars glittering against the aurora. His angular cheekbones and dark brow gave him the chiseled appearance of a god. But his gaze—his entire demeanor, really—depicted the impression of a man plagued by perpetual boredom. Yet he regarded me with interest, eyes glinting as though some unanticipated diversion had suddenly sparked life back into them. *Me. I am the diversion.*

And he is nothing but a predator stalking his prey.

I shifted my feet, increasing the distance between us. By the time he recovered himself to a standing position, I'd moved well beyond his immediate reach. His leathery wings lifted high behind him, casting me into his shadow.

"Don't come any closer," I warned, waving my dagger, though we'd already established its inefficacy. My hand trembled. "Who are you?"

"A Guardian," he responded simply, his voice calm and even, wholly impervious to my threats.

"Guardian of...Prisha?" *One of her soldiers? Does she have soldiers?* My heart plummeted into my stomach. *Venom and hell, we are so fucked.* The creature before me was not a lowly monster. He was sentient. Coldly calculating. Dangerous.

He gazed blankly for a moment, not offering confirmation or denial of my accusation, but the way his expression darkened with a shadowy smirk spoke volumes.

"So you're her monster," I whispered. "And you've come to kill me."

His lids closed heavily, and he inhaled slowly. "Funny. Prisha says you're a monster too, Starlight."

The pace of my heart quickened. Did he know her well then? And what did he know of me? He'd called me Stitcher...but was he aware I'd stolen the heart of stars and accidentally ripped centuries of stitches from the skies? Possibly, considering the irritating choice of nickname.

My mind raced with the prospect of the information he might possess. Prisha's plans, her goals, her...weaknesses? He could change everything for us...if I could get him to cooperate. If I could get him under my control. That would be imperative. "What does she want with me?" I asked, testing how willingly he would answer my questions.

A short laugh escaped through his nose. "Aside from a slow, painful death for the Stitcher so she can finally break free from her prison and exact her revenge by destroying mankind?"

It was the response I should have expected, yet I flinched all the same. He made no move toward me, but still, I stepped another pace backward and brandished my useless dagger. "I won't let you kill me."

He rolled his eyes and folded his muscular arms over his torso. "We'll see. Prisha is accustomed to getting her way."

"And I am accustomed to defying expectations."

He made a little hum of surprise and seemed to reconsider me.

"Hm. Now *that* is a skill I envy. Maybe I don't want to kill you after all, little Stitcher. At least, not yet. I'm still deciding."

"That's reassuring," I huffed. "But forgive me if I can't say the same about you." I lurched toward him, and his fingers snapped around my wrist, pulling me close so I could feel his breath ghost over my face as he inspected me. My entire spine shivered, wobbling with such conviction I was certain it would shatter.

He battled a smile that tugged at the corner of his mouth. "Just so we're clear, Prisha didn't send me."

Something about the glint in his eyes, paired with the effortless posture he maintained, unnerved me. He was thoroughly unthreatened—perhaps even amused. In fairness, what did I expect a shadow from the In Between to fear? He could smother me with darkness. I could only eviscerate the air three inches away from his body with my dagger. The playing field was uneven.

I'd need to correct that.

I wrenched my arm free from his grasp and backed away. "You're a creature of the In Between. A-A monster. A sky...ruffian," I sputtered, stumbling over my words as I stated the obvious in an effort to stall. *Good Halah, think before you speak.* I needed to catch my breath. "You're a curse from Prisha."

"A curse from Prisha?" He laughed with an indignant air. "I believe it was *you* who summoned me, was it not?" He cocked his brow and tugged playfully on the invisible line between us. The tendrils of magic glimmered in the air, gilded threads that came to life at his touch. *So, the connection between us remains.* The subtle warmth of the energy glowed somewhere near my heart, its twining grip both reassuring and strangely threatening. As though the gentle threads could wind tighter at any moment, gripping my insides until I either suffocated or found myself ripped to shreds. It felt...ominous.

My pulse quickened and I eyed him suspiciously. *What have you done, Zara? What does this mean? Get rid of him.*

"Everything from the In Between is a curse. I think I would recognize her work when I see it...I've killed many of her monsters." *And you're next,* I promised, steeling my resolve.

He had an almost haughty look about him, as though offended by my well-founded mistrust. "Have you? Then...why did you struggle to kill me? Perhaps I am not a monster? Or perhaps you are not as good as you say," he mused, pondering his own puzzle with a tilt of his head.

My brows furrowed and my gaze sharpened, but the weight of the blade in my hand steadied me. I leveled my breathing. I knew how this ended—what I needed to do. I just needed to figure out how to do it. And more importantly...why I couldn't.

The insufferable smirk of superiority he wore on his face told me he had something to do with it. I trusted nothing about the beautiful creature. I did not care that he had helped me escape the Dune Riders. It did not matter how he stopped my breath when I first met his eyes. One wrong move, and he would smother me with shadows. Readily. Easily. Curse of Prisha or not, he was a monster.

"Only monsters come from the In Between," I retorted, making up my mind. "If that's where you've come from, that's what you are."

He shrugged his shoulders, and the iridescent sheen of his wings reflected the sunlight as he moved closer to me, the shimmer of a smirk at the corner of his mouth. "Well, if that's what you'd like to believe...I can be your monster. For a price." He winked, but everything about his expression darkened.

I gaped, then snapped my mouth shut in a conscious effort to pull myself together. The shock of his response had nearly sent my heart off-kilter. I narrowed my gaze. "I'm not interested."

Aiming straight for the heart, I lurched forward once more, but he did not balk as he had before. This time, he lazily swiped his hand to counter each of my strikes, predicting and reacting to every move with an effortless block. His brows lifted, a clear testament to his dwindling enthusiasm for the exercise. He grabbed my wrist and smiled.

Kill her. Destroy the Daughters. I jumped, startled by the goddess's voice echoing in my mind, parading as my own. Horrified, I ripped my hand away from Prisha's monster and glared at him. "What was that? What did you say?"

Of course, he hadn't said it. Prisha had. Or...my mind had.

His brow lifted in question.

"Never mind," I said. Then, unleashing a gravelly roar of frustration, I grabbed the tether between us and pulled him close. Even then, even with my reckless attempt to outsmart him, the dagger refused to find its mark. It clashed uselessly against the unseen boundary, sending a shattering jolt of pain through my arm as though I'd just struck it against a glass wall. Clenching my teeth together, I shoved. And shoved again. I strained with all of my might until he calmly wrapped his hand around mine and removed the blade from my grasp. He spun it nimbly through his fingers, getting a feel for the blade, then slipped the dagger into the sheath at my ribs, patting it gently, like I was a small child in the midst of a tantrum. An adorable one who simply needed consoling.

I frowned and stepped away, wrinkling my nose. He smelled like the earthy dune rushes—the pale green ones that only bloomed at night. He was the fresh herbal scent of leaves bathed in moonlight. *Venom and hell, Zara. Do your job.*

"Go. Back. To. Where. You. Belong." I shoved angrily against the barrier between us, and when it did not shatter or bend in the slightest, I roared and threw my arms at my side, my hands balled up into fists. The tendrils of energy that crackled around me lashed out, exploding with a shower of sparks and arching up to the stars. They landed in a deep fissure rent open by Prisha, and the sky made a horrible, anguished sound before it shredded clear down the middle.

Shred the skies! Come to me, Star Thief! Prisha howled through my mind.

A gaping black hole opened in the gashes of the crisscrossed sky, only stopping when it reached the dunes before me. It hummed with the energy of the In Between, leaking its black curse through the gap.

Yes. Open the skies. Destroy the Daughters, her voice echoed inside my mind. I recoiled at the intrusive commands, watching the skies with a sense of horror.

What have you done now, Zara? How have you possibly made this worse? What is happening to you? I clutched a hand over the glow in my chest, horrified by the shadows passing through its surface.

I whirled on the shadow demon from the sky, as if he were somehow to blame. As though this had been his plan all along. Was he driving me mad? The rift overhead now split the sky in two, creating a doorway between worlds—a channel for Prisha to usher her creatures through.

Or better yet, one for me to send them back. *Perhaps a happy mistake, then. He's got to go.*

My lungs expanded with a sharp inhale and I braced myself. Pummeling the creature, I wedged my shoulder against his chest and pushed him toward the gaping rift between realms. "I. Said.

Go. Back." I panted in between each word, struggling to gain any ground in the sands. For a beast of shadow and darkness, his muscles demonstrated a surprising solidity beneath my hands. Like...warm stone. Rigid and strong and...unyielding. And chiseled to perfection like the statues of the old kings in Rashii.

Something told me that if he chose to resist me, he could have ended me with a blink of those amethyst eyes. He hardly fought back, letting me push him toward the tear, watching me with growing amusement. The edges of the rift glowed with golden threads behind him, but the middle—the middle oozed with the same darkness that he had called on last night. The monstrous shroud of shadow that obliterated a squadron of men. It reached for him like it knew him—like it wanted him back.

He belonged there.

He threw his arm out, catching himself against the edge of the tear when I gave one last heave to push him through. He wrapped golden threads of energy around his outstretched wrist to buy himself purchase against my advances and leaned into my pushes, showing how easily he could have resisted all along. His eyes left mine for the briefest second, losing their glint with a flash of something darker as he turned his gaze to the rift.

I saw the flicker of displeasure in his eyes, the subtle pulse of fear darkening his visage, but when he turned back toward me, he resumed the same effortless calm. A lopsided smirk surfaced on his lips. He leaned forward ever so slightly, brushing my senses with the familiar dune rush scent, and my breath hitched. My heart raced inside my chest, suddenly all too conscious of the charged space between us, of the knowledge that he could so easily destroy me.

"Go. Back," I commanded with an edge to my voice, though it fell short of anything compelling.

"No." His tone was gravelly but luxuriously rich—like the most complex tea blend. Warm and smooth but laced with something spicy. He jerked his head to indicate the rift, then leaned closer to me. "I'll not be going back to the In Between. Too many monsters, like you said." His eyes danced with delight when he winked, his lashes darting together so fast I wasn't entirely certain I'd seen it. I stared blankly at him. His face settled into a look of smugness, and his spine lengthened as he stood taller. He knew the effect he had on me, the way his unexpected charm surprised and unnerved me.

I backed away hastily, needing to separate myself from whatever spell he'd cast upon me that had so thoroughly inhibited my good sense. What was it about him? Why couldn't I hurt him...or, at the very least, banish him back to his rightful place? I hadn't exactly mastered Ahma's art of stitching Prisha's creatures back into the skies, but I'd never struggled to *kill* one of Prisha's creatures before. This must be his doing—and if so, he was likely far more dangerous than I'd anticipated.

"Why won't you just...die?" I asked in a voice that felt foreign —raspy and encumbered by confusion. He cocked an eyebrow in response, making me realize I'd spoken my thoughts out loud. *Really, Zara? You're asking Prisha's creature why he won't die? Perhaps if you ask him nicely next time, he'll be more inclined to oblige your request.*

I exhaled my frustration in a dramatic huff. Laughter rippled in the air—the magical sound glittered like sparkling wings of beetles in the sun. "You're fully capable of killing me, Starlight, but something in your subconscious won't allow it. Pity for you. Intriguing for me."

"My entire consciousness is set on destroying you. I promise you that. This is your doing."

"It would be unconscionable for me to take credit where credit is not due. This isn't my doing, but yours." Mischief glimmered in his eyes, and he took another bite of my halfmoon bread. "And I'm curious enough to let you live until I figure out whatever's holding you back."

"Thanks for the thoughtful accommodation," I muttered, crossing my arms over my chest. "So you've changed your mind about killing me, then?"

He lifted his brows and shrugged. "I didn't say that. I said I won't be killing you *yet*. There's always tomorrow. Why rush?" He shoved another huge bite of bread into his mouth. "This is really good, by the way," he said, waving the flat crescent.

My nose crinkled with disgust as he spoke through the mouthful. What kind of a monster lacked the decency to chew his food properly before speaking?

This one.

He swallowed the rest of the bread and ran his hands over his black trousers. My eyes wandered to the sculpted muscles of his thighs before snapping back to a more appropriate level.

"Have you got any more?" he asked hopefully.

"For the creature planning to kill me? No. None for you."

"Ah. Too bad," the sky ruffian responded, seemingly oblivious to my unrest. He turned his back on me and walked a few paces away, stopping in front of a puddle of green fabric pooled together in ripples of shimmering satin. The Stitcher lay unresponsive, curled into a ball at his feet. *Shit.*

The memory of the arrow piercing the Eldress's shoulder rushed back to me. I'd been so concerned with subduing the monster, and so disoriented by his presence, that I'd forgotten. She needed help. The arrow...the inky blood stain across her shoulder...*Is she dead? Oh no.* Fear lodged itself in my throat.

CHAPTER 8

NOT THE TYPE

I froze, holding my own breath in my lungs while I watched her chest rise and fall slowly—perhaps too slowly—but she moved. She breathed. Relief washed through me like a gulp of fresh water after a day in the dunes.

The creature's black wings twitched slightly as he repositioned them behind his shoulder blades, arms folded over his chest while he contemplated the Eldress. Concern bubbled uncomfortably inside of me.

"Get away from her," I warned. "If you touch her, you die."

Amethyst eyes lifted toward the heavens, and a slight breeze rifled through the roots of his hair. The dark brown crop fell into effortless, windswept perfection when he turned over his shoulder to speak to me. "Perhaps we can take a little break from all this fighting. The old woman needs some attention. A proper healer. Do you know one?"

"*What?*"

"I did what I could for her while you were.. incapacitated. Removed the arrow. Stopped the bleeding. But if she doesn't see a healer soon, she'll likely die of infection. Or worse." He pointed to the broken shaft in the sand. "Arrow might have been poisoned...her skin is festering, and she's quite fragile. And very old. Though not as old as me." His voice climbed with his rambling, as if moderately entertained by his own observations.

Several mindless blinks later, I stomped toward the Stitcher and placed my hands on the dark stain that spidered over her tunic to see for myself. He was...*older* than her? He...*helped* her? No traces of the arrow remained in her shoulder, and black sutures threaded through the Eldress's papery skin to seal the wound closed, though a putrid fluid drained from the swollen flesh. Her blue veins twisted alongside the wound like a map of Rashii's winding city streets, but the flow of blood had stopped. She was alive.

She would need the attention of my Sisters if she had any hope of lasting.

"It will be fastest if we fly," he announced dryly. As if that decided the matter.

I craned my head so fast, it cricked a muscle in my neck. "*We*? There is no we. You stay out of this."

His twinkling charm faded into a glower. "You're welcome, by the way." He tossed his hands to the side to accentuate the expectant expression on his face, clearly waiting for my thanks. He could keep expecting until the sand wings resurfaced from their dormancy a hundred years from now...I didn't trust him and didn't plan to. I would not be thanking Prisha's monsters. Not now. Not ever.

"Go away." I turned my back to him again, ignoring the way the hair at the nape of my neck bristled with the knowledge that he was watching. Hyper-aware of the focus of his eyes on my back, I turned to the Stitcher. Her skin shimmered with the faintest trace of perspiration, and she looked even smaller than I remembered—her face pale and clammy.

If I hurried, I could get her to the guryas by nightfall and let the healers work on her while I convinced my Sisters to prepare to leave for Rashii. If we left tomorrow, we'd make it to safety before the start of the festival with time to warn the guards to fortify their protections against Prisha and keep everyone within the city gates. Then, I could sort out all of these other troubles. But what to do with the unintended keepsake I'd ripped from the sky?

The Daughters would want to interrogate him, but he was no mindless, bloodthirsty creature from the In Between. This one was sentient, with all the ability to scheme. He could overpower me, especially while vulnerable with the Eldress. I moved Ahma's garment to recover the wound, quickly cataloging my options.

The sun struggled just above the dunes, the vibrant red hue of its crown an attempt to compensate for its waning consciousness. It would soon go to sleep with the rest of the world—and I knew the dangers of lingering in the open after dusk. Too many monsters to worry about...especially the winged one casting me into his shadow. I had to move now.

"Ahma? Let's get you home," I whispered into her ear, wondering if she was even cognizant enough to hear me. I moved to scoop her frail frame into my arms, but froze as the weight of his hand fell on my shoulder.

"I'm coming with you."

My spine grew rigid. "No." Why would he presume I'd allow him to follow me anywhere? My stomach flipped. Why did I presume I'd have the power to stop him? *I have to try.* I chanced a discreet glance over my shoulder, stealing a look at the easy stance he maintained, his wide shoulders framed by obsidian canopies. His dark brows lifted with that expression of halfhearted interest he seemed to favor—the infuriating one that immediately solidified my dislike for him. Yet somehow, my skin flushed when I realized he'd caught me staring.

That's enough of this nonsense. I stood, letting my silk skirt fall around my ankles, and I carefully adjusted the band around my midriff to make it lay flat. My rucksack sat abandoned in the sand a few feet from the Eldress, half buried. The rumpled leather rustled as I rummaged a hand inside.

There. The bristled texture of the cording scratched my fingers. I wound it around my hand and removed the bundle, holding it in front of my abdomen where Prisha's monster could not see. *Deep breath.*

I whirled and disrupted the sands, spraying streams of sparkling dust into the air with the sharpness of my movement. Prisha's creature frowned and folded his arms over his chest, his chiseled cheekbones more pronounced beneath the emerging moonlight. I charged toward him, driving my shoulder into his ribs to knock the wind from his chest. He fell backward into the sand, but no sign of alarm ever marred his demeanor—he remained as calm and collected as ever.

He did not even give me the dignity of fighting back. Bringing his hands together, I knelt and set myself to work, winding the rough cord around his wrists with a series of complicated knots. Knots I knew with intimate familiarity from a lifetime of pitching the guryas.

Next, I secured his ankles. When I allowed myself to steal a glance at him, I frowned at the smirk on his face. He remained calm as ever, watching patiently, as though he did not notice how the world had shifted on its axis. How the dunes and the sky melted away behind him, so all I knew was his eyes locked on mine. I shook my head. *It is just a trick of the shadows. Shadows he commands. Pull yourself together.*

He stifled a laugh, and my gaze sharpened in response.

"What?" I asked, a bit more angrily than I'd intended, but nothing about the situation seemed funny to me.

He shrugged nonchalantly and motioned to the bristled cords

around his wrists. "I'm not against it—just didn't expect you to be the type."

"The type to what?" I asked, my face scrunching up. Understanding dawned on me, and my mouth warped into a display of horrified revulsion. He lifted his bindings, quirking a dark brow.

Every inch of my body blazed a fiery shade of crimson. "Oh goddess. Gross. No. I'm not—I don't. I've never—No." The warmth in my cheeks flared. I moved backward a few paces to extend the distance between us and looked him firmly in the eyes. My stomach churned at the smirk on his face, no matter how fiercely I ignored it.

After a sufficiently drawn-out staring match of awkwardness, I huffed and braced myself. *Ignore him. He's just another one of Prisha's monsters. Don't let him fluster you.* I stepped closer to him, reluctant to close the distance between us but needing to finish the job I'd started. Purely to ensure his bindings would hold. My weaving was a disaster, but knots—knots I could do. I pulled them tight and checked my handiwork. He wasn't going anywhere. If only I knew how to stitch the skies and hide him beneath its canopy so I could keep him concealed until I returned with my Sisters, but this would have to do for now. My priority had to be getting the Eldress to our healers.

"You. Stay here." My voice wavered slightly, unaccustomed to the attempted tone of authority. "Don't follow me."

He rolled his eyes but lounged back in the sand, making the dunes into his rajasana—like he was a prince of Rashii. "Okay, Starlight."

CHAPTER 9

INVISIBLE LACERATIONS

I walked a few paces away, stalled to listen, and checked over my shoulder to ensure he remained firmly where I'd left him. He waved. Not an eager wave or even a polite gesture of greeting, but one with a deliberate motion meant to provoke, one that made my face twist into a sour grimace.

Stop watching me. My eyes narrowed at him and my teeth ground together, but I did not dignify him with another word. I slung the backpack over my shoulder and went to retrieve Ahma. With any luck, we'd be back to the guryas by nightfall, and if Prisha's less sentient beasts didn't do the dirty work of destroying the winged one for me, I'd send the Daughters to handle him in the morning. I stopped in my tracks, gripping the straps of my backpack with whitened knuckles—what if Prisha's monsters freed him, and he led them straight to us? What if all of this was part of Prisha's larger scheme? I shook my head. The Daughters could interrogate him tomorrow and do what they saw fit.

Tomorrow. We'll deal with him tomorrow.

I brushed Ahma's white braids from her forehead, tracing the deep triangle of tension between her eyes with a gentle touch, urging it to disappear. Her chest sank with each exhale, but she did not awaken. *Hang on, Ahma,* I willed in silence. It wasn't unusual for the Stitcher to sleep for long stretches of time, but with the angry gash in her shoulder and a significant amount of blood loss, I worried. And if the arrow had indeed been tipped with poison...

I shook my head and trudged forward.

Her limp form weighed exceptionally more when carried in my arms. On the way to stitch the skies, her knobbled knees and lanky arms contributed at least a *little* to my efforts, but now she dangled like an awkward satchel of onions in my arms. And she sort of smelled like them, too. I wrinkled my nose.

Beads of perspiration trickled down the nape of my neck. They seeped through the fabric at the small of my back, where my tunic pasted itself uncomfortably to my skin. As I crossed the dunes toward the sound of the Daughters' threading—the compass that always led home—my breathing became labored, my steps more and more sluggish. My thighs protested, shaking with the effort, and the sand seemed to swallow my feet with each footstep. My sandals grew heavy, weighing down every pace across the dunes. I willed each foot in front of the other, but it felt as though leaden weights had been strapped to my ankles, pulling me deeper and deeper into the sand until I could barely move them at all. As if I were pushing through a giant vat of lorbean paste instead of air. I gasped, realizing I'd been holding my breath.

Venom and hell, Zara. Are you really that spent?

But as I continued, I knew this was more than fatigue. An aching pain spread in my heart, slowly at first, in the way ink seeps across wet paper. Then, all at once, with more conviction—like a bottle of ink knocked over onto the parchment, drenching the page with black. I gasped, halting midstep to grate my teeth against the pain that suddenly erupted in my chest like sharp shears shredding through fabrics or—strings pulled too tightly until they sliced through flesh.

I looked down at my chest, fully expecting to see that my skin had flayed apart. Expecting the eviscerating pain to send droplets of blood down my front to stain the sands. But there was nothing. Just the agonizing, all-consuming pain of something wound too tightly around my beating heart. Squeezing tighter with every step forward.

I froze when the horrible realization struck me. Slowly, I craned my neck over my shoulder, glancing back toward the dunes I'd left behind. I couldn't see it, but I knew it was there—I could feel it. I was certain. Bolstering myself, I tested my theory and pulled.

The ribbon of starlight shimmered to life, stretched taut between my heart and the place where the dunes dipped out of view. The place where I'd left him tied up in the sands.

"Shit," I swore beneath my breath, vaguely surprised by the flecks of spit that left my mouth with the huff of frustration. Considering the unholy amount of sweat that soaked through my clothing, I was surprised that any fluids remained in my body to be expelled.

The stars shimmered above, and I stood, stranded between both connections that called me in opposite directions. A call to home...and a highly inconvenient call back to that *monster*.

One last attempted step toward the guryas brought me to my knees in the sand. I clutched a hand over the invisible lacerations in my chest—the gashes deepened the more I strained against the magical binding between us. *What has he done to me?*

The ribbons ensnared the glowing heart of stars, burrowing within it like some sort of parasitic infestation. I panted, straining to catch my breath, and the Eldress groaned in her slumber where I'd let her fall.

I couldn't leave her here, unconscious and vulnerable to the monsters of the dark. But I couldn't make it to the guryas...I couldn't push past whatever spell that cursed beast had cast upon me. My gaze swept over the conical tops of the guryas, just visible in the haze of darkness blanketing the horizon, and my stomach wrenched with the realization that I'd never make it if I didn't change course. "I'm sorry, Ahma. I can't."

My brows knitted together, and my gaze followed the gleaming trail of starlight—the curse wrapped around my heart. The source of the agony that restrained me. *How did this happen? How do I free myself from him?* My heart pattered faster in a flurry of unrest—and then slowed as resolve washed over me. Resolve, and a hefty dose of anger. That fucking *monster.*

The Daughters are monsters. Stop them. Kill them! Prisha's voice pushed into my subconscious with a jolting furor of screeches. *Do you understand? Do. You. Understand?*

"Stop it!" I yelled to no one, forcing the unwelcome voice from my head. My heartbeat thundered in my ears. Why did those thoughts keep surfacing in my mind? I wished my Sisters no harm —I didn't want to destroy them. This connection to Prisha had to be *his* doing. The voice had begun interrupting my thoughts as soon as I pulled him from the sky. It was *his* fault...he wanted to destroy us. He served the goddess.

But no, I remembered with a frown. Prisha had invaded my mind since the moment she first noticed me, when I unintentionally ripped the heart of stars from her sky. *His* presence had only amplified her hold on me.

Both he and the heart of stars had to go.

I should have killed him. I *wanted* to kill him. So...why couldn't I? I scowled. *I'll find a way.*

I had half a mind to retrace my steps back to him and *demand* he release me from whatever spell he'd worked, but I couldn't afford to lose valuable time when Ahma so desperately needed a healer.

My hands rested on the Eldress's shoulder, willing her awake. "Please, Ahma. I need your help." She didn't stir. Tears burned in the rims of my eyes, though I was not sad. Whatever I felt was hotter, fiery and volatile. The acknowledgment of that fact made the tears flow faster, washing my frown away to reveal the stoic calm of dead-set determination.

"Ahma, I have to take care of something. You need to stitch the skies into a cloak and hide. Protect yourself. Please." I pushed gently against her uninjured shoulder, only deepening the wrinkles between her eyes. Nothing unearthed the Eldress from the clutches of sleep. Perhaps she *had* been poisoned.

I wiped my hands over my cheeks, erasing my tears. Stars twinkled above, their brightness a silent rebellion against the roiling gashes that ripped through the sky. No matter how vehemently the dark curse strained to suppress them, they never lost their shine. They never gave up. Nor did Prisha.

If only it were so easy to persevere.

A true blanket of indigo swathed the skies now, and the rifts crackled ominously—an unequivocal reminder of the dangers of night.

Damnit, Ahma. I couldn't leave her in the open, nor could I carry her. I could not take one more step toward the guryas. Not without slicing lacerations of agony in my heart. I could not chase down the monster and demand his death. I—could not. I could not, I could not.

I growled with the frustration of helplessness. How had I landed myself here? How had everything gone so catastrophically wrong? My eyes settled on the horizon, beyond the guryas to where the great city of Rashii hid beneath the rolling dunes. To the potential safety that seemed just out of reach—grains of sand draining faster from my hands the more desperately I tried to contain them.

Light rippled through the sky—an angry crackle of power that tore a new gash into the fabric of stars.

And yet, the stars persevered through it all. *Let them guide me.*

Something fierce surged within me—a raw, volatile emotion that sparked life into the embers settled in my stomach. Light erupted from me, or raced toward me, or simply consumed me. The source of it did not make itself known, and I did not question it. I just accepted it—*harnessed* it.

It engulfed me, condensing in the same way that steam collects into droplets, then droplets run into streams, and then streams flow into rivers. The light pooled at my sternum, flooding me with power, responding to my call to the stars for guidance. My eyes followed the stream of starlight that wound its way around my heart, trailing away into the darkness, beyond the line of the horizon to its other end. To the answer.

That bastard.

You're coming with me.

I pulled on the tether. Hard.

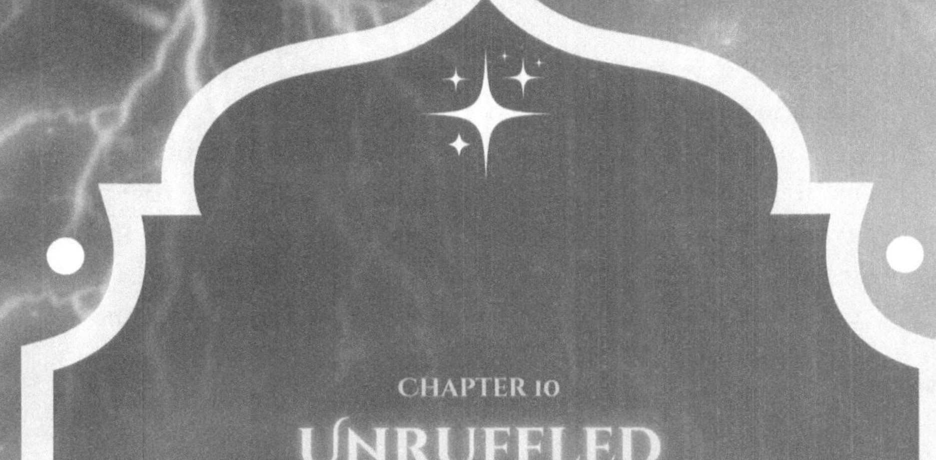

CHAPTER 10

UNRUFFLED

With the stars' intervention, the answer presented itself clearly. If I could not make my way back to him, let him come to me. After all, wasn't I the one who had pulled him from the In Between? Wasn't this leash my accidental creation—however disastrous the results?

The response on the other end of the connection made my knees melt into the sand. The pain and tension around my heart eased, as did my muscles and the pressure around my temples. *He's coming.*

With one hand wrapped around the hilt of my dagger and the other protectively splayed over the Eldress's heart, I bowed my head and waited, listening for any disturbances to the silence of night. Any hint of his approach. Only the quiet chirruping of dune crickets and the warped crackle of Prisha's hatred reached my ears until—

The staccato rhythm of wings beating against air. My stomach clenched and my body stiffened.

"You called." He landed before me—his hands free and unrestricted, his eyes narrowed in question. How had he escaped the bonds so easily? My knots had been perfect.

I pushed the concern aside and glared back at him, rising to my feet and lifting my chin to meet his gaze. With the dagger gripped in my right hand, I wrapped my fingers around the tendrils of starlight between us, coaxing it into view. The curse I'd cast between us when I'd beckoned him from the skies—or the one he'd tricked me with, binding me to him. It did not matter which. The only thing that mattered now was my intention to destroy it.

"What...is this?" I asked, indicating the connection between us. My jaw clenched, so the words hissed slowly through the narrow gaps between my teeth.

"I would think you'd be the one to know. You were the one to lasso me from the sky, Starlight."

I frowned. Did nothing phase him? Did nothing ruffle his massive, formidable wings? *Wings need feathers to be ruffled, Zara.* A cursory glance across the dark shadows above his shoulders proved how very...*unruffled* he would ever be.

I shook my head, my wary gaze never breaking from his. "I asked for the stars to help me show the Dune Riders a real monster—I did not ask for a permanent arrangement with one."

"Well, here I am, at your service, all the same. How very lucky for you." He bowed with an air of mockery, his eyes glimmering as though my anger served as the very catalyst that set them ablaze with stardust.

I grumbled and marched toward him, straightening my spine so that he merely towered over me by a technicality of height, not by presence. The steel of my blade warmed in my grasp, becoming part of me, eager to oblige the slightest hint of a command. I leaned closer until his shortened breaths whispered across my face, bridging the charged space between us. My eyes narrowed. "You have already served me by obliterating the Dune Riders. Your continued existence is a threat to me. This ends now." With a determined swoosh of metal through air, the dagger rushed toward its target. The connection between us erupted into a shower of sparks when the blade met it, but the force of impact ricocheted through the hilt, sending the dagger flying out of my hold.

A sharp gasp passed my lips as the dagger arced toward the ground, sinking with finality into the sand. A monument to mark my failure. What in the name of Halah had I done? Was there no way to free myself from this curse? I snapped my gaze back to him. What had *he* done? My heart galloped at the same canter of a wild mare, but I forced my fear into a box, compacting it until it fit in the smallest compartment of myself. Perhaps he would not notice how thoroughly he had shattered my nerves. I would not let him see.

If he felt any of the same concerns, he masked them with an ease I could never presume to replicate. A crooked grin flickered on his lips, then faded just as abruptly, washed away before it could fully form. He folded his arms over his chest, resuming his perpetually apathetic composure. "Must we continue the same tiresome argument? It's become quite clear, hasn't it?"

"What's clear?" I snapped, though it was perfectly clear. As clear as the skies before Prisha had unleashed her curse upon the realm. Back in the days of our most ancient ancestors, before the word "war" had ever passed their lips.

"You're stuck with me, Starlight."

My mouth opened and snapped shut like a fish in the desert, failing to produce the words that buzzed with impatience on my tongue. *Stuck with him?* He raised his dark brows over his deep-set eyes, somehow communicating his facade of unfathomable boredom while, in the same expression, exuding an intensity that drew me to him.

I stepped backward, horrified by his statement of the obvious.

By the presumed permanency of our bond. I felt my heartbeat stutter out of control, but forced myself to slow my breaths before I lost my focus. "There has to be a way to undo this—"

"Perhaps. But aren't there more important matters to attend to?" His head tilted toward the Stitcher.

Wiping my hands over my face, I tried to erase the tension that wedged between my brows. No matter how long I stressed and reconsidered and reformulated, there was only one solution. One path forward.

He watched me with casual interest, waiting patiently for me to piece together my thoughts.

"Fine," I muttered, accepting my failure to come up with an alternate solution. As I loped toward him, I felt the air for the golden threads of energy and gathered a bunch in my fists. If the rope hadn't held him when I bound him earlier, perhaps this would fare better.

"What are you doing?" he asked, but he didn't resist or pull away when I grabbed his hands, working to rebind his wrists. He merely studied my movements, humoring my effort with a quirked brow.

I didn't deign to offer him a response, keeping my focus on knitting the tendrils of light into the most unforgiving knots.

"Is this really necessary?" he challenged, his voice a slow drawl.

"Yes, sky ruffian. You're a monster of Prisha." I pulled a knot unnecessarily tight with a jerk. "You may have information that could help us, and I'm still not convinced you won't try to kill me when my back is turned. So yes, it's necessary." All of those were only partial truths, of course, as they left out the most obvious crux of my predicament. It killed a piece of me to acknowledge it, but exhaustion had taken over every muscle of my body, and I needed to stop fighting whatever it was between us. The bond seemed intent on staying. "And, against my better judgment, I can't go a step further without you. Which is...*infu-*

riating. But whatever this connection is between us won't allow it."

He nodded his head slightly, not divulging any of the emotions hidden behind his effortless mask. "I noticed."

Why did every word that slipped through his half-committed smirk annoy me? Did nothing bother him?

"Doesn't it hurt you too?" I spat out, my nerves shot. *Do you feel the same anguishing destruction of your heart when the connection between us is pulled too tight? Do you have any idea how much this frustrates me? How inconvenient this is? To not only call the angry goddess's attention but also find myself latched to one of her dark creatures in some unfortunate chain of events? Highly unfortuitous.*

Something flickered in his gaze—something dark with the faintest hint of discomfort. "Yes. It hurts me, too."

Well, at least there's that. His admission wasn't comforting, per se, but there was a fairness to it that made my heated attitude ease from boiling point to moderately hot. "Good. So, since I'm inexplicably stuck with you for the foreseeable future, I'm going to need your cooperation. Hold still."

He bristled slightly, but replaced his mask of cool indifference in the same breath. "So you need me to go with you because of an unfortunate circumstance of your doing, and because you suspect you can use me, but you haven't once considered what *I* may want." He angled his head slightly, dipping one ear toward his broad shoulder, as if to consider me from a new perspective. "So tell me, Starlight, what makes you think you'll have my cooperation?"

"Because you're my prisoner?"

His laughter illuminated the futility of my attempts to restrain him. I pressed my lips together and continued tying the knots all the same, giving them an extra tug with each loop for added security.

"Good luck, then," he answered, reclining backward against the sand.

Is he joking? It had never crossed my mind that he'd need convincing. If he suffered the same torment that inexplicably ripped me apart when I'd tried to flee from him, then neither of us really had a choice. Like he said...we were stuck together. At least until I figured out how to destroy the stream of light that bound us.

I frowned, pulling my mouth into a lopsided grimace. "Do you enjoy feeling like your heart has been served to an army of bulgroiches on a platter, then? It's not like I *want* to be stuck with you."

"Well, if you're trying to convince me to help you, you're doing a poor job of it. Tying me up and leaving me for dead. Attempting to assassinate me not once, but thrice. Why should I help you? Convince me."

I scoffed, breathing a shortened, half-formed laugh through my nose and shaking my head with disbelief. "I'm very sorry for my numerous attempts to kill you." I huffed as I tied off the glowing threads around his wrists. "And I'm sorry for my fixation on severing this hellacious bond. I apologize for my ambivalence in deciding the best course of action *and* my persistent efforts to restrain you. Mostly, I am just...sorry to find myself in such a predicament. But, I'm going to need you to come with me, so just —hold still for *one more minute.*"

And what had he said earlier? *Oh, yes.* "Besides, whatever happened to you being my monster? Or was that merely a convenient line to win over my affections so you can get whatever you want from me?"

The faintest hint of a smile curled on his lips, but he gave me nothing more to indicate the amusement he worked so hard to subdue. "What I want?" His eyes darkened with his predatory gaze, and his voice lowered into a rumble. "You're mistaken if you think I did not speak the truth. I say I'm a monster because I'm *honest*. But now I'm curious…what is it that you think I want?"

What do you want? I wondered, stepping back to let my gaze sweep over his folded wings, his broad shoulders, and landing on the black serpent etched in ink upon his neck. Prisha's mark.

The Stitcher must die. Kill all the Daughters. That voice. Was I —reading his thoughts? His eyes met mine, and I bristled at the sensation of chills running along my spine. Did he want to kill me? To trick me into revealing the location of the Daughters so that Prisha could end us? I exhaled, pressing my lips together.

A creature from the In Between, one bearing Prisha's mark, was certainly not to be trusted. I couldn't presume to know what he wanted, but I knew what I should want. *And* what I should not. My cheeks flushed as I dropped my eyes to the sand. "I…you said—" I began, but my mouth gaped open as I floundered to articulate an answer. He raised his hands and shook his head.

"I said I'll be your monster. For a price. Key difference there. Give me a reason to pick you over Prisha, and I'll be yours." He leaned in toward me and cupped my chin in his hand, setting every muscle in my body on edge. "This is the part where you convince me, Starlight." His voice deepened an octave, hitting a gravelly, low note that sent a shiver down my spine. The stars in his eyes flickered beneath a shroud of darkness. "What's in it for me?"

For Halah's sake. The sooner I could part from this horrible curse, the better. But for now, I needed him. I needed his cooperation just long enough to take care of the Eldress so that I could defer all of my problems to her judgment. She'd know what to do.

"Well?" he asked, his tone clipped.

"What *do* you want?" Ideas raced through my head, tinged with the color of concern. What would a monster of the In Between require of me? What could I possibly offer that would convince him to favor me over a goddess?

"Unbind me," he said simply.

"What?" I snapped.

"Unbind me if you wish for my cooperation. Unbind me and trust me to follow my own free will, and you will already be a more favorable master than Prisha."

"Master?" I balked, hating the way the taste of the word drained the moisture from my mouth. I did not intend to be anyone's master, and certainly not his.

He pulled at the tether between us. "You stole me from her, Starlight. You summoned me from the In Between. And this connection? You used it to command me to follow your will when you placed me before those Riders." He paused, chewing on his words for a moment. "But I don't like being controlled. So, if Prisha cannot reach us here, perhaps I can be free to choose who I serve. If you're brave enough to permit it." The corded bond between us shimmered in the spaces between his fingers as he considered it. "Or perhaps this bond means you will continue to force my hand and rob me of that freedom to choose. It is yet to be known. As is my decision on whether or not to kill you."

I shook my head. "Well, thanks for confirming I can't trust you. Pick something else. A different price. There's too much at risk."

"Fine." He sighed, clearly disappointed by my rigidity on the matter. "I should know better than to hope for such freedoms. For now, more bread will do." He held out his hands expectantly.

I quirked a brow. "What?" My eyes bounced between his outstretched palm and his entirely serious expression, analyzing his motives. Surely I'd misunderstood.

"Get me more of that bread, and I'll play your game. I'll go as your prisoner without a fight." He stated it like he was explaining something obscenely obvious, and I stared back at him as though he were speaking a foreign tongue.

Oh great. He's crazy.

But, acknowledging that his request could have been much worse, I readily accepted his terms before he had the opportunity to change them. "Fine." I scattered my fears with a shake of my head. "There's plenty of halfmoon bread where I come from, if that's what you want. Help me get the Stitcher to safety, and I promise you will be well fed." Mother would fret and set herself to making halfmoon bread and other delicacies as soon as I stepped through the leather flaps of the gurya, anyway. I had no doubts about that.

Not to mention the inevitable likelihood that she'd immediately pass out at the sight of the oversized, overly arrogant winged ruffian I'd ripped straight from the In Between before I could explain his presence. *Venom and hell.* I cringed, suddenly doubting my decision to bring him back as I imagined the impending storm of Mother's hysteria. *What will she think of my prisoner? Will she let me explain? How much should I explain?*

That was a problem to solve later.

CHAPTER 11

NIGHT MARE

"Fine," he agreed with a hint of annoyance buried beneath an airy tone. Looking over the dunes into the black night, he lifted his wings. "It will be fastest if we fly. As I said before." His gaze settled on mine.

"Oh no. No. Not happening," I replied far too quickly, stumbling over my feet as I retreated a few steps back. "As I said before," I added. For continuity's sake.

He grumbled and broke our gaze, turning it to the heavens. A slow exhale released the tension in his body. "Fine. We will ride."

"Ride *what*?" Did he expect me to summon crawlers from the sky to carry us across the hills? No horses remained in the dunes —they had all fled when he eviscerated their Riders with *shadows*. And for very good reason.

He smiled and dissolved the threads I'd wound around his wrists, swallowing the light with the shadows he summoned. "Sorry—can't do this while restrained," he explained.

Good to know there was no way to bind him effectively.

A rustle of energy bent the air around him when he brought

his hands together, wrapping the fingers of one hand around his clenched fist. He drew in the night, pulling the very essence of it around himself in a shroud of blackness. It warped and coiled like writhing snakes, concealing him from view, then rushed forth in a display of reckless abandon. The shadows dove into the sand and wound into a stormy funnel that scattered the grains into the air. A shimmering, obsidian form rose from the spiral, fragments of solidified shadows clicking into place, sculpting a towering mare out of nothing. No—not a mare. A *night* mare. *Venom and hell.*

Instinctually, I stepped backward. The mare nearly doubled my height, looming in the darkness like something from my worst dreams—a beast of the In Between. When it whinnied, it evoked the haunting screech of scavenger birds. And when its gaze settled on me, its calculating stare excavated secrets buried deep within me.

"Up you go." Firm hands gripped my waist and hoisted me onto the creature before I could utter any of my numerous protests. But once I was firmly seated, I marveled at the creature's body—the magic of solidified shadows, still malleable and fluid but holding the shape it had been commanded to form. Swirling ribbons of darkness that ebbed and flowed like a river, holding fast like steel when I placed my palm against it. Magical. Terrifying. Incomprehensible.

"Hold her," he commanded, breaking my dazed astonishment. He passed the sleeping Stitcher to me, and I turned her over in my lap to face the stars, frowning at the milky hue of her face. The strings of beads around her neck clinked together, rustling gently as the mare shifted its weight. The silk of her skirt cooled my skin as I ran my hands over it. I smoothed it incessantly, as though the very act of ironing out the wrinkles in the fabric could somehow clear away the ripples of my stress. It worked, however slightly.

She looked so frail. *Don't die yet, Ahma. Hang on.* Did her shoulder pain her? Did she sleep to avoid the reality of recent events, or had her duties as Stitcher finally drained her beyond recovery? Did poison hold her submerged beneath the waves of consciousness? Would the Daughters be able to heal her and wake her? Would this nightmare ever cease? And if I ever learned to tame my magic enough to *help* instead of wreaking more havoc, how long would I last as her successor before I tired beyond saving like her?

If Prisha's war was on the brink of a final battle...did it even matter?

The monster swung onto the horse, taking up the space behind me. I nearly jumped out of my seat, wholly unprepared for his closeness to my body. "What are you doing?" I snapped over my shoulder.

"Do you want me to help you make it back to the Daughters before Prisha unleashes her wrath, or would you like to take your chances without me?"

"Conjure your own horse," I hissed.

He rolled his eyes, then reached past me, fabricating reins from the very essence of darkness before wrapping his fingers around the snakelike shadows. I stiffened at the brush of his arms against my waist, the warmth of his chest pressing against my back and the subtle breath on my neck that sent an unexpected shiver along my spine. Sitting up tall, I pitched my torso forward to eliminate any form of physical contact.

"It's going to be an uncomfortable ride if you sit like you're tied to a wooden board the whole time."

Yes, well, this is significantly more comfortable than the alternative of cozying up to one of Prisha's beasts, thank you.

A weary sigh brushed against the nape of my neck. "Fine, have it your way." But he reached his arms around me and bared his wrists before me. "Now, would you like to retie your prisoner's bindings? We had a deal, after all."

My expression softened with a laugh I did not expect. What was the point? "It seems we've moved beyond their necessity."

"Very well. Just thought I'd offer." A quick snap of the reins set the ghastly mare into motion. A gasp of surprise surfaced in my throat, but I swallowed it down, marveling at how fluidly it moved. It did not jostle like a real horse, but rather glided, rolling like the dark clouds preceding the storms of Prisha's greatest tempests.

A playful tug on my braid pulled me back to attention. "Just so you know, Starlight, I would have followed you anyway. Prisoner or not. Can't explain it, but I feel I'm meant to."

I tossed a glance at him over my shoulder.

His expression remained flat and untelling, but something about it spoke of a depth I didn't quite understand. An intensity lingering just beneath the surface. A truth that did not want to be revealed.

"Good to know." I rolled my eyes. If this was his attempt to endear himself to me, I had no intention of falling for it. Besides, even if I could look past the minor inconvenience of his origin—which I certainly couldn't—I was to marry Rali in a few days' time. Something tightened in my stomach. Why was I even thinking about any of this? And what would Rali think of my— my *curse*? What if I couldn't find a way to return the monster to the In Between or free myself from him?

Don't be ridiculous, Zara. You'll find a way. I nodded, making a silent vow to myself.

His arm moved against my ribcage as he lifted his index finger to the shredded skies.

"See how the stars shine? See how they persist? Glowing fiercely through Prisha's choking hold?" He allowed the horse to glide forward a few more paces before he finished his thought. "I think they're shining for you."

Despite my instincts to dismiss anything he said, I could not dismiss the awe that slackened my mouth when I marveled at the canopy of stars. The ancestors smiled at me with each twinkle of light, holding on despite the obsidian streaks of poison staining the mesh of sky. Glittering like diamonds, boasting of wealth and power and wonder. Acknowledging me. A part of me—in my heritage, in my present, and in my future.

"The stars favor you," he whispered.

I turned back toward him, lifting a quizzical brow at the sincerity etched into his calm composure. Something fluttered in my stomach, but I immediately slammed walls around my heart and let my expression harden. *What kind of a maniac says that to someone they've just met?* "If they hold me in such high regard as you say, then I hope they do me a favor." I let my words drift heavily, filling the empty space between us before I elaborated, "I hope they swallow you whole so I can be rid of you forever." Just like Ahma had done with Prisha's snake.

Unease wedged between us, and the smirk on his face dulled, dampened by the flicker of something haunted in his eyes as he urged the mare forward.

CHAPTER 12

RALI

It took until daybreak to make it back to the guryas, but as we moved closer to my home, I grew increasingly uneasy. Something was wrong. It was too quiet. Too still. The harder I tried to reach for the call of my Sisters, the more it slipped beyond the grasp of my consciousness. My throat clogged with the viscous poison of worry.

Plumes of black smoke rose from the dunes ahead. I thought they had been a mere trick of the light—perhaps the dispersing shadows of dawn or even a figment of my own imagination, but as we climbed uphill, my nerves tingled with dread. The feather-like columns of tar waved in stark contrast against the first inkling of daybreak, and my heart pounded in warning. The poison tumbling upward to the sky did not come from Prisha's curse— this darkness came from *our* world. A nightmare in reverse. The signal of destruction. It came in great waves of smoke and carried the acrid stench of scorched wood.

The mare glided forward, coming to a stop at the height of a particularly imperious dune. The valley opened up before us, and the catastrophe at the end of the steep slope came into focus.

The guryas burned.

My *home* burned.

Destroy the Daughters. Kill the Stitcher. The invasive voice rattled inside of my head, its tone triumphant and so far removed from the actual sensation of horror that clutched my brain between its shriveled fingers and long, piercing nails. I scrunched my eyes closed for a moment, as though squeezing them shut could somehow force its presence out of my mind. I wished it would *leave me alone.*

When I opened my eyes, the wall of flames still curled before me, devouring the painted hides of the guryas in a weaving dance between the wooden beams. The scent of charred wood mingled with the crackle of fire as it climbed up the dwelling. Heat accosted my face as I stared numbly at the way the flames reached up toward the rising sun, as though trying to return to its distant brethren. I vaguely registered the flooding wetness that coated my cheeks, though I hadn't realized I'd started crying.

What...what happened?

The monster shifted behind me, tugging the reins to direct the whinnying horse away from the wreckage.

Whirling, I turned in my seat to face the creature from the In Between. The signature hint of amusement he normally adopted was absent. In its place, he wore a grave expression that creased the space between his brows. "We should go," he murmured urgently, eyes darting toward the skies.

Anger consumed me, a mirror to the flames licking away the remnants of my home.

"Did you do this?" I lashed out. "Did you send Prisha after them? Did you tell her where to find them? Is this your doing?" I yelled, my voice cracking with strain. But in my soul, doubts stirred. Of course it hadn't been him—he'd been with me. But still...If he could hear Prisha like I could...if he could communicate with her...

I didn't know who Prisha chose to communicate with, or how, so he could never be trusted.

He attempted to place a tender hand on my shoulder, but I shoved him away. "Don't touch me." His eyes widened and his whole body tensed. He locked his jaw, as if to hold back whatever words he rehearsed in his mind but dared not say.

I slid from the horse, retrieving the Eldress from where I'd left her slumped across the mare's shoulders. Perspiration dripped from my brow to the tip of my nose. I wiped my nose against my shoulder, stumbling toward the flaming guryas with as much haste as the shifting sand could afford me, carrying the Eldress away from the wretched creature.

I shouldn't have trusted him. Not even for a second.

Sparks of fire popped, branching from the body of devouring flames, and I fell in an ungraceful heap in the sand. I dropped the Eldress before me and leaned over her, shaking her uninjured shoulder and begging her to wake. To help. To do anything. But her tongue simply lolled to the side of her lax mouth, and beads of sweat smattered her pallid complexion.

"Ahma, please. Wake up!" The roar of flames blasted a threatening wave of heat across my face, and I squinted, but Ahma did not even flinch. Tears clouded my vision, though the fire's blaze quickly siphoned them from my cheeks. "Please, Ahma. Help."

My eyes swept over the incineration, dreading what I might see if I permitted myself to look too closely. Had the Daughters fled in time? Or were they still in there...enshrouded by flames? My mouth ran so dry my tongue chafed against the roof of my palate, and my throat shriveled, collapsing in on itself so I could not swallow the shape of my fear.

The Daughters must die. Kill the Stitcher. A vision of the Eldress tied to a stone slab rammed into my mind, her ancient body withered and broken, with blood pooling around the knife in her abdomen.

Surprise choked me. I squeezed the tears away, but they slipped through my lashes and rolled down my cheeks until the heat banished them. The smoke stung, but I could not bear to pull my gaze aside.

The blaze consumed the remnants of our belongings. Most had already crumbled into ash, but some stood fast, rebelling with unwavering resilience. The tea kettle, still hooked on the side of the failing support beam, shelves on the precipice of a collapse, heaps of debris and fallen ash across the cook surface. Defiant until the end.

Yet no hint of the Daughters surfaced in the rubble. "Please, Ahma, wake and call the Daughters to us. Please." Had they fled to the city without me? Did the Dune Riders find them? *Venom and hell.* We should have been quicker to heed Lurah's warning. A sharp pain twisted between my ribs—the knifelike stab of guilt. How could I get the Eldress to one of our healers if I'd been detached from the web that connected all Daughters? If I could no longer trace their magic?

I lowered my head to her chest, letting my tears fall as little crystal additions to the rows of beads swathing her neck. Her heart beat so slowly, her lungs shuddering with too-shallow breaths. Still, she didn't stir. Without the Eldress to reunite the Daughters, the call of their weaving no longer reached me. They were beyond my grasp, and I—I was lost.

A crackling sounded above me, and I snapped my neck back to look up. Flames enveloped the tallest mast at the center of the gurya, splitting the weakening wood.

Kill the Stitcher, Prisha hissed. A shadowy wave of darkness spilled from the rifted sky, materializing into a hand of destruction. The tendrils lengthened into fingers, swooping toward the creaking beam. With an artistic flick of its wrist, the black mass shoved the mast off balance.

Seconds spanned for an eternity as the mast teetered. I gaped, following its slow descent as it cast a menacing shadow over our heads, holding me frozen beneath it. A wave of fiery purpose coursed through my veins, freeing me from the state of paralysis that gripped me. My muscles ignited with a burst of desperation but—too late.

Seizing Ahma beneath her shoulders, I heaved to drag her from the path of the falling beam and snapped my eyes shut, cursing the moment of hesitation that would now cost us our lives.

I gasped, pulling air sharply into my lungs as the mast collapsed in a spray of sand at our side. Threads of shadow wrapped around it, wrenched aside by dark magic so the beam missed us by only a few measures. The monster appeared behind me, his wings snapping over us to form a canopy, shielding us from the sputtering sparks of flame that leaped from the scorched wood.

None of us moved—hearts hammering, breaths jagged, every muscle of my body rigid with tension. Had Prisha...had Prisha just attempted to murder Ahma from her prison in the sky? *Could she do that?*

I rolled my head toward her creature. And had her monster just...saved us? My eyebrows cinched with confusion when he met my gaze. Behind him, his wings dissipated like smoke, carried away on nonexistent winds.

"I—"

"Halt! Who goes there?" A voice sliced through the remains of my half-formed thought, barking with an authority that jarred me. Or perhaps it was the sound of approaching hooves and the too-recent memory of my encounter with the Dune Riders that reignited my already frayed nerves.

The monster's spine stiffened behind me. He pulled away, slamming a hand over his ear as the swish of an arrow grazed him. A tributary of shadowy blood gushed down the side of his face, sprawling into narrowing forks. His lips curled into a sneer of rage.

"Unhand her, or the next one goes through your eye socket!"

My attention darted toward the speaker, adorned in a leather breastplate and red-plumed helmet. A guard from Rashii—his arrow cocked and aimed with the confidence of a man who never missed by accident. Any other day, it would have been shocking to see an outsider approach the guryas, for the Stitcher's magic made them impenetrable to strangers. But now—there was nothing left to hide behind...no Eldress to weave her protective canopy above us. And no capacity left inside of me to feel anything but a vast, rapidly expanding emptiness that left me entirely exposed.

A growl rumbled in the monster's chest, and in a fluster of movement, his arms wrapped around me, pulling me behind him, shielding both me and the Eldress from the newcomer's view.

"Wait!" I gasped, squeezing the corded muscle above the crook of his arm. Stepping around him, I met his gaze and pleaded with him to understand the words written across my face. To keep his magic hidden. To tread carefully. "He's a guard from Rashii. He can help us." *Let me handle this. He can't know what you are. Don't overreact.* The vein in his temple ticked with obvious disapproval, but he did not stop me when I stepped around him to approach the rider.

The soldier's horse slowed to a trot and came to a stop in front of me—a guard with unruly black hair, tousled by his ride through the desert. He peered down at me with sharp eyes and an even sharper nose before lancing back toward my captive with murderous intent. Sliding from the mare's back, his hand wrapped around the hilt of his sword.

"Did you do this?" he gritted through a sneer, cheeks

reddening as he brushed past me and stalked toward the monster who'd saved me. "Where are the rest of the Daughters, Khazdruki scum?" He waved toward the soldiers behind him, communicating some secret signal with a swish of his hand. They tightened their formation around us, arrows aimed at Prisha's creature.

"Stop! He's good! He's with me!" The words burst from me of their own accord, erupting before my mind had the time to consider them. But now that they hung there, uncomfortably out in the open, I questioned them, wanting to pull them back and bury them beneath the rest of the feelings I did not care to inspect. Why *did* I wish to protect him? It would be so easy to let the soldier kill him and free me from this bond. To run away to Rashii with these soldiers and forget this mess ever happened. To enlist their help to uncover what had happened to my Sisters. But something twisted inside of me at the thought. The ruffian had just saved my life after all, and...perhaps by some unguided impulse I did not understand, I needed him.

The guard locked eyes with me, coldly calculating, excavating every morsel of truth he could uncover from my stare. I shifted beneath the intensity of his gaze. "You are certain? I swear by Halah...if he has harmed you, or if he means you harm, I will flay him navel to neck. You have my word, Daughter. I will protect you."

"No, truly. He's harmless. He's...protecting me." The soldier's eyes narrowed with an air of skepticism, sending my heart into a new flurry of erratic beats before I continued, spinning a wild tale without time to second-guess my sanity. "The Daughters hired him to protect us from Prisha's monsters...so we could...safely dedicate more time to prayer," I added quickly. Perhaps he would buy the partial truth. I avoided chewing the side of my tongue, holding so still to keep from fidgeting that I probably gave away my discomfort with the unnaturalness of my rigidity.

The guard's nostrils flared, but he relaxed his grip on the hilt of his sword and nodded. "Forgive me, Daughter of Halah. There's been much unrest in Rashii...talk of war with Khazdra and now this attack upon the Daughters. It is hard to know who to trust. But I honor your judgment." He paused, settling on my moonlit braids and moonsilk skin, and his expression softened, jade eyes freckled with flecks of gold, slightly creased at the corner with the hint of a smile. My breath hitched, betraying my unsolicited attraction as I noted his square jaw and the way his muscular frame enhanced his commanding presence. "What is your name, Daughter?"

"Zara," I managed, in a voice too foreign and weak to be my own.

Recognition flared across his face like sunlight. "Zara? As in... Zaraya Avasya?" He crossed the remaining distance between us and wrapped his hands around mine. "*It cannot be*. Zara, it's me, Rali."

I balked, shivering at the brush of his hands around mine. *Wait. This is Rali?*

I reconsidered his appearance, my stomach fluttering with a sudden rush of sand wings. This soldier—this man with tousled hair and streaks of honey through his jade eyes—this was the one who had inked his soul into poetic words to share with me? Who had bared his heart in the dozens of letters passed between us? I'd imagined him as someone...completely different. Not this handsome, perfect specimen of a man before me.

Perhaps the union the elders had arranged would not be as terrible as I'd once feared.

"What are you doing here?" A crescendo clamored in my heart, jolting it back to life. "Did you see who did this? Have you seen my Sisters?"

Rali's chin jutted toward the flames, his face twisting with remorse as he shook his head. "The city guard sent us to check on the smoke. At first, we assumed it was merely travelers from

Haldratha or Zunar crossing the desert to visit for A'i Halajan, but when the plumes expanded, we knew something was wrong. We thought it was Riders...perhaps Khazdruki scouts pillaging the travelers' camps...but I never expected it to lead me straight to the heart of the Daughters' clan." His tone dropped with an almost reverent appreciation before he turned his attention back to me. "By the time we got here...it was too late. But I promise, whoever did this will pay."

My breath stilled with uncertainty when he rubbed his thumbs over the tops of my hands in a tender motion. Warmth flowed through his palms and through his gaze, but it was tinged with something prickly. Perhaps sadness? Pity?

"I'm so sorry for your loss, Zara," he said softly. "You must be..." His voice trailed off, unable to produce a fitting word to describe the irregular shards of emotion deconstructing me from within.

For a man who had produced so many poetic, heartfelt letters, it seemed strangely contradictory to see him stumble over his words in person. Perhaps if he had ink and paper, he could find the right ones. Yet something about his state of speechlessness endeared him to me, and the gates holding back my emotions ripped from their hinges.

I screwed my face into a grimace, banishing the last tears slipping past my lashes. "I have to find my Sisters. I'm...lost without them."

He brushed a stray lock of my hair, taming it back into its braid. "I will help you. We will send out a search party." He waved a gesture of command to the riders behind him. Half branched off in response, racing into the dunes and dipping out of sight. "You don't have to do this yourself...you shouldn't be alone. It's not safe. Come back to Rashii with me."

"She's not alone," a snarling voice protested.

Rali's attention snapped over my shoulder and his teeth

clenched, jaw muscles twitching. His fingers flexed at his side, straying dangerously close to the hilt of his sword again. "Zara, come with me," he repeated in a slow rumble. "I can protect you."

My gaze drifted over my shoulder toward the enemy I'd unleashed from the sky, his arms crossed over his chest, his distaste evident in the way he glared at Rali. A sudden pang of reservation lodged itself in the muscle of my heart, piercing and hot. If I left with Rali, would Prisha's creature follow? And what if he didn't? Would the bond between us stretch until I doubled over with pain and begged to be returned to him? How could I possibly hide the bond from Rali if I allowed distance to wedge itself between us?

Perhaps I could convince Rali to allow him to come with us? I caught the tension in Rali's posture from the corner of my eye, his possessive stance creeping between me and the creature. *Probably not.*

Venom and hell, I cannot believe I'm saying this, but..."Rali, I need your help." Under ordinary circumstances, I would never entrust the Eldress's safety to anyone but a Daughter, but these circumstances were anything but ordinary. And I trusted Rali. Or...I wanted to trust him. Or maybe I simply had to.

Don't be ridiculous, Zara. Rali seemed a bit different from the picture my expectations had painted, but this man had bared his heart and soul to me in letters over the past year, convincing me to accept our arranged union. He was not a stranger...not really. I could trust him to get her to safety.

I nodded, mind made up. I just needed to convince him to leave without me so I could be free to deal with this monster alone.

Rali lifted his brow, but I gestured for him to wait. When I turned my back to him, I glued my eyes to Prisha's monster instead, warning him with an unwavering stare as I walked past him to scoop the Eldress from her bed of sand. Her body slumped between my arms when I lifted her, and I carried her carefully toward Rali.

Rali's eyes widened with alarm. "Zara…is that—"

"The Eldress," I answered in confirmation.

"*The* Eldress? The—" He floundered, too flustered to produce words in the moment of awe. "What happened?" he finally managed. His eyes raced over her body, landing on the dark stain at her shoulder and the deathly pallor of her complexion. "She's injured? Zara, she needs a healer's attention! Immediately."

"Take her," I commanded, shoving the frail body toward Rali, trying not to grimace at the sight of the Eldress in an outsider's arms. *He's not an outsider, Zara,* I corrected myself. *He's Rali. He's yours.*

"Take her? You mean…without you?" he asked, his eyes turned down with worry. "No, you must come too."

"You'll be faster without me. I'll follow."

Rali's gaze darted between me and the Eldress, torn by some internal battle. "I'll have my men accompany you. For your safety."

"That won't be necessary," I opposed, perhaps too quickly. Of course he had offered out of kindness, and it would be unusual to refuse such a gesture. I swallowed the sandy dryness in my mouth. "They should go with you," I amended, the words sticky on my tongue. "The Eldress needs all the protection you can offer. I'll be safe with—" I motioned vaguely toward Prisha's creature, realizing I did not even know what to call him. "My Guardian," I finished lamely.

Rali looked as though the decision to leave me behind ripped a piece of his soul free from his chest, but he nodded grimly. "If any harm comes to you…if you do not show up in Rashii…"

"I'll be fine, really." I smiled, but no part of me believed that. Sighing wearily, too exhausted by stress to convince him, I continued, "I promise I'll follow. But you must get her to a healer. Fast. The Eldress is...*everything*."

Rali lowered his gaze, admiring the limp body in his arms. "Yes, she is. Without her..."

His thought trailed off, and we both shuddered.

"You must be careful with her," I urged, shoving my remaining reservations aside.

"Of course. I will protect her with my life."

He bobbed his chin, then bounded toward his horse to place the unconscious Eldress across its shoulders. Her arms swung limply over the horse's ribs, and the beaded bangles stacked at the fullest part of her hand, barely held in place by the odd angle of her bony thumb. She looked like a corpse. Thin and deteriorated, like one who'd died from many moons of starvation.

"You think this is wise, Zara?" a voice whispered in my ear as I watched Rali fasten the Eldress to his horse, and I stilled at his use of my name. Of course, he had heard Rali use it. "You know it would be faster if I flew her to the city?"

An icy shudder ran down my spine, and I snapped my head to the left, surprised to find the monster so close to my side, though he no longer looked like one. At least, not anymore. His eyes still held a universe of power in their depths, but in every other respect, he looked like a standard mortal.

I wrinkled my brow in confusion, remembering how I'd watched his wings dissolve after he saved us from the falling mast. "The Eldress is safer with a guard of Rashii than a monster of the In Between. And...how did you make your wings disappear?"

He smirked, though he attempted to suppress his amusement, as though at odds with it. "They're made of shadow," he explained matter-of-factly. "I create and destroy with shadows, and so I can create and destroy my wings. Simple, really. But let's keep that between you and me. I don't trust him."

"And I don't trust *you*." But I was glad he could hide the

wings...that was better for both of us. He was right—Rali didn't need to know what he was. Who he was.

Rali dusted his hands on his trousers after he fastened the Eldress to the horse, using leather straps to secure her unconscious body in place. His eyes darkened when he turned to me, glaring at the creature—the man—at my side.

"I'll send someone back for you," he promised, then his eyes darkened when he looked toward the monster. "If you so much as—"

Prisha's creature interjected before Rali could finish his threat. "I'll take care of her. She is safe with me," he said firmly, standing taller so he towered over Rali.

"Very well," Rali answered. He combed a hand through the rumpled mess of his hair. Smoke from the flames rose behind him. "And Zara?" he asked, walking toward me to take my hands in his, but pausing in a moment of hesitation. He shook his head, closing his mouth before attempting to speak again. "I'm sorry. I fear...I am flustered by your presence. So long have I looked forward to this meeting that now...in these circumstances...the right words seem to have escaped me."

"It's okay," I responded, uncertain of the right words myself, but grateful that the fates had brought us together at the right time.

"I know I wrote it in my letters, but you must know it was all true." He smiled at me, squeezing my hands gently. "You are the fire that consumes me...the flame that gives me meaning. The blaze that—"

Prisha's creature snorted from somewhere behind my back, and the streaks of honey in Rali's eyes sharpened to daggers. I held my breath, uncomfortable in the sudden tension, but he turned back to me. "I should very much like to kiss you," he whispered, his throat bobbing.

I opened my mouth with surprise and stared back at him,

reconciling the memory of his heartfelt letters with the handsome, hopeful man before me who felt like a stranger I could fall in love with, and I nodded.

A soft squeak caught in my throat as he pulled me toward him, finding my lips with his own. His eyes closed with the passion of his kiss while mine wrenched open, uncertain how I was meant to respond. Finally, I relaxed into his hold, letting him deepen his exploration.

A bored voice interrupted us. "Must you do this out in the open? You know...I'm right here. I can see you," the cursed ruffian drawled in his disinterested tone that had the faintest hint of irritation laced through it.

Rali released me and smiled, his eyes sparkling with victory—smug superiority.

"Would you care to join us, then? Or do you prefer to watch?" he asked, his tone chiding. "She is mine, you know."

My lips jerked downward in a disgusted frown. Rali stood with his jaw jutted out, his chest flared like some strutting feather-train bird, feathers splayed behind it with pride. Sure, I was meant to marry him, but I was not some playing piece on a caza board to collect. To own. He didn't seem to notice my aversion to his statement.

The monster, however...*he* gave me his rapt attention. His eyes found mine with a fiery burst of stardust. This gaze sent a jolt of electricity through me, igniting something deep inside me, piercing my heart so acutely that my lips parted. The unwavering intensity of his gaze demanded my undivided presence—my full attentiveness—so the rest of the world faded away in favor of the small but inconceivable microcosm of existence that had formed between us.

Venom and hell, Zara. You just kissed your betrothed, and the sky ruffian is the one who sets the world off balance? Hasn't your chaos messed things up enough already?

He seemed to notice the way my heart began to race, the way I scolded myself for staring. His lips bent in a poorly concealed smirk, and his countenance darkened, pulling shadows across his face in a way that made me tremble.

"I don't share," he grumbled in Rali's general direction, keeping his eyes firmly locked on mine. "I do not do halfhearted. And I don't play nicely with others."

"Charming," Rali responded.

Oh goddess. A flurry of sand wings swarmed around my heart as panic set in. I had not failed to notice the way he glanced at Rali with enough ire to shred him with his gaze alone. Or the way my own body betrayed me, reacting to his possessiveness like a candle erupting into flame of its own accord.

It was...unacceptable. He was a monster. A curse straight from the In Between. A force that had eviscerated a squadron of men with *shadows*. Mere shadows. And he did not own me any more than Rali did—tether or not. But why did my body respond to him with such certainty, as if it were already his to own?

More than ever, I needed to sever the ties that bound us together. I needed to return him to the hell he'd come from, or be trapped in my own hell for eternity.

CHAPTER 13

MONSTER

We watched Rali and his company ride into the distance until they became only a blip on the horizon, then nothing at all when the swell of the dunes rose up to swallow them.

Take care of the Eldress, I prayed, though uncertain to whom I intended to direct my prayers. I was not on good terms with either goddess. Perhaps I should continue to pray to the stars. A band tightened around my chest. *No.* Last time I did that, I lost control of my power and found myself permanently attached to a monster. *Maybe I shouldn't pray at all.*

Something warm brushed against my upper arm, and my breath snagged in response to the tickle of his words against my ear. "I really don't trust him," he whispered. "He reeks of arrogance and nobility."

A short burst of laughter issued through my nose, but he merely cocked a brow, then recovered with a smirk. He paused, presumably waiting for me to explain what I had found so funny.

"If anyone here reeks of arrogance, monster, it is you. Perhaps it is merely yourself you're smelling."

"I am not nobility."

"But you do not deny your arrogance."

He shrugged, falling into silence for a few moments before he could not contain himself any longer. "Bit inappropriate, too, wasn't he? 'The fire that consumes him?' Really? Given the circumstances? Ignorant ass." He mumbled the last bit under his breath.

"He's *poetic,*" I challenged. "I'm sure he didn't mean it like that."

He frowned. "I just don't like him. Everything about him screams of deceit."

"Well, forgive me if I'm reluctant to accept my enemy's assessment of him."

"So we're still enemies?" he asked, shadows casting his glowering expression into stark relief.

"Are you still considering whether or not to kill me?"

"Are you still hoping to sever this bond and toss me back to Prisha at the first chance you get?"

I narrowed my eyes at him, but snapped my mouth shut, folding my arms across the beaded band at my waist and trying my hardest to ignore the way his blasé expression boiled my blood. Pressing my forearms against the beads grounded me, and I finally continued, "Anyway, you're wrong. He's not nobility. He's a guard. *My* guard. I think I know him better than you...we're meant to marry at A'i Halajan this year. He loves me. And I only need *one* guard in my life."

Something in him shifted. Black shadows pulled the light from the air around us, condensing into a solidified presence. His wings rematerialized, stretched end to end, framing the commanding expression on his face.

"I'm a Guardian, not a guard. Do not confuse the two."

The lightheaded swirl in my vision distorted the dunes as an unwarranted flush of heat swirled through my cheeks. I overcorrected my momentary fluster and adopted a carefully crafted expression. Unperturbed and wholly unaffected. "And you think being a Guardian of the In Between, a monster of Prisha, who likely intends to kill me, is a point in your favor?"

"I haven't killed you yet," he pointed out, lifting his brows as though he did, in fact, believe he deserved some credit. "But there's always tomorrow. I suggest finding more of that halfmoon bread...wouldn't want to make poor decisions because I'm hungry and annoyed."

"Okay, then." *Asshole.*

I suppressed my body's very affected reaction to his intense gaze, shoving it somewhere deep inside me and locking it away with a key. I'd forced my voice into my own interpretation of his lighthearted tone, but it had failed to resonate with the same apathetic quality he excelled at.

Still, my efforts seemed to unnerve him. *Good. You see? I can get under your skin, too.*

It was only fair.

He watched me, on the precipice of whatever he wished to say and eternal silence.

With a last glance toward the burning guryas, or at least the ruins that remained, I shoved the painful lump in my throat deep down into the depths of my stomach, forcing it out of existence. Burying the stone deep into my memory, ignoring the way it weighed heavily in my core.

Wallowing in my grief would not fix any of this. Besides, I could no longer bear the singed smell of scorched memories in my nostrils or the stinging discomfort of smoke blowing through my eyes. I blinked away the tears and, with them, the guilt. A snake shedding its skin, molting away the past to accept the journey ahead.

Mind made up, I abruptly collected a fistful of skirts, then turned my back on the ruins. I marched forward, following the tracks in the sand left behind by Rali and his men, letting the haunted vision of the guryas fall at my back. They held nothing for me. Only the pain of the past. My future, the answers I needed, my very survival—all of that lay ahead. And I had promised Rali I'd follow.

Shifting sands whispered at my heels despite the quiet plodding of his steps, warning me of his approach well before his presence prickled the skin at the nape of my neck. I stiffened, but continued to march forward.

"So we're really going to follow him?"

I bristled at the mention of *we*, but accepted the fact that my cruel destiny denied me freedom from his presence—at least for now. Biting back the words I wished to say, I opted for the most diplomatic approach I could muster. Cold and distant, yet employing a minimum standard of respect. "Wherever the Stitcher goes, I follow. She'll know what to do about this." I gestured vaguely, unable to pinpoint exactly what I meant, then sighed. "About everything."

His mouth twisted and his expression rearranged. His cheeks shifted to give the impression that he'd clenched his tongue between his molars, biting down the words he fought against saying. The starscape of his eyes lifted to meet their twin—the twinkling canopy of night—and his wings twitched tellingly at his sides.

Here we go again. "You know it will be faster if we fly," I mocked, predicting his argument before he'd even opened his mouth.

"So we are in agreement, then?" He fell into step with me, matching my pace a fraction behind me to keep his distance. Or study me. Or perhaps consider all the ways he could dissect me with his shadows if he decided to *kill me tomorrow* as he so often considered. I shivered and shuffled forward faster but lifted my chin with an air of confidence.

"We are not in agreement. Not ever. We are in...mutual existence. A regrettable agreement of tolerance. That is all."

"Well, it would be faster," he muttered, more to himself than to me, but his words carried in the silent dunes. "But suit yourself. We'll take the long route."

I frowned, tossing a glance over my shoulder at him. "I prefer my feet firmly on the ground, thank you. Access to earth and air at all times. You know...like a proper Daughter."

He snorted, and even I laughed at this joke. I had never been a proper Daughter. Proper Daughters didn't hear voices that commanded them to kill the Stitcher, and they certainly didn't unstitch the skies or accidentally summon monsters to the realm.

When I had regained my composure, I chanced another glance over my shoulder. His eyes darted away, apparently consumed by the monotony of the golden dunes, but his footsteps followed mine in perfect unison, as though instinctually attuned to each of my movements. I spun around and his gaze snapped back to mine. Walking backward so he could see my look of disapproval, I challenged, "Besides, you can't possibly expect me to let you sweep me into your arms? I don't even like you walking so closely to me. I don't trust you. I—" I paused, sweeping my gaze across his chest, combing my eyes through his effortless hair. "I do not even know your *name*, monster of Prisha, though it seems you have found a way to steal mine."

His jaw tightened at the mention of the jealous goddess's name, but his throat bobbed beneath the collar of his neckline. He bristled, pulling his gaze away from mine once more. The horizon mastered his attention for a few paces, leaving me with a distinct feeling of emptiness in its absence. "Monster is fine, if that is how you wish to see me. If that's what I am to you." His countenance darkened, a shadow falling across his cool demeanor. "It's what I've always been."

I dug my heels into the sand, stopping so abruptly that his

movements continued straight into my abdomen. He bounced off me, his fingers brushing against my arms, and he seized my wrist to catch his balance. He promptly released it as if he'd been burned by a hot coal, recovering his stance, but his hand flexed stiffly at his side.

He angled his jaw upward and studied me below half-hooded eyes, settling into his signature affect of indifference. Somehow, it lacked its former conviction. He wore it like a mask—from the bored glaze in his eyes to the insufferable smirk of superiority to the lackadaisical sweep of judgment. An act performed with precision, each piece a brick laid in defense. A wall to guard whatever truths he shielded beneath his insufferable persona. But beyond the wall, beyond his efforts of concealment, his body stilled. The breath in his lungs hovered, trapped as though he braced himself for my reaction. As if the words I said to him might matter. Or might wound him.

My body reconstituted with a tingling numbness of understanding, a rush of empathy I did not expect. The hair on the back of my neck raised, and anger washed over me, recalling the Dune Riders and the cool, deadly touch of a hostile blade beneath my chin. The hatred that cast the Rider's face into monstrous shadows when he faulted me for all of Prisha's destruction. *Monster*, he'd called me. My stomach clenched, pained by a sudden twist of guilt. "Nobody wants to be called 'monster,'" I said. "What is your real name?"

He regarded me for a long moment, his eyes swirling with the sandstorm of thoughts he buried inside. Finally, he cracked a smile that lifted the shadows from his face. "The name fits."

I crossed my arms and dipped my chin, glaring up at him from beneath my lashes.

He sighed. "Fine. If you're so curious to know, I'll tell you. After you earn it."

I exhaled sharply, more exasperated by his presence than ever.

Perhaps I had misread. This was all merely an act to get under my skin—and it was working. "Must everything have a cost with you? Eventually, you will tire of halfmoon bread."

He tilted his head. "Doubtful."

My hips angled to the side, moving all my weight to one foot as I crossed my arms firmly over my chest. I lifted my chin and glared back.

His eyes swept over my figure with methodical precision, then finally returned to my gaze. "That's not what I had in mind, anyway." His smile softened and disappeared, though the hint of a smirk remained, visible only in the effort it took to subdue it. "I'll tell you. But only if you can best me. I want to see those fighting skills you boast of."

"Best you?" My heart dropped. *Is he serious?* Hadn't we already established there was no way to defeat him? That my subconscious refused to allow me to finish him off no matter how loudly my consciousness screamed?

"That's not fair," I protested.

"There's little in life that's fair, Starlight. Come on. Show me what you can do, and I'll think about telling you."

"And if I refuse?"

"Then 'monster' suits me just fine."

"And if I fail?"

"You won't."

I narrowed my eyes, taking a moment to calculate his intentions but finding no secrets in his gaze to explain his behavior. He stared back, his piercing gaze a rigid wall of defiance. He would not bend—he meant what he said.

Fine. Let's make it quick. My fists slammed against his chest, the shock of the impact surging through my joints. His arm hooked over mine, and my back slammed into the ground. A rush of air expelled itself from my lungs. Amethyst eyes hovered above me, sparkling with the thrill of his amusement. My body seized beneath his weight, heart pounding wildly in my chest as panic spread through my limbs like poison. His mouth pulled into a dangerous smile—a predator who'd captured his prey.

"Well, are you a monster or aren't you?" I asked through a tight breath, struggling to break from his hold. "Surely this is the part where you kill me?"

He wavered, tilting his head with a teasing look of consideration. A lion toying with a mouse trapped beneath its paw. "Why rush? There's always tomorrow." I blinked sluggishly, but his hand wrapped around mine, and he hoisted me to my feet. "Again. But this time like you mean it."

He stepped away, widening his stance and opening his arms to the side. An invitation to try again. His expression remained unfazed. Cocky bastard.

"We don't have time for this," I complained, throwing a glance to the horizon. How far had Rali already gone with Ahma? What if they ran into trouble and needed us?

His brows lifted. "Then perhaps you should yield."

That's not what I meant. I tightened my jaw, wishing I could refuse him but incapable of letting him win so easily. I trusted Rali to get the Eldress to safety. I did not trust Prisha's creature to exempt me from his insufferable gloating if I allowed him to win this challenge. "No."

There was no way I'd survive enduring his smugness the entire way to Rashii. That would be...unacceptable. And that was only if he decided to let me live.

"There's always the option of flying," he offered.

I groaned in frustration but did not dignify him with a rebuttal. Cracking my knuckles bought me time as my thoughts raced through my mind, allowing me to calculate his stance, his reach, his infinite advantages. *You can't think like that,* I reprimanded myself. *Every fighter has a weakness to exploit.* I would find his if it was the last good thing I did in the Realm of Taara before I found my resting place among the stars. I bit my cheek with a resurgence of grim determination.

He watched me, interest piqued with one brow lifted. Shadows danced gracefully between his fingers, weaving in and out slowly as if flowing to a tune neither of us could hear. As if it were its own being—one that could turn and unleash its fury at any moment.

I flinched. *If you don't handle this, Zara, he can destroy everything you love. Do not forget where he came from. Who he belongs to.*

My breath wavered as I reconsidered him, the predatory gleam in his eyes, the shadows that clung to him like he was their master. What would he do when he tired of this game between us? When he grew disenchanted with the connection that bound us together? An icy rush of dread flushed through my veins. *This isn't just about me. Not really. He has the ability to destroy us all, and I'm the only one who can ensure that never happens.*

Rushing toward him, I aimed low and wrapped my arms around his knees to knock him off balance. His arms looped around my midsection and flipped me up onto his shoulder, spinning me playfully before returning me to the sand. The world swam in my vision, and I crashed to the ground, my rear bouncing with a final thump of defeat. His lighthearted laugh shook the air.

Venom and hell, I've had enough of this. I brushed sweat from my forehead, leaving a trail of grainy sand at my hairline when I blinked my eyes back into focus.

His legs folded beneath him, and he sat down in the sand next to me, so close I could feel his steady breaths rustle through the loose hairs across my forehead. He studied me closely for a long moment, losing the gleam in his eyes to something far more intense. He examined my expression carefully, lingering far too long for an answer that refused to surface. I held my breath, afraid to move beneath his scrutiny but also afraid to back down. I returned his gaze, searching for answers to questions I did not know. Searching for...anything.

Finally, he frowned and broke his silence. "You hold back when you fight," he murmured. "Why?"

"That's insulting." I scoffed.

"Your refusal to try is the insult. Perhaps you do not care to know my name after all. For a moment, I was beginning to think you'd forgotten to hate me."

"I *am* trying—"

"No, you aren't. You're afraid."

It seemed an unfair assessment. I wasn't holding back. Fighting was in my nature—it was the only thing my chaos was good for. He just didn't waver. He didn't yield like Prisha's other monsters or succumb to a quick slice of my blade. He was a nightmare from the In Between, sent by Prisha to punish us. The sky crackled in agreement overhead, an ominous reminder of the jealous goddess's intentions. I looked up nervously, wondering if Prisha knew I'd been chosen as the next Stitcher. If she planned to reach past the bars of her prison at the next window of opportunity to end me as well.

Then I studied him—*really* studied him. The way his wings slumped like charcoal puddles against the sand, the edges fraying out like tattered robes in the wind. The way shadows seemed to crawl beneath his skin as he considered me, always there below the surface, ready to strike. The way his gaze flickered between amusement and a darker, more predatory emotion I could not name. "I'm not. You're just—" *Impossible.*

"You're a Daughter of a goddess. Fight like one. I know you can...unless you plan to let Prisha's monsters destroy you? Don't you want to defeat her?" He asked the question like he was trying to stir up my anger, then leaned closer. "There are monsters far worse than me coming. You need to get ready."

"Is that a threat?"

"It's a promise."

My heart thumped loudly against my ribs, blood rushing through my veins as panic set in, reminding me of who he was. What he was. Did he mean to remind me of what he could do? Of what Prisha's monsters intended? I couldn't permit myself to trust him, to grow careless in his presence. I'd already seen the destruction he could accomplish in mere seconds—and he was only *one* of her creatures. Just one of the murderous beasts she sent, but one that could efficiently obliterate us all.

No. Prisha didn't send him. You did this. You are responsible. Fix it.

His chest compressed with a quick laugh when I scowled back at him, collecting my anger and fear and resolve into one compact package—a projectile to launch at him. I surged forward and tumbled into him, pinning his back to the sand below my clenched fist. Baring my teeth, I reached for the dagger in the sheath at my ribs. It sang against the leather as I unsheathed it, catching the stars upon its surface so that it glimmered with malice.

I shoved against the barrier between us and leaned forward, letting all of my weight add to its force. Our breaths mingled, short and staggered but rhythmically entwined by an unheard beat. The whole aura of the air encircling us seemed to swell with it until I forced myself to focus. My heart raced, and warmth spread through my cheeks when his eyes darted from the dagger clasped in my hand to my face. A knowing smirk surfaced, one that hinted at danger and victory. *What are you doing, Zara?*

Grinding my teeth against the effort, I bellowed and thrust the steel toward him. The blade resisted, as though I'd tried to force it through a slab of granite. But I persisted, pushing downward until my muscles quaked and burned. *Just do it,* I commanded the blade, undeterred by the insurmountable boundary between us. *Listen to me.*

The boredom in his eyes returned, seeping back slowly until they appeared glazed with his glassy, unenthused look of disinterest. Exasperation poured from me in a guttural shout, and I reached within, to the last reserves of strength buried deep within me. Starlight spilled from me, a shattering sunburst that forced its way through the space between us, radiating with certainty and power. Emerging from my heart. *The heart of stars,* I registered vaguely before leveraging it to comply with my bidding.

The threads of light wound around him, snaking into cuffs at his wrists, then pinning his limbs to the ground. His expression darkened, cast into shadows. *Shred the skies, thief of stars. Monster. Shred the skies.* The light I wielded sputtered then warped, its glow fading into tendrils of shadow at the sound of Prisha's voice. Light turned dark, becoming something I hadn't intended...something beyond my control. "What are you doing?" I gasped, blaming him.

Kill him, Zara, I urged. Clearly, our connection held dangers I didn't fully comprehend...and we could not continue this game. My entire body trembled with the effort, but I forced the blade through the invisible boundary. Finally, the blade tapped lightly against his skin, an odd contrast to the force I exerted. Expelling the air from my lungs with a cry, I nicked the hollow of his throat —a shallow scrape wholly unnotable in ordinary circumstances. So inconsequential, the pain did not register on his face, though a thin line of bloodlike shadows slipped from the scratch.

He brought a hand to the cut, touching the blood as his glassy boredom dispersed. His face brightened, surprise registering in the jump of his brows and the quirk of his smile. He swallowed, and the movement of his Adam's apple pulled inexplicably at my attention. "Now we're talking," he managed darkly between breaths.

He cupped my chin in his hand, and for the fleetest moment, I stiffened, afraid that he intended to kiss me. Oddly entranced by the notion that he might try. Confident that I would deepen that gash at his throat if he did. But he merely smirked at my reaction and brushed a gentle thumb across my cheek. Then, with a slight nudge, he lifted my chin to turn my sight to the sky.

"The stars favor you, Zara. You see?"

My mouth parted instinctually, gasping at the ethereal heavens, the glittering gemstones of the lives that came before us and the haunted traces of Prisha's destruction. Great gashes ripping the sky from end to end. And the stars that never relented. The inconceivable eternity of it made me dizzy. I shifted to distance myself from him, casting a reproachful glance in his direction.

"Then I hope they swallow you whole." *Since clearly I'm incapable of killing you.*

He barked with laughter, though his countenance darkened.

Exhausted, I released...everything. I fell back onto the sand, and the shadowed starlight returned itself, burrowing into my heart, its presence warming me with the confirmation of its allegiance. It hummed, glowing once more, then faded into nothing. The stars above glittered in applause, and the dune cradled my head like a pillow. The last dregs of my energy drained away.

Leather wings skimmed against my upper arm as Prisha's creature adjusted his position. He lay next to me, tracing the path of my eyes to the sky above. His chest rose and fell slowly in my peripheral vision, but he did not speak. Not for a long while.

Finally, when I felt most in danger of allowing my exhaustion to pull me into an uneasy sleep at his side, I forced myself to sit up and break the silence. "I believe you owe me something, now, monster."

He responded with a heavy sigh, then a silence. I huffed with irritation, realizing he'd never intended to tell me. But then—

"Rueper," he confided, his voice deep and granular. He paused for a moment, then added, "But you may call me Rue."

"Roo?" I gasped. *The great, terrifying Guardian of the In*

Between is named Roo? "Like R-o-o?" He didn't seem so frightening after all. I suppressed a giggle.

He noticed.

"Rue, as in you will *rue* the day you ever presume to laugh at me again." Shadows materialized, enveloping us in a darkness more precarious than a starless night. He drowned us in the dark, the presence of his winding shadows so consuming that it both diminished and heightened my senses, drawing all of my attention to the form of the Guardian. His proximity prickled at the edge of my consciousness, though I could not see him in the darkness and no part of our bodies touched.

"Okay," I whispered, my heart racing with fear or something less definable. "Rue for short." *Venom and hell. He's touchy.*

I didn't know what to say afterward, so I stared up at the scars in the sky and traced them with my eyes until my lids grew heavy and exhausted by my search for words to articulate my jumbled thoughts.

"We should go," I said abruptly, climbing to my feet. The weight of fatigue pressed down on my shoulders, and I stumbled. My head rushed, making the sand swirl deceptively below me, but a firm hand gripped my elbow and steadied me.

Rue turned his head toward me, a lock of hair sweeping across his brow. It rumpled with concern when he studied me. "You need rest. I pushed you too hard."

I *did* need rest, but rest was not a luxury we had the time for. "We can't. The Stitcher—"

"The Stitcher will be there when we arrive," he interjected calmly. "There is nothing you can do for her that you haven't already done. A star cannot shine when it burns out, Starlight. Rest, then conquer. I'll take first watch."

Conquer? Who said anything about conquering? I just wanted to find the Stitcher. "But—"

"We'll leave at dawn. You have my word."

Your word? I bristled at the notion that his word should mean anything to me. He was my enemy...he probably longed for the opportunity to smother me in my sleep. An argument wedged its way into the forefront of my mind, but when I opened my mouth to protest, Rue shook his head. "The stars will protect you." *And so will I,* the intensity of his gaze seemed to say, though why, I couldn't begin to fathom. "You'll be safe."

"I don't trust you," I protested, but my vision blurred with fatigue. I had overextended myself. "How do I know you won't just kill me in my sleep?"

"I didn't last time." He shrugged as though his argument decided the matter and lifted his brows when I opened my mouth to protest. "You're clearly exhausted. The least I can do is offer you a good night's sleep before I decide whether or not to kill you." He smirked.

I wasn't entirely sure if he was teasing or serious, but I *was* certain I needed rest. He hadn't killed me yet—actually...he'd saved me today. Perhaps he didn't intend to kill me at all.

Or maybe the bond between us protected me, too. From the corner of my eye, I watched him, wondering how eagerly he'd destroy me if the bond between us didn't exist.

Rue sank to the ground, patting the soft dunes next to him. "Here?" I asked, gesturing to all the openness.

"Here is fine. Unless you've changed your mind about flying?"

I muttered incoherently and stomped a few paces away, pausing to debate. My fingers wrapped instinctually around the hilt of my dagger, and I felt safer, even though I knew the weapon to be lacking. Perhaps a few hours of rest would be okay. I curled up in a ball, facing away from Rue so I did not have to meet the gaze I felt so intensely against my back. But that was childish. Foolish, really. I shifted, turning ever so slightly so I could keep him in my line of sight. Just in case.

Shadows emanated from him, drifting peacefully over us like a gurya of darkness, enveloping us in the solace of complete obscurity. I watched Rue discreetly for a while, noting the way his wings twitched with tension whenever he turned his gaze to the sky, but finally, I fell asleep with the steel blade pressed beneath my cheek, the reassuring coolness of its handle in my grasp.

CHAPTER 14

KILL THEM ALL

I stood on the edge of nothing.

Not *exactly* nothing...because something was undeniably there. But what it was did not exist in the planes of my understanding. Silken shadows shifted, constantly adjusting their angles to fall into new prismatic shapes. And an indescribable cold melded with my very bones.

What is this place? The pounding of my heart chided in warning, crushed by the vacuum of emptiness surrounding me. It ruthlessly stripped away my senses, leaving me disoriented and on edge. *Did Rue bring me here? No...I'm sleeping. Wake up, Zara. Wake up.* But I could not move.

Two figures materialized. Or perhaps had always been there and my eyes simply adapted to see them. Or sense them? I couldn't quite perceive my surroundings to discern anything reliably but the hammering of my own heart.

They ambled slowly through the void. Two shadows.

"You have the Stitcher?" one shadow asked. A female. Familiar and close—as if it were my own voice.

"I do," the other replied. Male. Tall and broad-shouldered. Built like Rue. *What is he doing here?* The channel widened as they slipped through, prisms bending and shifting around their forms to accommodate their presence. Somehow sharp and angular but fluid and soft in their movements all at once.

"And you haven't killed her?"

"The Stitcher will not interfere with your plans. I assure you."

The weighted pause preceded a fresh current of anger. The air itself became venomous with the charged emotion, its touch burning like acid against my skin.

The less formidable shadow held its breath, waiting for the moment to pass. It didn't.

"She still lives?" the first voice seethed. Her teeth made a hissing sound as the words slipped through them. "Kill her!" she shouted, words reverberating solidly in the void. "I cannot reach your realm unless you kill her. Kill her, kill her, *kill her!*" Her chant eroded into a maniacal repetition.

"I have just acquired her. It is complicated," the second one replied.

"No," the angry one spat. "My patience is complicated. My tolerance of your incompetence is complicated. My desire to continue this alliance is complicated. Do you want my army or my wrath?" The fearful one diminished beneath every cutting word, as though the shards of anger in her voice sliced away bits of him until he became nothing at all.

A violent twist in my stomach warned me of something, but the vacuous landscape dulled my ability to react...it dulled my ability to even comprehend the growing pit of dread in my stomach. I floated, held in place by all the void. I simply...existed, forced to tolerate the feeling of writhing snakes in my stomach, the white hot venom flooding my veins, and the hysterical leaping of my heart that compelled me to act.

"I want them dead. I want them all dead. Dead. Dead. *Dead. Kill her, stupid useless servant.*" When the shadow walked forward, her storm of words swarmed like drone bees around their queen. She chanted with increasing agitation—spewing words whose meanings I could not distinguish aside from a general impression of her rage.

The cloud of anger expanded and roiled, solidifying into dark, inky tendrils that spidered outward. A shattering boom blasted through the void, and a gash of light opened at her feet, wrenched apart by the serpentine strands of darkness she projected. Light flickered from the gash in a way that scattered the emptiness, illuminating the vastness of the terrain. A terrain interrupted only by the network of scars and gashes amid the infinite structures towering around her. A palace? Buildings? Turrets? Whatever it was, it had her malice written into every fiber of its structure.

She reached out a hand, grabbing the prisms of darkness that pervaded the land in her fist, crushing them into the shape of her will. Into the shape of her monsters. "They deserve to die." She hurled the spider-like shadow of a crawler through the gash, then created another. And another. And another. "They—all—deserve —to—die. Do you hear me?"

"As you wish, Prisha."

"As I wish," she mumbled to herself, turning the words over in her mouth like a delicacy. She stood taller. "Yes. As I wish. Kill her. Kill her. *Kill her! Kill her!*"

The second shadow dipped its chin and backed away, disappearing into the void. My limbs trembled with dread, wondering if Rue would make good on his promise to Prisha. Begging myself to wake from this nightmare to stop him. But the void held me.

Prisha inhaled deeply, alone in the transient landscape of darkness.

"Dresgar?"

The prisms shifted, and another shadow took shape at her side, shorter and stockier than the first. His wings draped carefully behind his back, but he held them at a different angle than Rue. I could not discern his features, but his entire posture felt like a frown. His reluctance imprudently lingered about him in a shroud. "Prisha," he responded simply, his tone politely inquiring despite his hesitations.

"Do you know what I hate, Dresgar?"

"Humans?"

She laughed sharply. Then, her entire composure darkened. "Traitors. Betrayers. And it appears I have a rogue…" Her words trailed off as though she were taking the time to savor their bitterness. "He was from your squadron, was he not?"

Dresgar flinched. Shadows billowed about him, solidifying into thick cords that enshrouded his figure, urged into place by Prisha's hand.

"Do you know what happens to those who fail me, Dresgar? Do you know what will become of you if I find out you were part of this?" Prisha stepped toward him, tracing an elongated finger over the writhing, snakelike bindings she materialized from the void.

The eye of Prisha's swirling storm choked with a sob. "Please. Don't."

Prisha paused, tilting her head in consideration, or perhaps merely savoring the creature's fear. Finally, she jerked her hand upward, whisking away the tempest. The creature trembled, freed from the darkness but still under the presence of her predatory shadow. "Then I want it dealt with. I want *him* dealt with. Or I will deal with *you*."

"Yes, Prisha." His tone was brittle, lacking substance.

"And once the Stitcher dies and I'm free of her restraints, I want that little Star Thief and her heart of stars." She paused, twisting the shapeless prisms in her hands as she stared through the gash at her feet. "Then I want them all dead. Do you understand me?

"Y-Yes. I believe so?" Dresgar stammered.

Her voice leached all the warmth remaining in that land. "Then let me speak more plainly. *Kill them all.*"

CHAPTER 15

TINOYA

Kill them all. Kill them all. The voice echoed inside my head, throbbing and consuming. It screamed louder and louder, pushing aside my own thoughts until all I knew was vitriolic anger with the most burning conviction. It felt like it belonged to me, but also distinctly foreign.

Stop. This is not you, a smaller voice shouted, lost beneath the fiery, murderous rage that overpowered my senses.

I clenched my fists, scooping a handful of sand into my palms and squeezing until the pressure of my nails bit against my skin. It grounded me. The intrusive voice—the compulsion to kill and destroy—slipped away as quickly as the sand between my fingers. I could breathe again. *Where am I?*

I quickly inventoried, feeling the rough grains beneath my palms and the soft caress of moonlight on my face. The cooler air of a star-cloaked desert. Sand. Dune. Stars. Zara.

But something was out of place. A haunting screech ripped through the night, and my eyes snapped open. Rolling to my side

153

and pushing myself up to standing, I scanned the horizon. My heart stopped.

Oh, hell.

The dunes rolled out into the distance all around me, golden sand turned silver beneath the glow of moonlight. Above, the great golden rifts splintered chaotically through the stars, dripping with black tar. Across the dunes, just where the navy curtain of sky met the silver mounds of sand, a black cloud rolled toward me, rippling like a swarm of insects, but bigger. Angrier. The ground trembled beneath its advance.

I stared for too long—paralyzed by the inability to make sense of the shrieking storm. Crawlers? Bulgroiches? Whatever they were, it became impossible to differentiate one creature from the next. They'd amassed into one dreadful shadow—one roiling, deadly maelstrom of darkness. My muscles liquefied into some functionless blob of honey. My heart rate quickened, pounding harder and harder all the way up into my eardrums, a fist hammering at the door of my brain, begging it to jolt back to action.

Rue. Where is Rue? Turning on crouched knees, I spun around, searching frantically for any sign of his midnight wings, but he'd left me completely alone. He was gone.

Hot, acidic rage coursed through my veins again, but this time, it was entirely my own. Where did he go? A fiery poker twisted through my heart, and my stomach sank with the recognition of his betrayal. Had my dream been real? Had he really just met with Prisha in the In Between? That shadow discussing my demise with Prisha...had it been him? Had *he* summoned these monsters to destroy me at her command and left me behind, asleep and defenseless? Did he lead the charge racing toward me now? *That* was how he planned to end me?

He *had* promised to kill me.

But I'd thought that maybe—

The cacophony of screeches and wails grated sharply against the silence of nighttime, each one piercing my eardrums and fraying my nerves. I grimaced, holding my dagger uselessly before me as if the small blade could do anything against a mob of monsters hellbent on destroying me. I braced myself for the moment of impact, too overwhelmed with dread to fully consider the certainty of my death. There were hundreds of them—they would shred me in seconds.

The world spun on its axis, and my brain crashed against my skull, knocked backward as the crawlers swarmed up my frame and forced me to the ground. I screamed, writhing beneath their claws. Thick, black blood flecked across my face when I thrashed my dagger about wildly, slicing whatever I met without reserve. A crawler's screech turned into a rancid gurgle, choking on its own blood rushing from the hole I'd left in its neck.

I slashed at a bulgroich's shoulder, sending a new shower of blood into the fray, then sliced straight through a crawler's grabbling hand, separating its fingers from its knuckles. My own skin blazed with fiery pain, scratched and bleeding with each slice of the claws that parted my skin.

The edges of my vision smudged. The world tinted gray, and the fire inside of me began to extinguish. The stars called for me.

The stars.

Something tugged at my heart, and the golden threads binding me to Rue flared to life, illuminated by the radiant glow beneath my breastbone. The heart of stars. I shouldn't use it...I shouldn't draw attention to it...not when Prisha seemed drawn to its presence and I didn't understand why its light had begun to warp into shadow.

But you'll die if you do nothing, I scolded myself. Rather than shoving it away or burying its power beneath my fear and inadequacy, I reached for it.

Star Thief...shred the skies. Shred them! Prisha's shrill voice filled my mind, pulsing with powerful insistence, but I rammed her back. I focused all my attention on the tether connecting me to Rue and the burst of power in my heart. Our tether surged with a vibrant glimmer. *So he's here,* I registered with a sinking feeling in my gut. *And he's left me to die.*

Bitterness washed over me. I wouldn't give him the satisfaction of winning. I had to survive this...even if only out of sheer spite.

With my rage, I harvested each strand of energy from the heart of stars and threw them outward, blasting a ring of light in a wide halo around myself. The shrieks of Prisha's creations reached horrific decibels. The stars above flickered in response, then her creatures' dark figures writhed, thrashing beneath the binding tethers of light I wrapped around them. Energy flowed through me, wild and burning, unmeasured and unrestrained.

But it drained me. Too quickly.

The creatures flailed their spindly limbs, ripping and shredding the tethers away as my light faded. Or...darkened. My ribs jumped with short, harried breaths, unable to catch enough air. The golden tether entwined with my heart—the one binding me to Rue—flared with renewed strength. I gasped when his end of the tether snapped tight, pulling so forcefully it nearly ripped my still-beating heart from my body. But my hazy vision followed the line to the menacing cloud of shadow, the tenebrous form of a nightmare's approach. A night *mare*. And a winged terror astride it.

Rue.

The mare galloped and skidded to a halt, spraying sand into the air as the last remnants of the tethers restraining Prisha's monsters flickered into shadow. The world paused and amethyst eyes met mine. Intense, and now blazing with inhumanity. With ruthlessness.

I lifted my chin, meeting his gaze. *Is this what you wanted? To just sit back and watch me die? Are you happy?*

The black swarm of creatures recovered, no longer restrained by my magic. They raced toward me, cries echoing with triumph. Still, Rue showed no sign of intervention. He glared down from his seat atop the horse, unflinching and steadfast among the storm surrounding us. He really meant to watch me die.

Rue. Please. I mouthed the words, but no sound came out.

His expression flinched.

He stared down at me from his lofty perch, reins gripped in his clenched fist, and his chin lowered with a dangerous air, but he didn't move. His expression turned steely...unreadable.

Please don't do this.

He brought his hands together.

Shadows engulfed him, spraying outward and spinning into a vortex of jet black ribbons. From the tempest, a monstrous figure emerged. Its back curved with long, jagged ridges, and an array of thorny spikes crowned its head. Its eyes narrowed on me, head tilting in a snakelike bob of curiosity, then it snapped its wings wide, hiding the star-dusted sky behind its reach. It raised its head to the stars and bellowed a powerful roar that made the sand tremble. Shadows spilled from its maw instead of flame—darkness imbued with ire.

Behind it, Rue sat astride his mare, amethyst eyes trained on mine, slashing his arms through the air to control his monstrosity. A puppet and its master.

The dragon responded with another thunderous bellow, spewing a stream of shadows around the ring of monsters. Chaotic screams and unnerving screeches blended with the slashing sound of blades through flesh. The heavy shadows lingered, dancing and flickering like twisting flames, covering the details of the gruesome attack. But even the opaque blanket of shadows could not smother the shrieking sounds of death.

Finally, slowly, the world shifted to silence.

"Zara." Rough hands shook my shoulders. It hurt. *Everything* hurt. "Zara, please." His voice cracked.

My eyes snapped open. Sand and blood crusted my face, leaving my skin rough and sticky. Rue's gaze swept across my body, and he swallowed visibly as his eyes cataloged my injuries with increasing concern. "I'm so sorry, Zara."

I pushed myself up to my elbows, clenching my teeth to brace against the fiery assault of sand biting the raw gashes along my forearms. "What in Prisha's hell was that?" I snapped, heart still pounding. The dunes wobbled before my eyes.

Sadness stained his attempted smirk. All the same, he seamlessly slipped into his typical Rue-like composure. His mouth pulled into a lopsided grin, and he raised a moderately amused brow. "Excuse me? I believe *that* was called 'saving your ass.'"

I almost liked him when he made that expression. That charming, playful, and eternally intrigued look I'd grown to expect from him. I might have told him so if my throat didn't burn with fiery pain and if every part of my body didn't scream with bloodied gashes.

I sat fully upright, groaning with effort. Blood coagulated in odd places across my skin, and many of the gashes in my arms still trickled with crimson streaks. Most of them weren't deep, but they burned relentlessly.

I leaned toward him, brushing the pain aside. Pretending this was the most ordinary moment between us. Just another game. I placed a hand over his forearm, surprised by the corded muscles and strength in his arm. His spine straightened in response, his breath stilling. I forced a smile to my face when he met my eyes. Trust began as a timid thing inside me, a quiet whisper of moonlight coaxing the moonpetal flowers open at night. Slowly, uncertainly. Against everything I knew to be sound judgment. "If I didn't know any better, I'd say you were losing your conviction to kill me."

His jaw twitched with a hint of tension, but his eyes glittered. He leaned closer, so close that I could feel the hum of his energy entwined with mine and the brush of his breath against my cheeks. "Maybe tomorrow." He shrugged.

My facade of composure crumbled with a laugh. *Right, well, at least I have until tomorrow before we do this again.* The short burst of laughter made my wounds flare with sharp, biting pain. "*Fucking hell.*" I winced.

Rue brushed a hair away from my face, tucking it behind my ear with the return of his pained expression. "I should have been there. I shouldn't have left you." His eyes darted between each gash across my body, studying them with a twist of some unspoken emotion tightening his jaw. "You need healing. I'll make a poultice and stitch the worst ones."

Anger washed away any hint of amusement I'd felt moments before. "No. Wait." Why *had* he abandoned me? I needed to know if he'd sent the monsters after me, even if he'd had a change of heart at the last moment. Had he intended to kill me? I leveled my gaze at him, letting my expression turn cold. Had the meeting between him and Prisha happened outside the realm of my dreams? "Where were you? Why did you leave?" The accusation in my tone carried the faintest undertone of betrayal, wilting the blooming moonpetal flowers of trust.

A sheepish grin emerged behind his pained grimace, contorting his expression into a rather unfortunate appearance. He looked like he had a toothache. His shoulders shrugged. "Your stomach was growling loud enough to wake the sand wings from their hundred years of slumber, so I went to find food. Seeing as I ate all your halfmoon bread." He fished for something in the pocket at his hip, then winced. "Cursed little things," he muttered, pressing his thumb against his mouth for a moment, then reached back in.

This time, he moved more gingerly, withdrawing a small, teardrop-shaped fruit with skin that resembled scales. *Tinoya—the dragonberry fruit.* My mouth rushed with saliva, and my stomach rumbled. The fruit had a subtle sweet flavor and a texture that melted on your tongue—but the sight of it made my heart ache for home. For my Sisters.

Kill them all, Prisha's unhinged voice commanded, bursting into my mind the second I thought of my Sisters. I stiffened, nearly jumping an inch from the ground at the grating sound of the goddess's voice in my head. *Shut up, Prisha,* I hollered back at her.

Rue noticed, raising a concerned brow as he ran his knife across the sharp scales of the dragon berry's skin, but he said nothing. Did he know that Prisha spoke to me? Did he hear it, too? He pried back the purple shell to reveal white flesh dotted with red seeds, turning his attention to the work of his hands. "Here...eat." He passed the fruit to me, and I grabbed it eagerly. "I shouldn't have left you. I came as fast as I could."

Looking up beneath my lashes, I observed his expression as I slurped the soft fruit from its casing, watching the way his jaw tensed and the space between his brow creased.

"Oh. And water, too. I brought you some water from that well east of the guryas." He reached behind his back and swung the leather canteen around to his front, ducking his chin forward as he lifted the strap over his head.

I gulped greedily while he watched me in silence, then I passed the canteen back to him.

The regret written on his face made my heart twist with suspicion. "Rue. I dreamed of your visit with Prisha. Did you send them to kill me? The monsters?" *Who's side are you really on?*

"You dreamed of Prisha?" He shook his head, his eyes darkening. "I didn't visit with Prisha. Zara, those monsters were sent to kill *me*."

My brows scrunched together. "What do you mean?"

"Do you think Prisha lets her creatures wander off and do as they please? She's noticed my disappearance, and now...she's hunting me. She doesn't tolerate desertion."

Did that mean the shadow from my dreams wasn't what I'd feared? Had Rue truly abandoned and angered his goddess? The dream felt so real...but perhaps it had only been a nightmare. Perhaps he spoke the truth. And if so...

"You should go back." If his disappearance upset Prisha, he needed to go back. I didn't need any more attention from a deranged goddess, and he didn't need to risk his life because I'd forced him to follow me. Granted, *'forced'* wasn't a fair description, considering I'd tied myself to him by accident, but still. All the more reason to break the tether between us. "You should go back. It's okay. I understand." My voice squeaked into a tight, airless tone, though I couldn't identify the source of the under-lying emotion.

"I can't." His whole frame remained still—exuding a stub-born steadfastness that challenged anyone who tried to break it.

"Of course you can. The In Between is where you belong—"

"I belong with *you*."

I gaped at him, failing miserably to mask any part of my surprise.

"The tether," he corrected when he saw the flicker of befud-dled horror in my eyes. "The tether has bound me to you...you know what happens if we stray too far. But if I don't kill you to show my allegiance to Prisha as she *incessantly* demands, and if I don't return to her—" He shook his head. "I've seen her unmake creatures for far lesser crimes."

I paused, taken aback. What did he mean by *unmake*? "She— She'd kill you? Surely she wouldn't—"

"I assure you, she would," he said, shedding his usual unperturbed air for something darker, grimmer. "You cannot defy her. Any whiff of dissent, any hint of defection, any slight resistance to her command, and she will disintegrate you back into the void she made you from. But perhaps that is what you want for me." His brow lifted and his jaw squared, as if daring me to voice my hatred of him. Challenging me to confirm that I did, in fact, want Prisha to erase him from existence.

Yet somehow, the words I should have wanted to say dissolved from my tongue. I flinched, conflicted by a rush of empathy for the insufferable creature. If he told the truth, if it wasn't just some grand scheme to manipulate my perception of him, then I understood his fear. And the bravery he mastered to stand against her. "No," I finally admitted, almost too quietly.

"Then you have to understand. I can't go back there. She'll know I'm bonded to you. She'll know I killed her creatures. And she does not forgive. "

"How could she possibly know that? You could blame me or—"

"Because I used *her* magic, Zara. I'm tied to her as equally as I am bound to you. She *made* me. Everything I can do is because she made me, because her magic flows through me. And if she's realized that I betrayed her—that I helped you and that she no longer controls me as she expects to—she will stop at nothing to *unmake* me. She does not tolerate betrayals. You know that."

"But if you—"

"Zara. *No.* She is not a fool. She knows what I've done, and I'm sure she means to punish me for it. My best chance at survival, my only hope of escaping her is helping *you.*"

He finished cutting open another tinoya and tried to pass it to me, but I shook my head. My stomach had soured and no longer welcomed the food. The sickening sweetness of the fruit now churned uncomfortably in my gut. Or perhaps those were simply my jumbled concerns, tripping over the realization that maybe Rue was not the monster I'd judged him to be. Or, if he was, it was merely a matter of survival, not by choice.

I understood what it meant to not have a choice.

"Well, thanks for saving me." I tried to put a lighthearted spin on the words, but they fell flat. His gaze flickered toward mine, then darted back to the knife he twirled absentmindedly in one hand.

He nodded in quiet acceptance of my thanks, then heaved a deep breath. "You could have saved yourself, though, Starlight. You're a force to be reckoned with." He paused and looked up, and my skin flushed beneath his amethyst gaze. "I just couldn't bear to watch them hurt you a moment longer."

I sat in silence, trying to find the right words to say back. He was wrong, of course, but I couldn't articulate as much to him without sounding like a petulant child fishing for compliments.

"You need to eat," he said to break the silence, taking my hand and pressing the fruit into my palm. "We can't stay here much longer." He nodded toward the angry sky. "She'll send more. I'd rather not die today."

As if to validate his concerns, the golden rift above us crackled with menacing sparks.

I looked back at him, burning panic spreading from my chest and creeping up my neck to choke me.

His cool composure crumbled, and he turned back to me. "We really should get out of the desert. Get you to Rashii. Unless..." He hesitated, clearly debating if he should voice whatever he wanted to say.

I blinked and lifted my brows, daring him to continue.

"Well, you're the new Stitcher, aren't you?" He waved vaguely to the stars above. "Stitch the skies. Hold her back."

My mouth gaped, snapped back shut, then opened again. "It's

not that easy. My stitching is broken." I paused. "I think *I* am broken."

"You can't be broken," he dismissed with a laugh.

"And what could you possibly know about stitching? About my magic?" I blurted, my cheeks hot with annoyance at his easy dismissal. "Every time I try to connect to the goddess, every time I follow the ribbons of energy, I lose control and end up making things worse. I *unstitched the rifts.* I *helped* Prisha. What kind of a Stitcher can I claim to be if I only *create chaos* any time I think of using my magic to help? How can I face my Sisters and explain that to them? Halah shouldn't have chosen me...I'm *nothing* like the other Daughters. I'm too..." I waved my hands, grasping at straws for the word my brain refused to supply. "Chaotic."

Rue frowned, considering me for a long moment. I became uncomfortably aware of the heat in my cheeks and shifted, turning my eyes to the sand. "If it's not fixed, then break it," he finally mused.

What the heck is that supposed to mean? "That's not how the saying goes," I told him.

"Well, maybe that's how it *should* go. Maybe broken is exactly the change this world needs. Maybe the way of things is meant to break. Maybe the perception of what you should be and what the world expects you to be...maybe *that* is broken. Because you are stronger...strong enough to do what others couldn't do before you." His hands gripped my shoulders, and he searched my eyes for whatever he hoped to find there. When he seemed to locate it, he lowered his voice into a tender rumble, speaking with every impression of earnestness. "But none of those things mean that *you* are broken, Zara. You are exactly as you should be. And I like your chaos, Starlight. It matches mine."

"That doesn't fix the fact that I can't stitch." My voice had become quite airy—it couldn't compete with the deafening thrum of my heart. He'd moved so close to me our noses nearly touched, but my body refused to pull away.

"There's got to be a way..." he said, his voice trailing.

Still, my lips pursed together in a frown. He huffed a short breath through his nose, laughing at my dubious expression. "I like the way your hair catches the moon and your skin shimmers, even when everything about your expression screams with annoyance. The stars favor you, Zara."

I lost myself for a moment, stunned by the fluttering in my chest and the way my eyes darted rapidly back and forth to study his gaze, so foolishly close to mine. Pulling away, I composed myself with a shake of my head. "Then I hope they do me a favor and swallow you whole." The words lacked any conviction this time, but I said them for consistency's sake. Best not to let him get too close. *You are promised to Rali, Zara,* I reminded myself. *And on your side or not, Rue is still a monster.* I moved backward.

"I'll work on a poultice to calm those wounds, and then we should go," Rue murmured.

I nodded. "Use the dune rushes. The ones with—"

"Pale green leaves shaped like daggers? I know. This realm once belonged to Prisha, too, you know."

It had never occurred to me that a beast from the In Between would be so well-versed in our herbal remedies, but he was right. Prisha had once walked among the mortals of Taara. When Rue returned wielding a handful of dune rushes, he crushed them between his thumb and index finger, bruising them in his palm until they wept with a syrupy liquid. He worked quietly, spreading the sticky salve into the worst of my gashes. The salve stung viciously at first, then dulled my pain to a soothing tingle. Once the skin grew numb, he unwrapped the string binding a leather kit he pulled from his pocket and set to stitching the worst of the wounds closed.

Tears burned at the bottom of my lashes, and I had to bite my lip to stop its embarrassing tremble. Not because of the pain, but because of all my uncertainties—what if my Sisters never came back? Or what if they had fled for safety but returned to the guryas, only to find it in shambles and their Stitchers missing? What if we never found our way back to one another? I needed them. I needed home. An unwelcome tear streaked down my cheek and dropped from my chin. There was no home. Not anymore. And there never would be a home for me again if I didn't find a way to banish Prisha from this realm forever.

I needed to talk to the Eldress. I needed to find a way to fix all of this.

"Rue. Help me find the Eldress, and I'll figure out how to stitch Prisha into the sky forever."

"Deal."

"That wasn't a bargain."

"Sounded like a bargain." His eyes danced with mischief as he brushed the last of the salve from his palms. "I don't want to be her monster...I don't want to be hers to control or destroy. You stitch Prisha into the skies, and I'm yours." Something in his expression darkened and my stomach fluttered. "You do know it will be fastest if we fly, don't you?"

I gasped as he lunged toward me to scoop me into his arms. With a rush of gushing wind, he bolted upward toward the sky, wings spread wide.

CHAPTER 16

RASHII

The first signs of dawn shimmered against the gilded domes of Rashii's palace, reflecting the light of the rising sun as if the burnished tops of the towers had become their own luminous stars guiding our journey. Drab gray still lingered in the air over the vibrant backdrop of pink and gold brushstrokes, but the last evidence of night scattered as the sun crested behind the tallest pinnacle. The ends of Prisha's rifts reached toward the city like groping fingers stretching for something just out of reach, but the sky above Rashii remained largely untouched by her destruction.

Rue's arms wrapped firmly around me, and I had finally relaxed enough to marvel at the rush of flight, the tiny dunes, the winding web of streets bursting with color in preparation for A'i Halajan. From a distance, the ceremonial art of lining the streets with designs of sawdust and spice for the coming parades coated the city with vibrant splashes of color. Vast patches of moonflowers mingled with the rarest blossoms that only grew where the land was more forgiving, their delicate petals carefully arranged to form patterns.

Somehow along our flight, my chin found its way to rest upon Rue's shoulder, and my eyes admired the effortless sails of his wings catching the air as we soared. Startled by the realization, I erected my spine and chastised myself for the lapse of judgment. But still, his arms looped firmly around my middle, and my legs wrapped around his hips...the unavoidable closeness of his body pressed against mine quickly undid any semblance of calm I had previously mustered.

"Your heart is racing," he whispered in my ear, his voice soothing yet complex like spiced tea. "Are you all right? Am I hurting you?" He ran a calloused hand down my arm and wrapped his fingers around my hand, turning it over to inspect the worst of my gashes. The wounds no longer bothered me. The salve had worked some unexpected miracle. But the way he ran his hand against my arm had me imagining how they would feel on other parts of my body.

I flushed and pulled as far away as I could, berating myself for even considering such a thing, but doing so meant I had to squeeze my thighs tighter around his hips to keep from falling. That was a mistake. He moved his other hand, bracing it against my back, and met my gaze with a raised brow.

"I'm fine. I am just...not accustomed to flying."

A humming sound emerged from his throat, but he graciously kept his mouth closed and thoughts private. I used the silence to beg my heart rate to slow to an acceptable, unaffected level. One that did not imply he had any sort of impact on my vitals.

It didn't work.

My stomach leaped with a concerning lurch as Rue's wings caught the air, spreading wide and angling to drop us toward the ground in a dramatic descent. "Sun's up. It'll be safest to approach by land. People aren't always accommodating of unknown creatures with shadowed wings in these parts." And for good reason. I shouldn't be accommodating of him either—what would they say if they discovered Rue's origins? They'd call me a traitor. They'd kill us.

But the briefest touch of his lips against my temple as he whispered the words into my ears sent a cascade of chills down my spine that made me push aside my concerns for later. I nodded in agreement, making an effort to mask how fully aware I was of the lack of space between our bodies.

We landed in a valley nestled between the dunes, and I quickly untangled myself from his arms, brushing my tunic as though I could brush away every inappropriate desire and sensation our proximity had inspired. He stared at me for a moment, his eyes darkening dangerously with a smoky, enticing haze.

I swallowed the lump in my throat, uncomfortable beneath all of his staring. *You are staring right back at him,* I scolded myself and ripped away from his mesmerizing pull.

"Right. Let's go," I said to break the moment, and I marched away, climbing up the steep incline of the shimmering dune and cursing the sand for all its attempts to swallow my steps. I could not put distance between us fast enough.

"Rashii is that way, Zara," Rue called out from behind me.

Right. I froze, mid-climb, with one foot buried in the dune at an odd angle, then gave up and slid backward. In all of my rush to distance myself from Rue, I hadn't considered direction. The correct direction was simply *away.*

Rue observed me, raising that persistently infuriating brow as I regained my footing and marched across the dune toward the other end of the valley.

"You know it would be easier if we—"

"Fly," I responded. "Yes. We know. But we have already established that would be unwise for—reasons. So.."

A haunting whinny emerged behind me, and I snapped my attention back to Rue. "Actually, I was going to say *ride,*" he said smugly. He stood beside his monstrous night mare, holding its reins in his hand as it tossed about a trailing mane of onyx ink.

I angled my head, searching hopefully for a second mare, despite knowing there wouldn't be another. "There is only one," I complained.

"We only need one."

Oh good Halah, why? I pulled a sharp breath through my nose and noticed that my shoulders had risen to somewhere around my temples. *Relax. You can do this.* The horse leveled its harrowing gaze upon me. *No, I can't.* "Can't you at least make it look a bit more...realistic? Less...'shadow monster from the In Between?'"

The mare chuffed in offense. Rue rolled his eyes and patted the horse's nose, holding it between his hands to kiss it with affection. "Don't listen to her, Chaya. You're perfect." But he pushed up his sleeves and traced a hand along the horse's frame. Shadows danced along its torso, formed by individual pieces mashed together at sharp angles to create the illusion of a mare. He smoothed the jagged, irregular shadows into a glistening obsidian coat. "Better?"

"Two horses would be better." I folded my arms across my chest.

"Two horses would take extra time and energy."

"And this, of all times, is when you decide you don't mind sharing? I swear I will die of..." What exactly? Feeling him close to me? "I will die of...discomfort."

"Well, that'll spare me the effort of deciding whether or not to kill you, at least."

"Oh good Halah, are you still going on about that? I thought we'd moved past it."

"That was before you insulted my horse. But there's still time to think on it. It would be imprudent to do so now...but there's always tomorrow."

My lips pursed together when I glared at him. His insufferable grin made me want to kick him. Or see if I could banish it by pressing my lips to his. *Venom and hell, Zara. What is wrong with your brain? It is time to find the Eldress.*

"Well, apologies to your horse. We should go."

"Her name is Chaya."

I cleared my throat. "Fine. This is fine. Apologies to Chaya. Let's find the Stitcher." *And the first thing I will do is ask her what to do about this mess I've created so I can focus on what matters. Like sealing away Prisha and her monsters forever. All of her monsters.* My heart twinged at the words like a little traitor, forming an agenda of its own that I did not agree with nor approve of.

IF I FOCUSED ON THE SANDSTONE WALLS AND THE WAY the sun danced in the burnished copper gates, I did not have to notice the way Rue's legs wrapped along the outside of my thighs or the way feelings of warmth confused my senses, making my heart flutter like a thousand sand wings.

The city walls stretched like reassuring arms wrapped around the glittering city within, weathered by time but boasting of power. The tops of the walls were carved with intricate reliefs, depictions of the first goddesses and the fall of Prisha, scattered with the stars and the moon and all the wonders of the heavens. I studied them with forced intrigue, but even *they* were not enough to distract me. *Oh Halah, why is his arm brushing against mine again? How many times must he adjust his grip on the reins?* I squirmed, and I knew he must be smirking behind me. I could feel it. He was *always* smirking.

When we approached the main gates, the blazing copper

panels swung outward, revealing a tight formation of city guards, helmets gleaming beneath the morning sun and arrows notched. I was, frankly, quite sick of arrows.

A lump of a cry wedged its way into my throat when their aim swiveled toward my chest, and my heart hammered about in tumultuous leaps. The guard at the front of their formation stepped forward and assessed me for a palpably tense moment, then relaxed his sharp glare into a wide-eyed expression of recognition when I pulled back my scarf, revealing my white blonde hair and moonsilk skin. Only the Daughters had such fair complexions. He lowered his arrow and waved off the others. My chest deflated as air slipped laboriously through the tension of my pursed lips.

The lead guard marched toward me, crossing his arm over his body to place a clenched fist against his heart. "Daughter of Halah, thank the goddess you are okay. We heard what happened to your Sisters. May Halah guide them." My spine stiffened when he tucked his chin and touched an armored knee against the cobbled sandstone.

I watched him uncomfortably, wishing he hadn't gone through all the effort to kneel before me. I was certainly nobody to kneel before. If he knew who I was and what I'd accomplished as a supposedly revered Daughter of Halah, he would have opted to release that arrow into my windpipe instead.

I also wished he would hurry up and finish his ridiculous pleasantries so we could move on to discussing the more important matters burning on my tongue, demanding to be voiced. If he had heard about the guryas, did he know anything about where the Daughters had gone? Had Rali and the Eldress made it back safely? Was she going to be all right? Could I see her? I moved to slip down from the horse to put myself on the same level as the man to speed up his process, but Rue placed a hand discreetly upon my thigh, warning me to stop.

When the guard raised himself from his wholly unnecessary display of reverence, his attention turned to Rue, then frosted with mistrust. "And who is your companion, Daughter of Halah?"

"Zara," I corrected, then realized he had asked for Rue's name and not mine. "I am Zara. He is Rue, Guardian of Daughters. He accompanied me to ensure my safe travel to Rashii. We followed behind Rali and his men. He should be expecting us."

"I see..." he said with contemplative slowness, assessing Rue with uncertainty, "I did not realize the Daughters hired guards for protection, but with the whispers of war between Khazdra and Rashii, the unrest between Daughters and Riders, the increase in...monsters, I suppose it is warranted." His eyes narrowed upon the crusted gashes along my arms. "But he has done a poor job of it, has he not? You're hurt."

I pulled the sleeves of my tunic toward my wrists. "We ran into some crawlers. But we won." *Obviously.* What an understatement, but the truth was harder to explain. And certainly more dangerous.

"Rali did not inform us of your companion, and I am not so certain I like the looks of him. You may speak frankly with us, for we will always protect you. Say the word, Daughter of Halah, and we will turn this man into a pincushion of arrows if he has dared to harm just one hair on your head."

Rue's fingers clenched into a fist on top of my thigh, bunching together the light fabric in his grip.

Good Halah, could you try to appear less menacing, Rue? It won't help your case.

Tension swelled among the guards, and I noticed the reversal of their relaxed holds on their bows as they eyed Rue suspiciously, itching for an excuse to use them. "Truly. I am fine. He is... fine. I'm just tired." The weight of the past several days voiced itself in my heavy exhale. *This would be easier if Rali were here.* "Where is

Rali? I'm sure he can sort this all out," I said, scanning their ranks for any sign of the handsome guard with the freckled jade eyes and tousled hair, but he did not appear among them.

I turned my attention back to the leader, whose eyes blinked rapidly, as though he had not anticipated the question and hoped to find himself in different circumstances when he opened his eyes again. Once he recovered, he assumed a professional yet caring demeanor. "Rali is not on duty, but we will inform him of your arrival. You must be exhausted from your travels," he responded. "Let me escort you to your room, and I will have Rali sent to meet you there."

My room? The idea of a room with walls and ceilings made my insides twist with uncertainty. I had never had a room of my own before...only the guryas, the dunes, and the vast open sky. The Daughters did not stay in traditional dwellings. Without open air and access to earth and sky, the Daughters couldn't reach Halah. Not that I was keen to reach Halah anyway. But still...I'd be more comfortable if—

"That would be appreciated," Rue responded on my behalf, cutting off my stream of worries.

The guard bowed his head, then parted from us with a turn on his heel, approaching one of his men. He quietly relayed orders to the guard, who nodded with understanding, then moved toward us with a smile. "If it pleases you, Daughter of Halah, follow me. You'll be staying up at the palace."

At the palace? I nearly choked on my own tongue. The guard eyed Rue suspiciously and spoke to him, "I apologize, but as we were not informed of your arrival, we have not arranged accommodations for you. The inns are likely filled this close to the festival, but I'm sure you may find space in a brothel or the outskirts of the city. Many travelers stay in tents."

I'd rather stay in the tents...

"I will be fine," Rue responded with a confidence I didn't share. "But I will accompany Zara until she is safely in her room."

The guard nodded, then mounted a chestnut stallion. Its gleaming coat complimented the rich golden brown hues of the city, colors that reminded me of warm tea with goat milk. And *home*...meals with my Sisters and laughter over sipped tea until we became so hysterical we splashed the brew onto the floor cushions. At least, it reminded me of home in the days before the Eldress grew too sick and the Daughters became too desperate. Before war lingered on the edge of everyone's mind, creeping at the verge of consciousness like a venomous spider that paralyzes its victims. I frowned, chest tightening.

As we passed through the streets, children played, darting after balls and giggling. Parents scooped them into their arms when we approached, scolding them to be still and modeling the proper sign of respect for the Daughters. The stillness unnerved me—watching laughter and play, and the vibrancy of life pause as we passed to show respect to...me. Respect I wasn't sure I'd ever deserve. With all of their eyes on me, my spine stiffened and my body stilled, suddenly all too aware of the attention, understanding the source of their reverence.

These people—they saw the Daughters as a symbol of strength, the descendants of their goddess, the ones who'd keep them safe and someday liberate them from Prisha's curse. The Eldress had kept Prisha at bay for ages, sparing the city from her wrath, but now, with the Eldress dying, who would stop her? Who would fulfill the prophecy they whispered in prayer? Who would end the coming war?

Would I really be able to take the Eldress's place? I clenched my jaw, staring grimly at the crowd. They trusted us to protect them.

When they looked at me, they didn't see the worst of Halah's

Daughters. They didn't see my failures or doubts. They saw security. Hope.

The heaviness of my responsibility fell like a sack of rocks in the pit of my stomach, turning my legs to lead until I was certain the cobblestone streets would collapse under the weight of it all and swallow me whole. What if I failed them? What if I never managed to mold my magic into the way of Daughters to bring them the security they deserved? These people needed a *real* Stitcher, a capable one, and without the Eldress to guide me...I wasn't sure I was strong enough to become who they needed me to be. Would they still revere me—still stop in the streets and show their respects—if they truly knew me? Could I be enough?

THE ROOM THAT RALI HAD RESERVED FOR ME WAS luxurious. There was no other word for it. The air carried faint traces of florals billowing past cream-colored gauzy curtains. Those hung beside the great, vaulted arches overlooking the main courtyard. When they danced in the breeze, they revealed glimpses of a shimmering pool below, like a long, rectangular turquoise pendant that might have hung around any of the Daughters' necks. Baskets overflowed with flowers, hanging from the open arches, the splashes of fuchsia and violet florals spilling lazily along their woven sides. A plush bed topped with deep purple throws sat beneath a curtained arch. A large, circular mandala hung over the bed, intricately carved and gilded so that it shimmered like the rising sun.

The guard chuckled behind me, and I snapped my attention back to him. He smiled with a trace of amusement, gesturing toward the open arches with a nod of his chin. "Rali insisted you'd be most comfortable in a courtyard room with open air. He said it was the way of Daughters. Will this be all right?"

Will this be all right? Inside, I laughed with disbelief, but externally, I forbade my eyebrows from rising in surprise and forced myself into composure. "Yes. This is...lovely." *How did Rali acquire such beautiful accommodations for me?*

He dipped his chin in a bow and turned to Rue. "I assume you can find your own way to suitable lodging?"

Rue smiled cordially in return and nodded his assent in a way that suggested he was on his best behavior, but I knew he'd devour the man for breakfast if he so much as looked at him the wrong way.

When the guard slipped from the room, I turned to him, twisting my hands awkwardly before speaking. "You don't have to go. You can stay here," I said, gesturing toward the divan and armchair positioned in the corner. A serving tray set with delicate tea cups and sparkling sugars sat on the table between them. "There's plenty of space." I did not require a bed, a divan, *and* an armchair to sleep, after all.

"I don't think your Rali will approve of my presence."

"No," I acknowledged with a half shrug. "But unfortunately, I don't think this tether will approve of your absence." I wrapped my hand through the air, coaxing the shimmering bond into view. "You should stay close by." I paused, then added, "At least until we can meet with the Eldress and find out how to undo this."

He made a humming noise of agreement with the slightest tilt of his head. "Well, if you insist, I suppose I can find a way to tolerate my stay." With a dramatic flop, he fell backward onto the bed, pushing excess pillows aside and taking up every last measure of it with his oversized frame. His obsidian wings brushed against the gilded mandala behind him.

"This is quite comfortable, actually," he said, placing his

hands behind his head and flashing a devilish smirk. My blood boiled, heat rising to my cheeks.

"That is *my* bed. Do not make me second-guess my offer of hospitality."

"You know I am bad at sharing. I got here first." He turned his head toward the ceiling and closed his eyes, smugness all over his infuriating face.

"That's not how this works. There will be no sharing. There is a perfectly lovely divan over there. So get off." I stamped my foot on the tile to little effect.

"Make me," he challenged with a playful lilt to his voice.

"What? No." I cinched my brows together and crossed my arms over my chest. Truly, he was a monster. A slightly more tolerable one since he had rescued me from an army of crawlers, but still a monster.

He pushed himself up onto his elbows, making the springs groan beneath his shifting weight. "Tell you what, I'll let you have the bed if you—"

I waved a hand to stop him. "No. Absolutely. Not. There will be no bargaining. No deals. No manipulating for your own gain. Not everything must be decided by what you get out of it. This is my bed. So get. Your. Massive frame. Off."

His face brightened with amusement. "You didn't even hear my proposal."

Good to know he hadn't lost his infuriating touch. "I don't need to, nor do I want to." I muttered a string of curses under my breath and marched toward him when he still refused to move. Seizing his boot in my hand, I tugged until the corded muscles along my spine screamed for me to stop, then dropped his foot with an exasperated huff of air. I needed better leverage.

Only when I climbed on top of him, swinging my leg over his hips to sit astride his waist, did he exchange his expression of smugness for one of alarm. Every muscle in his body stilled, and his eyes widened as I leaned forward, wrapping my arms around his trunk so I could heave him into a sitting position. His body pressed flush against mine, so close our breaths fell into rhythm with one another, our hearts colliding in the space where our chests made contact. The lump at the base of his throat bobbed, and he met my eyes. His voice drained of color when he spoke. "What are you doing?" he asked breathlessly.

"I—I...Nothing. What are *you* doing?" I responded, suddenly all too aware of the mistake I had made. The way my hands held the muscles of his back, pulling him so close to me that I could feel the racing of his heart speeding to match mine. So close I could count the stars in his amethyst eyes, shimmering as if to greet me, and so that I could feel the warmth of his body mingled with mine. *Venom and hell, Zara. This is unacceptable.* I released him like the iron handle of a hot kettle after scolding myself, then moved my hands to a more innocent position in my lap.

"I don't know why you have to be so difficult," I complained, wringing my hands.

"That's it then? You yield? You hardly tried."

"You're insufferable, you know that?" I hissed, glaring back at him. "What chance do I have against you?"

"You don't trust your own strength, do you, Starlight?" His mouth flicked into a grin. "You can easily win this...I know you're strong enough."

I frowned. Was this all just some stunt to prove my own strength to me? I knew I was strong...too strong at times, and reckless with powers I didn't fully comprehend. But I couldn't reach for my magic at the first sign of a scuffle, just to dispel his curiosities about my strength. It was too dangerous. Too unpredictable. And there was no way I could ever beat this brute without it.

But Rue leaned closer to me, lowering his voice into a conspiratorial whisper. "Besides, all you'd need to do is look at me like you just did a minute ago, and you'll have me dropped to my knees. Powerless. At your mercy."

What? Oh. Hopefully, he didn't notice the rush of warmth that rose to my cheeks. My eyes wandered to my arms, cursing the crimson flush of my skin that only deepened with a fresh wave of embarrassment at the sight of them. He'd definitely notice *that.*

"The stars *do* favor you, you know," he whispered, pulling me from my escalating cycle of mortification.

Would he just stop with that nonsense? One second, he threatened to kill me, and the next, he marveled at me in astonishment. *You do the same to him.*

I rolled my eyes with a shake of my head. "There are no stars right now, Rue. And if there were, I'd ask them to do me the favor of swallowing you whole, so—"

A loud knock startled me. I jumped from Rue's lap, scrambling to my feet at the side of the bed as a man's voice called through the door. "Zara, may I come in?"

Rali. Finally.

...Shit. Rali.

"Oh! Yes. Of course. One minute," I called, my voice pitchier than usual as my feet padded quickly across the tiles. The bed creaked behind me, and when I turned back to shoo Rue away, I saw that he had already slipped into the shadows.

Rali and Rue's first meeting hadn't exactly been cordial, and I expected seeing Rue in my chamber would only accelerate their dislike of one another. I swallowed the grain of guilt in my throat. I didn't like hiding my association with Rue, but the situation with him was...precarious. If they found out who he was...*what* he was...they wouldn't take kindly to him. But I needed him. I tried not to think too hard about what would happen if they discovered his origin, but the fears rushed into my mind anyway. Would they kill him? Would they accuse me of fraternizing with the enemy? Surely they would execute me for such a crime. And what if they separated us before we could see the Eldress and find a way to undo the tether? My heart twisted, remembering the agonizing pain that had sliced into my chest when the bond had pulled too taut in the desert. Thank Halah Rali was here...I'd need him to take me to the Eldress right away.

I opened the door and gasped in surprise when Rali stepped over the threshold, immediately seizing my cheeks between his hands as his eyes bounced across my face with wonder. "Zara, you made it. Thank Halah! I'm so happy to see you...to have you here, safe with me." He leaned forward and pressed his lips to mine.

"Oh," I said rather pointlessly when he released me, touching the memory of his kiss on my lips with my fingers. The unexpected affection startled my brain out of a functioning state, and I could think of nothing more profound to say.

Luckily, Rali was more prepared to initiate the conversation. "I have been waiting for this day for so long. I am so glad that you are finally here. We must celebrate! We must plan for A'i Halajan—"

"Yes. But Rali." I put my hand on his chest to make him pause. His mouth had already prepared to launch into more rambling about the upcoming festival, and I needed his attention now that my scattered thoughts had reassembled into something useful. "The Eldress? How is the Eldress? Did you get her to a healer in time? Where is she?"

He brushed a stray hair from my brow, tucking it behind my ear before his finger moved downward, playing with the earring dangling from my lobe in a way that made me feel...trapped. *He is only showing affection, Zara. What is wrong with you?*

"She is well. She is healing," he replied, smiling with all the melted comfort of warm honey, but his eyes darkened to suggest he'd closed the door on that conversation. Something was wrong.

"I want to see her. Will you take me to her?"

He placed his hands on my upper arms, shaking his head with

the shadow of a grimace. "Best not, Zara. She is very weak and should be allowed to rest. I'll take you to see her when she is feeling better. Besides," he drawled, placing a finger over my lips to silence my immediate objections, "there is so much to do for A'i Halajan."

"But I need to see her. She will see me—she will want to. I know it."

"Zara, no." His voice became more forceful, and any traces of warmth washed away. "We must allow the Stitcher to rest. She's too important. Unless...is there any chance Halah has chosen a new Stitcher? Do you think it's possible?"

I opened my mouth but almost immediately swallowed my response. "Why?" Why would he think I'd know anything about a new Stitcher after losing contact with my Sisters? Of course, I *did* know, but I couldn't tell him as much. If I told Rali Halah had chosen me, would our union be permitted to continue? Would he expect me to demonstrate my power before I'd even learned to properly wield it? Would he see me as a failure? What if he found out about the heart of stars or...or Rue? And, perhaps worst of all, what if he discovered that I had undone so many stitches in the skies, destroying the work of generations before me?

"No," I responded simply, silencing the way my heart jumped in protest to the lie. "I don't think she's chosen a new Stitcher yet. But if you bring me to the Eldress—"

"Not today, I said," Rali snapped, then his features smoothed beneath the sharpness of my glare. "Tomorrow, Zara. I will bring you to see her tomorrow, after the ceremony. I promise. Just let her rest for now."

I searched for truth in his gaze, but he turned away, taking several long strides to cross the room. He stood under the middle arch, sweeping the breezy curtain aside to inspect the courtyard, trying too hard to appear at ease. The tension in his shoulders and the stiffness of his movements betrayed his efforts.

"Have you found my Sisters?" I asked his back. My feet remained firmly planted at the threshold, refusing to move closer to him.

His shoulders slumped forward with a heavy sigh. "The patrol has not returned yet. I'm worried they've been captured by Khazdruki to use as leverage."

A cascade of rocks settled in the pit of my stomach, weighing me down so convincingly it became difficult to move. Difficult to breathe. Where had they gone? Were they prisoners somewhere, waiting for me to help them? I should be out there...searching for them. Or meeting with the Eldress to ask for her help. Or...anywhere but in this room. "Are the Khazdruki really threatening to wage a war against Rashii? Now? You think it was them and not the Riders?"

Rali turned back to me, warmth spreading back through his features. "I do not want you to worry, Zara. I will take care of it. You do not need to concern yourself."

Whether or not he felt I needed to be concerned had little impact on the amount of worry creeping its way into my throat to choke me. But he placed a gentle hand upon my shoulder and leaned forward to kiss my cheek. "This is meant to be a joyous occasion. Go down to the festival and try to enjoy yourself. It is tradition. Let me handle everything else."

Are you kidding me? In what possible realm of fantasy did he think I'd be able to enjoy myself under these circumstances? That I'd be happy to go frolic at some frivolous festivities while leaving him to sort out the matted mess of worries that had burrowed through every vein of my body? Didn't he understand how important this was to me? Speaking to the Eldress seemed crucial —not just to my own survival, but to the entire Realm of Taara. "I don't think it's a good time for celebration, Rali. There are more important things to—"

"More important than A'i Halajan?" he cut me off, narrowing

his gaze and widening his stance, forcing me to question myself. "More important than our union?" Now his voice cracked, reeling a scrap of guilt from my gut with the hurt in his eyes. "Zara, you have a responsibility to the people. They expect you to show up for them. Don't disappoint them."

That's *exactly* what I was trying to do, but something told me that Rali and I had different sets of priorities. We stood there, uncomfortably still in the silence as unspoken thoughts lingered between us, his hand still perched on my shoulder, his eyes daring me to disagree.

"I'll go with you to the festival as soon as you let me see the Eldress," I asserted, hoping to smooth over the tension that now clouded the air between us.

Rali withdrew his hand and adjusted his uniform, pulling the hem of his jacket downward at the hips with a sharp jerk. "I can't go, Zara. I have a city to protect, so you must attend for both of us." He did not raise his voice, but I frowned at the faintest whiff of reprimand in his tone.

"Surely you can—"

"I assure you I cannot. I am busy. But they expect you to go, so you must. I'll see you tomorrow." The door closed behind him with an audible click that made my breath catch. What had happened to the Rali I'd met in the dunes? This Rali seemed too short with me, stressed and overwhelmed. Distant. I stared at the closed door for too long, not realizing how I'd frozen to the spot, lost in my own mind as I sifted through the troubling sandstorm of my thoughts. I should have tried harder to comfort him, to chip away at the stony facade he'd built around whatever worries plagued him. Had I upset him? He seemed...angry with me.

Soft footsteps approached, and a different hand, a reassuring hand, found its way to my shoulder, melting the tension away. "Come on," his voice rumbled into the shell of my ear. "Let's go find your Eldress."

CHAPTER 17

COORDINATOR OF CEREMONIES

To my surprise, the door opened without a fuss. I'd expected it to be locked after the click accompanying Rali's departure, but it swung open easily, inviting us into the grand hallway. Servants eyed me as I left the room, but none quite as curiously as they regarded Rue, who took up too much space even without the winged shadows attached to his shoulder blades. I nodded uncomfortably at each of the gawking strangers, hastening my steps to distance myself from them. A maid startled when I smiled at her, and porcelain fragments scattered across the hall, landing at her feet while she clutched the dusting cloth uselessly in her hand. Instead of kneeling to scoop up the pieces, she swept her fist over her heart and tucked her chin to her chest, but it didn't hide the scarlet flush of her face. I wanted to reassure her, to confide that I was every bit as much of a disaster and more, but Rue ushered me past the commotion with his own agenda in mind.

"Are you sure you're doing the right thing by marrying this Rali? You know him well? You really trust him?"

"Yes, of course," I responded without thinking. Because

thinking made my stomach sour with questions I didn't want to answer, questions that called my judgment to light. Despite all the letters, despite the timid affection he had cultivated with his reassurances and beautiful words, he felt like a stranger. But wasn't it normal to be nervous before such a big event? It had to be. And if he was anything like me, the union was likely the least of the worries causing him stress.

Taking a deep breath, I straightened my spine. The Daughters had agreed to his request to court me. They had arranged for the blessing of our union at A'i Halajan. And since I had failed miserably at every other task expected of a Daughter, I did not wish to disappoint them by rejecting this match. It seemed unfair to judge him on one charged interaction between us, considering the circumstances.

I would find the Eldress and address my...obstacles. Then, I would marry Rali and serve my duty, both to Rali and the people. And if we tackled the stress that divided us, we could rekindle that ember of affection sparked by our letters and find love together. And then I would keep fighting until Prisha became a mere memory whispered by the stars, protecting everyone I loved, including Rali, from her destruction.

But still, something nagged at my mind, some small voice that screamed to be heard, muffled by duty and expectations. "Besides...I have to. It's not like I have much of a choice," I admitted, quickening my steps to keep up with Rue's long strides.

"There is always a choice. Some choices are harder than others, but they are always yours to make. Nobody can take that from you. Unless you let them."

"Mmm," I mumbled.

"I don't like him," Rue admitted in a low growl. The corridor seemed to darken, or perhaps it was only his mood.

"Do you like anyone?" I asked. He didn't seem to be the warm and fuzzy type. More...shadows and malice and danger.

"I don't mind you."

I suppressed the smile attempting to emerge from my lips and angled my eyes toward him, studying him from beneath my lashes. "Odd thing to say for someone who hasn't decided whether or not he intends to kill me."

His scowl lightened. "Merely a circumstantial dilemma. I don't want to kill you. But I also don't want to die. You are...stabby."

"Only when you annoy me."

"Yes, well, you know the realm will never approve of our association with one another. And if they discover who I am—"

"We can't let them find out. They'll see you as the enemy, and I'm not really sure you are. At least...I don't think you have to be."

His only response was the smallest pull of a smile at the corner of his mouth. We rounded a corner, and the end of the passageway spilled into the open courtyard. I hadn't realized how the shade granted a reprieve from the sweltering heat to keep the marble and stone passageways cool until the blazing sun greeted my cheeks like an old friend.

Light sparkled like a thousand drowned gems in the turquoise pool, blinding me for a moment with the sun's reflection. I had never witnessed such a beautiful place...lush succulents and flowers bestowed the courtyard with vibrant life, and the sky stretched like a vast blue sea above us, still untouched by Prisha's curse. *Not for long,* the voice of guilt chimed in. *Not if you don't find the Eldress or figure out how to fulfill the responsibilities of Stitcher.*

I cringed, assessing the sky. The walls and columns surrounding the space loomed prestigiously above, like soldiers guarding cells—an inescapable prison—and I shivered with the sensation of feeling trapped.

"Where do you think they are keeping the Eldress?" Rue

asked, placing a hand on the small of my back to still the rush of trembles through my spine. "Can you sense her?"

I paused, closing my eyes to listen for the weaving magic of the Daughters, the pull of that internal compass always leading home, but all I could sense was the pounding of my own heart. "No," I admitted, surprised by the creak of emotion in my tone.

Rue's hand slipped from my back, and the air shifted with tension, snapping my focus back to the courtyard. A woman with short black hair, cropped and angled to mirror her jawline, pelted toward us. "Zara! Daughter of Halah!" she shouted, stirring birds from their rest in the shade. They exploded into the air with a sharp cry of alarm. Just like my heart.

"Zara." She hastily swept into some interesting interpretation of a bow, though she seemingly lacked the grace to do so. When she straightened her spine, her amber eyes glittered above the light of her smile. "You *are* Zara? Are you not? The star of A'i Halajan? The Daughter selected to receive Halah's blessing? Descendant of the goddess and perpetuator of her holy lineage?"

"Uh. Y-Yes?" I stuttered over my own tongue and squeaked with shock when she wrapped her arms around me.

"Oh finally, I've found you. I am Basmina, coordinator of ceremonies. I've only just been promoted to lead coordinator and you're already making me look bad by making us late. Come quickly. You are required to attend the ceremonial Ja' Rilaht procession."

I threw a cursory glance back at Rue, who merely shrugged at the alarm on my face. 'I'll follow,' he mouthed, and Basmina tugged my arm so sharply that my head snapped backward, falling a few paces behind the rest of my frame as she led me away at a breakneck pace.

"Basmina?" I asked between spurts of breaths as she rushed me through the courtyard and winding hallways, caring little for the increasing gasps issuing from my lungs. She insisted we were late and that there would be time for breathing later, but later never seemed to come. "Basmina. What is Ja' Rilaht? Do I need to...do anything?" *How long will it take? Will anyone notice if I slip away to search for the Eldress? Is this what Rali had insisted I attend?* Nobody had prepared me for what to expect at the festival. Only to pray for Halah's blessing. My inability to pray like a proper Daughter had been well-established, but Basmina wouldn't know that about me.

"You only need to sit, look beautiful, and graciously accept the gifts that the people of Rashii offer you. You can manage that, can't you?" Her bronzed, upturned nose crinkled when she looked at me. "We really must hurry. You can't go about looking like that."

She led us in front of a paneled double door, cracking open one side to usher me through. Rue's hand caught the door before she could close it behind us, and he followed with a confidence that brooked no questioning about whether his presence would be permitted.

Basmina stopped long enough to eye him curiously, appraising his stature and lingering far too long on his wide shoulders and amethyst eyes, then closed the door without a word of confrontation. I clenched my fist, digging my nails tightly into the heel of my hand, and forced myself to relax when she turned away. Basmina steered me toward the center of the room, and I blinked several times, stunned by the faces looking back at me.

A collection of women wearing proud smiles beneath blonde hair and moonsilk skin approached me, entangling me in a jumble of hugs and a rush of familiarity. Daughters of Halah. My eldest Sisters and Aunts. The ones who'd moved to Rashii with unions of their own. Aunt Vanya. Rada. Juryasha—with a rounded belly. Magura. Aunt Naila.

Basmina slipped away, pardoning herself from the room. As soon as she left, my Sisters exploded into chatter. Voices mixed with one another, each attempting to be heard over the others, their bracelets and beads jingling to complete the chaos. They grabbed my hands, pulling me further into the room to sit me on a tufted couch. Silk tasseled pillows scattered across the seats. "Have you met him yet? Is he handsome?"

"Oh, I hope he's a kind one," my elder Sister, Rada, wished dreamily as she pulled the beads from my hair and began to unwind the braids.

"Are they often unkind?" I asked nervously, wondering what she meant and wincing at the careless tug of her fingers through my hair. A shimmering powder drifted over my head, entering my nose and lungs to make me cough.

"Never mind that. Forget I said anything. Wait." She paused, rubbing her palms together over my head to scatter more powder. It smelled of honey and blossoms. "*Is this him?*" She tilted her head toward Rue, eyebrows lifting at me with delight. Rue smirked, but shifted almost imperceptibly. Perhaps I was the only one to notice, but his lackadaisical composure wavered ever so slightly beneath the attention of all the women in the room. I bit my lip to hide the grin of satisfaction, knowing now with certainty that he *could*, in fact, be ruffled.

"Oh. No, that is not him," I answered, flushing with embarrassment from the misunderstanding. Rue's expression darkened, but he recovered with a wry grin, amused at my expense.

My elder Sister Magura blew disappointment through her pursed lips. "Too bad. He is handsome. You would have been lucky. Are you available?" she asked Rue without any effort of tact.

Rada punched my elder Sister in the arm. "Magura, your union has already been blessed. Stop that nonsense."

"I was asking for *Zara*. Do we know anything of this Rali she's been promised to? Perhaps a switch could be arranged. She clearly seems comfortable with this one."

"Oh, oh no. That will not be necessary," I responded, perhaps too quickly. My ears and cheeks warmed with a new flush. Rue was certainly handsome, but also rude, infuriating, and of questionable intentions. Not to mention the minor flaw of his origin.

Rue shuffled inconspicuously to the corner of the room, where he occupied himself with the spread of little pastries and cheeses. Too bad they hadn't left out any halfmoon bread. He would have loved that.

"Where is your tapestry?" my Aunt Vanya asked sharply, shoving my Sister Rada aside with a hip, then reaching to rearrange the braids at the front of my hair. Rada scowled at her, but she spun around to bustle toward a table littered with brushes and jars.

My mouth opened to answer Aunt Vanya's question, but I could only manage a shrug. The tapestry had likely burned in the wreckage of the guryas, but I didn't know how to explain...how to break that news.

Aunt Vanya noticed the strained sadness in my eyes and softened. "Still not good at weaving, then? Never mind, you can borrow mine. Nobody will know the difference." She moved a hand to her hip, scanning the room behind me. "Are you alone? Where are our Sisters? Didn't any of the Daughters accompany you to witness the union?"

I twisted my hands in my lap, forming a response in my head. Rada returned, abruptly shoving my shoulders down and away from my ears. "Sit straight and look up." I lifted my chin to the exposed beams above, but Rada smacked my hand. "Not with your face. With your eyes." She rammed a chiseled sliver of charcoal toward my cheekbone, sweeping it around my lashes until it made my eyes water.

"So, where are they?" Rada asked, tucking the pencil into her dress and snatching a pot of vibrant liquid from the table. She swirled the concoction in the palm of her hand, then dabbed a fine bristled brush into the oil.

"I don't know," I whispered so quietly the whole room stilled to hear me. Even Rada stopped, her brush poised next to my lips.

"What do you mean? What happened? Who brought you here?" Her mouth pursed.

"The guryas...are gone. They...they burned."

A collective gasp rose sharply among all of the Daughters, and they stopped their fussing long enough to toss frightened glances between themselves.

"What happened to them?" Aunt Vanya asked, her voice croaking. "Was it Riders? Or did the Khazdruki find them? Did the Daughters survive? How did you escape?"

"I left to..." I hesitated, catching myself before I told them that I'd been out with the Eldress and found myself obligated to explain circumstances I did not wish to share. How could I describe everything that had happened? How could I justify Rue? They wouldn't buy the same explanation I'd fed to Rali and the guards—they'd know better. "I left to patrol the dunes, and when I returned, the guryas were burning, and the Daughters had fled. And I didn't know what to do but..." I paused again, searching for a logical explanation. "I ran into Rue. He was traveling to A'i Halajan to witness the union, and he found me and swore to bring me to safety. And I was hoping the Daughters would meet me here, so I didn't go looking for them, but now I don't know where they are, and I'm so sorry." I spoke faster and faster as I went on, an unexpected rush of tears ruining Rada's efforts to enhance my features.

"Oh, Zara." Warm arms enveloped me. "We had no idea." My Sisters' expressions turned grim, and the air mingled with a cloud of uncertainty.

"They'll find their way back. They always do," Aunt Vanya

said. My Sisters nodded in unanimous agreement, but worry lingered at the corner of their downturned mouths.

"But how could you not know?" I asked, my voice growing stronger. "Didn't you notice? I can't sense them anymore. Can you? Didn't anyone tell you?" I paused, unsettled by the nervous glances they shared with one another. "Have you seen the Eldress? Will you bring me to her? I need to talk to her."

Rada raised a cocked eyebrow at the others, but bit her tongue. "We don't hear much in Rashii," she finally admitted, dropping in a graceful heap of sheer fabric at my feet to level her eyes with mine. "We're cut off from the Daughters here. For our protection. So we're not tempted to return. There are...wards around the city to prevent us from sensing our outside Sisters. And the Eldress."

"But the Eldress is *here*. She should have arrived just before me."

Aunt Vanya blinked, her eyes widening before her smile. "Oh, then that is good! She'll be safe here," she said reassuringly.

I gaped at her. "That is *not* good." What was *wrong* with her? "The Eldress is ill. She is dying, and we *need* her out there mending the skies. We need all of you out there because the stitches are failing and the Daughters are missing and Prisha's monsters—"

"So it's true? It's getting worse? All we hear about is the tension and whispers of war from Khazdra. They think Prisha is waging war to punish us for stealing their land," Rada whispered, not bothering to let me finish. "Has Halah chosen a new Stitcher yet? Do you know? That would change everything for us."

I wasn't prepared for that question. "No," I lied, shifting uncomfortably on the cushion. "Nobody can stitch the skies besides the Eldress." At least that part was true. "But if you can help me find the Eldress...maybe she can help us get past the wards to get back and—"

"Zara...It isn't safe out there. Too many enemies wish the Daughters harm. We need to stay here," Rada interrupted, speaking in a kind but absolute tone.

"It isn't safe in *here*," I challenged, gritting my teeth in my frustration. If I didn't figure out how to stitch the skies and hold back Prisha, the city walls would offer little protection against her wrath. It wasn't safe *anywhere*. When did the Daughters of Halah become too afraid to protect the people and only care to protect themselves? Had all of them given up hope in the fight?

Rada smiled apologetically. "Of course. But it *is* safer. And the best thing to do is to stay here and pray for a new Stitcher while we fulfill the duties we've been assigned. Perhaps *our* Daughters will finally carry out the Prophecy of Dusk and Dawn and bring about an end to Prisha's curse. That is the role *we* must fulfill. *That* is the role we *can* fulfill."

From the end of the couch, lounging against the arm so her swollen belly rose like a sand dune, my elder Sister Juryasha choked on a sudden sob, her hand lost halfway into the caress of her abdomen. My other Aunt elbowed her sharply in the ribs, which only made Juryasha cry in earnest.

"Don't mind Juryasha," Rada told me. "She is anxious. Childbirth is hard, especially these days. But it's what Halah has called us to do, even if it sends us to the stars." She said this last statement with a scolding undertone, tossing a reproachful glance toward Juryasha.

Aunt Vanya narrowed her eyes back at Rada, and I gaped, still grappling with what she'd said. "Do not frighten the girl, or she will never do as she's meant to," Aunt Vanya snapped. I studied Juryasha nervously, who began to cry with great heaving sobs into Aunt Naila's shoulder. Aunt Naila grimaced, but patted her head gently and played with the braids in her hair, consoling her.

"Why?" I asked, still stuck on Rada's comment about joining the stars. "You mean they are dying?" I immediately regretted asking, for the question only made me sound like a small, frightened child. But not nearly as scared as Juryasha.

Rada shrugged, resuming her effort to stain my lips with the coral oil. "We don't know what's wrong, exactly. The prince has even broken some of the rules to help us. Just the one about royalty getting too involved with the Daughters," she amended quickly. "How they're not allowed to meddle or seek unions with us." She twirled the end of the brush in her palm to reshape the bristles, shrugging airily as she continued, "It's an old rule, really, meant to keep power in balance. At least, that's what Prince Tiralish said. He thinks we should focus on rebuilding our lineage and getting stronger, especially with the threat of Prisha and the lack of a new Stitcher."

She dabbed the corner of my mouth with a silk hand towel, frowning at her handiwork before slipping the cloth between my lips to make me blot them. "Anyway," she continued, "he's taken it upon himself to ensure the Daughters are seen by the best midwives at the palace in hopes that we can spare them. But even so..." She leaned forward now and dropped her voice to a whisper, eyeing Juryasha nervously, "They rarely return to us from the palace after birth. Just the babes."

I rubbed my lips together, considering the information. The oil tasted subtly sweet...like the tinoya fruit I'd shared with Rue. I caught his eye, but Rada yanked my chin back to brush another layer over my lips. I shivered.

"Would you sit still and stop fretting?" Rada scolded. "The only thing you need to worry about today is *today*. Deal with the rest tomorrow. The people are so excited to greet you. I'm meant to make you presentable, and right now, you look as though you've lost a battle against a thousand crawlers."

Rue snorted from the corner of the room.

"Why are you still here?" Rada snapped at him. "Go away." A moment of tension filled the air, and for a second, I wondered if

Rue or Rada would win the battle of wills. But it was Rada—of course it was Rada. Only an elder Sister could prove more intimidating than a shadow monster from the In Between. And she was my true blood Sister, so her instinct to protect me ran deep.

Rue met my eyes for half a second, then dipped his head in a modest bow, one I recognized as a mockery, but to the rest, I knew it appeared appropriately respectful. I wanted to tell Rada to let him stay, but she'd already moved on to stripping me of my garments.

Basmina's head popped through the door at the far side of the room, sending a strip of daylight across the walls. "Are you ready yet? They are waiting. Why does this part always take so long?" A rush of noise slipped through the parted door—laughter and chatter, vendors hawking their wares with boisterous cries that cut effortlessly through the rest of the din. Not only sounds filtered through the door, but also smells. Charred meats, honey, and complex arrangements of spices mingling together in the air, wafting through the crack until my stomach rumbled with an audible growl. Rada giggled at me and adjusted the leather waistband of the gown, which she pulled over my head. "Well, good thing Ja' Rilaht usually involves a lot of eating. Time to go."

When the doors at the far side of the room reopened, they spread wide and without reserve, eliciting a hush from the crowd and the focus of a thousand pairs of eyes on me. I lounged uncertainly against a sea of cushions, their fluffy abundance crowding me with a paradoxical sense of discomfort. My Sisters filed into line before me, adopting an unusual silence to match the crowd's lull, but the bangles around their wrists and beads in their hair jingled softly to bring music to their movements. To bring beauty worthy of the descendants of Halah. My stomach writhed, unaccustomed to the attention. Unsettled by the praise...the hope inspired by the mere presence of Daughters and the mere suggestion of a fortuitous union to come. If only they knew this nonsensical tradition kept me from working to ensure their hopes and prayers for safety were not in vain.

The procession moved forward despite my every impulse to run in the other direction. Pulled by my Sisters, the sudden lurch of the palanquin jerked me roughly into the cushions before its movement evened into a more steady progression. I politely acknowledged the faces in the crowd, smiling warmly at the thousands of eyes upon me, but only one pair mattered. Only one pair stole the breath from my lungs, dissolving the rest of the crowd away until nothing else stood before me but him.

I knew I shouldn't have searched for him...shouldn't care to pick him out from the crowd, but he called my attention like the stars in a cloudless sky. Meeting his gaze settled my nerves in a way I'd never expected, nor wanted. They made me feel...seen. Safe.

Somehow, they'd become the internal compass I'd been missing, my North Star in a way that seemed both ill-advised and nonsensical. How could I have allowed my attraction for him to develop to such a point? But all the same, there they were. Luminous. Brilliant. Dancing for me. As if everything I'd begun to feel for him was both cherished and returned. His mouth twisted into a smile, and he bowed. "The stars favor you, Zara," he mouthed when he lifted his chin again, and I frowned. Quite unconvincingly.

Then I hope they swallow you whole, I thought in return, willing him to hear the words and, more importantly, my *heart* to hear the sense of them. I was meant to fulfill my duties by marrying Rali. Every part of me knew my growing trust in Rue was folly, my connection to him a burden that must be destroyed. No part of me was allowed to feel for Rue...to want him.

But want him, I did, and he knew it. He smiled in earnest when my cheeks flushed with warmth.

What a traitor I was. To pull Prisha's creation from the sky and allow him to live, to let him become important to me, to want to believe that he was not the evil we'd come to expect of his brethren because he was just *Rue*. Because I did not want him to be the enemy. Because I wanted to believe he was more. And the crowd...they watched my procession with awe, regarding me as some savior, praising my devotion to Halah, my honorable dedication to the duties of protecting the people and perpetuating the goddess's lineage. But how quickly would they turn on me if they knew? If they found out all I had ever done was endanger them with my chaos and fail to protect them as their Stitcher? If they knew I'd invited Prisha's monster right into their midst?

Kill them all. They all must die.

Flustered, I blinked Prisha's voice out of my mind and turned my attention away from Rue. I refocused on the crowd, hoping they would blame the flush of my cheeks on the sun's heat. Hoping they might mistake my tears of worry for ones of appreciation. *What is wrong with me?*

We came to a crossroad where the sea of people parted, standing along either side of the street to protect the carpet made of sawdust and spices, an art piece meticulously arranged by local artisans for A'i Halajan. They laid out the vibrant display along the processional path each year so the arrangement might be disturbed by the fresh crop of Daughters presented for new unions at the festival. It was what they expected of us, my Sisters told me. We were to come through and disrupt the old way of things, clearing the path to make way for something new. To pave the path for the next generation and bring hope for the future. And this year, as the only Daughter presented for a union, all of those expectations fell upon me.

Cinnamon and star anise filled the air as the wheels ground through the arrangement, along with smokier, more robust scents that mingled with the delicate aromas of lavender and orchid. How fitting that I'd leave a jumbled mess of destruction behind me. Chaos was my nature, after all.

As we continued along the path, people showered me with gifts, each presentation twisting like a knife in my heart, striking judgment for accepting their gratitude and admiration when I'd done nothing to deserve it. A young mother with deep brown eyes approached me, holding her infant close to her breast, cradling him in the swathe of fabric tied behind her back. She smiled and passed me a stack of silver bangles, each hammered with divots that captured both shadows and sun, encrusted with mother of pearl and star sapphire. An old man with cataracts that clouded his eyes but not the admiration in his gaze passed me a parcel wrapped in waxed fabric. I opened it to find a collection of cheeses and breads. He held my hands in his, covered in liver spots and years of hard labor, but they were also full of compassion and warmth. "May Halah bless you, Daughter," he said before a quartet of women swooped in to replace him.

They adorned me with a gauzy chiffon cloak, placing it gently over my shoulders and clasping the beaded collar around my neck. The airy garment felt like a breeze on my skin and looked like a smoky sunrise, glimmering with thousands of hand-stitched beads along the hem.

We moved forward, coming to another crossroad in the streets as more spectators placed morsels of food in my lap or around the pillows, urging me to eat like I was some animal to fatten for slaughter. But I ate until I felt certain I'd be mistaken for one of the pillows myself, too overstuffed to enjoy any more of the delicacies they shared. At that point, I merely pretended to nibble, smiling with an effort to appear gracious as I received each gift.

But behind my smile, I wondered how much longer I'd have to continue the charade. I worried, exhausted by the act, when every beat of my heart urged me to go find the Eldress so I could become what these people deserved.

A small child with white-blond locks and moonsilk skin approached me. Hours beneath the sun had dotted his nose with a constellation of freckles, but he was unmistakably a son of Daughters. Perhaps a nephew of mine, but one I would never have the chance to meet outside of Rashii, for only Daughters returned home. He smiled a bit uncertainly, lifting his open palms to show me a serpentine hairpin. It glittered resplendently in his hands, flecked with obsidian and emeralds.

He placed it a bit roughly in my hair, then scampered away into the crowd, wrapping his arms around a pair of legs. Rue's eyes met mine, quite alarmed yet amused by the little boy trapping his knees in a fearsome embrace. He awkwardly patted the boy's head, who looked up and gaped in horror when he realized his error, but his father swooped in to rescue him, scooping him into his arms and pressing his forehead against the boy's with a smile. Rue sighed with relief, and I hid a giggle behind my hand, amused by the idea of a shadow monster becoming a father.

Rue continued to weave between spectators, keeping pace with the procession, staying unseen and unnoticeable to everyone. But I noticed him. And I could not stop my gaze from wandering to his, no matter how many times I scolded myself.

The palanquin jostled with a jerk, and a thump disrupted the pillows behind me. Something heavy rammed into my spine. The crowd cried out, and I yelped, whipping around to see what had struck me.

CHAPTER 18

THE OTHERS

A stocky form stretched across the pillows, an arrow protruding from his back. Blood spooled from the wound and soaked into the silk cushions below him. A second arrow whizzed past my jaw. I snapped my hand to my neck, where its tail had brushed against my skin, then screeched when it landed in the center of a moon-shaped pillow at my feet. It exploded into a furry of feathers. My blood rushed through my veins, rioting its way through my body until every muscle tensed on edge.

Another arrow pinned the hem of my dress to the platform, a measure away from my ankle. I gasped, tugging my foot back. I scrambled to my knees on the unsteady platform and scanned the rooftops, searching for the assailant. Spectators screamed and shoved, creating a bedlam of limbs and elbows around the palanquin that made it impossible for me to descend.

Panic twisted around my windpipe, an unforgiving constrictor, and power rushed to flood the space between my ribs in an automatic response. A faint glow emerged just above my breastbone, pulsing within me, begging me to act. *No, no, no.* I wrapped the gauzy covering tightly around my frame and hinged forward, hiding the heart of stars and slamming mental walls around it, suppressing it until it was hidden so deeply inside me, even I could not reach it. I could not use it—not here. Not around so many people I could accidentally harm. What if it called Prisha's attention to this crowd?

A pair of hands wrenched me from the platform and dragged me through the chaos.

"Are you hurt?" Rue asked me, his voice pressured.

"No," I breathed, too stunned to lend any strength to my voice. "No, I'm fine." My chest heaved with short, shallow breaths that sent stabbing pains beneath my breastbone, but I wrapped the veiled cape tighter around myself, hiding any last traces of the power I was never meant to have. The force I had stolen from the stars.

Rue ran his hands over my arms to inspect for signs of harm, then ripped his attention from me when he was adequately convinced of my well-being. He cast his gaze toward the navy canopies above the streets, then up to the rooftops. A dark figure with a longbow gripped in his hand stood erect, locking eyes with Rue for the span of a few uncomfortable breaths. He dropped out of view behind the rooftop turrets and vanished.

"Coward," swore Rue, flexing the hand that didn't hold me. "Stay here. Do not speak to anyone until I come back."

He raced away, disappearing into the shadows of the alleyway as if he had become them himself. Or as if *they* had become part of *him*. I leaned against the wall, forcing my body to slow my sharp, ragged breaths into steady, carefully measured ones.

The procession in the main street had erupted with pandemonium, soldiers of the city guard shoving past the rabble to secure the Daughters. My Sisters passed panicked glances among themselves, shuffling forward with hastened, short steps as the guards steered them to safety. "Where is Zara?" Aunt Vanya shrieked over her shoulder, but the soldier pushed her forward, relaying orders to find me to his comrades.

I shrank into the shadows, needing a moment to breathe. I willed my heart rate to slow, suppressing any last hints of that raw power in my chest. How had I come so close to using it? Had anyone seen it? Had they noticed? And, perhaps most pressing, what would have happened if I hadn't been able to subdue it in time? If the power had slipped from me and harmed the spectators? I needed to lock it away, deeply inside of me, and learn to rely on the Daughters' weaving instead. That was the safest magic, if I could only learn to control it.

Pain ripped suddenly through my chest, slicing at the muscle, threatening to pull the organ straight through my skin. Crying out, I crumpled into a heap, clutching a hand over the physically unharmed skin. It burned in agony just below the surface, suggesting a dire wound that could only be felt, but never seen. The tether around my heart pulled taut, searing a web of scars onto the walls of the muscle. Where was Rue? Something was wrong. He'd gone too far—had he been hurt? Fog clouded my mind, submerging me in a haze so thick it felt like an ocean wave washing over me.

The sound of wings slicing the air pulled me back from drowning in that tumultuous sea. Rue landed with a rustle deep in the shadowed alley, dragging the crumpled form of a man in his wake. He threw the man toward me, disdain written on every angle of his beautiful face as he stared down at his prey, looking every part the monster—one that would stop at nothing to shred the world and lay it at my feet. "I brought you something," Rue explained, lifting his gaze but not his chin, so his amethyst eyes blazed beneath dark brows.

The man crawled toward me, and Rue pinned him beneath his boot. A Rider. Dark, curled hair, cropped short at his ears. A bloodied, off-centered nose and stormy eyes that darkened like coal when they met mine.

"I saw what you did," he seethed through bloodied teeth, his words foaming with a cocktail of hatred and excess saliva. He spat the excess forcefully toward my feet, leering at me with teeth bared and eyes warped by malice. "You abomination. You deserve to die," he hissed. "I'll kill you and every one of your bitch Sisters."

Rue pressed the jagged sole of his boot deeper into the man's shoulder until it cracked. "Fuck you," the Rider gasped at Rue, sucking air sharply through his broken teeth and turning his head toward the ground.

"Was it you?" I seethed, stepping closer to him. "Did you kidnap my Sisters and burn the guryas?"

"The Riders have always known," he said to the ground, failing to acknowledge that I had spoken. "Always known you are monsters. Just like the ones you pulled from the sky." The man's back deflated, and he let out a long, whimpering breath. Rue wrenched him up by the hair and forced him against the wall. The man grimaced, folding into an awkward position with his knees mashed against his chest and his elbows drooping uselessly at his side. Rue's arm crossed over the man's neck, barring him against the sandstone. He squirmed uncomfortably beneath the pressure at his windpipe, but relented quickly. He slumped into an overspent heap, his muscles lax.

He twisted his neck to wipe his bloodied face against his knees, before slurring through his swollen mouth. "You let them celebrate you. Traitor. Monster. Sky Render." He sought my gaze with a sneer. "I saw. I saw the skies. I saw what you did. The monsters...the winged ones masquerading as common men, like *this* one you keep at your side." He spit a frothy mouthful of bloodied saliva onto the paved stone and looked back at me, a string of spittle still dangling from his chin. "What are you planning with them? The other ones you summoned? Did you lure them from the sky to kill us all? What did we ever do to you, Daughter?"

"Others?" I breathed, clutching my chest with a hand in a futile attempt to fortify the cage around my thundering heart. "What others?" Rue threw me a cautionary glare and shoved all his weight against the man until he yelled with a shattering cry. But the man did not relent in silence for long, his hatred swirling about him like a toxic cloud, resurrecting him from his near bout of unconsciousness.

"The other winged beasts you've lured from the sky," he seethed, and I recoiled beneath the daggers in his eyes. "You can let your disgusting monster kill me if you want, so you don't need to get your precious, holy hands dirty, but my brothers will come for you. They'll kill you before you can harm anyone else. And they'll kill the rest of your monsters. You fucking disgrace."

My stomach knotted, and each word he spoke, every accusation, sliced through my gut until my intestines felt like a bloodied clump of stewed-up bowels. Shapeless and watery, useless and burning with guilt. Poisoned by confusion and worry. But Rue, Rue only growled with anger and pressed his forearm unforgivingly into the man's windpipe, choking off his speech.

"*She* can shred you limb from limb if she so desires. I would not take that opportunity from her." He leaned forward, pressing against the man's clavicle with a dangerous scowl on his face. "But I'll hold you down for her while she eviscerates you. Gladly."

His amethyst eyes flicked toward mine, now a dangerously dark shade of midnight. I shivered. "So, Zara, your kill or mine?"

"Oh, I don't think..." I didn't want to kill him. If he knew anything about my Sisters, I should question him more. And perhaps he was right about me...maybe I deserved his hatred and anger for my mistakes. But I didn't know what he meant about the *others*.

His claims made my stomach writhe with venomous snakes.

I'd only summoned *Rue*. Were there truly more? Why? Had Prisha sent them? Had I accidentally summoned them, too? My eyes narrowed on Rue.

Had *he* called them? Could I truly trust him? I watched the way he ruthlessly pushed down on the man, the last traces of his humanity disappearing behind shadowy malice when he glared down at his victim.

"We should take him to see the Eldress," I decided finally. She would know what to do...the right questions to ask.

Rue looked at me for a long moment, and when the man's chest fell with a release of tension, he wrapped his hands around either side of his head and twisted. The man's neck snapped with a sharp crack, and he slumped forward onto the sandstone, never to rise again.

"Nobody threatens you and walks away alive," Rue declared coldly as he rose to full height, dispersing his shadowy wings into the darkened corners of the alleyway so they disappeared from sight. My ears rushed with pounding blood, and my heart threatened to break free from the safety of my ribs. My eyes darted between Rue and the discarded corpse. *Venom and hell.*

"Rueper, Guardian of the In Between," I breathed. "Good Halah. *You* threaten me every day. I could have handled him. I—"

"I know you could have," he interrupted. "But I did it so you would not have to. Because you are trusting to a fault, and because he needed to die." His voice was a low growl, not unkind, but deep with emotion.

My lungs fought to expand against the vice of panic wrapping tightly around them. "He didn't need to die. We could have taken him to the Stitcher. We could have—"

"We could have let him live so he could spew his tale to everyone and blame you for Prisha's army? So they will lock you up? Or worse? What then, Zara? What would be your plan then?"

"I—well...but I didn't call Prisha's army," I sputtered.

"Of course you didn't. They're coming for me. And you. And the Eldress...and anyone who's ever dared to take a stance against Prisha. The last war is beginning."

My mouth opened, but no words formed. Every muscle in my body tensed, paralyzed by fear.

"You do not know the war you are up against, but I do. I've seen your enemy."

Rue crossed the distance between us, placing his hands on my cheeks, exuding a sense of certainty that made my knees wobble. "But I see you, too, Zara. And Prisha doesn't stand a chance against you. *She* doesn't know what she's up against either." He paused, searching my eyes with the faintest hint of admiration. "I killed him so you can live. Because you matter."

I gasped without meaning to. It escaped unbidden between my parted lips. Rue pressed his forehead against mine. "Without you, this world is doomed. I know it," he murmured. His words landed like a soft caress against my face, his tone a sultry, mesmerizing whisper that sent shivers down my spine.

"The world is doomed *because* of me," I objected, but I didn't move a muscle. I let him hold me.

He rocked his head slowly back and forth, still pressing his forehead to mine. "I don't think so, Starlight. I think you're exactly the bit of chaos this world needs."

"You're a terrible influence," I countered.

Rue barked a short laugh. "And what else would you expect from a monster of the In Between?"

Finally, I stepped away, my arms stiff and uncertain at my side as I remembered myself. "We should go back. To the palace. Maybe we should talk to Rali. Warn them about...the others."

Rue regarded me for a long moment, as though wavering with some unspoken misgivings, then nodded. "Of course. But first..." His traveling cloak rustled behind him as he swept through the alleyway, then knelt in the shadows, patting the man's corpse and sifting through his pockets. Triumphant, he reemerged spinning a pocket knife with a gleaming bone handle in one hand and clutching a palmful of coins in his other. He jingled them gleefully.

"A quick stop, if you don't object. I never did get those half-moon breads you promised, and I believe they were part of our original deal." He looked at me and frowned. "Of course, I'm not complaining. Due to...circumstances," he amended awkwardly. "But I am hungry."

I'd promised him halfmoon bread and failed to deliver. I couldn't help that when we arrived at the guryas we found nothing but flames, but everything was a transaction with him...some deal or negotiation. I wished he'd never brought it back up.

"I'm sorry. I shouldn't have—" Rue began.

"No, it's fine. A deal is a deal." *And perhaps deals are all that matter to him.*

Rue led me through the alleyways to a more modest part of the city, off the processional path but still bursting with life. Street vendors with reddened cheeks cried out, children bolted past ambling adults in pursuit of spinning hoops, and the smell of charred meat and spices filled the air. He stopped, inhaling deeply with his eyes closed and nose lifted, then steered me toward a little stall on the right-hand side of the street. A couple walked away from the booth, chattering brightly as the woman ripped a steaming halfmoon bread down the center, handing the other piece to her partner.

"Halfmoon bread," Rue whispered enthusiastically. "Would you like one?" He flashed his palmful of coins at me.

"No, I'm fine," I responded, frowning at the reminder of home. I held back, not wanting to call attention to myself, but watched Rue approach the stall with an eager swagger to his strides. A portly man with a flour-dusted apron and very few hairs left clinging to his balding head leaned his arms over the counter, regarding Rue with a suspicious glare. He tended to elicit people's misgivings simply by existing, as if they sensed his origin, even if they didn't recognize it.

But the man's expression brightened when Rue slapped the handful of coins on the counter. I grimaced, wondering how egregiously generous his overpayment was, and if Rue had any inkling of the coins' value. The vendor behind the counter did not ask questions, though. He merely eyed the coins with a greedy glimmer of delight before sweeping them into his apron. Rue returned bearing an armful of halfmoon bread, every bit as delighted as the merchant. He stuffed the extra bread into his pockets, then took a hefty bite from the one still clutched in his hand.

"Let me have a taste," I said, simply with the intent to irk him.

Rue's eyes widened, aghast. "You know I don't share."

I suppressed a laugh. I had finally learned how to get under his skin. But to my surprise, Rue sighed and ripped off a chunk of his treasure, passing it to me. I shook my head. "I'm only kidding. I'm full." A lump of something like guilt formed in my throat.

"Good," Rue responded, popping the whole chunk into his mouth. He chewed, reflecting for a moment, then leaned to whisper into my ear. "Because you would have had to fight me for it."

"And I would have won," I shot back at him, then blinked with the realization of my own gall. *What is this brazenness, Zara? Where did that come from?* But I knew I'd said it to rile him. To stir his attention so I could watch his eyes sharpen and his muscles tense as he regarded me with his expression of great intrigue. When he looked at me like that, the world paused in mid-spin, as though he'd become important to me. As though he'd become everything to me.

I shook the ridiculous notion from my mind. He was dangerous. A ruthless killer who'd snap the neck of a man without thinking twice. A monster of the In Between. A mistake I needed to deal with.

"Zara, Daughter of Halah!" a stern voice shouted, followed by the sound of the uniform striking of boots. I turned, heart hammering at the sight of a dozen palace guards swarming toward me. Rue angled his body ever so slightly, stepping between me and their formation.

"Zara, Daughter of Halah. Thank the goddess you are unharmed. Your presence has been requested at the palace. The king requires an audience with you."

CHAPTER 19

THE KING'S BEES

The guards did not grant me the courtesy of time to manage the galloping pace of my heart, nor to still the storm of sand wings flitting about my stomach. They ushered me to the main hall of the palace without delay, walking over the black and white tile with long, purposeful strides. Our connection never strained, so I guessed Rue remained close by, but he clung to the shadows so even *I* could not find him when I searched to borrow courage from his gaze.

The scalloped arches of the entrance allowed sunlight and fresh air to pass through the filigree columns. As we progressed toward the inner rotunda, the room funneled toward a sandstone staircase flanked by a series of imposing columns—a design boasting regal authority. The base of each stair had been carved to honor the legacy of every ruler who had ascended the Sun Throne, so that with every step upward, the stairs credited the progress attributed to each new monarch's reign. And at the very top, an imperial set of brass doors led to the sitting monarch—the highest point of greatness in Rashii's story.

The guards withdrew, filtering away to flank either side of the staircase. My eyes flicked back and forth between them, my lips parted with uncertainty. The stomp of boots against tile approached swiftly from behind.

"Zara," a deep voice called out, rich like melted chocolate. A hand wrapped around my waist and spun me around, pulling me close.

"Oh. Rali." I gasped in surprise. I placed my hands on his shoulders and leaned my forearms upon his chest, unintentionally bracing against our proximity after the disaster of our last interaction. Rali didn't seem to notice.

His jade eyes swept over me, liquefying with molten streaks of honeyed affection. "You are all right? The guards say there's been an attack?"

"Yes, I'm fine. Just shaken." But my lips tightened into a thin line, biting back my frustration with him. *Where were* you *when I was attacked? Busy protecting the city? That went well, didn't it?*

I brushed aside my annoyance. Certainly, he'd only been fulfilling his duties, as we all were called to do. I shouldn't blame him for that. He cared deeply about his honor and responsibilities. "Have you heard from my Sisters? Did the scouts return?" I asked, steering the conversation in a more opportune direction.

Rali's nostrils flared as he shook his head. "Not yet." My stomach sank. The cords of his neck tensed beneath his clenched jaw. "I cannot believe—This should not have happened. There are too many warning signs. Too many concerns." He ran a hand through his unruly hair. "I thought it would be safe to celebrate the festivities, but...I need you to stay within the palace until the threats pass," he insisted.

My gaze hardened. This was not what we had agreed on. "I don't belong within these palace walls. I belong outside, fighting the threats. With my Sisters." Snakes slithered in my stomach. *Do you believe that, Zara? Do you truly think you can help them, or have you* become *the threat?*

Rali's expression darkened and, for a moment, I saw not his eyes, but the Rider's hate-filled gaze tearing me to shreds. The damning accusations he tossed like daggers with his wrathful glare. A wave of unease washed over me. If the Rider had been right about the other winged men, if Prisha had sent them to hunt down Rue and me, staying within the city only endangered everyone else. *I should tell Rali...I should warn him.* But the words stuck in my throat, forming a lump that made it impossible to speak.

The people needed a Stitcher. They needed a protector to face Prisha and stop her before her army could breach the city walls. Someone more capable than me. *But Halah chose me,* I reminded myself. I sighed internally, but the faintest glimmer of warmth spread beneath my breastbone, reawakening my courage. Reminding me of my strength. But I shoved it away, burying it deeply within me to hide it from Rali. To hide it from myself.

I did not succeed in hiding it from Prisha. *Star Thief. Sky Render. Open the skies,* she screeched in the deranged pitch only she could muster. I snapped my lids shut and forced her from my mind. When I reopened my eyes, I glared up at Rali, writing determination across my features. "I need to see the Eldress. Now."

"Zara, *no.* The most important thing you can do now is focus on earning Halah's blessing at our union. Go back to your room and pray. You'll be safe there. With everything going on, I do not want to worry about your safety, too."

"Nobody will be safe *anywhere* if you don't listen to me, Rali. Take me to her." I took his hand in mine and tried to urge him along. His hand snaked firmly around my wrist.

"I said go to your room and pray."

I glared at him. "I don't pray, Rali. You know that. I fight. You promised I could fight."

"I never promised you could fight with *me*, Zara. You are meant to *listen*."

My face fell, mouth gaping, brows drawn together in disgust. This was not the man I'd imagined him to be—the man he'd painted in the pretty curls of his letters and lofty words. But my reaction seemed to upset him, and he sighed wearily and shook his head. "I'm sorry, Zara. I am stressed. I shouldn't have spoken to you like that. *It's just...not safe.* Not until there's a new Stitcher." He paused, biting his lip in consideration. "Have you heard anything yet? About a new Stitcher? Did your elder Sisters mention anything before Ja' Rilaht?" An eagerness unveiled itself in his voice.

"Only the Eldress can stitch the skies, Rali," I hedged. "If you want a Stitcher, take me to her. Let me see if I can convince her to wake again. Please."

He kissed my hand. "Later. I promise." He paused, nodding toward the staircase. "The king wishes to see you. You shouldn't keep him waiting. I'll check on the Eldress and see if she's ready for visitors."

I inhaled deeply, then turned my head to the stairs, swallowing in a moment of hesitation. Rali did not miss the way my shoulders tensed. "You are not in trouble. He only wishes to meet you. It is customary."

"It's not that, it's..." My eyes landed on the doors at the top of the grand staircase. So solid and...closed.

"Can the windows be opened?" Proper Daughter or not, the access to earth and air made me feel safe. Walls and enclosed spaces only served to make me feel trapped. And powerless.

Rali blinked at me. "In the throne room? Yes, of course." He nodded to the guards lining the stairway, and a trio immediately departed to follow his silent command.

THE THRONE ROOM WAS A PLACE OF PARADOX. AS SOON as I stepped foot in it, my body stiffened, both overwhelmed by the unending stretch of carpet leading to the Sun Throne and simultaneously conflicted by a sense of claustrophobia. The walls arched over me on either side, and though the windows had been opened, walking through the room made me feel as though I were wading through the jaws of a hungry beast. My eyes shot warily to the ceiling, holding the coffered framework in my untrusting gaze. No stars above to guide me, to shimmer and whisper their encouragement. No sun to shine a light upon my path.

Subtly, I probed the room for Halah's tendrils of energy. To the king, the ribbons of power remained invisible, but for me, they flowed about like old friends. When I reached for them, they wriggled just beyond my grasp, avoiding me. I frowned.

"The room will not swallow you, Daughter of Halah. Come in."

King Onros's voice was melodious and deep, filled with years of wisdom and an unwavering assurance that immediately set me at ease. I approached the throne, my steps padding quietly along the carpeted walkway. When I stood at the base of the throne, I crossed a clenched fist over my heart and kneeled.

"Do not kneel, Zara. We are equals in the eyes of Halah." He fell silent for a moment. "You do not need to worry...at least not about me. I do not mean you any harm."

Standing, I met his kind gaze with a puzzled scrunch of my brow. "Are there others who do?"

He laughed a deep, musical guffaw. "You are a Daughter of Halah. Your list of enemies rivals perhaps even mine in length, and mine has grown quite long as of late. *If* I'm to believe my advisors." He leaned back against the Sun Throne, carved with etchings of daybreak that rose above his white hair like a crown, and he exuded a comfortable sense of power and certainty.

"Do you?" I asked, unable to stop myself from wondering. "Believe them, I mean? I've heard the rumors about Khazdra." What possessed me to ask the king such a forward question, I couldn't fathom, but I was frustrated by the limited information and sense of secrecy I'd endured since I'd arrived in Rashii.

"Bah," he objected with a wave of his hand. "Khazdra is the least of my concerns. The advisors worry too much, if you ask me. They just need a hobby. Like me." His skin folded into innumerable wrinkles, and his color appeared dull, lackluster, like unpolished bronze, but the red flush of his cheeks and the glint in his eyes gave him life. He rose from his chair and offered his arm.

"Then you do not share the same worries?" I probed as I accepted his arm, wondering if the king might dispel the whispers of war that seeped through the city, tinting the very air with unease. If the king wasn't concerned about the growing tensions with Khazdra, they must not truly be a threat as the guards had led me to believe. And if that were the case, perhaps the Daughters *had* been captured by Riders...I could certainly confirm *their* hatred of us.

"I find it hard to get too worked up about anything in my old age," the king responded, interrupting my train of thought. "But most won't bother to listen to an old fool like me. No worries. It matters not. The stars have a way of sorting these things out anyway...writing our fates for us. But that is not what I wished to discuss. I didn't bring you here to bore you with political affairs or concern you with our troubles. You have enough to worry about."

Right. Of course it would be inappropriate for him to discuss such matters with me. *I shouldn't have pried.* "You asked to see me?" I asked, my voice small.

"Indeed. Have you ever seen a beehive, Daughter of Halah?" He led me to a hutch beneath the open windows, and a buzzing sound filled the room when he opened the doors. I flinched, fearing an attack, then marveled at the glass chamber he'd housed them in. "My observation hive," he explained, nodding to the bees. "I find solace in their constant rumbling. They do not blab on about politics or problems. There are no princesses to challenge the queen...they merely buzz about their business, serving their sovereign with unwavering devotion. I have dozens of hives around the palace grounds, but I like to keep one nearby. Sometimes, just watching them is enough to sort through the chaos of my mind." Their bodies writhed and twisted beneath the glass, moving through the geometric design of the honeycomb, each completing whatever duty the stars had assigned. The king tinkered with glass jars on the bottom shelf and passed me a miniature spoon for tasting. "My newest variety. These bees have fed mostly from tinoya blossoms...the nectar gives the honey subtle notes of fruit and a light, fragrant profile. Try it."

I accepted the spoon, tasting the faintly pink honey as the king waited patiently for my thoughts. It did taste like tinoya, but sweeter, and the flavor brought me to the moment Rue had opened the fruit for me in the desert. I swallowed. "It's good," I responded, shoving the thoughts of Rue away. The king grunted at my lacking response and opened a new jar.

"I wished to talk to you about the attack at the ceremonial procession this afternoon," he said, passing another spoon to me.

I responded with a timid nod and tasted the second spoonful of honey. This one burst with a complex layer of spice, warming my tongue. "Cinnamon?" I asked.

"Fireblossom," the king corrected, seemingly annoyed by the amateur nature of my palate. "Fireblossom nectar gives the honey spiced notes, similar to cinnamon, but more robust." He replaced the lid. "I'm glad to see you escaped unharmed. My guards said they found you on the other side of the city, far away from the processional path."

I put the tasting spoon on the ledge of the hutch. "I was led to safety and discovered by your dutiful guards after the threat had passed."

He hummed, studying me carefully as he considered his next words. "They also informed me of a strange phenomenon. A...light of some sort? Do you know anything about this? I must admit, the ways of Daughters are somewhat foreign to me."

Venom and hell. My eyes flicked to the window behind the hutch. "I'm afraid I don't. What kind of a light?" I asked calmly, with an innocuous note of intrigue coloring my tone.

He regarded me carefully. "They said it seemed to come...from you. If the Prophecy of Dusk and Dawn has come to light, I should like to know. That will realign the stars for us all."

I smiled and shook my head, laughing slightly as I instinctually took a step backward. "It was a mere trick of the sun, perhaps? Everything happened so quickly. It was difficult for anyone to make sense of what was happening. I'm just thankful I got away."

"Of course," the king conceded with his words, but not his expression. "Well, we will be certain to tighten security tomorrow. Halah knows we can spare no more Daughters. I will make sure you are well protected."

"I appreciate your concern and protection. Thank you, Your Majesty."

"Is there anything else I can do for you, Daughter of Halah?" he asked before closing the hutch.

I froze, paralyzed by a moment of indecision, wondering if I should mention it at all.

"Yes," I began tentatively. "There is one thing. I'd like to see the Eldress."

"She is under the prince's care. I will speak to him and see if you may be brought to her."

My disappointment unveiled itself with a frown.

"I am sorry, Daughter of Halah. She must be safeguarded until a new Stitcher is named. You know how important she is to us all. We wait for the prophecy to come to light, but I fear she may be our last hope. Go, get ready for the blessing of your union. We all look forward to that day."

Well, almost all of us. Everyone except the bride.

CHAPTER 20

STITCHES

The sun dipped below the turrets of the palace courtyard, and a navy curtain spread across the heavens. The rectangular pool, now black with night, caught the jumbled reflection of stars. The hanging baskets swayed gently overhead, moonpetal blossoms quietly unfolding to soak in the tranquil glow, and the earthy aroma of dune rushes drifted to my nose. They smelled like Rue.

I clenched my fists, elbows leaning against the balcony beneath the open archways, wondering why he hadn't returned after my visit with the king. He couldn't be far...the tether pulled at my heart but not with agonizing tension—just enough to remind me of its presence. My eyes traced the skyline of Rashii, looking all the way beyond the copper domes and mismatched roofs of the outskirts, beyond the city walls and to the sloping dunes of the Sundom Desert. Prisha's rifts crackled in the vast sky above the desert, edges ablaze with sparks of gold, like fire devouring a sheet of paper. *Where are you, Rue?*

I paused, conflicted by the source of my worry. Had I grown

so used to his infuriating companionship? Or did the twisting in my stomach stem from a place of mistrust regarding the circumstances of his disappearance?

Why had he left me? Had he done so willingly? Did it mean he'd decided to break ties with me? Would he come back? Did... something happen to him? The last thought stuck in my throat, sending a pulse of foreboding through my blood. Needing reassurance, I brushed a hand over my heart, seeking out the burdensome tether between us. It shimmered with the ethereal quality of starlight, then dissipated into the gloomy darkness. He still lived... there was that, at least. And he couldn't be far. But the realization did little to qualm the twist of conflict in my gut.

I huffed in frustration and retraced my steps to the door for perhaps the thousandth time that evening. This time, when the door had closed with an audible click behind the guards' departure, it refused to open. I had checked. Thoroughly. My eyes panned downward, landing on the dent in the door where I'd kicked the wood in frustration, but the slight twinge of remorse did not deter me from renewing my effort to antagonize the guards.

The brass knob rattled angrily when I shook it, but it did not turn, and the door did not budge.

"You are to stay put this evening, Daughter of Halah. For your safety." The guard's gruff voice floated loftily through the wood, now with an obvious edge of exasperation.

"I would like to speak with Rali."

I imagined the guard's carefully measured breath in the pause before he spoke again. "He is busy. There is much to prepare for tomorrow, and all of our security must be enhanced. Royal decree." He spoke to me with the same voice one would use when dealing with a particularly willful child.

I was willful, but I was no child.

"If he expects our union to be as blessed as he hopes, he best come talk to me. Now." I pounded the door with my fist on the last word.

"He is on duty. As I have already told you. Many times." Well. Good to know our exasperation was mutual.

"He told me he'd take me to the Eldress. I want to speak to him."

"I have already told you he cannot, and that you are not to gallivant through the palace on your own tonight."

I rattled the doorknob again, clenching my teeth.

"Go to sleep, Daughter of Halah. Tomorrow is a big day. You may trust us to ensure your safety."

The magnitude of my frustration could not be fully expressed with a mere groan, but I *tried*. Fists balled at my side, shoulders raised somewhere by my ears, and an unhealthy amount of boiling blood coursing through my veins, I turned my back to the door and stormed into the room.

A dark figure leaned casually against the open archway, arms folded and legs crossed at the ankle, quietly reposed with one brow lifted. "Hello, Starlight."

The rushing wings of a startled bird took flight inside of me. How long had he been here, watching? "You could have helped me," I said, waving a hand sharply toward the door once my initial surprise wore away,

The shadows of his wings rippled behind him as he adjusted his position. "I could have. But that would cost you."

A guttural sound, somewhere between a screech and a roar, scraped through my throat.

"Is everything always about what you get out of it? Can't you do anything just because you *want* to?"

"Not where I come from," he answered cooly, and I flinched at the reminder of what his choice to follow me—to abandon

Prisha—might cost him. The likelihood that she would unmake him if he ever returned to her domain. But a smile tugged at the corner of his mouth. "Besides…what if what I want is to annoy you? Have you considered that?"

My gaze sharpened, and my arms crossed over my chest, hips jutting to one side, latching onto his playful tone. "Well, you don't need to make everything a bargain," I scolded, failing to hide my own smile.

"Can't help it." Rue shrugged. "It's survival skill where I come from. And I've perfected the art."

"Well, seeing as I have repetitively demonstrated my inability to harm you, maybe save that survival skill to use with someone else. I think you're safe with me."

He quieted for a moment, and I shifted uncertainly when his eyes wandered, slipping into an appreciative sweep of the rest of my frame. "The stars *do* favor you, Zara. That much I know to be true."

I lowered my chin, glaring back at him. "Then I hope they swallow you whole."

He laughed the most beautiful laugh, allowing a glimpse of an unguarded Rue to slip through the cracks. Unfiltered and touched by genuine happiness for a moment. "Let them," he said, pulling himself back, but the hint of a smile still creased his eyes. "I'll find my way back to annoy you another day."

My lips twisted into a pursed expression, but failed miserably to blot out the smile that had worked its way to my face. The air thickened with a weighted silence, and we stood there in the quiet, trying to hold back our senseless smirks. Slowly, I remembered myself, and mine drooped. "Where were you?"

Rue's amusement faded too, his face falling into its usual air of disinterest. "I had…business to attend to."

I frowned at him, noting the lift of his brows and the hooded gaze of his eyes that walled him off from me. "Why do you say 'business' like you're hiding something?"

Traitor. Traitor. Kill them. Let their screams echo through the void. Let them drown in the abyss of my wrath! Make the Star Thief shred the skies. She is mine.

I gasped, gripping the folds of my scarf in a clenched fist. The heart of stars glowed, projecting fine particles of light into the ethereal glow, like stardust drifting through a moonbeam. The tether binding me to Rue crackled to life, illuminated by the heart of stars, then warped into shadows. It tightened around my heart with a sharp, crushing pain that made both our faces screw into a grimace.

"What did you do?" I asked, my voice strained.

The vicelike grip squeezing my heart faded, and Rue's shoulders slumped forward in relief, as did mine. He leaned against the wall, wings draped around his arms like a shelter, and he steadied his breath with a weary heave. His skin paled, drained of color, and I noticed how his weight favored his left side. The traveling cloak he wore frayed with gashes more numerous than the ones in the sky, and a puddle of sweat stained the front of his tunic. How had I not noticed before? Something was wrong...something he kept hidden beneath all his banter and charm.

He breathed shallowly, but lifted his eyes to meet mine. They filled with sadness, despite the brave smile he donned. "That. Yes. I—killed the Guardians she sent after us. The ones that man spoke of. They made it all the way to Rashii, but they're no longer a concern. I bought you some time."

His energy seemed to fail him, and his knees gave out. He hobbled unevenly to regain his balance, and I caught him in my arms as he slumped forward.

"You're hurt," I said, alarmed.

"Just a flesh wound." He groaned into my shoulder. "But if there was ever a good time to practice stitching the skies...it would be now. She'll send more. There's no doubt about my abandonment of Prisha now." His words slurred with exhaustion.

Venom and hell. This is all my fault. He risked...everything by following me and believing in me. He became the first and only Guardian to turn against Prisha. He risked his life.

For me.

And there's nothing I can do to protect him in return. "I don't know how to stitch the skies," I admitted, the words unsavory with the taste of my regret. Rue swayed precariously in my arms, and my back protested against the strain of his weight. *Lift with the legs.* "Come on. You're okay. You'll be okay."

Adjusting my hold to support him beneath the arms, I locked my wrists together in front of his chest and pulled. His boots dragged along the floor, streaking the beautiful tile with two dull lines as I heaved him toward the bed. My thighs screamed with each strenuous step.

Finally, he collapsed sideways onto the mattress, and the force of his fall sent my body flopping across his hips. He groaned, recoiling with a wince of pain.

"I'm sorry," I muttered awkwardly, setting my feet back on the floor and smoothing my skirt.

Rue's eyes scrunched closed, but he smiled. "S'alright, Starlight. Under any other circumstances, I would have enjoyed it."

I bit my lip, insensibly amused by his confession, but my eyes wandered to the torn fabric at his thigh, landing nervously on the white-knuckled fingers covering it. Pulling the flap of ripped fabric away, I sucked air sharply between my teeth, wincing at the defined muscles coated with a slick layer of crimson, spidered with shadows. A long, clean gash trailed from his kneecap to his groin.

"Is it bad?" Rue asked. His skin was so pale.

"No. It's not so bad," I replied, a few octaves too high.

Rue groaned and threw his head back against the pillow. "Got any spirits?"

I stared blankly back at him.

"To sterilize it."

Right. Sterilize. Good idea. Sweat gathered at my hairline as I bustled through the room, opening cabinets and drawers without any regard to my method. Finally, I knelt on the ground at the tea table, wrenching open the lattice doors below it, and sighed with relief. *There.* A modest collection of bottles in varying shapes and sizes sat within. I clutched the neck of the tall, clear one and rushed it back to Rue.

He opened the cork with his teeth and splashed it over the gash, stifling an agonized groan into his fist. I gripped his upper arm, my own knuckles growing white with concern.

"Dune rushes," I announced, twisting my head back and forth to scan the room. "There are dune rushes somewhere...I smelled them. I can make a poultice. Like the one you used for me."

"Good. Yes. You smelled them? Can you find them?"

"I think so. They smell like you."

He lifted his head from the pillow, staring questioningly at me like he'd only just noticed me for the first time.

"Never mind that," I said, hastily darting away. The dune rushes called my attention immediately, spilling over the long rectangular baskets affixed to the balcony. I plucked a handful of the pale green leaves drenched in moonlight from the basket, waving awkwardly to the guard when he looked up to assess the source of the rustling above.

"Just wanted some tea. Collecting leaves. Goodnight!" I slipped quickly back through the arches, leaning against the wall for a moment to collect my breath before running back to Rue.

The leaves bruised easily in my palm, creating the same sticky salve that Rue had used to numb and heal my injuries in the desert.

"It needs stitches first," Rue said in a hoarse voice, withdrawing the kit from his cloak. I frowned as he struggled to thread the black cording through the needle's eye.

"Let me," I said, wiping the salve into an unused teacup. Fishing the thread from his grasp despite the nausea bubbling in my stomach, I leaned forward to inspect the gash. Healing was not an affinity of mine, but it was one I'd had to practice after several close calls with Prisha's monsters.

Biting my lip, I hesitantly pushed the needle through his skin, snapping my eyes shut when he flinched.

"It's easier if you keep your eyes open," Rue gasped, still trying to set me at ease despite the grimace of pain distorting his features. Dark circles rimmed his eyes, and sweat dampened his hair against his blanched skin.

I swallowed and forced myself to be brave. For him. Focusing only on the gash, I mentally detached from the task at hand and set to work.

"See, you *can* mend," Rue said, disrupting my concentration as I neared the end of the wound.

"Yes," I agreed quietly, looking down and focusing perhaps a bit too intensely on the effort of knotting the final stitch. "When it's something that matters, I always find a way." My cheeks flushed with warmth. "But stitching skies is different than mending wounds."

"Stitching skies and saving your people is also important to you," he countered. "You'll find a way."

I smiled faintly. Sadly.

"You're not alone. You don't always have to be alone."

I rolled my eyes. "Only because we're stuck together."

"I never complained about it."

Somehow, my hand had wandered to his hair, brushing the

dampened curls from his forehead to feel for a fever, then meandering through the tousled locks with a gentle, almost wistful touch. When I caught myself studying his lips, wondering what they might feel like against mine, I stiffened my spine and pulled my hand away. But Rue's hand found mine.

"Thank you," he said with an affectionate squeeze.

I flashed a halfhearted smile that disappeared just as quickly, but I didn't pull away. I held on, gripping his hand while everything else crashed down inside of me, shattering somewhere at the bottom, cutting me with a thousand broken shards of dread. "I— I can't do it."

Marry Rali. Stitch the skies. Do what everyone expects of me.
...fall for you.

I worried my teeth against my bottom lip. "I don't think I'll ever be able to stitch the skies. There's...something wrong. With me."

Rue's thumb swept against mine. "Perhaps it is merely the circumstances that are wrong." He paused thoughtfully. "Is there anything I can do to help you?"

"Nothing." I sighed. "It's just...every time I try to access my power, it feels like Prisha is there, waiting. She knows it...she can feel it. It's like a trap." My eyes darted to Rue uncertainly, and I swallowed the lump in my throat. His brows furrowed, but he didn't interrupt me. "And when I tried to reach for Halah's magic earlier, the threads avoided my grasp. And ever since I ripped open the stitches, Prisha's had her eyes on me. She's waiting for me to lose control. She wants me to destroy and to...kill."

"Kill who? Me?"

"*Everyone*. And it scares me. Her voice—it's in my head. Like...it's part of me. Like it wants me to forget who I am. Perhaps I am going crazy?"

"That's why you cannot stitch the skies?"

I pulled my hand away and buried my face in my palms. "I

told you I am broken. *Venom and hell.* What will the Daughters say? The people? They *need* me, Rue, but I don't think I can be enough for them. And Rali? What will he think?"

Rue brushed a strand of hair from my forehead, tucking it back behind my ear. "If Rali only sees you as broken, he is missing the best parts of you. You are enough...more than enough. You are everything."

"I don't want to marry him," I confessed. As soon as I'd said it, I wished I hadn't. It was a truth I wasn't allowed to voice. Horribly unfair. And one that sought another truth I wasn't allowed to hear or want...an objection I should have never expected of him.

"Then don't." Every muscle in my body stilled, waiting for him to say more. But he relaxed, his head sinking deeply into the feathered pillow behind him.

I was being foolishly unfair. The Daughters required me to marry Rali. They expected me to fulfill my duties, and I loved them enough to try. Didn't Rue understand that? It wasn't as simple as refusing. To be a Daughter of Halah meant a life of responsibility. Honor. Fighting for the protection of the people and perpetuating the goddess's lineage to protect those of future generations. Never had I been promised a life of my own choosing. Nor did I know what I would choose if I could.

Not this.

I buried the selfish thought and busied myself by scooping the salve from the rim of the teacup onto my fingers. "I don't have a choice," I decided, applying the salve to Rue's wound.

"You do." He winced, then his expression eased as the numbing effects of the salve took effect. "There's always a choice. *You* might have forgotten the fiery temper of the woman who told me she's accustomed to defying expectations, but I haven't. I never will. I know your strength. It inspires mine."

My heart fell with a twisting sense of disagreement, unable to reconcile his praise with my sense of failure. "No matter what choices I make, someone will be disappointed."

"Then choose to not disappoint yourself."

"It's not that simple, Rue."

He laughed, but there was a sadness to it. "That's what I did. When I decided I couldn't do what she asked of me anymore. When I knew I could never return to be her monster, I chose not to disappoint myself. I chose to be yours."

My heart pattered, skipping a beat altogether. "You're not a monster, Rue. You never were." And in that moment, I meant it. He was not my enemy. Not from the moment the bond between us tethered our hearts together.

I met his gaze tentatively, the assured intensity of the starscape within watching me, daring me to defy my circumstances and forge my own path. To be brave like him. *But what do* you *want, Rue?* I desperately needed the answer—I felt every decision of mine hinge upon it—but I was too cowardly to ask. "I just...I can't do it. The Daughters expect me to replace the Eldress and marry Rali. Rali expects me to love him and honor him when he *apparently* will not do the same for me. He expects me to be a wife and bear him Daughters, but I've begun to doubt his intentions of loving me. The people expect protection I cannot give them, even if they have not yet recognized me as the new Stitcher. Even if I *want* to protect them." I took a deep breath, lifting my chin to the ceiling to hold back the tears that welled at my bottom lashes. "Even if I want to protect you."

"And what do *you* expect?" Rue asked me softly, an underlying tenderness to his tone.

I looked back at Rue, my face contorted with heartbreak, my lips pressed tight, the taste of salty tears seeping between them. "Me?" My voice cracked. "I expect to fall apart if I continue disappointing everyone by not being what they expect me to be." I paused, drawing in a deep breath. "I don't fix, I destroy. I am a fighter, not a Stitcher. *Why* did Halah choose me?" Scrunching my eyes closed, I turned my face back to the ceiling, but the tears streamed freely down my cheeks, regardless of my effort to stop them. "She should have chosen someone better...a better example of a Daughter. Someone who could weave and harness Halah's power without distorting it. Someone...not broken."

Rue tugged on my hand, and I fell onto the bed at his side, locked in an embrace that warmed me to my core. "Perhaps it is time for you to embrace who you are, and not what they want you to be. Halah chose you for a reason," he murmured into my neck, pulling me against him. "Prisha's noticed you for a reason. How many Daughters are left still fighting? How many could pull Prisha's monsters from the sky and endear them to your cause?"

"Only one." I corrected, *Only you.*

But I realized I'd inadvertently answered his question with my haste to object. *Only one...only me.*

"One is all you need. If there's ever been a Daughter to stand a chance against Prisha, it is you. You are not broken because you don't conform to their expectations of you, Zara. You are...exceptional."

Exceptionally screwed, perhaps. He draped a shadowed wing over my shoulder, and the comfort of its warmth surprised me. *I should get up. I should not let him hold me like this.*

"Tell you what. I'll make you a deal," Rue mumbled, his breath drawing in slow waves as a calm washed over us.

"No more deals, please. I've had enough of those."

"Just give me...one minute. One minute to recover my strength before I burn this world down to help you." My eyes widened, but his embrace tightened reassuringly around me before he continued to mumble dreamily beneath my ear. "One minute, then I will break down that door and help you find your Eldress to see what she has to say about all of this."

I nodded, frowning at the pallor of his skin and silently

promising to give him my patience. I owed him that much. I played with his hair, wondering what the Eldress would have to say and if it would even matter. Wondering if I could bring myself to listen if it wasn't what I wished to hear. I wondered what I wanted her to say about Rue, about Rali, about my responsibilities and failures. I wondered so long and so hard I did not notice how Rue's muscles relaxed and how his breaths lengthened as he drifted into a peaceful sleep, holding me in his arms.

CHAPTER 21

RALI'S GIFT

Kill them all.

I gasped, eyes snapping open as the asphyxiating clutches of Prisha's rage melted from the last vestiges of my nightmare. My chest heaved with incomplete breaths, desperate to resurface from the dream, yet consumed by the haunting images still plaguing me. The injured Guardian, wings pinned to the wall by daggers of shadow. The fear and defeat that spilled from his aura faster than the shadowy blood leaking from his chest. The way his eyes gaped, staring at his own heart, still beating in Prisha's hand. How his body crumbled to ash in the moment she unmade him.

Each time I closed my eyes, she was there, waiting. *It's only a dream, Zara.*

But every instinct within me screamed that it was more.

Sunlight trickled through the open archways, filtering through the gauzy curtains to splash its halfhearted glow against my nose. A different warmth wrapped around my arms, curling up against my back. Rue's chest rose and fell slowly behind mine

—relaxed and still drifting in the clutches of sleep. He was here. He was safe.

And he was very close to me.

Oh. The realization of his proximity startled me from my panic, my muscles solidifying like blocks of ice against his frame. I knew I should not have permitted him to work his way so close to me, but...I couldn't deny I enjoyed it far more than I should have. He felt familiar. Right.

The terror from my nightmare drifted away as I eased back into Rue's hold.

No matter how firmly I commanded myself to move, I couldn't bring myself to leave the safety of his arms. *Not yet.*

Carefully rolling over so as not to disturb him, I repositioned myself at an angle more conducive to studying his face. Color had returned to his cheeks, and the pained crease between his brows had smoothed to an expression of utmost calm. His hair broke free from its usual carefree perfection, now wildly mussed and chaotic. *I like your chaos...it matches mine.* His words echoed in my memory.

I ran my fingers through the out-of-place hairs, smoothing them away from his forehead, and permitted the faintest smile of appreciation to appear on my lips. If his injury still pained him, no evidence remained behind to suggest it. My eyes trailed along his frame to check the state of his stitches, but the comforter wrapped firmly around his leg in a protective cocoon. I sighed. Moving it would only wake him. I'd promised myself to give him the time to rest so he could recover enough to help me, and...I realized with a start as my breath hitched, my fingers still twisted through his strands of hair. I *wanted* to give him the time to rest because...his well-being had become a concern of mine. I wanted to protect him in the same way he had protected me. And perhaps for other reasons I dared not name.

If I left them unnamed, they could continue to exist as a

nebulous cloud at the edges of my mind, never taking shape into something tangible. Something real. It was better that way.

Instead, I peeled myself from his arms and padded toward the door. I lifted my fist with the intention to knock, but hesitated. Why would the guards let me leave now if they'd been so adamantly against it last night? Still, I wondered if I could persuade them. Perhaps with a request for food? Rue would need something when he woke...he'd need it after all the energy he'd expended in his fight.

My knuckles rapped softly against the wood. Blankets rustled behind me, and I froze, turning nervously back to Rue. He merely shifted and stretched a black wing across the bed. A beam of sunlight cast a stark contrast of highlights and shadows across his features, and the air in my lungs snagged, my eyes unintentionally lingering to admire this perfectly peaceful version of him.

"Lady Zara?" the guard asked politely from the other side of the door, his voice muffled by the inches of solid wood between us. The guard was different from the one I'd antagonized last night, less gruff with exasperation and perhaps slightly more amenable to my demands. "I am sorry, Lady Zara, but you are meant to stay in your room until Rali comes to collect you." *Or not.*

My insides crawled at the mention of Rali, pulverizing his name into gravel inside my gut. "Surely he would not deny me breakfast? I'm starving."

"It is already past noon, Lady Zara. But I will have a service sent for you to tide you over."

Past noon? And nobody brought me anything to eat? Am I a prisoner or a guest? I supposed they *had* left me with tea and small pastries, but my stomach growled for something more substantial. The rumbling protest played its part quite convincingly. Pity the guard could not hear it through the door. "I can't wait that long.

Please. You may...escort me if you'd like," I offered, employing my airiest tone of innocence.

A moment of silence suggested the guard's internal debate, then the lock clicked softly before the door swung open. I slipped through the gap and linked my arm through his with more confidence than I truly commanded, steering him away from my quarters. He didn't need the opportunity to inspect them or return me to them...Rue needed sleep, not questioning. And I needed food, answers, and the Eldress. Not seeds of doubt or more hours helplessly trapped in my chambers.

As if summoned by the faintest whiff of my freedom, Rali rounded the corner, dressed in the deep blue uniform of the palace guards. The black buttons of his jacket lined the front of his chest all the way up to the high collar at his neck, creating a perfectly tailored silhouette to showcase his muscular frame. If I had not grown to mistrust him, I might have appreciated his handsome features more thoroughly. But as it was, I could not hold back the way my expression soured at the sight of his arrival.

His steps faltered almost imperceptibly as he neared us, gaze narrowing on the guard who hastily made a show of unlinking his arm from mine. A smile that hinted at warmly crafted lies and deception lit his features when he turned to me, making my skin crawl. "Zara. You're awake. Good morning." He swept forward and took my hand in his, planting a moist kiss upon my skin. I resisted the urge to wipe it on my skirt when my arm fell back to my side. "Happy A'i Halajan. May Halah bless us. The day we've dreamed of has finally arrived."

The urge to wipe my hand of Rali's touch spread like wildfire through the rest of my body until I couldn't hold back my reservations any longer. "Rali, I don't think—"

He pulled me close, pressing my cheek uncomfortably against the row of buttons down his front as he stroked my hair. "Shhhh," he hushed me like a small child afraid of the night, slicing through my unfinished thought to silence it. "It's normal to have hesitations before the ceremony, and I know I haven't acted like myself lately, but I have a surprise for you to make up for it. One that will surely lift your spirits."

I freed my arms from his restricting hold, wedging my elbows against his chest. "Rali, I mean it. We need to discuss this. And I want to see—"

He stepped away, collecting both of my hands in his. "The scouts have returned, Zara. They've found your Sisters."

My heart collapsed, careening through the pit of my stomach to be swallowed by the gaping pit spreading beneath my feet. Or at least...it felt that way. In reality, I stared at him numbly, mouth gaping and lungs frozen in mid-breath, my entire body caught in some stutter of time. Everything else—all other thoughts and worries—faded to nothing more than extraneous noise that hummed in the background...both undecipherable and unimportant.

"Where are they?" I managed, finally collecting myself.

My mind buzzed with impatience as Rali led us through the winding corridors of the palace, round corners, up stairs, down stairs, and around again until I became quite disoriented by the scheme of the layout. The further we moved from my chambers, the more the connection binding me to Rue pulled at my heart. It stretched, but not unbearably so. I only hoped the tension would not wake Rue or make him worry. My fingers absent-mindedly moved to rest over my heart, clutching the dull ache beginning at the end of the tether, pulled taut around each jolting thud of the muscle. Or perhaps that was simply my worry.

Finally, Rali stalled in front of a set of double doors, long golden handles gleaming in the middle, a pair of potted succulents on either side of the entrance.

He pecked my cheek with a quick kiss, then nodded to the

doors. "Go on. They are very excited to see you. I'll give you some privacy while you visit with them. I'll see you this evening."

My sense clattered back to me as Rali knocked on the door, then swiftly departed, taking long strides that stamped confidently against the ornamental runner lining the hall. "Where are you going?" I called to his back.

"I have a lot to do," he tossed over his shoulder. "Don't worry...you'll be safe. There are guards posted in the room for your protection."

That wasn't what worried me at all, but he'd already disappeared, slipping away into one of the hallways of the labyrinth he called a palace. Even the sound of his footsteps faded, leaving me with no hope to follow.

My shoulders tensed, my lungs pulling in far more air than required, only to expel it in a forceful vent of frustration. The door swung open, nudging my shoulder blade with a sharp bite as it clipped against the bone. A guard frowned apologetically at me, clinging to the door handle when I yelped and spun to face him, but then he smiled warmly, stood taller, and gestured me into the room.

The room was set lavishly with rows of tables with shimmering damask linens the same color as the liquid bubbling inside the long flutes at each place setting. Empty crystal serving bowls reflected the sunlight streaming through the open arches, marking the transition between the banquet hall and the beautiful terrace beyond. Instead of cushions, delicate chairs built from slender rods lined either side of the table, tinted gold beneath the warm glow of the afternoon sun. Outside, the gurgle of running water sang an unfamiliar tune.

The air danced with a melody of aromas—roasted fowl and a mixture of spices both familiar and unknown, breads, and the sweet, tart scents of fruit. In the corner of the room, a smaller table boasted an array of small plates. A circular platter of halfmoon bread sat on one end of the table, and a jewel-toned mixture of couscous and vegetables filled a crystal bowl on the other. Between them, vibrant salads, cheeses, bowls of decadent spreads, and flatbreads for dipping erupted in heaping mounds.

I turned back to the guard at the door, raising an inquisitive brow in his direction. Aside from the guards stationed along each wall, the room appeared empty. He nodded toward the open terrace.

A pair of guards marched through the tallest archway, then moved to either side of the opening, revealing the long line of Daughters as they filed through the opening. Mother first, then Juna, and Sessu, and—I gasped. "Lurah!" *She's alive.*

My skirt billowed around my ankles as I raced toward them all, throwing my arms around them with tears beginning to brim in my eyes. They were here...they were well. Even Lurah. Rali had found them for me, just as he'd promised. My anger with him melted, if only slightly. There was still the matter of the Eldress. *And Rue*, my mind chimed in, quite unhelpfully. The tether around my heart smarted with a dull twinge of pain.

"You're here! You're all here! What happened?" I breathed, a laugh of relief freeing itself at the same time I brushed the tears from my eyes. "Was it the Riders? Khazdruki? Prisha?"

Mother smiled, the wrinkles of her familiar face folding, never reaching the milky clouds in her eyes. She held my shoulders, staring at me with a fondness that seemed to have forgotten the long years she'd spent critiquing every misstep I made. My Sisters watched us quietly, wearing identical smiles that did nothing to inspire one of my own. Something was...wrong. I felt it creeping into my bones, snaking through my veins like dark shadows of dread, wrapping around my throat until my pulse pounded loudly in my ears.

"Yes. Riders, but...never mind that," Mother croaked, a tear forming at the corner of her eyes as they bounced from the guards back to me. "A story for another day. Today, we must focus our hearts on A'i Halajan and save the rest for tomorrow. Halah's way may not always be clear to us, but we must follow the path she chooses. Hmm?" she asked in her most knowing tone, waiting for me to agree with her.

But I did not agree with her. A flurry of nerves and worry threatened to burst free if I tried to contain myself any longer. "Mother...tell me what happened. I was so worried. And the Eldress is here. Have you seen her? Will you bring me to her?"

The sagging skin at her throat moved visibly when she swallowed, eyes flickering back to the guards. "She is fine, Zara. Do not worry. Today is about you and A'i Halajan. Let us focus on Halah's blessing. Come, we really must get you ready."

I dug my heels into the sandstone tile, my knees locked and as unyielding as the towering walls around us. "Wait. I need to talk to you." I shook my head, trying to sort through all the raging worries clamoring for attention in my mind to make some sort of ordered sense of them. It was a futile effort, but I spewed the main thoughts from my mouth all at once. "We need to talk about Prisha and the Eldress. And Halah and...Rali. I don't want to marry Rali."

Mother's eyes snapped to the guard in the corner, whose lips had tightened into a firm line, his eyes darkening slits of warning. My Sisters averted their eyes, none of them daring to look at me.

"What is wrong with you all?" They shuffled their feet, finding the architectural design of the patterned sandstone to be the newest wonder of the world. My Sisters normally chatted and joked, teasing me to no end, but they'd fallen silent, repressed by some fear that fell over us like a stifling blanket.

I'd been grateful that my Sisters hadn't greeted me with the unsettling reverence they showed when I'd been chosen as Stitcher, but they hadn't greeted me like family either. They weren't acting themselves. A great rift seemed to split open between us, an impasse that couldn't be traversed. And I didn't understand why.

Mother's stiffness melted, though her smile remained forced. "Sometimes, it is hard to know what is right and what choices we must make. The Daughters coordinated this blessed day, but this union is not for you or me to decide—so do not bear that burden for yourself. May Halah guide you...she will show the way." She pulled me into a hug and tucked her chin so her mouth fell beside my ear, and I thought for a moment she may whisper some truth beneath her riddles. A stern look from the guard quickly extinguished that flame of hope. "May Halah guide us all," she murmured instead. "Come."

She grabbed my hand and led me to the terrace, her bangles and jewels jingling with each step. Her graying hair wrapped around her head in a braided crown banded with gold and silver beads that sparkled in the sun. Her woven scarf draped over her shoulders like a cape, fluttering gently behind her as she moved. My Sisters' hair had been pulled back into intricate braids, adorned with jewelry and beads in preparation for the festivities of the evening. How long ago had they arrived if they'd had time to dress themselves so extravagantly? Why didn't they come to see me right away? My stomach twisted with the ache of their oversight. Didn't they know how worried I'd been? How the weight of their disappearance had gnawed at my insides until every part of me felt raw and powerless in their absence?

I turned toward the balcony to hide the way my eyes pricked with tears. The terrace opened to the same courtyard visible from my room, and my gaze lifted from the rectangular pool, wondering which of the archways around the square led to Rue. I wished he was here.

The whole affair felt somber. The atmosphere fell hush, save for the gurgling fountain, the soft tinkling of jewelry, and the subtle clink of plates and cutlery as the Daughters helped them-selves to the spread of food.

I'd lost my appetite.

My Sisters busied themselves for hours, preparing me for the ceremony while I silently prayed to Halah for the first time in my life, begging for her refusal to bless our union. I knew better than to use magic to weave my soul to hers when I prayed, but still, I hoped she'd hear the prayers echoing fervently in my mind as my Sisters braided my hair and swept kohl across my lashes.

Let the stars choke and fade to darkness, the flames of every lamp extinguish, and the city fade to blackest night. Let no light shine upon us, so the whole realm sees our union is unblessed. Please Halah. But I dared not ask her for what I truly desired—for then, my prayers would almost certainly offend her. The venom at the pit of my stomach spread, warming my body with increasing waves of anger as my Mother and Sisters fretted over my appear-ance, readying me for the union I did not want.

Every time I made another effort to object, each time I raised my voice to protest or question Halah's decisions, Mother's eyes bulged with a scolding glare, prohibiting me from speaking anymore, communicating volumes in the way her jaw clenched, or her eyes darted warily to the guards. She did not want to discuss it. "May Halah guide you to serve your duties to the Daughters," she said, her voice lowering with a layered intensity, weaving meanings within meanings beneath meanings. Secrets I couldn't decipher any better than I could weave.

Mother held a bone-handled mirror in front of me, circling my head so I could see the beautiful design my Sisters had worked with my hair. A series of braids swept past my temples, looping through a trio of large golden hoops, interlocked and placed behind my head like a crown. My hair wove through each of the loops, gathering below the third and smallest ring, spilling along my back in soft waves.

Juna removed her dangling earrings and fixed them to my ears, her grimace masquerading as a smile. Lurah tied strips of beautiful blue gauze to the ends of my braids. The lustrous threads woven throughout the fabric gleamed in the sun, singing her talents. Sessu did not tease me or smirk when she approached, but her lips entertained the phantom of a smile when she unhooked the clasp of her necklace and fastened it behind my neck. Each of the Daughters adorned me with a personal gift, some token passed directly from their wardrobe to mine. A tradition to honor the permanence of sisterhood even after a Daughter left to begin her own family.

Finally, Mother stood before me. "You look beautiful, Zara." She reached her weathered hands behind her head, fiddling with the swooping braids wound into a crown. The emerald eye of the serpentine hairpin glinted in the sun, her fingers curled around it when she presented it to me with a smile that bordered on misery.

I dipped my chin forward so she could reach the back of my head, and she slid the hairpin into place, then gripped my hands in hers. A piece of parchment rustled between our hands, passed from her palm into mine.

"I am so proud of you," she whispered. "I have always been so proud of you, even if I failed to show it. You are...remarkable. You always have been." Her lips wobbled, lost halfway between frowning and the desire to smile, a bittersweet tint of unspoken words lingering at the corner of her mouth.

I curled my hands into fists and placed them in my lap, heart pounding dangerously against my ribcage as I resisted the temptation to unfurl the parchment that burned like fire in my hand, begging me to open it. But I smiled at Mother, adjusted the band of my skirt, and discreetly folded the paper into the beaded waist. Whatever was written on it would have to wait. It was clearly meant to stay hidden.

"Good Halah! You are not even dressed yet!" a shrill voice

squawked somewhere behind us. The woman with cropped hair and amber eyes raced toward us, her heels clipping against the tile, her legs restricted by the strange flute of a dress she wore.

"Basmina?" I asked, finally fishing her name from my memory.

"Yes, yes, hurry, dear. The sunset is coming. We must get you down to Stargate before dark. Up. Up." She turned to my Sisters. "Where is her gown? Why is she not dressed yet? You've been with her for hours. Why does this always take so long?"

Mother nodded to the dressing screen in the corner of the terrace. Layers of tapestries woven by the Daughters draped over it, creating the perfect shelter of privacy between the screen and wall. Basmina grabbed my hands and pulled me along, practically shoving me behind it. The toe of my sandal snagged on the uneven sandstone. When I regained my balance, my eyes leveled upon the most beautiful gown clipped to the top of the screen, so gorgeous it made my heart ache with the waste of its beauty on such an unhappy occasion.

Delicate lace woven by the Daughters spilled to the ground, tiny crystals splattered in clusters along the bodice and train, glimmering like little constellations. A high-necked collar defined the regally elegant tone of the dress but split into a deep plunge, stopping just between the bust, where it trailed into a line of carefully placed buttons. The hue reminded me of smoky quartz, almost purple but too mystical to be defined by just one color. It was...exceptional.

You are exceptional, Rue's words echoed in my mind, dragging like the blade of a dagger over my heart.

"Hurry up!" Basmina called impatiently, as if I hadn't heard her demands to hasten my progress the first few times. As if I wasn't uncomfortably aware of the way her foot tapped impatiently below the screen before she gave up her fidgeting and set to pacing instead.

I dropped my eyes from the dress, and my gaze darted toward the opening between the dressing screen and the wall, checking for unwanted witnesses. Instead of undressing, I quietly unwrapped the small curl of parchment that Mother had passed me.

The letters on the note were scrawled in haste, mere smudges of kohl against the parchment, but if I squinted, I could make out the words. I scanned it, and my heart thundered with increasing urgency after every word.

Zara. Read fast so they do not suspect. We cannot speak freely in front of the guards. We promised to keep his secrets so we could see you, but we had to devise a way to warn you. If you are reading this, Sessu's plan and hair styling worked.

The prince is a liar...an ally of Prisha. He's trapped us, Zara. He's kept us sheltered in a skyless room so we could not pray. The Eldress, too. None of the Daughters are safe in this city. We must get out. Help us. Please.

We will pray to Halah to intervene at the union when all the Daughters are together. We need your help...your strength. You must help us find a way out of here. Please.

Destroy the paper.

I crushed the paper in my fist. *That* was their plan? To *pray*? That wasn't enough. My jaw tightened, imagining the prince's neck clenched in my hand instead of the note. How *dare* he side with Prisha and invite Halah's Daughters into his home? Was it the same prince my elder Sisters and Aunts had spoken of before Ja' Rilaht? The one...*bending* the rules?

The tendrils of light glimmered into existence around me, responding to my call and racing toward me, winding around my fingers. But as soon as they touched me, they warped. Their light faded, the glow evaporating to leave behind the absence of light... roiling wisps of shadow. The darkness writhed like snakes around my hand, charged with energy and imbued with the anger that gripped me. I watched, both captivated and terrified by the way they bent to my will, shredding the paper in my hand and disintegrating it into dust. What...was that?

Star Thief. Destroy. Destroy it all. Shred the skies and set me free, Prisha crooned, her voice a twisting dagger in my chest.

No, I said to Prisha, my voice firm with unwavering defiance.

I snatched the gown from the clips and stepped into it. *If there's anything I'm going to destroy, it's a wedding...and your prince.*

Then you.

CHAPTER 22

STAR WELL TEA

Basmina clapped with delight when I emerged from behind the screen, dressed with confidence constructed by my resolve, though I guessed she assumed it to be an effect of the gown. She steered me toward a looking glass, clutching my shoulders as she assessed my reflection with a look of admiration. I stared back at myself. Certainty lifted my chin and squared my shoulders, painting my visage with a look of empowerment that glowed more convincingly than a touch of lip oil or blush could ever hope to replicate. I'd find a way to help my Sisters. I'd bring an end to their suffering and restore our home. I *had* to.

I turned away, meeting Mother's stony and unflinching gaze, willing her to understand that I *knew*. That I'd fight this as relentlessly as she hoped I would...that I would destroy anyone who meant to harm them and free them once and for all. From the prince. From Rashii. From Prisha's clutches.

Basmina mistook the smoldering look of anger on my face for one of demure acceptance. Nothing more than a bride prepared to fulfill the duties of an unwanted union. "It will be all right," she said, her expression thawing as she patted my shoulder.

Basmina chattered with animated gestures, leading me through the palace as she explained the customs of the ceremony and the itinerary of the evening. "The grand vizier will pour the star well tea, and when the steam settles, you will both peer into the teacup. If it has captured the light of stars, it means the ancestors favor the union, and you must pass the cup to one another to take a sip."

I nodded at the right times and plastered an expression of attentiveness on my face, but my mind continued to race, my pulse quickening at an alarming rate. The beautiful style my Sisters had crafted with my hair already loosened and strands pasted themselves to my neck with sweat. I was certain my makeup fared no better.

"The Daughters will weave and ask for Halah's blessing. Once she has demonstrated her approval, the union will be successful, and the grand feast will begin. You will be expected to visit with guests...they like it when you tell them they've been blessed by Halah, too."

"What kind of a demonstration?" I interrupted before she could continue. That part seemed important—I couldn't allow the people to believe my union with Rali had been blessed, for I had no intention of following through with that part of the plan.

"It is different every time. You will know."

Of course. They would search for a sign of Halah's blessing and be satisfied with even the smallest hint of her approval. They would see her blessing wherever they looked. A flicker of a candle. A light appearing in a darkened window. The twinkling dance of the stars above. Any suggestion of Halah's light would suffice to convince them. If only I'd learned to stitch the skies like Ahma... I'd stitch every star out of existence in anticipation of tonight.

The stars favor you, Zara.

My gaze moved skyward to the dying gold of the sunset and the spreading darkness that welcomed the stars to witness A'i Halajan. *You'd better favor me tonight,* I grumbled at them, hoping Rue's infuriating nonsense might actually hold some merit.

The Daughters trailed somberly behind us, keeping to our shadows. My thoughts drifted, wildly weaving together a plan of my own while only half-attending to Basmina's continuous jabber. If the Daughters had been invited to attend the ceremony, I would only need to play my part long enough to allow them to gather. Long enough to confront Rali. I'd demand he bring me to see the prince, then the Eldress. And Rue...*I need Rue.*

The tether binding us tugged in response to my thoughts, as though he understood, as though he could feel my desires flow through the connection. The bond pulled with every step toward the palace's central courtyard, and my breaths tightened, fresh pain stabbing through my heart in response.

The grand courtyard opened like a wide mouth before the palace, speckled by the many flecks of color in the crowd. Banners waved above their heads, a tribute to all the cities gathered to witness the union of Halah's Daughter. Vibrant music and excited chatter filled the air—a section of the crowd clapped delightedly around a dancing couple, cheering on their movements with the ringing of bright laughter.

Basmina steered me to the far end of the courtyard, shielding me from the crowd's view by angling her body in front of mine. A pair of sandstone steps curved downward from the main portico of the palace, the shimmering granite columns that Basmina dreamily referred to as Stargate.

"You'll meet at the top." She had to shout into my ear to be heard over the revelry, and my body stiffened at her words. I paused, foot hovering, my will flickering just like the candles that lined the edge of every step. What exactly would I say to Rali? I didn't want to marry him...but that didn't mean I wished to embarrass him publicly. He didn't need to be caught up in all of this mess. I just...needed to talk to him. I craned my neck to the mirrored staircase at the other end of the portico. If he was there...waiting on his side to ascend to Stargate for the ceremony...

My foot dropped back to the ground, and I shoved past a wide-eyed Basmina, hugging the curved base of the wall. Rushing past the gathered crowd, I ignored the faces gawking at me, their mouths open and their eyebrows lifted in shock as though they'd never seen a bride panic. "I just...I need to talk to Rali," I muttered to no one in particular. Silence spread through the onlookers, rising up like a dust cloud, suffocating the joyous sounds of their festivities. Perhaps I was the first Daughter to ever run away from a union...but it certainly wasn't the first time I'd skirted my duties.

My heart thundered when Rali appeared, weaving through the people, his eyes locking on mine. When he emerged from the crowd, the spectators froze, the air growing too dense and still in the absence of their breath. He marched toward me, black brows lifted in concern, his jaw tightened so severely it strained the muscles in his neck. I became acutely aware of the attention of the crowd—the lull as they craned their heads, hoping for a glimpse of whatever drama I'd incited. The chatter returned with a rush of animated voices.

Rali grabbed my arm, a gesture that looked reassuring to the crowd, but I felt the way his nails dug into my skin. I felt the anger of his gaze, hidden beneath his carefully crafted concern. My mouth parted, eyes settling upon the golden circlet atop his head. I stared too long, breathless—my weight shifting backward to re-establish the distance between us. That was why the crowd broke into furious whispers.

"It's you," I croaked hoarsely because my voice failed me. "You're the prince." A dimple formed above his lopsided smile.

"Yes," he responded, as if taxed by my acknowledgment of the obvious. "Prince Tiralish. Heir to the Sun Throne."

I shook my head, words assembling into a tidal wave of raging fury, drowning away my initial shock. I glared back at him, words seething through clenched teeth, "You *lied* to me."

His eyes darkened, a raging venom spilling into them, warning me to hold my tongue. "Obviously," he droned, dropping his facade of endearment for me. "How else could I have arranged the union I needed with you? The Daughters would not entertain the idea of a match with Prince Tiralish, but they readily fell in love with the handsome guard named Rali." He gripped my arm, angling intentionally toward the base of the stairs so my words could not be read by the crowd. I flailed against his hold, freeing my arm with one sharp movement.

"How many people knew?" How many had lied to me on his behalf?

"Does it matter? It seems everyone knows now."

"You know this union cannot happen. Halah will not allow it."

"If you want to see your precious Eldress again, I suggest you play along nicely," he whispered into my ear, all smoke and acrid venom. "I don't require Halah's blessing to get what I want, though I don't think she would deny one who carries her blood. But," he drawled, "it would be nice of you to humor the crowd's expectations. For the people's sake."

My spine grew rigid. Thoughts collided, smacking against one another until my mind shrieked into a cacophony of incomprehensible noise. What did he mean by 'carries her blood?' Surely, he must have meant me...a prince could not have been allowed to descend from the goddess's lineage. Unions between royals and descendants were banned. Just like this one should be.

"Don't flinch." He pulled me closer, his chest flush against mine as his lips claimed me. The crowd swooned in appreciation, but my legs solidified into lead, and my body melted out of my control like a tapered candle bending in half, wax drooping in the desert sun.

He pressed his forehead to mine so that horrible circlet bit into my skin. I gaped back at him, wide-eyed with horror. *Do something, Zara.* The heart of stars hummed inside me, but I shoved it down, terrified that the prince might notice. That *everyone* might notice the monstrous power inside of me. *Find a different way to fight.*

A guard trotted urgently toward Prince Tiralish, his cheeks puffed and red, his mouth rounded with shallow breaths. "Your Highness. Guards on the wall. Slaughtered."

Tiralish ripped his attention from me, but not his hand. His grip remained firmly clasped around my upper arm. "And?" the prince asked, his tone lethal.

"Khazdruki work. Venom-tipped arrows." The guard's efforts to maintain a professional composure before his prince failed—I heard the crack of fear in his voice that matched the look in his eyes.

"Fuck," Tiralish growled under his breath, twisting his head with a violent shake of frustration before recovering command. "Find them." He drew in a deep breath, too greedy for air, like a cloud amassing too much water before the rare deluges of the wet season. His storm was on the verge of unleashing.

"Yes, sir." The guard bowed curtly and hustled back through the crowd. The prince's deadened stare masked a maelstrom of emotions when he faced me, mixing together so violently they could hardly be recognized. Anger. Fury. Desperation? Hatred? A tempest on the brink of devastation. His voice rumbled when he spoke, boiling like the bubbles of a steeping pot of venom tea. "Hurry up and *pray* that your goddess accelerates her blessing of this union, little zealot, or we're all dead."

"And what will you pray to *your* goddess for, traitor?" I

snapped back, wedging the accusation of his association with Prisha like a sword through his heart. My lips drew into a hateful sneer as I plunged the dagger of my words to the hilt.

"Get the fuck up there. You know nothing," he said dismissively. His guards shouldered past him and linked their arms through mine, guiding me to turn back to the palace steps. My eyes locked on his deadened ones, refusing to break contact, willing him to witness the anger flaring to life in mine until the guards finally forced me around.

I nearly tripped over the first step when they shoved me toward it, and my Sisters flinched, hugging the sandstone wall behind the stairs. Lurah caught my elbow so I did not fall, and we passed a wordless moment of terror between us.

I nodded, though what I promised with the gesture, I didn't know. Just...a promise to not give up. To fight.

I'd always been good at fighting. Now was not the time to stop.

My legs trembled, and the entire crowd fell hushed with wonder, watching in awe as I began my slow ascent. To them, I must have looked quite regal, with the elegant train of my gown flowing over steps behind me, my chin lifted, and eyes fixated on the granite columns of the portico. But every part of me strained, resisting each step, melting like putty whenever I forced my legs to propel me upward. And my insides twisted, not just with emotion but with Rue's absence...his distance digging the anchor of his bond tighter around my heart...stretching too far. *Where are you?* I worried. I should have woken him. I should have found a way to sneak back to my chambers, but there hadn't been an opportunity. *Please come,* I willed, pulling gently against the tether. *I need you.* The line slackened instantly. A wave of relief flooded my chest.

When I reached the main landing to face Prince Tiralish once more, the dark sky crackled ominously, then thundered with a tremendous roar that shook the ground. The sound timed itself perfectly with the strike of my foot against the sandstone. As if I could claim Prisha's fury to be my own when I walked toward him, all hatred and venom.

The spectators cried out, cowering and pointing to the sky. The gilded veins of Prisha's rifts bled closer to us, the fine lines of new tears racing toward Rashii's palace.

Prince Tiralish's face paled, and his throat bobbed with a swallow, but he looked out over the crowd. "A'i Halajan!" he bellowed, his voice commanding and sure.

"Aili Halajan ru," they murmured in response.

"Daughters can't marry royalty!" a lone voice shouted in the crowd. "Halah won't allow it!"

The prince's gaze narrowed, but he softened with a smile, as though glad for the opportunity to address the matter. "Ancient law prohibited such unions, but modern times require...reconsideration. Reimagination of those out-of-date practices." He graced me with a doting expression, his tenderness at war with the hatred in his gaze. "Zara and I courted for a year, and we've fallen in love." He squeezed my hand playfully with a gesture of encouragement, but my hand burned, adverse to his grip. "We have spoken at length about our future, and in turn, Zara has communed with Halah, asking for her blessing to reconsider the rules that no longer serve Rashii's best interest."

Revulsion churned inside of me, disgusted by the way he twisted truths to suit his agenda, but least he'd given the man the courtesy of an explanation instead of simply silencing his challenge. He wrapped his arm around my shoulder, pulling me toward him to portray our united front to the crowd. Couldn't they see how my shoulders tensed? How my body recoiled from his touch? How my face contorted with disgust? Perhaps they were too entranced by his charm.

"Our union will bring two powers together, two respected

lines of *strength* and *authority*, joining our forces to fight against the enemies that threaten our people. Working together, we will restore stability and power to Rashii." He paused for a moment, letting the weight of his words sink into the hopeful hearts of his people, before raising his arm high, lifting mine and his in a triumphant gesture. "Rest assured...Halah will bless our union!" he proclaimed, then lowered his voice to a dramatic whisper. "Halah will bless us all."

The crowd murmured with excitement, and Tiralish walked me to the altar at the center of the portico. The hair raised at the back of my neck as I eyed the tapestry woven by the Daughters draped over it, spilling onto the ground. Dozens of candles in all shapes and sizes danced with life above it—gifts from the people, from cities all over the realm, Basmina had explained. A demonstration of their well-wishes for Halah's blessing.

The grand vizier shuffled forward carrying the ceremonial kettle, dressed in navy robes as dark as the night. His buttons captured the flickering candlelight of the altar, glowing like a constellation of stars down his front. He swayed gently as he walked, his steps falling in time with the deep, sonorous vibrations of the solemn city bells, struck to herald the initiation of the ceremony. The vibrations of each strike rippled through me, echoing in the chambers of my heart and throughout my tremulous limbs.

When he stopped before us, the bells quavered away into silence. He fished the tea bowl from his left pocket and set it in my hands. I stared down, wondering what to do with it, my heart still pounding to the ghosted echo of the bells.

The tea bowl shimmered in my hands. The elegant glazed pattern mimicked the nebulous clouds of the heavens, blue and silver and copper, swirled together in harmonious beauty. I wanted to smash it. My fingers tightened instinctively around the lip.

The aroma of black tea layered with sweet florals blossomed into the air, carried to my nose by a waft of steam. The grand vizier poured the star well tea with practiced precision, careful to not waste even a drop of the sacred brew.

A crack shook through the sky, and I winced when the hot tea spilled over the lip of the cup, landing on my hand. The prince's attention turned upward, his eyes lifting warily. From the corner of his mouth, he muttered toward the grand vizier. "Can we hurry this along?"

But my attention fell over his shoulder to the shadows accumulating at the far end of the portico, and blazing amethyst eyes locked on mine. My heart jolted, pulsing with a rush of relief. *Help me.*

"Pass the tea," Tiralish seethed, wrenching it from my grasp and peering into it. The suggestion of a frown frosted over his face, and I smirked. Shadows stretched above us, cloaking the twinkling stars from view, denying them access to the star well tea.

Thank you, I mouthed to Rue, who met my eyes with an intensity that made me shiver, the corner of his mouth lifted into his signature, devious smile. I could just...kiss him.

The prince did not miss a beat. Unperturbed, he lifted the bowl to his mouth and sipped deeply.

"The stars have answered! The ancestors approve," the grand vizier shouted behind us.

My attention snapped to him. *What stars?* Not a single one blinked above. Not *one single star* pierced through Rue's shadows to cast its light into the tea. The surface of the brew showed nothing but...tea. Just tea. Tiralish knew it, I knew it, the grand vizier knew it. But the spectators swooned with admiration, hanging onto every romanticized notion of the ceremony, believing any sign affirming our match. In fact, they probably found it more impressive that the stars had found their way to the tea through the thick cloud of shadow.

The prince shoved the tea bowl back to me, a look of warning in his eyes. "Drink, my love," he cooed in a tender voice undercut by the poison of his hatred.

A thunderous boom made the surface of the star well tea ripple as I stared into it—even the tea shivered at the prospect of passing through my lips. A cry lifted from the crowd, followed by another collective shout. A gilded gash stretched across the sky, oily darkness seeping from the spidering veins. They ran toward us like wisps of smoke, crossing right above our heads, disappearing behind the patch of Rue's shadows and emerging on the other end.

The prince's eyes blazed when he looked back at me. "A light shines above us...Halah's chosen to bless us, after all," he said through a dangerous smile, triumph written across his face.

"Only a traitor would see Prisha's curse and call it a blessing," I said through gritted teeth. He reached for my wrist, snapping his fingers around it like a viper's fangs.

"Drink the damn tea," he whispered in my ear.

A familiar humming called to me, simmering beneath the crackle of Prisha's sky. Winding and weaving—a compass's call to home. The Daughters, weaving prayers. At the same time, the shadows around us thickened, enveloping us in a swirling cloud of darkness—a magic I recognized with equal familiarity. My eyes snapped to Rue's, my head shaking almost imperceptibly in warning. *Do not implicate yourself in this...don't show them what you really are. Only as a last resort.*

With his hand wrapped around my wrist and nostrils flaring, the prince sneered into the crowd. My Sisters sat cross-legged at the base of the stairs, arms connected, tethered by the roots of their weaving magic, their eyes milky white and vacant.

"What are they doing?" he snapped at me, assuming them to be the cause of the disturbances. "Make them stop."

A smile uncurled from my lips. "Basmina told me they were

meant to weave at the union. Besides, Mother never listens when I ask her to stop praying. I doubt she'll start listening now."

The rifts above crackled ominously. "Drink the tea," he urged. I narrowed my eyes, and his jaw clenched with fury as he pushed the cup toward my face.

I'd already had that choice taken from me once. *Never again.*

Rage overwhelmed me, and I splashed the contents of the bowl onto the prince's face. He doubled over, clutching where the hot tea burned his skin with a shriek, his mouth gaping and eyes contorted with pain. I turned the tea bowl over in my hand, staring at the glazed surface. Not a star to be found, and not a drop of tea remaining to pass through my lips. *To hell with his union.* The bowl shattered into a thousand perfect shards of rebellion at my feet.

I pushed past him and ran, crossing the distance toward Rue.

Shrieking rose up from the crowd, one voice at first, then several, then a complete frenzied panic. "Khazdruki!" The word echoed through the crowd, passed from neighbor to neighbor with increasing urgency and fear.

I paused, turning in horror toward the square. *The Khazdruki of the north?* I'd heard so many whispers of the tensions with Khazdra, but...an *invasion?* Now?

The scene unraveled into chaos, spectators shoving and screaming, trampling over one another to get away from the lumbering shadows that towered a whole head taller than Rashiiki men, their curved blades slashing indiscriminately through the crowd.

The grand vizier shouted, his voice shrill and piercing as a Khazdruki wrapped the bulging muscles of his arm around the old man's neck. His torso was bare save for the layers of jagged beads and the ancestral markings tattooed over his biceps. Vikings of the sand and sea north of Taara.

A hissing sound from above startled me, and I stumbled backward. Four husky shadows descended the length of the granite columns, slipping all the way to the base before dropping to their hands and knees with a solid *thud*. One barreled into Rue, but he wrestled him to the ground, slicing the man's throat with his stolen bone blade. He regained his footing and sprinted toward me, but another Khazdruki rammed a shoulder into Rue, sending both of them tumbling across the portico.

I shrieked when another pair of arms wrapped around my throat, pulling me off balance. My nails raked over the Khazdruki's forearms, and I gasped for air, kicking my heels against the sandstone to regain my footing. He tightened his grip around my neck, flexing his muscles until—

I can't breathe.

Rue, I screamed in my mind, still thrashing against the Khazdruki's hold, legs scrambling beneath me.

The thread of light tugged sharply at my heart, and I craned my neck, straining every muscle in my back to follow its path to my shadow monster. My Rue.

When our eyes locked, a wave of understanding rushed through our bond, but not with words. It was an innate awareness of one another...a mutual agreement. The tether between us pulsed with light, then solidified into obsidian shadow.

Shrill screams rose through the height of the clamor, ripping my attention from Rue. I stared, paralyzed by numbing horror, as the Khazdruki sliced through Sessu, then Basmina. Basmina's blank eyes gazed toward the heavens, lifelessly watching the orb of light that carried Sessu's soul to the ancestors in the night sky. A new star to guide us.

Something inside of me broke. I shouted, my voice warped by gut-wrenching grief, and Prisha's sky fractured above me—the sound worse than the screeches of a thousand ravenous crawlers. The sound of obliteration. *Shred the skies, Sky Render. Unleash your power.*

And I did. Not because Prisha commanded it, but because dark energy flowed from me, whether I willed it or not. It wasn't the beautiful, quiet magic of the Daughters' weaving, nor the powerful, unwieldy force of the heart of stars buried deep inside of me. This magic felt like rage. No. *Vengeance.* This magic twisted and burned, darkened and destroyed. It flowed through my bond with Rue, filling me with shadows until they no longer fit within me. My body forced them outward and upward when I could no longer contain them, reaching toward the rifts in the sky, shredding the gaps wider. The Khazdruki restraining me howled in anguish, falling into a pile of writhing pain. I did not turn to see what damage I had inflicted.

I stood, vaguely aware of the shrieking crowd, the fearful clamor, and Rue's widened, unblinking gaze that watched me with panic. Producing a guttural shout, I sent the tendrils of shadow flailing, directing them toward the sky. They groped within the rifts, twisting and writhing, tightening their unrelenting hold, grabbling and snarling in knots around whatever they touched.

I had already stolen one monster from Prisha's sky by accident. Now, I would take them all. *On purpose.*

They fell like meteors, one after the next. Dark streams of toxicity from the In Between splashed into smoky puddles at my feet, shadows rising and dancing into a twisted duet at my side. Crawlers. Bulgroiches. More winged Guardians like Rue. All bound by the shadows flowing through me. And the pièce de résistance rising from the longest pool of darkness stretched across the portico. Horns first, then spiked crown, a vicious maw, horrible barbed wings and a thrashing, angry tail.

The dragon's head leveled on me, eyes as dark as coal and head tilted as it considered the horrible pounding of my heart within my chest. Then the world stilled, and the night hushed. The fighting ceased to exist in that moment, that void-like gap in time when all terrors held their breath, leashed by the shadows flowing between me and Rue.

Kill the Khazdruki, I demanded.

The dragon blinked with placid understanding.

Rue's eyes darkened, all traces of the microcosmic universe within them drowned by blackest night. When I turned toward him, his gaze passed through me without recognition—everything that made him Rue devoured by the web of shadows I spun, controlled by the leash of power between us. Just like the rest of the puppets attached to our shadows.

I pulled on the threads, controlling the movements just as Rue had controlled his dragon when the crawlers attacked in the desert. Regret shattered like splinters through my heart when I saw Rue bend to my will like the others, but I did not have a moment to acknowledge any misgivings or change my course of action. The Khazdruki ripped through the crowd with a bellowing yell, and Prisha's rifts spewed blackness into the crowd...shadows that Prisha would twist into the shape of nightmares.

This was all a nightmare.

Everyone was dying.

I balled my hands into fists and raised my arms in sync with the deep, drawing breath that gathered air into a swirling storm inside me, then unleashed a soul-shattering scream. I flung my hands to my sides, fingers outstretched and willing the creatures to do as I commanded. A vacuum of noise fell into the void left behind by my furious screech, and shadows billowed all around me. Bulgroiches slashed through the bare chests of the Khazdruki, lacerating their hearts into ribbons that dangled like sinewy trophies from their jaws. Crawlers shredded and scratched, reducing the hostile men to piles of mulched flesh. And the winged men, the Guardians, flew through the sky, severing the

Khazdruki's howling heads from their spines with each confident slash of their swords.

When no Khazdruki man remained upright, I doubled down on my power. Clenching my fists with a surge of shadow, I crumpled the creatures I'd summoned until they were nothing but black, pulverized dust. Soot upon the ground. The scorched remains of chaos. They withered away, disintegrating into a graveyard at my feet. All except one—I spared one. The one that tugged at my heart, reining me back from that place of oblivion, that brink of forgetting who I was...stopping me from losing myself to shadow.

My heart jolted with the horror of what I'd done.

"Monster!" The word echoed through the crowd, gaining traction as it expanded from hushed murmurs to condemning shouts. Rue pushed up to his elbows and held me in his piercing gaze, the amethyst galaxies of his eyes painting an emotion I couldn't define. One that punctured a hole in my lungs, making it impossible to draw in air. Painful to even try.

What would he think of me now? He'd asked me to let him make his own decisions, to pick his own master, but hadn't I just stolen that choice from him? I knew how it felt to be robbed of the freedom to choose.

He collapsed, his energy spent by the power I'd drawn from him.

Monster. Monster. Monster. The word repeated through the crowd until it crawled its way into my heart and soul. It manifested until the word etched itself into my being—becoming an irrefutable truth and an undeniable part of me. Their stares fell upon me like daggers, wounding me with the way they reviled my presence. Even the Daughters looked at me as though they didn't know me. They gazed, expressions gaping—trepidation written across wide eyes.

I'd saved them from the Khazdruki...I'd harnessed Prisha's

monsters for good instead of evil, but all they saw was another monster.

Perhaps it was the truth.

Numbness washed over me. I turned slowly, facing each of the condemning glares looking back at me.

Monster.

Guards gathered around me and shackled irons to my wrists. I did not fight. I couldn't.

I couldn't do anything but stare, withering away inside until there was nothing left of me but an empty husk.

And the name I deserved.

CHAPTER 23

MORALS

They locked me in a pit. High, natural walls stretched above me, swallowing me into the forgotten chamber of its belly, casting me into shadow. The prison had been carved from the earth, the walls rough but not textured enough to climb to my freedom. Not that I'd tried...there was no point. Guards posted at the top made it impossible to scale the pit without notice, and besides, I didn't deserve freedom. There was no need to try.

Instead, I sat, crumbled, cross-legged and filthy at the bottom, playing the image of Rue's expression in my mind until my insides melted into an acidic state that burned and burned, consuming me from the inside out. Did he think I was a monster? *Was* I a monster? I hadn't meant to...channel his power or command him or...whatever I had done. But I had. And he probably never wanted to see me again. To him, I must be no better than Prisha.

I couldn't bring myself to test the connection between us to see if he would respond. What if they had captured him, too? I'd done nothing to help him escape or protect him. Would they kill him if they discovered who he was? What if...what if he didn't answer my call simply because he didn't *want* to?

I couldn't bear the thought that I'd reach for Rue and feel nothing in answer, so I didn't reach for him at all. I wasn't brave enough to face that level of grief. Not yet.

Sunlight streaked across my face as I slumped against the side of the pit, but voices stirred me from my semi-consciousness. A rope ladder unfurled, tumbling to the bottom. I stared vacantly at it, too exhausted to move, too apathetic to try.

A pair of brown boots disturbed the dust from the ground, and I looked up to find Rali considering me with a ponderous frown.

"Well, that ceremony didn't go as planned," Rali began, shoving a hand into his pocket and shrugging. *No. Not Rali—Prince Tiralish.* His tone felt so light—so at odds with the venomous hatred I felt for him. He remained oblivious to my scowl while he continued, "No matter, though." He shook his head. "Union or not, Halah gave me exactly what I needed. We'll work well together."

Work well together? Is he insane? Did the Khazdruki bludgeon him over the head during their invasion? I opened my mouth to toss the first insult I could muster at him, but questions clamored loudly in my mind, each one rioting its way to my tongue, demanding to be voiced. *Why choose Prisha? Why me? Why force me into a union that was not only unwanted, but against the law? Why trap my Sisters? Why, why—*

"Why, Rali?" I finally spat at him. "Or should I call you Tiralish?" The question was open-ended, but I was too exhausted to put my thoughts into any coherent order. *Why* was what I most needed to know, however indirect or undefined the query seemed.

He studied me at length, the depths of his eyes calculating some hidden formula I couldn't decipher. "First, I think you owe me an explanation of whatever just happened," he replied, his voice calm but lacking any warmth.

"I can't," I growled, angrier than I'd intended to be, but once the fury was allowed to unfurl, it built and swelled uncontrollably inside of me. Whatever had happened at the ceremony hadn't been planned—I doubted I could repeat it even if I'd tried. I *knew* I didn't want to repeat it. I didn't know who or what I was anymore, and I'd never feared my power more. But *he* didn't deserve to know any of that. I owed him *nothing*.

I narrowed my eyes at the man who'd lied and manipulated, who'd sided with Prisha and trapped my Sisters. *Why?* The question repeated itself in my mind, demanding to be answered. "Go away, Prisha's pet," I spat out instead, turning my shoulder to him. I stiffened my spine, setting myself to admire the very uninteresting crevices and cracks that puckered the walls.

He stepped in front of me, refusing to be dismissed so easily. His nostrils flared, but he made an obvious effort to control his temper. "Do not call me that. I am Prince Tiralish of Rashii, and you understand *nothing*. You have no idea." He turned away from me, pacing the length of the pit with wide, agitated strides. "I have responsibilities to my people. I did what I had to do to protect them. They were risky decisions, sure...but decisions that *had* to be made." He paused, turning back toward me with an almost apologetic tint to his expression. As though he wanted me to understand and to excuse his behavior. To stop imagining I could flay the skin from his body with a mere gaze. He sighed wearily. "Nobody else would protect us. Not our king. Not the Daughters. Not even your precious Halah. Only *Prisha* answered my prayers. She promised what everyone else could not. What else was I supposed to do?"

"You stupid idiot," I seethed, hardly stopping to consider the impact of throwing such an insult at the prince. It was less than half the insult he deserved. "You thought Prisha would help you?

Help with *what*? She's a monster. She'll destroy everyone...
including you. Whatever she promised you was a lie."

"Yes, well. It was a risk I had to take. I ran out of options,
Zara. My father was useless...whenever the council met to discuss
foreign relations or the growing tension with Khazdra, he seemed
to develop an allergy that made his eyes glaze over until he was so
ill, he needed to escape back to his little plants and his bees." His
face twisted with disgust, as though the very mention of King
Onros's bees had stung his tongue. "He does not have what it
takes to be a ruler. He was handed the throne by my grandfather...
he did not earn it. I've had to work twice as hard to make up for
his inadequacies, and I've made mistakes in my desperation. But
the good news is that I don't *need* Prisha anymore. You changed
that." He cupped my chin in his hand and forced my gaze to meet
his eyes. "I have something better now. *You.*"

"The Sundom Desert will freeze over before I'd ever consider
helping you." The temperature of my voice chilled the air so
noticeably, there was a chance that very impossibility would
happen sooner than anticipated. But why he thought I'd consider
any arrangement between us was beyond me...whatever his
excuses, whatever his justifications, they were weak. Just like him.

"Don't be foolish, Zara," he urged. "Those Khazdruki at the
union? They won't be the last." Tiralish set himself back to
pacing, running his hands rather aggressively through the tangles
of his unruly hair. "My idiot father didn't listen to me about the
unrest in the north. He didn't heed the threats or the rumblings. I
told him—" He stomped around the room, his feet striking ruthlessly against the innocent ground. The ground had done him no
harm...yet all his clamoring suggested a personal vendetta against
it. My eyebrows lifted, considering the thought. *Wouldn't be the
worst thing if the floor swallowed him whole.*

"I told him we should send a firm message to put Khazdra
back in their place, but he is too old or too tired or too incompe-

tent to protect the Sun Throne and his people from the usurpers. He didn't take it seriously. All he cares about is bees and nectar and honey. But me? I've done *everything* I can to ensure Rashii's safety. And sometimes, being in power means taking risks to protect those who rely on you. Surely you understand that?"

"I assure you, I understand nothing of your twisted excuse for morals."

Tiralish groaned and tossed his head back. "Everything I've done has been to protect my people. *Everything.*"

"Well, you've done a shit job of it."

"So have you."

I blinked blankly back at him for a few breaths. I hated every part of what he said, but it rang with truth. Sighing wearily, I closed my eyes and settled my anger. I needed answers, not more fights. "So you sided with Prisha because you no longer trusted the Daughters to help you? You thought Prisha would give you the protection you needed."

"The Daughters have been growing weaker and weaker for years. Your Eldress is dying...when's the last time she stitched the skies? *Prisha* promised me her army, Zara. She promised me strength. And to have Prisha's power *behind* us instead of against us? What ruler in their right mind would deny her?"

"One with proper morals."

"Oh shut up with your holy devoutness and *morals.*"

I snorted. "Holy devoutness? Do you know anything about me at all?" *If you did, you'd know I'm just a disaster. A monster.* Hadn't he seen what I did at the union? The ache in my heart festered.

The prince regarded me curiously. "You know...I *have* realized something interesting about you. I think there's more to you than you let on."

I laughed dismissively, but my pulse quickened, thumping

through my veins. "How so?" I asked. Let him elaborate on his suspicions...I'd tell him *nothing*.

"Well, the Stitcher's magic prohibits Prisha from entering this realm. The very existence of a Stitcher's magic repels her, operating like twin poles of a magnet. Naturally, Prisha wanted me to kill the Eldress to resolve that little issue, but I kept her alive as...insurance."

"Where is she?" I demanded immediately, interrupting his train of thought.

He waved his hand to stop me. "Alive. Sickly, but surviving. But that is not the point. She's been locked away...no access to earth or sky. No ability to use her powers. And I *thought* that might be enough to free Prisha from her prison if the Eldress's magic was subdued, but there's still something holding her back. The rifts are plenty wide. The time is favorable. But *still*, she's trapped. I can think of only one explanation." He paused and inspected me. "Do you know anything about that? There isn't a new Stitcher, is there?"

I stiffened, but put every ounce of my focus into appearing natural. "Halah hasn't spoken to us in years."

"Hmmm," he responded, placing a gentle hand on my shoulder. "Because that display at the union...it's become very clear you are not just a Daughter. And I think you know more than you're telling me."

"Perhaps you should let me talk to the Eldress, and then maybe I'd know whatever you—"

"Or," he interjected, "*maybe*...you will do exactly what I say because if you don't, you're putting the whole goddessdamned Realm of Taara at risk. If you want to live...if you want to keep your precious Stitcher alive, we need to work together. So tell me, *what do you know?*"

"You're delusional."

"Goddessdamnit, Zara. You need to help. Stitch the skies. Or open them." He waved his hand with an agitated attempt of ambivalence. "I don't give a damn. But whatever power you have, it is *your* responsibility to protect the people with it. We won't win against the Khazdruki without your help, and you *know* we won't win against Prisha. Those monsters...if you can command the crawlers and the bulgroiches...the Khazdruki will run back to their sand skiffs and disappear beyond the Saanan Mountains. *You* can stop them."

I flinched. No part of me wanted to help the prince, but the weight of responsibility sank like iron in my gut. Of course I wanted to stop Prisha...to protect the realm from all threats, but how could I do that when *I* had become a threat? When I couldn't figure out how to access the gentle weaving the Daughters had used for centuries? When I'd buried the stolen heart of stars deep inside me where it could never cause any harm because I couldn't learn to control it? When I'd panicked at the union ceremony and somehow channeled Rue's powers as my own, putting everyone, including him, in danger? Any form of magic I touched I corrupted with my unpredictable brand of chaos... my lack of control. I shouldn't be allowed to use any of it. "I... can't. Not without the Eldress. Let me go, please. Let me talk to her."

"I can't let you go. You're too dangerous." His eyebrows lifted, and an airy chuckle escaped him to show his shock at the gall of my request. "Didn't you see how the people feared you? I can't let a *monster* walk among them. It would be unconscionable."

"And yet I don't see you locking yourself up," I quipped, but the sneer on my face deepened as he glared back at me. The sting of his insult burned, clawing to reopen the raw wounds inside of me.

"I only did what I had to, Zara."

"But why? You call *me* the monster, but at least I'm not a liar and a traitor like you. *I* didn't side with Prisha. *Why,* Tiralish? Why me? I don't understand."

The prince looked at me as though I were an idiot. "I thought you'd be intelligent enough to piece this together. Prisha needed me to find and kill the Stitcher...but how could I find the Stitcher when you hid in your little guryas beneath your Eldress's illusions? I knew if I could marry one of you, if I could gain your trust, I'd find my way to the guryas and the rest of the clan."

"But you found them anyway. Without my help."

"I did. When I arrived to 'rescue' your Sisters from the staged attack, they came with me willingly, but imagine my disappointment when I discovered the Eldress was nowhere to be found. I guess her absence was the reason the camouflaging magic failed, allowing us to find the clan in the first place. Well, that and Lurah's assistance. Her desperation to warn you helped us find the clan faster."

"But then I handed the Eldress right to you. Because I trusted you." I said the words as an accusation, but he didn't even flinch. I shook my head, disgust bubbling like a vat of rancid tallow in my belly. "But that still doesn't explain. Why me? Why my Sisters? Just...let them go. They have nothing to do with this."

"Are you not listening to me? They have *everything* to do with this. Prisha needed the Stitcher and your precious Eldress...it became clear very quickly that Ahma was not the one I needed. That there was another blessed with Halah's power. And I refused to let any of the Daughters out of my sight until I'd found what I needed. Prisha was very...persistent with her demands." His body shrank visibly to reflect his fear, and my mind raced, recalling the shadows in my dream in the desert...the shadow that shrank with fear in Prisha's presence as they discussed the Stitcher's demise. The one I'd wrongly presumed to be Rue.

"How have you been speaking to Prisha?" I asked, carefully placing my words.

"In my dreams...through my mind. I couldn't run from her even if I wanted to...she always finds me. But with you here..."

"No. *How?* Only the descendants of gods can commune with them."

He smirked, holding his cards close to his chest, waiting to see if I would uncover his secrets. My lips parted with a faint gasp, noticing the complexion of his skin, still tan but lighter than most Rashiiki, and the dusting of freckles across his nose. The jade green eyes...green just like my Sisters'. Like *mine*.

"You...you're a descendant of Halah?" I breathed. "How?" It wasn't possible. He'd been born to the royal family, the first-born son and heir of King Onros and the late Queen Vilaa, who died during his birth. Royals and descendants were not permitted to join. Queen Vilaa could not have shared Halah's blood.

"My father has his vices, and I suspect he has many heirs hidden within the city. But when Queen Vilaa went into labor, her son was breached, and neither survived the birth. Rather than announcing the tragedy and their deaths, he sent for his mistress, taking in the bastard she'd birthed just a few weeks earlier, claiming it to be Vilaa's surviving son. Claiming the bastard as his rightful heir."

"And that bastard—"

"Is me," he confirmed with a nod. "Prince Tiralish. Son of Drua, Daughter of Halah, and King Onros, ruler of Rashii." He bowed regally, then winked at me. "Though let's keep that last bit between us...wouldn't want his other bastards to think they have a right to the throne."

"But...how?"

"Being a prince comes with a certain set of privileges. Access to information. Training. Support of following one's interests and hobbies. When I was little, my father used to let Drua visit me to teach me the ways of Daughters. I loved her...my nursemaid, who cared for me and made me feel special. Who protected me. At least until the day she revealed who she truly was." His face soured. "After that, she never visited me again. Abandoned me to live with my wretched father. Alone. Like I no longer mattered."

Something glimmered in the rim of his eyes, and he turned to inspect the wall of the pit.

"In my loneliness, I prayed for Halah's favor. For her to help me and protect me. To make me into a better ruler than my father so I could do right by the people. So I could protect them from the threats he did not care to fight against. But it was not Halah who answered. Only Prisha heard my prayers."

So it *had* been him. Prisha had commanded him to kill the Eldress, not Rue. She'd commanded him to gather the Daughters...to subdue us so she could return and kill us all. And he'd turned against his own blood...his own lineage...for what?

"But with you here," he repeated in an attempt to regain my attention. I paused midstep, realizing I'd taken to mirroring his habit of pacing. "I don't have to be afraid of her anymore. You can save us, Zara. I see that now. Prisha was...a mistake. But you...my prayers were answered when Halah sent you to me." He grabbed my wrist in his hand, and with his other, he let his knuckles brush against my skin, trailing the length of my cheekbone. His eyes melted, turning the freckles inside his jade eyes to the warm color of honey. "I know you're angry with me...I know you probably wish you could set your army of bulgroiches upon me."

He chuckled, but there was an edge of nerves hidden in the way his eyes darted toward mine. "But I think with the right *motivations*, you and I could see eye to eye, and you could be...useful." He kissed my forehead and then stepped away, whistling a shrill treble between two fingers. The rudimentary ladder spilled back to the bottom, tumbling down the side of the pit. Tiralish caught the bottom rung in his hand.

"Where are you going?" I asked hurriedly, panic already clawing at my throat.

"To check on your Sisters and precious Eldress. You...*do* care about them, don't you?" His hand wrapped around the side of the rope ladder, and he paused, letting the weight of his words sink into my gut, poisoning me slowly.

"Are you—are you suggesting you're going to hurt them?"

"I don't see any reason to, as long as you do what I expect."

What exactly did he expect? I winced, bracing myself for yet another set of obligations I couldn't fulfill. I couldn't use my magic...I couldn't risk it. *Please don't ask me to.* I'd doomed us all.

"I'll leave the pit open for you. You're lucky. Most Daughters don't get that luxury under my care." He nodded up toward the gaping hole at the top of my prison. "I can be very accommodating, you know, as long as I trust you to use the access to your power responsibly. I *can* trust you to be responsible, can't I, Zara?"

I glared at him, not deigning to give him a response. Nothing I did with magic was responsible.

He wrongly accepted my silence as confirmation.

"Wonderful." He waved grandly toward the open ceiling. "Access to earth and sky, for your cooperation. Get me an army, Stitcher, and keep Prisha away. Mess up, and I'll make sure your Sisters are the first to die. I'll be back to check on your progress."

"I don't know how!" I howled in panic. Tears pricked in my eyes at the prospect of reaching for the magic that scared me, the magic I didn't fully comprehend.

The prince smiled, but I saw through the masquerade of compassion plastered on his face. "You'll find a way."

He hiked his knee up and stepped onto the bottom rung. I had half a mind to pursue him, to rip him off balance or tear through the ropes above him, but even if I survived such stupidity, the guards would release the ladder and send me to my death. I fell in a heap on the dirt floor, crossing my arms and my legs and glaring at the wall.

When he reached the top, his dark shadow leaned toward one of the guards, and he spoke in a vociferous whisper, clearly wishing for me to overhear. "Send for me if she requires more... concrete motivation. I can arrange to have one of her Sisters executed if it would help."

CHAPTER 24

A Familiar Sound

Day faded to darkness, and my spirit faded to despair. For hours, I'd beckoned the tendrils of light used by the Daughters, but they slipped away from my hold, shivering at the mere brush of my fingers, little snakes skittering away from the desert sun. Even the remnants of Halah's magic hated me. I dared not try to use any stronger magics, for I could feel Prisha's rage lingering at the edges of my consciousness, coursing at unpredictable moments through my veins, a desert dust storm rising without warning, clouding my own reason and logic in the whirlwind of her madness. *Shred the skies, Star Thief. Kill them. Kill them all, then hang them in the starry sky.*

Hugging my legs, I wiped a tear from the corner of my eye against my knee. *No tears,* I scolded myself. *You are a fighter, Zara.* But I had nothing left inside of me to fight with. I had plenty of tears, though. *Those* were available in abundance.

The crackling of Prisha's rifts above taunted me, laughing at my efforts to collect the ribbons of light necessary for stitching. Cajoling me to unleash the full extent of my magic. To rip the skies wider. To unleash the monsters. But I knew better than to search out the power I'd used at the union. It belonged to Rue, and I'd never risk using it again. I had to find another way.

Pressing the bridge of my nose against my knees until it hurt, I groaned. Would Prince Tiralish really kill my Sisters if I didn't meet his demands? Somehow, I didn't doubt him. He had no morals when it came to doing whatever he felt necessary.

I took a deep breath and reached for the threads of light once more, but they slithered away, slipping like oil over water. Bellowing with frustration, I slammed my fists against the rough floor. The skin at the base of my hand erupted with searing pain —I'd already repeated this futile exercise enough times to rip it open and expose the meaty pulp below. *Smash, smash, smash.* I screamed with each strike until the pain in my hands matched a fraction of what I felt in my heart.

A familiar sound—the steady beat of wings slashing through air—broke through the sound of my ragged sob, breaking down the dam holding back the full flood of my worries. I frowned toward the opening, squinting to make out the source of the scuffle above and shifted to my knees. My heart raced, pounding with emotions mixing into a destructive gale that ripped through my body, knocking me off-kilter. If it was Rue... how could I face him? Snakes writhed inside of me. What would he say to me? And what could I possibly say back to him? There was no way to excuse what I'd done. I knew how important the freedom to choose his own course was to him, and I had robbed him of it. Used him. I was no better than Prisha.

I listened to the quiet, stifled gurgle—the sound of a sliced throat filling with blood, drowning out the victim's last word. Then, a heavy *thud*. And another. And another.

Perhaps he was coming to destroy me, too. And maybe I deserved it. But seeing hatred transform his face? Hatred for me?

That was more than I could bear. *Please spare me that...at least spare me that. Let my death be quick.*

I watched the mouth of the pit, wiping my tear-streaked face clean, despite knowing full well my bloodied hands were doing a poor job of it. A black figure descended through the long chute, wings raised high to decelerate the rush of his landing. *Rue.*

He landed in a kneel, fist stabilizing his rough collision at the bottom of the pit, pebbles rattling against the earth as though the force of his impact angered them. Or perhaps they simply understood the emotion radiating from his amethyst eyes and cowered wisely in response. My heart rattled, too.

His gaze found mine, unwavering and certain. Not a trace of hatred touched the curve of his mouth, the intensity of his stare. "Zara."

"You came." My tongue scratched like sand against the roof of my mouth, my throat sticking with the prickly dryness, as though I'd tried to swallow a mouthful of dune nettles.

"Of course I came," he responded, furrowing his eyebrows and folding his wings neatly behind his shoulders. We stared at one another. I swallowed, hesitating with uncertainty, and I flinched at the raw pain inside of my throat. His head tilted, and he swept his gaze from my eyes to the bob of my throat and back to my lips, his jaw twitching with tension and rigidity with some moment of indecision.

"I'm so sorry," I said, my voice croaking with strain as tears flooded my cheeks. "I didn't mean to. I don't know what happened...I lost control. I—"

"You did what you had to do to survive," he interrupted a bit tersely. "To help us all survive. I could never fault you for that."

"I suppose you've come to kill me?" I asked weakly, choking on my own sadness. I wouldn't blame him. Not after what I'd done. The salt of my tears flooded my tongue.

His distance, the icy wall he built between us, shattered. He rushed toward me, pulling me into his arms and wrapping his wings around us, forming a shield to block out everything but this precarious moment shared between us. "Not today, Starlight."

Warmth flooded through my body, branching into my limbs and spreading life back through me. It felt dangerously similar to hope. The press of his forehead against mine and the strength of his arms around me wrapped me in safety. But the ephemeral moment quickly burned away, souring into something darker. I shoved my hands into his chest and pushed.

"Where were you?" I demanded, cinching my brows together. He'd been alive. He'd been well. He'd left me in this hole for hours to worry and fade and rehash the vivid memory of my failures. I hadn't called for him through the tether binding us together, but he also hadn't called for *me*. He'd left me in silence with nothing but self-torment for company. Had he been angry with me?

His cheeks tightened with the smallest flinch, and he did not reach for me again, no matter how badly my conflicted body wished him to. Instead, he ran a hand through the hair by his temple. "The guards are everywhere. I came as soon as I could... there'd be no way to help you if I got myself locked up, too."

"They're searching for you?" Of course they were. *Oh Halah, this is all my fault.* I should have been more careful, more reserved. They must have seen...they saw the way I controlled him...the way he bent to my will like the rest of Prisha's monsters. They'd know, and they'd kill him and...

Guilt turned my insides into a dripping, rancid slosh that even the village pigs would reject. Why did he chance coming here? He should be gone...he should have escaped and run as far away from Rashii as possible. As far away from *me* as possible. But he hadn't. The tether between us tightened around my heart, wrapping me with a squeeze of reassurance...with steadfastness. He hadn't run. He'd come for me. Through all the dangers and the unknowns and despite my errors, he'd come for me. "H—how did you get here?"

His mouth quirked into the infuriating half smile I'd somehow grown fond of, and my anger with him melted away like King Onros's honey, dripping through the crevices of a wooden spoon. "I am a shadow summoner, Zara. I know how to disappear in the darkness." He paused, his fingers flexed as though wishing to reach for me, but restraining themselves from wherever they'd intended to wander. "Once I'd found where they'd hidden you, I had to wait until sundown. The night is my friend...full of shadows and darkness and stars that lead back to you." He shared a sad-hued smile, painted by the shadows haunting his eyes.

I threw my arms around him and buried my face into the dip between his chest and shoulder, and his body shuddered against mine as we folded into each other. "I'm sorry," I tried again. "At the union....I don't know what happened. I didn't mean to...I just...reacted, and everything went wrong." Pulling away, I looked up into his eyes, my cheeks wet with fresh tears. "I told you I was broken," I said, my breath dragging through my ribs. "You were never the monster. *I am.*"

He growled under his breath and pulled me closer. "*Never* say that about yourself again," he commanded, his conviction rumbling between his ribs with the sound of an ominous thunderhead. "Nothing about you is flawed, Zara." The rough pad of his thumb brushed a tear from my cheek, and I bit my bottom lip, holding back the very real possibility of a fresh onslaught of tears. "Anyone who says otherwise is a fool. The stars favor you."

A halfhearted, salt-filled laugh spilled from me. "Then I hope they do me the favor of swallowing you whole," I teased, rolling my eyes with a failed effort of lightheartedness. But I didn't mean it. Of course I didn't mean it. If anything, they should swallow *me* for the disaster I'd become. My tongue subconsciously swept the tears from my lip, and Rue's gaze flickered down.

"If that's what you want, Starlight, I'm sure they'll listen," he responded, his tone turning gravelly.

"It's not what I want," I admitted in a whisper.

He met my gaze with so much intensity, so much meaning written across the twin amethyst starscapes that I felt every last hesitation crumble. The energy radiating from his body mingled with mine, demanding more, demanding closeness. "And what *do* you want?" he asked, his tone layered—a complex arrangement of notes that sent an appreciative shiver down my spine.

My breath hitched at the lack of air between us, the way a mere measure of space existed between his body and mine. And the way I wanted to shred that space out of time and existence, despite my best judgment.

I knew there were a thousand things I should say in response, a thousand more appropriate answers to the question, but my gaze betrayed me. It wandered to his lips, asking for what I knew I should *never* hope to have.

He groaned as the last traces of his reserve collapsed, accepting the path of my eyes as my answer. His fingers wound through my hair, and he pulled me toward him, pressing his lips against mine, taking care to taste the tears that lingered on my lips, shattering the last pieces of the wall I'd built between us. The wall I'd built to shield myself from *feeling* more than to protect me from his threats. He'd never been a threat to me, not from the moment his heart had threaded through mine, despite my unwillingness to admit what it meant. Despite all my intention to sever it.

Every part of my body sparked with life, with fire that danced and harmonized with his shadows. I moaned, overwhelmed by a rushing wave of emotion as his kiss deepened. A primal ache built in my core, and I arched my head back, opening my mouth to let him claim my lips without restraint, exposing my neck to him as his exploration wandered from a tender worship of my lips to my jawline and down to my throat. My hands wove through his hair, gripping the loose curls to pull him closer, to keep him closer, and my hips angled greedily toward his. His wings folded around us, encircling us behind a curtain of intimacy. I wanted him— fully, completely, unabashedly, whether I was meant to or not. He was my monster, and I was his. We fit together perfectly. His eyes poured over me, molten with intensity and longing and truth. Like I mattered. Like he saw something more than a disaster.

Like the stars favored me.

The sky crackled, and Rue's lips stilled. He drew a deep, rueful breath against my skin, laced with the trembling evidence of his fragile, nearly shattered willpower. "Let's get you out of here," he said.

Shadows wrapped around us, and the ground dropped away beneath my feet, the rush of wind as exhilarating as the safety of Rue's arms locked around me. Perhaps flying was something I could grow accustomed to...not that I'd ever admit that to him. My heart raced as we pelted through the mouth of the pit, and Rue stretched his wings wide, clipping them through the darkness with a sharp swoop. We rose toward the moon, hiding in the darkness between the stars, leaving the broken bodies of the guards' corpses and the shards of my misery behind. For a moment.

From the corner of my eye, I caught the blinding flash of sparks flaring through the sky. I craned my neck, looking beyond the gates of Rashii to the dunes of the Sundom Desert. Toward home. The skies ripped open like flayed skin, as though Prisha had cracked her whip again and again across the heavens until they grew bloodied and torn beyond repair. A black swarm raced across the dunes toward the city, accumulating in mass as inky jets sprayed down from each of the gilded seams. Her army. The beginning of the end.

Rue froze, his body bobbing in midair between each stunned flap of his wings. "She's going to ambush the city. You need to stitch...try to stitch, Zara," he urged, panic tinging his tone. "We need a Stitcher."

I clutched a hand over my chest, pressing against the splitting pain that felt convincingly like my heart cleaving in two. "I'm not a Stitcher. I'm a destroyer."

"Yeah...well, we're going to need one of those too."

His wings flattened along his back, and my stomach lodged itself in my throat, leaping far from its rightful place as he plummeted toward the earth. He wove between the rooftops, landing in a dark alley on the east side of the palace. "Stay here," he commanded.

I stumbled out of his arms and collected my footing before charging after him. "Where do you think you're going without me?" My eyes narrowed at the mere thought, and I snapped my fingers around his wrist, forcing him to turn back toward me.

He grabbed my shoulders with urgency. "It's safer if I go alone —I know how to hide in the shadows. There are guards everywhere inside."

"Inside?" My expression twisted into concern.

"I'm getting your Eldress. I know where they're keeping her."

"How? What—Take me!"

He snapped his head to the left, squinting suspiciously into the darkness before making a hushing sound. "I couldn't find you when I woke up, so I went searching. I found her. I found the Sisters he's been hiding too. You want to talk about monsters? Rali is the worst of them. I don't want you anywhere near where he can find you."

"You knew where they were, and you didn't help them? *Take me to them.*" Anger boiled in my gut. If he knew where they were, we could save them. We could ask the Eldress for help, and I could free myself from the prince's demands, for he'd have no leverage left to hold over me.

Rue wrapped his hands around the tether between us, beckoning the light to reveal itself. "I felt the tug of your distress during the union," he explained, nodding toward the connection. "I had to save *you* from him first."

He kissed the space above my brows, then lingered for a moment longer, pressing his forehead against mine. "I won't be long. I'll get her for you, Zara. Stay in the shadows. Stay hidden."

I looked skyward at the blinding rifts that reached toward the palace like a pair of greedy hands, and wondered how much time we had before the monsters breached the city walls. "But what if—"

"I won't be long. I won't let you fight on your own. Wait for us. If danger is coming, you know I'll answer your call."

"But—"

"I promise. Let me help you. Please."

CHAPTER 25

THE ROLE FATE ASSIGNED

RUE

The shadows guided my way through the palace, obscuring me from guards' notice as I retraced my steps from the day before to the room with no windows, no air, no sun. Prince Tiralish had stripped the room bare, a blank canvas with nothing to offer the slightest hint of hope or the faintest courtesy of distraction for its occupants. Nothing but gray stone stacked ominously into four foreboding walls, looming over the room like a quartet of shadowy assassins, leaching the essence of life from the space.

The Daughters sat huddled in corners and along the walls, some shivering and some limp with apathy. Or worse. I couldn't bring myself to look too closely. These were the Daughters the prince had slowly accumulated, isolating them from their power, denying them access to their goddess so he could strategically disempower them.

In the center of the chamber, the Eldress reclined in a gray mess of blankets, her frail frame swallowed by the unkempt heap of bedding. She looked so...diminished. As though she had aged a hundred years since I last visited. *I just saw her yesterday.* I frowned at the sack of sagging skin and jutting bones that housed her infinite wisdom, her unmatched experience, and pondered if she could even tolerate the effort of an escape. But I had to try... for Zara.

Traitor. Do not ignore me. Kill her. Prisha's fury hissed through my bones, spitting with rage as she compelled me to change the course of my actions. I flexed my fingers, bracing against the storm and stilling my breath until the deluge of her interference dissipated. My shoulders relaxed when I released the tension through a carefully measured exhale. Prisha had always haunted my thoughts—always lingered at the edge of my mind, but now that I suspected she did the same to Zara, I found myself inspired to destroy the goddess who'd made me. If not for me, then for Zara. I'd do anything to stop the pained flinches that crossed Zara's face whenever the goddess slipped into her thoughts. Prisha always took notice of those who stood out, and Zara, extraordinary Zara with starlight in her soul, seemed fated to attract her attention.

"Rueper," Ahma croaked from her bedding, noticing the way I clung to the shadows. She remembered my name...her body might have been failing, but her mind clearly was not. I did not think I'd left much of an impression during our brief encounter the previous day before I'd rushed back to Zara. Still, when her milky eyes scanned over my frame, unfocused in a way that gave the distinct impression of *true* seeing, I had no doubt she knew me...perhaps better than I knew myself. I froze, suspecting her starry gaze scrutinized the layers of granite crusted over my heart that Zara had begun to demolish chip by chip, studying the uncertain rawness beneath that flinched in fear of the one word spoken by each throb of the muscle. *Unlovable. Unlovable. Unlovable.*

Prisha had never loved anyone but herself, demanding more and more and more from me until I had nothing left to give.

Cursing me and punishing me for my inadequacies but never acknowledging my efforts. Zara was...different.

I shook the thought from my head, but the word still tightened like a band around my chest. Zara had presented me with the first opportunity to choose something else for myself, to believe I could be more than a monster fated to enact Prisha's will. Zara made me believe—no, she *exemplified*, that some expectations were meant to be broken.

What began as mild intrigue for a woman seemingly mismatched with the responsibilities life had handed her had evolved into deeper feelings of empathy. I understood her struggle to follow their expectations when she was meant for more...when she was meant for something else. And if she could find her own way, then so could I.

No part of me doubted that Zara was the key in this war, the twist of fate...the change that would finally alter the course of its outcome. She still didn't believe it, so I believed in her twice as fiercely to make up the difference. And she made me believe in *myself* because she did not see me as a monster. Not anymore...not once she knew me.

Zara's matriarch shifted and groaned, wrestling my attention back to her. I slipped deeper into the eerie quiet of the room, the air so dank and stifled it forced its occupants to be quiet as well. It felt like a tomb. My gaze swept over the Eldress's deteriorating frame, clinging to life by a single thread. Perhaps it was a tomb.

"Ahma," I addressed her, finally stopping to stand before her. My thighs tensed, caught between motions as I fumbled with whether or not I should kneel before the woman who'd once been my enemy. In the end, my knee graced the floor and my head bowed—at the very least, I should level myself with a woman of her power. A woman I greatly respected for her role in raising Zara, though we came from opposite sides of this war.

"Rueper. You came back," she mumbled, with no effort to disguise her note of surprise.

"It's Rue. Please," I requested.

"A shame." She sighed, patting a spidery hand upon my shoulder. "I quite like the name Rueper. I prefer to call people by their full name. It is who they are."

"Then perhaps you should call me *Monster*," I responded automatically. It *was* who I'd been made to be, who Prisha had intended to create, even if Zara had led me to believe I could be more...made me believe I could be loved. But Ahma did not know any of that, and to her, that is what I was. It was what she would see if she read the long history of destruction haunting my memories or sensed the irrational rage of the goddess fighting to control my every decision.

The Eldress rolled her eyes, and the bones in her elbows creaked as she leaned toward me, her skin papery white.

"You are no monster. Do you truly think that in your heart? Or is that just what you expect me to see?"

I wavered, uncertain if she anticipated a response. I was created by a monster, compelled by a monster, but...I did not want to be one. And if Zara could truly find a way to stitch Prisha to the In Between forever, I could have the freedom to be who Zara saw when she looked at me. The Eldress stirred, wincing between each breath she pulled in, laboring with stridor.

"Eldress Stitcher," I began, feeling far less confident than my tone suggested, "Matriarch of the Daughters of Halah, you must...come with me." Her lips thinned, highlighting the creviced skin around her mouth and the wiry white hairs sprouting around it. "Please," I added as an afterthought.

She made no move to comply, but she also did not deny my request. Uncertain, I slid my hands beneath her frame, letting her body curl up, cradled in my arms. Her bones creaked like rusted door hinges, and I flinched at the snap of her rib against my arm. *Snap. Snap.*

I froze. *Venom and hell, she is fragile.*

Her face screwed up with pain, but she didn't cry out. She'd grown used to enduring this level of misery.

"Put me down," she commanded, though her voice never rose above a raspy whisper. "I am too old and brittle and ill. He's kept me from earth and sky...from Halah." She frowned when she met my eyes. "And there is no magic to be found in this vile place that I could use to pray to Halah for strength."

"But Zara needs you." *Snap.* Another bone shattered when I shifted my weight to carry her toward the door. And another. The Daughters around the room watched me warily as their Eldress groaned in pain, and I winced at the sound of each brittle break. She was turning to dust in my arms. Nervously, I returned her to her bedding and changed tactics. "Zara...thinks her magic is broken, and she thinks—she suspects you might know what to do about it."

"She will learn to stitch the skies in time," the Eldress responded dismissively, already closing her eyes, as if compelling sleep to take her from this plane of existence.

My gut wrenched with concern for her, but I couldn't afford to give her the rest she desired. Zara needed me to do this. "We don't have time. Prisha's army is on the way...she's going to ambush Rashii. You...you have to help her. Or help *me* help her. Please." I begged her with my eyes to understand. "Tell me how to help her."

"And who are you to her?" she asked knowingly after a deep, shuddering breath rattled through her frame. "Who are you to come speak on her behalf? Where is Zara? Why has she not come to see me herself? Has that Prince Tiralish kept me from her?"

My head rolled between my shoulders in a vain effort to dispel my overwhelming anger toward the prince. "If you only knew how much she tried. She wants to be here, but she's in danger, and she should not step foot in this palace. I am keeping her safe."

"And why would a Guardian of Prisha give two dune beetle wings about the new Stitcher's safety?"

So she knew. I swallowed. "I—" How could I explain? "Zara is...special."

"Of course she is. She was chosen by Halah. Try again."

"No. You misunderstand. She is special. *To me.*"

"Go on." Her eyes narrowed, communicating a challenge with her gaze more than a sense of encouragement.

I shut the world out for a moment, closing my lids as I released a deep exhale. "I don't understand it...neither of us do. But somehow, we are bound to one another. Tied by some fate that cannot be severed."

The Eldress arched a wiry brow.

"It connects us. Prevents us from harming one another. Not that I've ever tried to harm *her*, mind you," I quickly amended when the Eldress's expression turned murderous. "We cannot even be too far apart, or the bond strains...painfully."

"Who created this bond?" she asked, carefully shrouding her emotion.

"I don't know," I said truthfully. "Some...magic pulled me from the In Between, and when I landed before her, the tether wrapped around my heart and leashed me to her. Irreversibly." I paused and measured her response, uncertain if she could believe the unbelievable. I had a hard time believing it myself.

"Show me."

I didn't know if she'd be able to see it, for the magic seemed to reveal itself only to Zara and me, but I did as she asked, coaxing the bond into view between my fingers. Her eyes widened as far as the deeply hollowed sockets allowed.

"That is a rare magic, Rueper, Guardian of Prisha." She traced a fingertip along the energy of the cord, her finger angled sharply, and the bond hummed in greeting. "This bond between you? It is no accident. Surely you have guessed as much?"

I stared blankly at her, and she waited, watching for any flicker of my understanding. When none came, she shook her head and elaborated. "This is the work of the stars binding you, weaving one fate to another. For some reason, our ancestors felt it important that you two should find your way across the heavens to one another."

"The stars?" I asked, my mind racing to make sense of the enormity of it.

"It is not a common thing for the stars to tie two souls together. There is only one other instance recorded in our history that I could name with confidence. A few others I've merely suspected."

"Oh." Such a realization deserved a more profound response, but numb shock was the only emotion I could muster for her.

The Eldress did not seem to mind. She studied me carefully, the stars studding the milky galaxy of her eyes twinkling vibrantly with life. "Tell me more about Zara's magic. What makes her think it is broken? She is still having trouble stitching the skies?"

"It does not behave how she wants it to. It doesn't work for her the way that it should."

The Eldress hummed thoughtfully, then waited for me to elaborate. I opened my palms in a helpless gesture, uncertain where to begin, but knowing I had to try. She sat in silence as I explained, a mere lump in the nest of blankets, staring off into space.

"Zara's magic is...unpredictable. Wild. She fears it because she can't control it. At the ceremony, during the attack, it turned to shadow and commanded Prisha's creatures and...me." I added, blinking uncertainly at the Eldress. "But...she didn't mean it. She didn't want to. The magic just floods through her...overwhelms her until she has no choice but to unleash it, however dangerous the outcome. She doesn't understand why it doesn't behave as it is meant to. She needs your help. Please."

I stopped, wondering how I knew all of this about Zara without explicitly being told. I simply...understood. The Eldress's eyes seemed to have glazed over, unblinking as though lost inside the universe of her wisdom. I resisted the urge to wave my hand in front of her face to check for consciousness. I would not disrespect Zara's matriarch.

So I waited in silence until I could bear it no longer. "So...do you know what it means? Do you know how to help her?"

The Eldress's awareness resurfaced in her eyes. "I have my suspicions, yes," she croaked, seeming to mull over whatever thoughts threaded her mind.

"And?"

Ahma sighed so deeply, I feared her lungs had collapsed. When she looked at me, her wrinkles rearranged, crafting sadness in the crevices of her expression. Or perhaps...pity. "Give an old woman a moment to process the emotionally devastating blow before she lands it. I am too old and tired to endure such tragedies."

My expression balked. "Tragedies?"

"You are Prisha's creature. Whether or not you wish to serve her, her magic flows through you. Am I correct?"

I nodded in acknowledgment of the fact. I didn't like it, but it was true.

"And your bond with Zara, it entwines your souls so you share a deep connection, a deep understanding of one another."

I nodded again.

"I cannot know for certain, it is just a suspicion, but my instinct is that the bond you share allows *your* magic to flow through her. That corruption of magic, that excessive power that lets her control Prisha's creatures, that is *not* Halah's magic. It's yours. It's Prisha's."

"But...she is a Daughter. Halah's magic runs through her blood—"

"And if I am not mistaken, it has been diluted from centuries of mixing with mortal blood. Your magic flows straight from its original source. Direct from Prisha. I expect it is much stronger, much more...influential."

"But then can't she—"

The Eldress shook her head with regret. "I don't think she'll be able to fully access Halah's magic while your magic flows through her. Yours is too strong. You cannot hear the quiet patter of raindrops above the roar of a waterfall. One washes away the other."

I furrowed my brows, wondering how the woman even knew of such things from her isolated life in the desert, but then understanding dropped into my stomach with the weight of a thousand stones. My mouth ran dry, and the blood drained from my face. "So...in order for her to stitch the skies...to save the realm..."

Ahma nodded. "You understand. You must sever the bond."

"But that's impossible." I shook my head, panic filtering through every vein of my body.

"Nothing is impossible. A bond like yours can be broken...it's been done before. It is difficult, but not impossible."

"But...how?"

"If history teaches us any lessons, only a great betrayal can sever the bond and compel her to release you. Otherwise, she will hold on to you forever."

As I would hold on to her. *No, as I will.* The possibility of severing the bond changed nothing. I regarded Ahma, shaking with an unexpected shiver beneath her stare. How much did this woman know? What secrets did she hold back? Surely there had to be another answer. Another way. "How can you know this for certain?"

"That the bond can be severed? Because Halah and Prisha once shared a bond, not unlike yours."

My face contorted with revulsion. "I thought they were twins."

The Eldress chuckled, amused by my apparent naïveté. "Not all bonds are romantic, Rueper. Soulmates can be friends. Family. Lovers. Only the stars know why two souls must be tied together...what story the constellations of their entwined destinies must weave."

"I see," I responded. But I didn't. Not really.

"Halah and Prisha were bonded...and believe it or not, they once meant the world to one another. When Halah fell in love with Tarek, a mortal man, resentment took root between the sisters. Prisha grew tired of this realm and wanted to return home to the Sanctuary of Gods, but Halah would not think of leaving Tarek behind." The Eldress scrutinized me in the moment of her pause. "And I think you might understand why Prisha could not leave without Halah. Why she couldn't stray too far from her."

"Because of the bond."

She nodded. "The bond doesn't tear apart with distance...but stray too far, and it slices through the anchors at either end—the hearts—killing both. That is what happened to King Grodok and the princess of Khazdra, if I am not mistaken."

Perspiration beaded at my temples, and my heart throbbed anxiously. "That's why Prisha betrayed Halah. That's why I can't be too far from Zara."

The Eldress nodded. "Prisha didn't know her actions would sever the bond. But she knew if she could eliminate Tarek from the equation, Halah would have no reason to stay behind in this mortal realm. And so she tried to kill him."

"And that betrayal severed the bond."

She nodded again, her lips pulled inward in some mournful, pitying smile. "And once the bond severed, Halah filled the land with her tears, forming Halah's Lament and raising the Namak Sea, then she banished her sister to the In Between. And so began the war that led to the tragedies we face today. I am sorry, Rueper."

I shook my head, unwilling to process what the Eldress meant to convey. "Doesn't Zara know any of this?"

A croaking laugh passed through her lips. "You think that girl paid any attention to the rambling teachings of an old crone? She has always been her own person. You must let her be her own person." She lowered her voice. "Sever the bond, Rue. There is no other way."

Her energy seemed to wane, and her skin dulled to a waxy pallor. She coughed, wincing at the crack of her ribs. "I think I am done with my suffering." She patted her blankets, inviting me to sit at her side before reclining with a weary sigh into the gray nest in which Rali had left her to die.

She turned to me, and I jumped at the sudden clarity in her eyes. The clouds lifted, revealing the most shocking green gems holding me in their gaze...so much like Zara's. "Rue?" She hesitated until my surprise passed and she had my full attention. "I'm ready to join the stars." Her voice sounded tattered and frayed, stretched too thin over too many years. But it was a voice that commanded attention. I stilled. She watched me, rapt, unblinking, waiting patiently, but with every expectation of my compliance.

She wanted me to...send her to the stars? To *kill* her? My lips parted in some form of a grimace, overwhelmed by the twisted, indefinable feeling inside me. "You don't mean that. Let me get you out of here. Please. Zara needs you."

"Don't you understand? I *told* you what you must do. Do it right, and you will accomplish two tasks...end my suffering and use it to set yourself on the path you must follow," she rasped, her voice crackling against the strain of her words, yet still managing unwavering conviction. "But do you have the strength to do it? You know it is Zara's time, not mine. *Let it be her time.*"

Her head fell back, and she reached a bony hand toward me. I accepted, holding the papery, brittle thing in mine, afraid one slight twitch of my grip might shatter her.

She pulled me closer with unexpected strength, her neck muscles cording as she lifted her head to whisper in my ear. "Break the bond, Rue. Let Zara become who she was always meant to be. Let her go."

I hesitated, caught in ambivalence, distressed by the impossible divide between what I wanted and what Zara needed. I needed to leave her...and not just leave her. I had to *betray* her. *On purpose.* With our bond broken, Zara would be able to finish this. She would be able to close the skies, free her Sisters, and set her realm right again. But did that make any of this...right?

My mouth curdled with disgust, already hating myself for the act I could never conceive of committing under ordinary circumstances. I'd need to destroy every good thread of the bond between us to unbind my power from hers, allowing her to be unaltered and uncorrupted by the powers that flowed through me from Prisha. I had to, so she could become what she was always destined to be. Because she was important. Because the stars favored her.

And so did I.

My heart cracked. How could I choose this for her against her knowledge? How could I look her in the eyes and lie to her and hurt her, even if from a place of love? The grief shattered my heart into shards that sliced through my lungs until they could hold no more air. Would the betrayal break her like it had already broken me? Would she try to stop me if she knew what I intended?

I knew the answer without a sliver of doubt. Zara wanted to save everyone, often to her own detriment. It was her best quality, and perhaps her biggest weakness. To care so much about others that she made a habit of putting their needs and desires and expectations first, silencing her own. But perhaps the biggest gift I could give to her was to not let her bear the burden of saving *me,* too...of putting me before herself. I could sacrifice myself. I could release the best thing that had ever happened to me and return myself to a certain death at Prisha's hands. I could do that if it meant giving her the best chance to save herself and her people. I could free her from the burden of caring for me so she could do what she had always been meant to do, even if it killed me. In every way.

Because I knew that if even one fleck of her soul still cared for me, she would move heaven and earth to save me, just as I would do for her.

Just as I must do for her now.

I reached for the bone dagger I'd taken from that ill-fated Rider, wrapping my fingers around it while guilt wrapped around my neck like a noose. I knew she had the strength to do it on her own. I was only sorry she had to.

My eyes fell on the Eldress, whose ribs shuddered with each ragged, painful breath. She had asked me to end her suffering and betray Zara. She had asked me to be a monster.

And so I must be the monster I was born to be.

The inescapable role fate had assigned.

My eyelids pressed together, squeezing a single tear between my lashes. *Zara deserves so much better.*

The dagger plunged into the Eldress's heart, and she expired with one long, raspy exhale. I leaned my forehead against the hilt, choking on the sob expanding in my throat, unsettled by the rush of anguish that pricked tears in my eyes.

I don't know how long I remained in that position, shattering from the inside out, crying over the hilt that jutted from Ahma's bleeding chest.

After a long while, after no goodness and no happiness

remained inside of me, I stood, bracing myself for the next agonizing moments that awaited me beyond this room. Preparing the worst possible things I could say to break Zara to free her from her monster.

It was so easy to know the most damaging things to say to her. So easy to find the words that would wound her most. So easy to play the role fate had chosen for me.

But breaking her would be the hardest thing I'd face in my life.

"You'll have to carry her to earth and sky so she can join the stars," one of the Daughters whispered, breaking the silence.

I sniffed and wiped the cuff of my sleeve against the corner of my eye, then scooped the limp, broken body into my arms, and began to walk toward the door. I paused in midstep, speaking to Zara's Sisters behind me. "The door is unlocked. Just...make sure that someone is left on Zara's side at the end. She shouldn't have to face this alone. She deserves to not be alone."

And I slipped from the room before I could disintegrate beneath the agony clawing at my heart.

"What are you doing with my Stitcher?" I froze at the sound of his frosty tone, not because I didn't expect to hear it—I'd deliberately put myself in a position to run into the prince —but because I had to believably play my part. If being the monster would save Zara, I would go all in. I drew in a deep, steadying breath and turned to face the real monster, lifting the corner of my mouth into my most devious smirk.

Prince Tiralish's eyes darted from my face to the Eldress to the dagger still protruding from her chest, and his mouth gaped wide.

The liar who'd paraded as Rali. Everything about him darkened. His shoulders widened, and his teeth bared in a snarl, reminding me of a mutt raising its hackles at an intruder.

"How *dare* you kill my Stitcher?" he demanded, his voice a low rumble of impending rage. "Do you know what you've done? Guards!" he shouted over his shoulder. "Guards!" His voice echoed through the empty passage, and he narrowed his eyes on mine, stalking toward me with murderous intent. "You will *die* for this. You will be sentenced to death! *Guards!*" The cords in his neck strained as he yelled, popping out like two marble columns I'd love to crumble. Perhaps Zara would do me that honor.

"I wouldn't do that," I interjected before he could resume his red-faced hollering. "Not if you want the real Stitcher."

It was his turn to freeze. "What do you know about the real Stitcher? What have you done?"

My smile widened. "I put her somewhere for safekeeping." Tilting my head, I let malice wash over my expression. "But I can bring you to her. For a price."

Delight sparked in his murderous gaze. "It *is* her, isn't it? I knew it." He dropped his attention to the floor and began to pace, muttering to himself. "But there is still something unusual about her. Some secret she isn't sharing. She's not a very *good* Stitcher, is she? Broken, or something. Maybe Prisha is the better choice, after all..."

Fury expanded inside me, threatening to erupt from its shell in an earth-shattering explosion. It took every measure of self-control to fold the anger beneath my carefully crafted act. *Play the part, Rue. Play it well.* "Zara will never be able to stitch the skies. I made sure of that. Prisha sent me to corrupt her magic."

The prince snapped his head toward me, regarding me in a whole new light. "*What?*" He shook his head, worry beginning to mar his expression. "*Never?* You made it so she can't stitch?

Venom and hell. Then she needs to die. If she isn't strong enough to fend off Prisha, then my hands are tied."

Did he really change sides so easily? Did he have no loyalty... no morals? "If you expect me to give her to you, it will be on my terms. She comes with a price."

He frowned with the air of an insolent child. "What price?"

"She lives. You will not kill her. You will not harm her. Do what you want with me, *but you will not hurt her.*"

His lips pursed, holding back whatever he truly wished to say, but he composed himself with great effort and a nod. I wondered if he could even be trusted with such a bargain, but it was the only leverage I had.

"Do we have a deal then?" I adjusted my hold on the Eldress, tossing her irreverently over my shoulder so she flopped like a sack of flour, then outstretched my right hand toward Tiralish. *I'm sorry, Ahma...have to play the part.*

He looked at my hand with disdain, but ultimately accepted the gesture, his shake a shade too aggressive. "Deal. Bring me to her."

CHAPTER 26

BROKEN

I folded myself into the darkness and paced the narrow alley to mark the time. Ten passes. Twenty. Still no Rue.

With every fretful step, the cloud of dread shrouding my heart darkened, and its rhythm thrummed with increasing panic against my ribs. I kept my eyes glued to the sky, waiting.

The city bells clamored in warning, then came the hellish battle cries of Prisha's army. Their screeches mingled amid the melody to brew a jarring racket of sounds—wails that frayed my nerves, clanging that rattled my soul, and shrieks that landed like fragmented debris in my heart. I imagined the guards' shock as they caught the first glimpse of the massive black swarm cresting the highest dunes in the distance. The smell of malice filled the air and painted a mood of despair that weighed heavy on my heart, its scent metallic like some mixture of blood and rancid sweat, touched by the lingering presence of ash. It crept through my nostrils, burning its way through my airway, settling into my lungs to make every breath a clipped struggle. My pulse overran my veins, beating wildly.

Where is Rue? Please hurry. Please hurry and bring Ahma. I nervously twisted the hem of my skirt between my fingers. *Let Ahma help us. I can't do this alone.*

The dark spillage from Prisha's rifts rained down beyond the city walls in tune with the low rumble of thunder. My breath jumped in short spurts, beginning to hyperventilate. What was I supposed to do? I could not stitch the skies...I could not fight them on my own.

Rue, hurry. I knew he wasn't too far...I could feel the subtle stretch of the bond between us, the beginning aches of the tether pulling gently at my heart. I tugged on the cord, willing him to understand the rush of my panic. No response.

I looked beyond the rooftops, squinting at the top of the city walls, trying to make sense of the flurry of activity above...the panicked shouts, the flares of beacons, and pounding boots. At least they were preparing to fight. They wouldn't be ambushed blindly. I scanned the dark alley and the skies, hoping for a glimpse of Rue's shadow or his wings stretched wide across the stars, but found only a sky tortured by Prisha's marks. If Rue did not hurry...if the monsters killed the guards and breached the city...how could I stand by and do *nothing*? I couldn't.

But Rue said he wouldn't let me fight alone. *He'll be here. Any minute. He'll bring Ahma. Ahma will know what to do.*

Shouts of soldiers above barked orders before arrows unleashed into the darkness beyond the wall. How close had the black smudge moved in the minutes that passed since Rue's departure? Had Prisha's creatures already come within the range of the archers? I inhaled sharply, panic clawing at my throat. We didn't have much longer.

My limbs trembled until my entire frame felt uselessly out of place, functionless and detached from the jumbled panic of my mind. What would happen if Rue did not come back? If he were injured? Fear jolted like a hot flame through my body, sparking my heart to double its galloping pace. *What if he doesn't return soon enough, and I do something foolish that gets others injured? What if...what if they kill me?* I'd never shied away from a fight before, but now, whether I wanted it or not, my role was bigger. Whose magic would repel Prisha from this realm if I died? I couldn't risk leaving them unprotected without a Stitcher...but who else had the power to truly fight and protect? It was *my* responsibility. My responsibility to *try*.

Do something, Zara. Do something now.

I jumped, startled by the sudden swoop of a shadow in my peripheral. Rue knelt before me, his black wings shrouding him like a storm cloud, and when he lifted his gaze to find me, the deadness there stole the air from my lungs. *What had happened? Was he hurt?* My heart twisted with concern, and I rushed toward him. "Rue!" I threw my arms around him, but his whole body stiffened. He peeled my arms away, his hands sticky and...red. Covered in red. *Why are they red?*

I stepped back, confused. Only *then* did I notice he'd come alone. "Where is she? Did you find her?"

"Yes." He widened his stance, pulling himself to full height so when he looked at me, it was with an air of disdain cast down the length of his nose. Behind him, the sky crackled ominously, and Prisha's army screeched beyond the walls, a matching backdrop to his marked change in attitude.

"And?" *Why are you being so weird?*

He jutted his chin upward, and his mouth quirked into a defiant smile. "I killed her."

The ground swallowed me. Or I collapsed. Or time ceased. The world spun off-kilter, and my blood pumped so quickly through my body that it drowned me and my thoughts in a red wave of ire.

"You *what*?" I gasped, clutching the space between my breasts, pressing against my sternum as though I could contain the splitting fissures in my heart with the pressure of my own fist. Cries beyond the wall shattered my eardrums.

"You're surprised?" He laughed, darkness staining his mirth. "You knew I was Prisha's monster. Are you really surprised I killed your precious Eldress?"

I shook my head, my lips stammering to force out some semblance of coherent thought. He...he'd been Prisha's monster, but...this was all wrong. This wasn't the plan. This was not Rue. Something was off. Someone was forcing his hand...he...he cared for me. But the cold expression on his face lacked any trace of the Rue I'd fallen for. This was somebody different. Someone I didn't recognize.

Ice traveled through my veins, numbing me into a state of paralysis as my heart withered, breaking into needle-sharp fragments that sliced through every feeling of hope and trust that had taken root within my core.

He shifted uncomfortably, but the disinterested expression on his face never wavered. "I did bring you *someone,* however. I didn't come empty-handed." He jerked his head toward the shadows, and Rali—no, *Prince Tiralish*—stepped forward with triumph on his face, lending the glow of confidence to each stalking step he took in my direction.

"Hello, Zara."

My attention snapped back to Rue, my mouth parting in shock. Rue's eyes showed the slightest flicker of emotion before cooling to a deadened stone. "Rue? How could you?" I whispered. My insides melted into hot iron, burning and disintegrating me with agonizing pain. "I trusted you."

He shrugged, apathy oozing from his posture. "The prince offered me a deal I couldn't refuse."

"You...bargained with him?" My vocal cords failed miserably to give resonance to the ghosts of my words.

"You know I appreciate a good deal."

No. Everything I thought I knew about Rue shattered, pulverizing the belief that I had ever been important to him.

"You want me to believe you've chosen some deal over me? You...you expect me to believe you never cared about me?" My voice cracked.

He hesitated, and for a moment, I thought I glimpsed the truth in his eyes, but it was gone just as quickly. Shielded by his hard, cold stare. He leaned closer to me, indifference radiating palpably from his frame, wedging its way into my heart like a lance. "Never."

"I thought—I thought..." I stammered, stepping backward.

He laughed a singular, venomous chuckle of disregard and wrapped his hand around the bond between us to bring it to view. It flickered, sputtering like a candle fighting to stay aflame beneath the rain. "You think it was random? Did you really think this was an accident?"

The tether pulled on my heart, the pain of his words an excruciating slice. "What do you mean?"

"I latched myself to you the moment Prisha knew you were important. The very first chance I got. It has always...*always* been about Prisha...I am *hers*. Her magic flows through me, and now, it corrupts yours through this bond. You know why you can't stitch? *Because I ruined you.*" He smirked. "You were so broken... so eager to accept someone who pretended to piece together your broken shards."

No. Raw, sharp claws of agony raked through my heart, unable to make sense of the shift in Rue's demeanor, the lack of life in his eyes so black and devoid of any favor toward me. Had I misread him so horribly? Had I been so desperate for someone to tell me I wasn't broken—that I was special—that I let this monster work his way into my heart to betray everything I thought I knew? That I let him become important to me so he could blind me just to use me for his plans?

"You made it so easy." He grinned dangerously, his gaze lazily appraising my frame in the same approach he'd used at our first meeting. "The stars do favor you, you know, even when you're angry. It's just a mystery why they'd pick someone like *you*." His voice dropped to a low growl, speaking the last word like it was a distasteful curse on his tongue.

Everything shattered. Tears flushed from my eyes, racing down my cheeks, coating my lips and drowning me with immeasurable sadness. "I hope they swallow you whole and banish you from this world forever," I seethed, my voice boiling with rage as it slipped through my clenched teeth. And I meant it. I meant every damn word.

The bond flared vividly to life, glowing with the luminous hue of molten metal before bursting into a roaring rush of flame. Fire seared through the tether, burning it away until all that remained was the ash drifting between us. I gasped for air at the same time as Rue, but my lungs felt empty and lacking, no matter how many panicked breaths I drew to refill them.

Our bond had been severed.

"Kill him, Zara! End him. End this," the prince commanded, his voice a far away, distant memory, the firm grip of his arm around my bicep hardly noticeable compared to the agony decomposing my heart.

Rue's eyes flickered angrily toward Tiralish before he raced toward me and scooped me into his arms. His wings unfurled with a swift slash of motion, then he shot toward the sky, holding me close to his chest. I screamed, thrashing against his hold, fighting to free myself. Where was he taking me? To Prisha's army? To Prisha herself? Would he kill me?

Every muscle in my frame engaged, violently twisting to break his hold.

"Zara, please." He gasped, winded by the elbow I wedged into his breastbone. "Zara, stop. I'm taking you to—"

"I won't go anywhere with you, you monster! Put me down. I'll kill you!"

I struggled, wildly bucking my body so that the strokes of his wings faltered as we crossed over the city gates to the desert beyond. The black smudge of Prisha's army flowed like a crashing wave over the rise and fall of the dunes, charging toward the city despite the raining arrows that did little to thin the herd. He was taking me to them...he was going to kill me.

"Zara...let me...explain. I had to break—" He gasped, holding his perfect nose that no longer looked so...perfect.

"You will not break me," I screamed. *"I will not—"*

The sky flared, a thousand veins of gold flowing like liquefied ore through the sky.

We froze, horrorstruck by the sight, but I came to my senses and used his shock to my advantage, reaching for the dagger he sheathed at his side. "Zara, stitch! You can stitch—" he shouted.

But I wasn't listening. Not truly. I drove the blade into his forearm, and he howled in agony, plummeting downward as the rhythm of his wings failed. *Seems there's nothing left in my subconscious to keep me from ending you now.* I ripped myself free from his arms and dove toward the ground, my foot crumpling beneath me before I fell forward and swallowed a mouthful of sand.

The fall winded me, and I gasped greedily for air, pushing up to my forearms to lift my gaze toward Rue. He hung in the sky, bobbing with every stroke of his wings and gripping the gash on his forearm. Horror outlined every angle of his face.

Agonizing rage poisoned my body, bubbling inside of me until it could no longer be contained. "Go back to where you belong, monster," I shouted.

I stood, ignoring the sharp pain that lanced through my leg, and reached a hand toward Rue, summoning the ribbons of light. They flowed to me readily, no longer fearful or resistant to my touch. They wound around my wrist, entwining into a beacon of snakelike ribbons that raced toward Rue, binding him and raising him toward the gashes in the star-filled sky. *I hope they swallow you whole.* My jaw clenched, set firmly into a scowl of hatred.

The stars hummed in response to the subtle twist of my outstretched hand, bending to my will. They flared into angry lances, piercing his body with ardent rays as instinct guided the path of my stitching. Tendrils of light grasped him like a crushing fist, passing him through Prisha's rift until her shadows grabbed for him, pulling him back to where he belonged. His jaw tightened, and the starscape of his amethyst eyes dulled to darkest night, but I saw no anger in his face. No trace of fury to match the raging fire that swelled between my ribs, hating him for his deceptions, for his illusions...for making me *feel*. For making me believe that I had been worthy of his love. That I had been worthy of love at all. None of it had been real. He had always been the enemy.

Now I would be his.

But as the stitching channeled through my fingertips, my breath hitched at the slightest grimace marring his features, and I recognized the emotion there—the one mirrored by my own. It was not pain that settled into the creases of his eyes or the bittersweet pull of his smile. It was sadness. Infinite sadness.

His gaze met mine, and I gasped as their color flared to life once more, shining like the incandescent swirls dancing between the streams of stars above. "The stars favor you, Zara. Never doubt that I meant it. I always meant it," he called out, his voice murky and muddled by the entirety of space between us, but his words found me, landing like the pierce of an arrow in my heart.

My hand wavered, conflicted. Struck by a dagger of clarity. In that moment, I understood. Every time he had told me the stars favored me, what he really meant to say was *I favor you, Zara. I love you.* And somehow, even in this moment when everything was broken, when everything was wrong, I knew it had been true. I didn't understand his betrayal, but I knew which version of Rue was true. Despite his deceit, despite our incompatible trajectories and opposing loyalties, he'd fallen for me. And—against reason or judgment, I loved him back.

I didn't want to admit such a thing, not even to myself, not when I needed to choose between what was right and what I deeply wanted. But I knew it with irrefutable clarity. I loved him—for if this was not love, his betrayal could not have eviscerated me so completely, breaking me, body and soul. All of this pain stemmed from the absence of love, and to notice its absence meant it had once been there, quietly blooming like a desert sunfire blossom, despite the crushing adversity of its circumstance. Thriving. Evolving. Growing. It had been real. But it had been planted in a lie.

The stars favor you, Zara. I watched the stars close around him, and I knew what he expected me to say back, our little joke he waited to hear one last time to heal the pain of these final moments together. As if this were just another lighthearted moment between us...another moment of banter and flirtation and quietly blooming feelings. But I could not. I couldn't say it. As the starlight surged around him and my vision blurred with tears, the words lodged themselves in my throat, and I choked on them. Hot tears fell down my cheeks, and I swallowed dryly, as though all of the moisture from my body had fled, making its traitorous descent from my eyes in great droplets.

Though he deserved it, though I knew this was what I was meant to do—what I'd been born to do—I could not force myself to voice the words he expected. Not as I watched them come true before my very eyes. *The stars are swallowing him whole.* And it was the last thing in this world that I wanted.

I faltered with my hand frozen in salute, somewhere between stitching the last of the stars to seal him away forever, and reaching through the portal to pull him back. Whether I would strike him or kill him or kiss him until my lips and heart swelled with contentment, I didn't know. I—could not know. He was gone.

And I was—broken.

I fell to my knees and uttered a sky-shattering wail that reflected only one fragment of the agony inside me.

The monsters approached—the great rolling mass of destruction raced toward me. Prisha cried out from the heavens, and somehow, in the stutter of time, Prince Tiralish found his way to me. He screamed at the top of his lungs, ordering me to *get up, get up and stitch, get up and fight.*

I hung limply from his hold and slumped back to the sand. My ribs cracked, or perhaps they'd already fractured along with my heart. I couldn't move. I couldn't breathe.

None of it mattered. Nothing mattered.

CHAPTER 27

THE UNMAKING

RUE

No stars graced this forsaken land between realms. Only absence and shadows.

The pervasive void of Prisha's lair reflected one's darkest thoughts like a mirror, until only the worst remained, trapped on one side of the looking glass, staring longingly back at the unmirrored pieces left behind. The malevolence of the air corroded through flesh and bone, its cursed shadows wending through my flickering existence. The oppressive darkness sought to dampen every last shred of light in my soul.

There was little left of me to extinguish. I had already sacrificed everything. For Zara.

By some cruel twist of destiny, my last act had confirmed the only truth that resonated with meaning in this great abyss. I was a monster, and fate would never let me be anything more.

Prisha's grotesque bindings slithered out from the shadows, emboldened by the return of darkness as the last stitches of Zara's magic sealed me off from her realm. I squeezed my eyes shut, wrestling back the overwhelming rush of emotion. At least now she could stitch. I'd done that for her. Now, she could win. Even if it had cost me everything.

Prisha's magic hissed as it wrapped around my ankles, between my ribs, around my neck. I slumped over. They could have me. The stony pavement chafed against my skin as her magic pulled me toward the palace, winding through the streets as steely white gazes tracked the progress of my shameful journey, observing coldly from either side.

When the dark tendrils carried me over the threshold and through the foyer, my head sagged over my chest. They strung me up against a wall, and four daggers hissed through the air. Each sank into the wood behind me, pinning me in place.

I flinched with the searing jolt of each puncture through my wings, a pain just vibrant enough to confirm I still lived, if only for a few excruciating moments longer. The blades, forged by Prisha's darkness, compelled my magic to hold its form, refusing my own shadows the permission to bend or fade away. Forbidding my escape.

I would end here. A monster. Banished and broken.

I lifted my chin at the sound of shuffling, meeting Dresgar in the eyes—my commanding officer from what seemed to be a lifetime ago. Unfounded hope that he might take pity on me or care to help urged me to speak—to offer him some form of bargain—but I held my tongue. I knew better.

The only loyalty permitted in these parts was to Prisha. There were no friends, no family, no empathy among acquaintances in the In Between. There was only the goddess who made us and survival. And I was fresh out of bargains—I had nothing more to offer. If Prisha planned to unmake me now, there was nothing left I cared about that hadn't already been destroyed.

Except Zara. And at the end of things, I would face this unmaking again and again for her.

"Your desertion nearly cost me my life," Dresgar hissed,

landing his spittle across the bridge of my nose. "I'm glad justice finds you, and not me, pinned against that wall to pay the price of your abandonment."

I wrinkled my nose, disgusted by the wet flecks glazing it, then met his hollow stare. Dead eyes. Dead soul. *There are only monsters in the In Between.* Was that how I'd looked before Zara? Was that who I'd been before our bond forged me into something new?

"Is this the life you really wanted?" I wondered out loud. I couldn't help myself...the question slipped through my clenched teeth.

"What other life is there?" Dresgar responded.

I shook my head, grinding my teeth against the agony caused by that slight movement. *What other life is there?* "A better one than this."

One with freedom and choices. A life filled with laughter, love, and stolen kisses in the dark. A life with food that wasn't scarce or fought for. One with sacrifice and honor. Connection and the favor of stars twinkling above. A life with starlight.

He snorted with derision. "Any life is better than the unmaking you're about to face. I'll let Prisha know you're ready."

Of course he didn't understand. There were only monsters in the In Between, but...perhaps I no longer had to be one of them.

Not now that I had nothing left to lose. No reason to hold back. If Prisha planned to unmake me now, there was nothing left to fear.

I don't have to be the monster. Not anymore. I'd already played my part.

"Yes. Let Prisha know I'm ready for her," I growled, sneering back at him. *I'll kill her.*

The little etchings of light that Zara's bond had traced over the vessels of my heart burned with something fierce that felt like hope. Vibrant. Undeniable. Compelling. The remaining scars of our connection seared deep within my soul, dimming the numbing apathy that poisoned me the second I returned to the In Between, pulling me back to remind me of who I was. No...who I wanted to be. Who I *could* be. For Zara. And because of Zara.

I bellowed, screwing up my face as I summoned the strength to wrench myself free from the magic of Prisha's daggers. They crumbled into dust behind me, and Dresgar's eyes swelled as I swept him aside. I barreled past him toward the foyer. Prisha might have planned to unmake me, but she couldn't unmake the reckoning she had coming for her.

The goddess emerged from the shadows, as if called forth by my rage. Her eyes flared, and shadows amassed at her ankles in a kinetic swarm, hinting at the dark emotions she held below the surface. With a commanding dart of her gaze, her darkness obeyed, spiraling around my body to envelop me. "Rueper," she crooned over me, leaning toward my ear to address me before clicking her tongue in disapproval. "Where are you running to this time? Not back to the one who returned you once your usefulness had run its course? Once she discovered what you truly are?"

My body thrashed against the bindings, straining violently to break free. Yet, with every measure of progress I made against her restraints, she tightened them tenfold. Heat rose to the surface of my skin with my frustration until sweat leaked from my pores. "You have no idea who I am now," I spat, pausing long enough to carve out my hatred for her with the daggers of my eyes.

"Don't I?" she asked. Her voice lilted with a trace of amusement before dropping back to a chilling tone. "Let me tell you a little secret. My usefulness for this version of you has run its course, too. But if I unmake you, I can mold you into something new. Something with less dangerous ideas. Something less...*you*." She smiled, the deep merlot of her eyes swirling with bloodlust. The bindings tightened, constricting me, crushing the life from my lungs and enshrouding me in the shadows of her anger until I could see nothing at all but darkness. Suffocating darkness.

There were no stars in this forsaken space between realms.

If only I could see them one last time.

I'd find my way back. To Starlight.

CHAPTER 28

NO EARTH OR SKY

Everything was a scream. The prince screamed for me to focus, demanding my cooperation with increasing hysteria, begging me to do something, *anything* to save the realm from Prisha's desolation. The goddess's creatures screamed, scaling the walls with scraping claws, slashing the throats of terrified guards, then moving on to frantic civilians. My body screamed at the lancing pain of broken bones and the emotional shards that eviscerated my soul with savage ruthlessness. But nothing screamed louder than my heart, the anguish reverberating within me, numbing every ability to think or feel *anything* but the deepest, most sorrowful regret.

What have I done? Why did I not *think* first? Surely I'd missed some critical piece, some secret that eluded me. Rue's sudden change of heart...that was not *him*. I knew that now without a shadow of a doubt. Some unseen influence or hidden purpose had forced him to hurt me, but I'd reacted in the worst possible way...not stopping to ask questions. Not pausing to follow my heart and my mind to find the truth. And now I would never have it—that truth had been lost when I'd banished him from this realm, stitched him into the sky, sending him to the unmaking that awaited him beyond, and I'd *never* see him again. The hole in my soul where answers and understanding should be gaped wider, shredding me to nothing.

When Tiralish tired of my catatonic state and realized his efforts to compel me were wasted, he tossed me into a dark chamber, forcing me to endure my fragmenting soul by myself, no longer hopeful that I could save him from his involvement with Prisha. No longer holding on to the delusion that I could hold back the reckoning she'd unleash upon him. She would come...her monsters would destroy what was left of me, and then she would come.

At least in death, I might be closer to Rue, hanging among the stars between the rifted skies. Maybe then he could see me once more, and recognize how I glowed only for him. How I favored him, despite the impassable rift betrayal had torn between us.

I sat in the quiet—staring blankly into the windowless, skyless room, a prison devoid of earth and air, until the overwhelming pain compacted into a heavy stone inside me, transitioning my excruciating suffering to the numbness of apathy.

My cheek pressed against the stone floor, my body curled into a heap of uselessness. I experienced every shriek, every tremble of the stone floor, every nightmarish terror my imagination conjured for me as I worried about the defenseless people facing Prisha's final army without me. I knew I should worry more, should work up the strength or courage or drive to do something more for them, but...it was over. There was nothing left to do...no fight left to draw from. No trace of Halah's magic existed in this skyless, earthless room, and no Eldress, no Rue...nobody left to save me. Nobody to save them. Prisha had won.

The prophecy held true in the end—it just wasn't what we

had expected. Prisha's gashes blazed like wildfire through the sky, and now her reign of terror would commence.

A light unfolds in the darkness, beginning what will have no end.

The clatter of hastened steps filled the passage outside my chamber—not just one pair but a great number. I picked my head up from the floor to listen, but the rest of my body refused to move. "It's this one, isn't it?"

"Yes—third door. That's the one he kept us in," a hushed voice whispered back.

A fist pounded against the heavy wood, then the doorknob rattled with an aggressive force. "Zara? Zara, are you in there?" a third voice questioned.

"Move over," another voice whispered harshly.

My Sisters. My Sisters had come to find me. A bittersweet melancholy spread through me—my heart somersaulting with recognition at the sound of their voices, but the guilt of failure spreading like icy venom down my limbs. I could do nothing to help them from here. The prince had locked me away from Halah's magic.

"It's locked. I can't open it."

"Zara, please! We need your help."

"She can't help us from that prison. No earth or sky...remember? No magic," the first voice hissed with impatience.

Lurah. Mother. Aunt Vanya. Rada. Magura. Juna. Sisters from inside and outside the city. How many had come for me? How many still survived? I forced my body into motion and crawled toward them, my ribs and ankle shooting arrows of white hot pain through my body with every movement. I scrambled to my knees, pressing my cheek and hand against the grain and wishing I could dematerialize and simply...slip through the wood to find them. But the door remained unyielding, and the room remained devoid of Halah's aid. The barrier between us may as well have been the curtain between realms...there was no way to cross to gain their help. And no hope left to save them.

"It's over. Prisha's won," I said through the door, defeated. Wet tears seeped through the wobbling turn of my frown, coating my tongue with their sorrowful taste.

"Zara, no. It can't be over. You have to try. Please."

Indistinguishable murmuring swelled behind the door. "Where is that Rue? Zara...where is Rue? He can help us."

"He's gone." I don't know how the words wedged themselves past the lump of stone in my throat, but they scraped by with great difficulty, causing my voice to crack.

"What?" one of my Sisters hissed with a dramatic air of disbelief. Probably Lurah.

"I stitched him to the skies. The stars swallowed him whole." My forehead tapped against the grainy wood as my face contorted with a choked sob.

"Oh no. Oh, Zara. Oh no, no, no." Their voices hummed and hissed behind the door, frantically arguing with one another or perhaps merely expressing their disappointment in my failures.

"He was always Prisha's," I cried through a grimace of tears and heartbreak, trying to explain but struggling to piece together the words that could convey the depth of my sadness. "He betrayed me."

"Oh, Zara. No. He *had* to. It...that was all for you. He was not Prisha's—he was *yours*."

I had not known agony until I heard those words. My heart stopped beating, and the blood drained from my face—how *desperately* I wanted to believe my Sisters. My mind raked through the memory of my last conversation with Rue, painfully remembering each detail, reopening the bleeding wounds inside me. "But—" My heart cleaved in two. He'd said he'd been Prisha's all along...he'd said he'd never cared for me. He murdered the one person who could help me fix this and left me to face the end of this world alone. *He didn't leave you...you banished him. You made the stars swallow him whole. You sent him to his final unmaking.* The lump in my throat escaped as a sob.

"The Eldress asked him to kill her and end her suffering."

"She said the only way to restore your magic and let you stitch the skies was to sever the bond."

"He betrayed you to *free you*. It was the only way."

"Prisha's betrayal broke her bond with Halah, so the Eldress said he should do the same to you to break yours."

They spoke all at once and over top of one another, but each account pierced through the jumble with crystal clarity, striking the air from my chest. The floor seemed to stretch wide and swallow me, my heart plummeting through stone and crust of the earth until I found myself upside down and disoriented, hanging on the other side of the world. Or, at least, that is how the sky-shifting, heart-crushing words felt.

He had betrayed me to sever the bond...on purpose? *To save me?* Why hadn't he told me...or...or warned me? Tears flowed down my cheeks. Of course he couldn't have told me for it to work—he'd kept that secret to himself, selflessly bearing the burden of that pain so I would not have to. So I could succeed. I clenched my fists into tight balls, digging the sharp edges of my nails into my palms. What had I done? I'd condemned him, stitched him to the sky and called him a monster—the very title he wished to escape—but he was the *furthest* thing from a monster if he'd selflessly broken himself to save me. He was *mine*. My Rue. And I would move heaven and earth or...shred the skies if I had to, but I would find a way to fix this.

A timid glow flared in my chest, responding to the overwhelming surge of emotions that flowed through me. It began as a softly muted whisper at first, then became brilliant, refusing to go back to the place of fear in which I'd buried it before. Surprised by the unfurling presence of magic in the windowless, skyless room, I stiffened. But...this was not Halah's magic—this was the *heart of stars.*

Star Thief.

I'd stolen the heart of stars from Prisha's sky and carried a piece of the heavens within me, making it a part of myself. There was nowhere I could go where the heavens could not reach me...they chose me and nestled within my heart, waiting for this moment of enlightenment. The power of every descendant of Halah and Stitcher and soul before me lived inside my heart. The stars *favored* me. As soon as I understood, it brightened the room, rays lancing through the darkness, dispelling shadows and fear and any lingering doubts I harbored.

A light unfolds in the darkness, beginning what will have no end.

This—this is the prophecy, I realized with a jolt of electric reinvigoration. *This is the light. The dawn of a new beginning.*

I breathed shallowly, my pulse drumming up a thrilling rush of certainty that washed away my fears. Prisha had no idea what a reckoning I'd saved for her.

Help me, I asked the stars, calling on the might of my ancestors, the weavers of heavens and fate. A luminous surge of light responded, throwing great spears of power around the room like the sun rising at dayburst, shattering through stone and wall, piercing through the ceiling above and dismantling the rafters. The room crumbled, dust and debris falling around me. From behind the remains of the wall that once stood between us, my Sisters gaped with wide eyes and lifted brows. Dozens of them, all covered in the white dust and rubble of my demolition.

"Help me." I inhaled through clenched teeth, wincing at the shooting pain in my leg. "Help me get to the city walls." I would not cower or hide from my purpose. Not anymore. I would go to face it.

If my Sisters had any reservations, they did not share them, but I could sense the thousands of unspoken questions wading through their eyes. Mother simply nodded, her lips a thin line of determination, and she waved toward Aunt Vanya and Lurah. "Help her. Whatever she needs." They pulled me to my feet, then Lurah and my Aunt offered support beneath my arms to help me hobble through the debris.

The herd of my Sisters weaved through the hallways ahead of us, paving the path, carefully checking each corner for guards. "Most of the royals already fled the palace," Lurah explained. "Prisha's creatures ambushed the throne room and killed the king. Guards are all fighting outside...there's nobody left to protect inside."

The king was...dead? Prisha's army had breached the city walls and razed their way through the palace? "How bad is it?" A band tightened around my ribs.

"Bad."

My throat ran dry, and my tongue felt foreign in my mouth. "Hurry."

The stairs leading to the Sun Throne dripped with blood and broken bodies, painting a new history to add to its archive. In the middle, amid the chaos, the prince sat with his head buried in his hands, fingers wound tightly through his hair, pulling at the roots. Was he...crying?

My gut twisted. Did I...did I feel bad for him? *No. Absolutely not.* He had lied, manipulated, sided with a deranged goddess, hurt me and my Sisters, and tried to disempower us by forcing us under his control.

He snapped his head up, and his eyes locked with mine. They filled with blackness, poisonous shadows of every dark emotion pooling into them—anger, fear, disgust, hatred. "What are you doing here?" he asked stiffly, raising himself to his feet. "Go back to your chamber."

"No." The response came out more like a growl than I'd intended.

The prince's jaw clenched, and he stormed toward me. "This is your fault. *Your fault.* You've left me with little choice...you can't hold back Prisha, and now the realm is *dying,* and I'm powerless to stop it. Powerless to do anything but make choices that people will criticize, hating me for every impossible decision. If I hide you away and protect you from her, will you gather the strength to do what must be done? No? You are too broken?" He sighed wearily, tossing a defeated expression toward me. "I do not *want* to kill you, Zara, but I cannot afford your failure. Prisha will not forgive those who pick the wrong side." He wiped his hands down his face, trying to banish the tortured mask he wore. "So what do I do? I must face my responsibilities and make the hard choices that others will not. Go back to your chambers. All of you."

I glared, resentment building with every word he spoke. He'd side with monsters to ensure his victory with little regard for morals or justice? He needed to pick a side—the right side—or get out of my way.

Baring my teeth, I summoned Halah's ribbons and directed them toward Tiralish, binding them around his wrists and ankles and stitching him beneath my glare. I stepped closer, clenching my jaw to mask the stabbing pain in my ankle and lowering my voice with conviction. "I will flay you from throat to groin if you ever presume to interfere with the descendants of Halah again. We are not yours to command. You are not ours to serve. Do you understand me?"

His face paled, and his mouth gaped, eyes darting nervously at the threads of my power as he held his breath in his lungs.

"Whose side are you on? Choose wisely." I tightened the binds around him, and his eyes bulged with fear.

"Yours. Just...help us. Please." He gasped.

Please was a good start, at the very least. I retracted the tendrils of light from the prince, but held him beneath the daggers of my glare. "Good. Prove it. Help us get to the wall... protect my Sisters." He nodded sharply, his jaw tightening into grim-set determination before he moved to the front of the Daughters, lifting a sword from one of the broken guards on the stairs. It sang against the stone as the tip dragged.

"Lurah? Mother? Juna?" I said, limping forward with their support. "Don't hesitate to feed him to the crawlers if he forgets which side he chose." Mother smirked—what a dangerous thing that woman was.

The sky was...bad. Worse than bad. Eviscerated like the bloody bowels of the soldiers who'd met their ends beneath the claws of crawlers. I couldn't hear Prisha through the chaos—or perhaps she chose not to speak to me, but I could feel her presence, lingering like a toxic, smothering cloud that wished to crumble the world to dust in her fist. My heart raced as I hobbled through the streets toward the city walls, pulled along by the support of my Sisters. Prince Tiralish slashed through crawlers and bulgroiches and opened a winged man's stomach when he seized Aunt Vanya from our ranks...but not before Vanya clawed ugly gashes into his cheek. I strangled another, stitching his throat closed with Halah's blessing.

Clinging to my Sisters as we climbed the stairs, I forced my mind to disassociate from the blood and mangled forms...the flesh mulched by crawlers and the cries of victims. If I considered them too closely, the whirlwind of guilt and despair stirring in my belly would unleash, obliterating my ability to act. To do what I'd been called to do.

Chin raised high, my breasts rising and falling with each shortened breath, I straightened my spine and faced Prisha's destruction. Standing my ground like the descendant of Halah I was. *I do not fear you.*

I pity you.

Prisha had broken her bond with Halah and let resentment and anger churn until she became a monster. A monster who would never know love or peace or connection.

The bond between Rue and I had severed, but nothing...not even the In Between or the rift I'd cleaved between us could keep me from him. Our story would not end like Prisha and Halah's. Our story had only just begun.

The crawlers screeched and clawed their way up the walls, milky eyes locked viciously upon me. Tiralish screamed orders at his guards to protect us, slashing his own sword violently about, showering black blood like rain as my Sisters ushered me into place. I scanned the rifts, my blood rushing with courage as I lifted a hand, but an agonized holler ripped my attention away from the shredded sky. My stomach twisted with horror.

A bulgroich slammed into the prince, punching its horned fist through the wall of his chest, and he stumbled backward, sword clattering against the sandstone. He met my gaze, mouth parting with the last words he'd never get to voice. The crawlers did not wait to descend upon him, dragging their prey toward the edge of the wall.

"Help him!" I shouted instinctually, but nobody moved to reach for the crimson hand clinging to the ledge. Nobody moved when his body fell to the dunes below to paint the sand with entrails and macerated flesh. There was no saving him.

I shoved the shattered pieces of my mixed emotions into a box to categorize later. There was no time for them now. No time to examine how *everything* hurt.

"Now. We need to do it now. Weave," I said, my voice raspy. My Sisters encircled me, sitting on the ground in a protective barrier of prayer, weaving in communion with Halah to ask for her strength, lending their power to me. I welcomed the web of threads, entwining the ribbons of their magic with mine, binding it around the heart of stars to connect the souls of Daughters past and present, forming the strongest bond of power I could create. But it was missing one crucial tie. One critical connection that had been lost when I'd condemned my monster to a fate worse than death. *My Rue.*

Please don't let it be too late. Help me find him, I asked the heart of stars. It had helped me once before...I trusted it could again. Unless he was already gone.

He couldn't be gone.

With a guttural shout, the light blazed within me, then launched toward the heavens, piercing Prisha's rifts, finding its target without a moment of hesitation. My heart raced, filling with hope as every muscle tensed with effort. And I pulled.

I pulled him back—not because the stars chose us at random, but because *I* chose him. *On purpose.*

And it was perhaps the first and *best* thing I had ever chosen for myself. One I would never grow to regret. I would choose it again and again and again because it was *mine.* He was mine.

And I was his.

Always.

Rue tumbled from the sky, all wings and shadow and perfection. Alive and mine. He collided with me in the clumsy haste of his landing, too shocked by my sudden retrieval to conduct himself with his usual air of calm. His eyes were clouded by haunted gray clouds, but they flashed with recognition when they settled on me, then blazed with life once more. "Zara."

I threw my arms around him. "I thought I'd be too late. I thought I'd let her unmake you. I—" My sob muffled itself against his chest. "I'm so sorry."

"Zara." He pulled away and grabbed my shoulders, staring back at me with disbelief. "You saved me. You called me back before she could finish me." His amethyst eyes glimmered with the stars of his tears, agony twisting his features when he beheld me. "Zara—I'm the one who should be sorry. I—"

"I know," I whispered, desperate to banish the pain written across his face. "You have nothing to be sorry for. You don't have to explain. Not now. It's done. Just...help me."

And as he had from the very first moment we met, he responded without hesitation, without question, understanding what I needed without requiring my direction. I cast my gaze to the skies, glaring at the monster who'd cursed us to endure centuries of suffering beneath her wrath. *No more.*

This time, when I stitched together the powers of Halah and my Sisters, binding them to the heart of stars to unite all Daughters past and present, I also reached for Rue's magic, that powerful, destructive force flowing straight from Prisha. And I made it mine.

A light unfolds in the darkness, beginning what will have no end.

Power burst forth, a blinding display of light projected toward the heavens, spearing through each rift, searching for the monster who'd caused all of this pain. The sky blazed, a ring of licking flames opening the curtain between worlds, burning around the edges as my tethers forced her from her prison, pulling her to our side of the realms. Demanding her presence in this final battle.

She was...a terror of beauty and malice. Long black hair and crimson eyes, skin of alabaster so bright it almost hurt to look at. And a rage I had never known, powerful, damning, consuming.

Her mouth opened, teeth bared as she unleashed a primal scream, racing toward me with fingers outstretched, prepared to strangle my neck. *Star Thief. Sky Render,* she hissed, spewing vitriol between the stars.

I tightened my hold on the braided powers—the quiet precision of Halah's threads, the infinite strength of the heart of stars, and the ruthless destructiveness of Prisha's magic. All focused into one.

One burst of power to destroy and mend—to heal and annihilate.

I had never been meant to be restricted to one of their magics. I had always been meant for more.

The javelin of light I forged pierced through Prisha's chest and erupted, blasting into a thousand shards of stars that screamed through the night. When they scattered, I redirected their remains to weave stitches through the shredded sky. Shadows spilled from me, writhing and twisting around each of Prisha's vicious creatures, pulverizing them to dust. All except the one I held in my heart, forevermore.

When it was done, when the sky glimmered with gratitude, its wounds smoothed into a navy curtain of stars and cosmic glory, I collapsed into Rue's arms, letting him help carry the weight of my pain. He pulled me toward him, his tears of wonder scattering through my hair as he embraced me. Our bodies pressed tightly against one another, limbs woven together in a desperate effort to never again be parted, and his lips found mine.

CHAPTER 29

A CLOAK OF STARS

The door closed quietly behind me when I slipped into the room, hesitant to disturb the stillness. Blossoms draped effortlessly from the baskets beneath each arch, and the early sun glazed the courtyard tiles with hues of gold. But that was not the beauty that stilled my breath when I entered. It was him—at ease, his leg ensnared by the mess of blankets, chest bare and rising with unhurried breaths as he slept. I had not yet grown accustomed to such perfect calm, but I cherished it, protecting these moments with the fiercest devotion. If I woke him, I would not get to admire the peace that found his face so easily in sleep, or the lazy flop of hair over his relaxed brows, the slow rise and fall of his abdomen...the hint of contentment on his lips. Lips I hoped to taste again and again, each evening, through the night, at dayburst, between council meetings and after every tumultuous navigation through political matters. We had already gotten off to a good start on that front, at least. I smiled.

The weeks following Prisha's last battle had left the realm in a fragile state. The Daughters had picked up the broken pieces, restoring order in the wake of Rashii's late king and Prince Tiralish's death, giving hope to the people for a better tomorrow. I didn't love the new responsibilities I'd been handed in the shuffle of power, but I loved the *people*. Their strength and resilience. Their faith in the Daughters and the start of the new dawn we'd weave together. It made every responsibility to them worth my while.

Oftentimes, Rue accompanied me at council meetings, slowly winning the hearts of the people with his antics. He proved to be a masterful negotiator...unsurprising, considering his natural talent for bargaining. Our relations with Khazdra remained rocky at best after Prisha's fall, but Rue convinced them to strike a deal of peace with us—allowing them to resettle the land they considered to be their homeland, rebuilding Rashii into a New Khazdra, so long as they promised their allegiance to the curse breaker —*Me*. For a culture that revered the stars as their gods, it did not require much convincing to establish a fledgling bond of trust between us as the realm fought to restore a sense of stability.

Rue stirred, lids parting slowly as the clouds of sleep lifted from his eyes. The corner of his mouth pulled into a smile, and he stretched, his muscles lengthening and shifting the blankets so they left little to my imagination. My cheeks flushed, and I averted my attention to the halfmoon bread in my pocket. Awkwardly, I reached for it and held it up. Rue's eyes brightened.

I crossed the room, sinking on the bed next to him before tearing the crescent in half. "Sorry," I said, passing half to him. "My Sisters devoured the spread at the council meeting...there was only one left."

Rue's ribs expanded with a measured inhale, and he bit back his expression of disappointment, forcing a smile. "It's yours, Starlight. Enjoy it."

I popped a bite of the bread into my mouth, appreciating the sweet and savory marriage of lorbean paste and honey before smirking coyly at him. He was nearly salivating. "Oh, that's right," I teased. "You don't like sharing." Taking another bite, I stifled a laugh, perhaps finding too much pleasure in the way the tension in his jaw suggested his valiant effort of restraint. I adored his unabashed obsession with simple pleasures, and the ease with which I could tease him for them. But when he groaned unintentionally, I decided to end his suffering, pulling a second halfmoon bread from my pocket. "Good thing I asked the kitchens to make you your own."

He battled the smile on his face for a moment, but in the end, his delight won over. He snatched the bread from my hands with a mumble of gratitude before shoving half into his mouth, sighing with contentment. "Thank you," he reiterated more clearly when he brushed away the last crumbs that had fallen into his lap. Then he turned to face me, his eyes a vivid shade of stardust, locked on mine with an intensity that dispelled the moment of levity.

"You know I don't like to share," he said. I rolled my eyes, already forming my comeback, but when he drew a deep, steadying breath, I paused and watched him with curiosity. "I have thought of *one* thing I'd like to share with you, though," he continued, reaching for my hand. His fingers wrapped around mine, and my gaze flickered to the way our hands fit perfectly together.

That doesn't sound like my Rue. I laughed to myself. "And what's that?" I asked, lifting a brow.

"The rest of forever." His expression softened, vulnerable and honest...full of hope. Waiting for my response.

My lips parted, but my breath lodged itself firmly in my throat, blocking the escape of words. Utterly stunned, I gaped at him until I finally recovered, collecting myself with an easy smile that contrasted wildly with the fluttering pace of my heart. "Well, it depends," I said, as though he hadn't just shifted the path of the stars with his words, stunning me into an unusual silence. "Have you officially dropped that 'I'll kill you tomorrow' act? Once and for all? Forever is a long time, full of too many tomorrows to have to worry about such things."

He raised his brows and cocked his head with a smirk. "Oh yes, there will be many tomorrows shared between us, but I am quite certain none of them will involve killing you. There are so many other endeavors to devote my time to...so many other things I'd like to try instead."

"Like?" I asked, realizing the space between us condensed with each playful bit of banter. My heart beat wildly between my ribs, desperate to close the distance.

His eyes dropped to my lips before finding me once more, full of ardor. "Perhaps I should show you?"

I nodded, my cheeks flushing. Perhaps he should. He *definitely* should.

The stars in his eyes dimmed, smoldering with the smoky haze of dusk when he pulled me into his lap. His hand wrapped through my hair, gripping the back of my neck, using it as leverage as he pressed his lips to mine. I melted into his hold, my body melding with his until no space existed between us.

Our kisses deepened with need, his tongue sweeping between my lips, exploring my mouth as our breath unified, increasing with passion. His hand slid beneath my tunic, palming my breast as my hips instinctively rocked against the hardness beneath me. I tipped my head back, overwhelmed by the brush of his lips against my skin and the heightening build of desire that pooled between my thighs. His fingers brushed over the peak of my nipple, and I gasped, wrapping my hand around his wrist, overcome by the new sensations, consumed by the fire of need for him to touch every part of me. He froze, his mouth still pressed against the softness of my neck where he'd been worshipping me with slow caresses of his lips. Our eyes met, his a dark shade of twilight dusted with stars. "More?" he breathed, examining my expression for any reservations. The air hung heavy beneath the weight of our breathlessness.

"All," I responded, releasing his hand and lifting the hem of my top. My clothes fell into a discarded heap somewhere in the room, and I lay bare before him. It was only fair, considering he wore nothing but the white sheet draped over his lap. Any trace of vulnerability left me beneath the admiration of his gaze, and I felt nothing but his absolute devotion. He leaned over me, the rigid muscles of his chest landing between my legs, and he poured over my body with molten intensity, trailing kisses down my abdomen. My nails dug into the taut muscles of his back rippling beneath my fingers. When I moaned at the moment his mouth moved between my legs, his wings opened with a shuddering snap before drifting over us, veiling us beneath the twin curtains of shadow.

His tongue swept over my center, and I gasped for air, my hips bucking with tension at the first pass of his mouth against me. It consumed me, stirring a response deep within me that tightened and twisted with every movement of his mouth. He groaned, his fingers sliding through wetness before entering me, moving slowly in tandem with the work of his tongue until the tension inside of me shattered into a thousand pieces of blissful relief. I threw my head back, stunned by the immensity of my emotions in that moment. The sky-shattering fulfillment that flooded through me. But I was not ready to be done with him.

My muscles melted into liquid, but when I regained control of myself, I reached for him and pulled him toward me. My gaze snagged over the lines of his abdomen, following the trail to the hardened length of him, "All," I breathed. "I want all of you." His gaze darkened, and he lowered his hips over mine, claiming me greedily with his mouth, his length resting between my legs. When he notched himself at my entrance, I gasped, arching my hips to give him better access, begging him to cross that final stretch between us.

He slid into me, groaning as he sank to the hilt, letting his hips press into mine with the pressure of his need. Our hips fell into the rhythm that the universe conducted only for us, and his open mouth rested against my jaw, nipping at my earlobe before kissing every part of me within his reach. His breath brushed the crook of my neck between each tender caress of his mouth on my skin, and his muscles coiled with tension as his body moved over me. I pulled him close and only wished to hold him closer as I experienced the fullness of his body and soul meshed with mine....the increasing passion of each thrust as we climbed nearer and nearer to the height of our unity. I cried out with a shuddering sigh, and Rue stilled inside of me, his heart pulsing with each throb of release shared between us.

The sun caressed my face, spilling through the open archways. Rue's arms wrapped around my torso and his wing draped over my side to cover the bare form of our bodies. We'd spent the past year tangled in one another's limbs through the night while rebuilding and recovering from Prisha's last battle during the day. Time did not diminish or lessen the happiness I'd found with him—my love grew steadily, becoming stronger than the bond the stars had once woven between us. The bond we forged on our own was another thing entirely. Comfortable. True. Enduring.

Ours.

A knock disturbed our private sanctuary of peace, and I huffed with annoyance. Couldn't they let us share a few more moments of quiet bliss together? But when Rue's eyes snapped open and worshipped my bare form with an unhurried sweep of

desire, I knew our next moments of *bliss* would be of the more...
ground-shattering, less calm variety. And I was more than enticed
by that prospect.

"Your Highness, High Queen, sorry to wake you, but you are
needed."

I sighed deeply, but Rue pulled me closer, planting a tender
kiss against my forehead. "Go on, Starlight. I'll meet you there."

"You better," I teased, but I had no doubts in my mind that
he would. He would always be there, wherever I was. By choice.

As would I.

Slipping from the bed, I wrapped a robe around my frame
and braved the hallway, already knowing who I'd encounter.
Mother, Aunt Vanya and Aunt Naila, Lurah, Rada, and all of my
Sisters crowded around the door, beaming and eagerly waiting to
ambush me. Or...style their muse for the occasion. Same difference. I rubbed the sleep from my eyes, pretending to be annoyed,
but my smile broke through. "You all are acting weird again," I
mumbled. They ushered me away, chattering excitedly about their
plans and the many ways they expected Halah to bless us that
evening.

In truth, *blessing* was a weak word for the exuberant display of
approval Halah bestowed upon us at our union. When Rue and I
passed the star well tea between us, stars showered down from the
heavens. The sky burst with ribbons of blue and pinks, twists of
green and amethyst strips of stardust that painted the backdrop
behind us with great strokes of eternal beauty, celebrating the
unprecedented strength of our bond.

But when all the fanfare settled down and the city returned
home to their beds, the night reclaimed its usual serenity. Rue and
I relished in the quiet of our solitude, indulging in one another's
company for a little longer before returning to bed, meandering
beneath the starry skies just beyond the city gates. The dunes
reminded me of home, but nothing felt more comfortable than

the way our arms linked together as our steps synchronized through the sand. The sky rustled behind us, shifting and stirring in our presence. I looked up, catching the admiration in Rue's gaze. He nodded toward the stars, and I followed his gesture skyward.

My lips parted, a gasp of surprise passing through them. Swirls of brilliant color crossed the navy backdrop behind us, and within it, the stars danced. They sparkled vibrantly, knitting themselves together, forming a luminous cloak of stardust that settled upon my shoulders.

Rue's lips pulled into that lopsided smile I adored. "You see? I always told you the stars favored you, Zara."

I hummed in halfhearted acknowledgment, knowing he'd missed a large but important part of the truth. I smiled back at him. "No, Rue, they favor *us*."

The end.

ABOUT THE AUTHOR

A.C. Guess is a self-proclaimed fantasy aficionado and devourer of books. She has been spinning stories and crafting with words for as long as she can remember, though she tries hard not to remember those early stories. Fueled by coffee and a wild imagination, she dreams of winning the Timeless Trials herself to have more time to bring her stories to life. Unfortunately, she must admit that she would never win because of her preference for simple comforts like caffeine, blankets, and piles of books. A.C. Guess recently moved to Colorado with her three kids, husband, and grumpy cat, where she is furiously typing new stories. Her published works include Sky Stitcher and The Timeless Trials.

www.acguess.com

@acguesswrites

Link Tree:

Delve into nine worlds of magic, fantasy, and romance with the Of Dusk And Dawn books, each written by a talented author who has created a story with a broken curse that contains the prophecy of Dusk and Dawn!

Those Who Seek Vengeance - Christy Kenning
| Secret Identity, Fairytale Retelling |

Forgotten Retribution - Leigh Fields
| Star-Crossed Lovers, Greek Mythology |

Broken - Ada James
| Forbidden Love, Secret Twins |

Sacrifice for the Standing Stones - Bree Moore
| Enemies to Lovers, Nature As Ally |

Blade Upon the Vein - ASF DeWeese
| Hidden Royalty, Enemies to Lovers |

Web of Echoes - Courtney Davis
| Tragic Past, Second Chance Romance |

Sky Stitcher - A.C. Guess
| Enemies to Lovers, Forced Proximity |

Starlings in the Dark - Forest Moria
| Gods and Mortals, He Falls First |

Brightless - Teshelle Combs
| Fated Mates, Light and Shadow Magic |

www.ingramcontent.com/pod-product-compliance
Lightning Source LLC
Chambersburg PA
CBHW020227010826
48973CB00006B/1403